"The world is full of obvious t
chance ever c
— Arthur Co<

CW01082764

Table of Contents

The Clockwork Murders

Chapter 1: The Silent Ticking

1. The Arrival of the Stranger

The quaint town of Hawkesbury-on-Thames lay quietly under the soft glow of the early evening. It was the sort of place that seemed almost frozen in time, where nothing out of the ordinary ever happened. The church bell tower stood tall against the dusky sky, and the narrow cobblestone streets wound through rows of ivy-clad cottages. It was a town of routine and familiarity, where everyone knew everyone else's business—or so they believed.

But that evening, as the clock struck six and a thin mist began to rise from the river, a stranger arrived in Hawkesbury, setting in motion a series of events that would unravel the very fabric of the town's peaceful existence.

The man appeared suddenly, almost as if conjured from the mist itself, stepping off the London-bound train that rattled into the tiny station. There was something unsettlingly peculiar about him that made the handful of townsfolk present pause and glance twice. He was tall and gaunt, with a slight stoop to his shoulders, as if he bore the weight of an unseen burden. His overcoat, though fine and tailored, seemed slightly worn at the edges, and a black bowler hat cast a shadow over his pale, angular face.

His eyes, however, were the most striking feature—cold and calculating, like those of a clockmaker examining the intricate mechanisms of a device. He held a small, battered leather suitcase in one hand, and with the other, he adjusted his silver-rimmed spectacles. Without so much as a nod of greeting, he turned and began to stride purposefully away from the station and into the heart of Hawkesbury.

Mrs. Tilly Prentiss, the stationmaster's wife and an ardent observer of the comings and goings in town, watched the stranger's departure with a frown. "Now, who could that be?" she murmured to herself, peering through the window of the station's small office. There were not many visitors to Hawkesbury, and the man's abrupt appearance had stirred a faint unease within her. She prided herself on knowing every soul in the village, yet this man was entirely unfamiliar.

As he walked down the main street, the stranger's eyes flicked from side to side, taking in his surroundings with an intensity that was almost predatory. His gaze lingered on the weathered facades of the old buildings, the dimly lit windows behind which families were just sitting down to supper, and the shrouded alleyways that threaded between them. It was as if he were memorizing every detail, filing away every corner and shadow for future use.

He paused in front of a small establishment, the only one that showed signs of activity—a modest inn by the name of The King's Arms. The warm light spilling out from its windows cast a welcoming glow onto the street, and the faint murmur of conversation drifted out through the slightly ajar door. The stranger hesitated for a moment, his hand tightening on the handle of his suitcase, before he pushed the door open and stepped inside.

The chatter inside the inn ceased almost instantly as the stranger made his entrance. Heads turned, eyes widened, and a few whispers flitted through the air like startled birds. Mr. Edwin Cooper, the innkeeper, rose from behind the bar, wiping his hands on a rag. He was a stout, affable man, accustomed to greeting travelers with a smile and a hearty welcome, but something about this visitor's demeanor gave him pause.

"Good evening, sir," Mr. Cooper said cautiously, the habitual cheerfulness in his voice muted. "What can I do for you?"

The stranger removed his hat, revealing a thinning crown of iron-gray hair. His eyes swept over the room, assessing its occupants—regulars, all of them—before settling on Mr. Cooper.

"A room," he said simply, his voice low and clipped, with just a hint of an accent that was difficult to place. "I'll need a room for the night."

"Of course, sir," Mr. Cooper replied, though the request was somewhat unusual. The inn was rarely occupied, and most visitors to Hawkesbury preferred the more modern establishments in the neighboring towns. "Sign the register, if you would."

The stranger set down his suitcase and picked up the pen with a thin, elegant hand. He paused for a fraction of a second, then wrote in a flowing script: Mr. James Blackwood, London.

"Welcome to The King's Arms, Mr. Blackwood," Mr. Cooper said, though the name rang no bells. "May I ask if you're here on business?"

"Of a sort," Mr. Blackwood replied with the faintest hint of a smile that did not reach his eyes. "I have matters to attend to in the area."

He did not elaborate further, and Mr. Cooper, sensing that further inquiry would not be welcome, handed him a key. "Room three, up the stairs and to your right. Breakfast is at seven, if you're interested."

"Thank you," Mr. Blackwood murmured. He picked up his suitcase once more and made his way up the narrow staircase, his steps eerily quiet, almost like the ticking of a clock.

As the door to his room clicked shut behind him, the murmur of conversation resumed in the common room below, more hushed and urgent now. Who was this man, and what business could he possibly have in a place like Hawkesbury? Speculation spread like wildfire among the patrons, each theory more outlandish than the last.

Meanwhile, in the privacy of his small, sparsely furnished room, Mr. Blackwood set his suitcase on the bed and unlatched it with a click. He drew out a small, intricately designed pocket watch and held it up to the dim light. The hands of the watch were stopped at exactly six o'clock—the same time he had stepped off the train.

He smiled then, a thin, enigmatic smile, as if he had just confirmed something of great significance. He carefully placed the watch on the bedside table and reached back into the suitcase. This time, he withdrew a small, well-worn notebook. Flipping it open, he scanned the pages, each filled with neat, precise handwriting and cryptic symbols. His finger traced a particular entry, and he nodded to himself.

"Soon," he whispered softly, the word barely audible in the stillness of the room. "Very soon."

The following morning dawned cool and gray, a fine drizzle coating the cobblestones with a sheen of moisture. Mrs. Tilly Prentiss was at her usual post outside the station, fussing over the flower beds, when she noticed Mr. Blackwood exiting The King's Arms. He moved with a deliberate calmness, glancing briefly in her direction before turning down the lane that led to the center of town.

Curiosity piqued, Mrs. Prentiss watched as he disappeared around the corner, then bustled into the station to fetch her husband. "George," she hissed, shaking his arm. "That stranger from last night—he's up to something, mark my words."

George Prentiss looked up from his newspaper with a frown. "Now, now, Tilly, let's not jump to conclusions. He might be a businessman or a—a writer, even."

"A writer!" Mrs. Prentiss scoffed. "With a face like that? No, he's here for something else, something... sinister."

But despite her misgivings, the day passed uneventfully. The stranger, Mr. Blackwood, kept mostly to himself, strolling through the village and occasionally pausing to make a note in his small notebook. He seemed to have a particular interest in the older parts of town—the churchyard, the abandoned mill by the river, the derelict house on the edge of town that had been vacant for as long as anyone could remember.

By evening, the townsfolk had begun to weave their own stories about him. Some said he was an inspector from the railway company, here to assess the station. Others whispered that he was a private detective, investigating some long-forgotten crime. The most fanciful rumor, however, was that he was the ghost of a man wronged many years ago, come back to exact his revenge.

But the truth, as it often is, was far stranger than any of their imaginings.

It was only on the third day after his arrival that the first body was discovered—Mrs. Margery Collins, a widow who lived alone in a small cottage near the edge of the woods. She was found in her parlor, a look of sheer terror frozen on her face, her hands clutching an old-fashioned mantel clock that had stopped at precisely the time of her death: six o'clock.

The town was thrown into an uproar. The constable, a portly man named Jack Havers, did his best to maintain order, but it was clear that the situation was beyond his experience. The villagers clamored for answers, for justice, but there were none to be found.

Only Mr. Blackwood remained calm, standing at the edge of the gathered crowd, his expression inscrutable. He glanced once more at his pocket watch, nodded as if in satisfaction, then turned and walked away.

It was time.

2. The Clockmaker's Secret

IN THE QUIET TOWN OF Harpsden, the mere mention of the clockmaker's shop stirred a sense of both admiration and unease. Nestled on the corner of the cobbled High Street, the shop had stood there for over a century, its windows forever dimly lit, filled with the rhythmic ticking of its wares. Yet, the true charm of this unassuming establishment lay not just in the delicate craftsmanship of the timepieces, but in the enigmatic figure who owned it.

Jonathan Pembroke, the clockmaker, was a man of quiet disposition and meticulous habits. He rarely ventured outside, preferring the company of his intricate mechanisms to that of people. Those few who had the privilege of watching him work spoke in hushed tones of his extraordinary talent. Every clock, every watch, seemed to have a life of its own once it left his hands. The townsfolk claimed that time itself seemed to obey Pembroke's command.

Yet there was a shadow that lurked beneath this veneer of precision and perfection, a hidden truth that few dared to contemplate. For as long as anyone could remember, Pembroke's shop had been linked to mysterious disappearances and unspoken tragedies. Some said that his family had been cursed, that every generation produced a clockmaker of unparalleled skill, but one who would invariably be driven to madness.

It was a chill autumn morning when the story truly began. The wind whispered through the trees, carrying with it the first hints of the coming winter. A thick fog rolled in from the moors, cloaking Harpsden in a shroud of white. Inspector Archibald Hart stood outside the clockmaker's shop, his gaze fixed on the faded sign that hung above the door: Pembroke & Sons – Master Clockmakers Since 1832.

Hart was not a man easily given to superstition, but there was something about this place that set him on edge. Perhaps it was the silence that seemed to swallow every sound, or the way the fog clung to the building as if trying to conceal it from view. He took a deep breath, steeling himself, and pushed open the door.

The shop was much as he had expected—cluttered yet meticulously organized, filled with the gentle ticking of clocks. The scent of wood polish and oil hung heavy in the air. Shelves lined the walls, each one bearing a variety of timepieces, from grandiose grandfather clocks to the most delicate pocket watches. All of them ticked in perfect unison, as if bound by an invisible conductor.

"Good morning, Inspector," came a soft voice from the back of the shop.

Hart turned to see Jonathan Pembroke emerging from behind a curtain. The man was tall and slender, with a slight stoop to his shoulders. His hair, once dark, was now streaked with gray, and his eyes, a startling shade of blue, seemed to miss nothing. He moved with a deliberate grace, every gesture measured and precise.

"Mr. Pembroke," Hart replied, tipping his hat. "I'm here about... well, you know why I'm here."

The clockmaker smiled, a faint, almost sad expression. "Yes, of course. You wish to speak about the incident."

Hart nodded. The "incident" in question was the disappearance of young Thomas Greene, a bright boy of fourteen with a penchant for tinkering. He had last been seen entering Pembroke's shop three nights ago, and since then, not a trace of him had been found. The townsfolk were already whispering, casting sideways glances at the clockmaker's windows.

"I know it looks bad, Inspector," Pembroke said quietly, his gaze drifting to a wall-mounted clock that ticked softly behind him. "But I assure you, I had nothing to do with the boy's disappearance. He came to me asking for guidance, eager to learn the craft. He stayed for a while, watching me work, and then... he left. That's all I know."

Hart studied the man carefully. There was a sincerity in his voice that was hard to doubt, and yet... something felt off. "You say he left, but no one saw him. There's no record of him exiting your shop. And the last place anyone saw him was right here, talking to you."

Pembroke's expression remained calm, though a flicker of something—regret? sorrow?—passed through his eyes. "I'm aware of how it must appear, Inspector. But I promise you, I would never harm the boy. I have no reason to."

Hart glanced around the shop, his gaze lingering on the countless clocks that filled every available space. "You've been known to keep secrets, Mr. Pembroke. Your family... your history... it's all rather mysterious, wouldn't you say?"

The clockmaker's lips tightened, just for a moment, before he nodded. "Yes, my family has its share of secrets. But nothing that would explain what happened to young Thomas."

"And yet..." Hart's voice trailed off as he moved closer to a particularly ornate grandfather clock. It was a beautiful piece, its wooden surface polished to a mirror-like sheen. But what caught his attention was the face of the clock—it had no numbers. Instead, strange symbols were carved where the hours should have been. "This is... unusual."

Pembroke stepped forward, his fingers tracing the edge of the clock's face with a reverence that bordered on obsession. "This is one of my father's creations. A masterpiece, though few understand its significance."

Hart arched an eyebrow. "And what is its significance?"

Pembroke hesitated, his gaze locked on the clock. "It's... difficult to explain. My father believed that time is not a straight line, but a series of interlocking circles, each one affecting the others in ways we cannot perceive. He spent his life trying to prove it, to create a mechanism that could... synchronize with time itself."

Hart frowned. "You're saying this clock... controls time?"

The clockmaker shook his head slowly. "Not controls, no. More like... resonates with it. It's just a theory, of course. My father's theories were often considered... eccentric."

"Eccentric or not, this clock is very strange. And I can't help but wonder if there's more to it than meets the eye." Hart leaned closer, his eyes narrowing as he examined the intricate carvings. "These symbols... do they mean anything?"

Pembroke's hand tightened on the clock's edge, and for the first time, Hart saw a hint of fear in the man's eyes. "They're... a form of notation. A language, if you will. One that my father believed could be used to... align the mechanisms of the clock with certain... events."

"Events?" Hart echoed, his curiosity piqued. "What kind of events?"

The clockmaker took a step back, his gaze shifting to the window, where the fog still pressed against the glass. "Moments in time," he whispered. "Moments of great significance. He believed that if the clock was tuned correctly, it could... influence these moments. Change them."

Hart felt a chill run down his spine. "Are you saying this clock can alter the past?"

Pembroke's laugh was soft, almost bitter. "Nothing can change the past, Inspector. But perhaps... perhaps it can guide the present. Or at least, that's what my father thought. I never truly understood it myself."

The inspector straightened, his gaze still fixed on the strange symbols. "And what about you, Mr. Pembroke? Do you believe it?"

There was a long silence before the clockmaker spoke again, his voice barely audible over the ticking of the clocks. "I believe that time is not as immutable as we think. That sometimes, under the right conditions, it can be... persuaded."

Hart felt a surge of frustration. "And what does any of this have to do with Thomas? Why was he here, Mr. Pembroke? What did he want from you?"

Pembroke closed his eyes, his shoulders sagging. "He wanted to learn, Inspector. He wanted to know the secrets of the clocks. He was... special. More talented than any apprentice I've ever had. But he grew impatient. He wanted answers that I couldn't give him."

"Or wouldn't," Hart muttered.

"Perhaps," Pembroke conceded softly. "Perhaps I was afraid. Afraid of what he might do if he understood too much."

Hart stepped back, his mind racing. "You're not making any sense, Mr. Pembroke. What aren't you telling me? What happened to Thomas?"

The clockmaker's gaze turned to the strange clock once more. "I don't know," he whispered. "But I fear... I fear he might have tried to... synchronize."

"Synchronize?" Hart repeated, his voice sharp. "With what?"

"With time itself," Pembroke breathed, his eyes wide with a terror that seemed to come from deep within. "I tried to stop him, but... something went wrong. There was a... a shift. The clock... it wasn't ready. And then... he was gone."

"Gone?" Hart echoed, disbelief flooding his voice. "What do you mean, gone? Gone where?"

Pembroke's gaze was distant, lost in some unfathomable memory. "I don't know, Inspector. All I know is that one moment he was there, and the next... he wasn't. The clock stopped, and he... vanished."

Hart felt his pulse quicken. "You're saying he just... disappeared? Into thin air?"

"Yes," Pembroke whispered. "Or... perhaps he didn't disappear at all. Perhaps... he simply moved... somewhere else."

"Somewhere else?" Hart's voice was tight with barely contained frustration. "What does that mean? You're speaking in riddles, Mr. Pembroke. I need answers,
   not cryptic nonsense."

But the clockmaker only shook his head slowly. "I wish I had answers, Inspector. But this... this is beyond me. My father's work... his research... it was always dangerous. I tried to destroy it, to keep it hidden. But I fear... I fear it has found a way to continue... without me."

Hart stared at the man, a mix of anger and confusion churning within him. "You're not telling me everything, Mr. Pembroke. There's more to this—more to you—than meets the eye."

Pembroke met his gaze, his expression one of profound sadness. "Yes, Inspector. There's always more. But some secrets... some secrets are best left buried."

Hart's jaw clenched. "I will find out what happened to Thomas, Mr. Pembroke. One way or another, I will uncover the truth."

"I hope you do, Inspector," Pembroke murmured. "I truly do. Because if you don't... I fear we may all become lost in time."

The inspector turned on his heel, storming out of the shop, his mind reeling with questions that had no answers. As he stepped into the fog, he glanced back at the clockmaker's shop, a sense of foreboding settling over him.

Something was very, very wrong in Harpsden. And whatever it was, Jonathan Pembroke and his cursed clocks were at the heart of it.

Little did Hart know that this was only the beginning—a beginning that would unravel not just the mystery of Thomas Greene's disappearance, but the very fabric of time itself.

• • • •

3. An Ominous Package

THE AIR IN THE SMALL village of Alderwood was still that morning, as if nature itself sensed that something unsettling was on the horizon. The early autumn mist hung low over the cobbled streets, and the sun, though it had risen hours ago, remained hidden behind a stubborn layer of cloud, casting a pallid gray light over the village. It was the sort of day that seemed to suck the vitality out of even the most cheerful of souls, leaving only an undercurrent of quiet apprehension.

At the far end of the village, nestled behind a wrought-iron gate, sat Hargrave House—a grand but aging manor that had seen better days. It stood with a stoic dignity, its stone facade covered in ivy and its windows looking out like weary eyes surveying a world that had long since moved on. Inside, the scent of old wood and faded lavender hung in the air, mingling with the dust motes that swirled lazily in the drafty corridors.

On this particular morning, Mrs. Beatrice Partridge, the long-time housekeeper of Hargrave House, was making her usual rounds. With a stern expression and a back as straight as a ruler, she moved through the rooms with the efficiency of a clockwork mechanism. Everything in its place, just as it had been for the past twenty-five years. The occupants of the house had dwindled over the decades, but Beatrice's commitment to maintaining order had never wavered.

As she descended the grand staircase, a loud, echoing knock resonated through the entrance hall. It startled her—visitors were rare these days, especially at this early hour. She paused, her hand on the bannister, listening intently. The knock came again, this time more insistent. With a frown, she adjusted her apron and made her way to the front door.

Opening the heavy oak door with a slight creak, she was met with an unexpected sight. A young man, no older than twenty, stood on the doorstep, his cheeks flushed from the chill. His cap was pulled low over his brow, and he shifted nervously from foot to foot. In his arms, he cradled a small wooden crate, secured with rough twine.

"Morning, ma'am," he mumbled, his eyes avoiding hers. "Got a delivery for Hargrave House."

Beatrice's frown deepened. "We're not expecting any deliveries," she replied, her voice clipped and precise. She eyed the crate with suspicion. There was something about it that set her on edge—the way the wood seemed darkened and worn, as if it had traveled far and through unsavory conditions.

"Just doin' my job, ma'am," the young man insisted, shoving a crumpled piece of paper towards her. "Sign here, please."

Beatrice hesitated, then took the paper. It was a simple receipt, bearing no sender's name or address—only the words, "To be delivered to Hargrave House. Urgent." She glanced back at the crate, then at the boy, whose gaze darted anxiously around the mist-shrouded grounds.

"Very well," she murmured, scrawling her name with a firm hand. "Leave it on the table just inside."

The young man obeyed, depositing the crate on the small table in the foyer. Beatrice could hear the faintest of rattles from within as he set it down. Before she could ask any further questions, he gave a quick nod and hurried back down the steps, disappearing into the fog that clung to the lane like a ghostly shroud.

Closing the door behind him, Beatrice turned her attention to the crate. It was no larger than a breadbox, yet it seemed to possess a weight far beyond its size. She stood there, staring at it for a long moment, the hairs on the back of her neck prickling with an inexplicable unease. Something about it felt wrong—dangerous, even.

Taking a deep breath, she moved closer. There was no return address, no indication of who had sent it or why. Only the word "Urgent" scribbled hastily on the side. She considered leaving it for someone else to handle—perhaps Mr. Davenport, the butler, or Miss Clara, the last remaining member of the Hargrave family still residing in the house. But curiosity, combined with a sense of duty, compelled her to act.

With steady hands, she took a pair of scissors from her apron pocket and began to cut through the twine. The strands snapped under the blade, one by one, and she carefully pried open the lid. Inside, nestled in a bed of crumpled paper and straw, lay a small, intricately crafted clock. Its casing was polished wood, inlaid with delicate patterns of brass and silver. But what caught Beatrice's attention was not its craftsmanship, but rather the fact that the clock's face was entirely blank—no numbers, no hands—just a smooth, featureless disk.

Beatrice stared at it, confusion mingling with a growing sense of dread. Why would anyone send such a thing? And what purpose could it serve?

Her musings were interrupted by a soft chime. Startled, she glanced down at the clock. It had made no movement, no sign of ticking, yet the chime reverberated softly through the room. She took a step back, a chill running down her spine. The clock chimed again, and this time, a thin line appeared in the center of the blank face. Slowly, almost imperceptibly, it began to etch its way outward, forming a pair of hands.

With each chime, the hands moved, as if marking some invisible passage of time. Beatrice could only watch, transfixed and unnerved, as the hands completed their circuit and came to a stop at precisely twelve o'clock. There was a final, louder chime, and then silence.

The air in the room seemed to thicken, the shadows deepening. Beatrice blinked, shaking herself free of the strange trance the clock had cast over her. She reached out, hesitantly, and touched the smooth surface of the clock's face. It was cold—unnaturally so. She drew her hand back, a shiver running through her.

Whatever this clock was, it was no ordinary timepiece. And she had a sinking feeling that it was not meant to keep time, but rather to mark it—perhaps even to count down to something. But to what?

With a determined expression, Beatrice closed the crate and left it on the table. This was a matter for Miss Clara. The young woman had a keen mind and an even sharper intuition—she would know what to do.

Gathering her composure, Beatrice made her way through the house, her footsteps echoing in the empty hallways. She found Miss Clara in the library, a large tome spread open on the polished mahogany desk. Clara Hargrave looked up as Beatrice entered, her pale blue eyes bright with curiosity.

"Beatrice," she said warmly. "What brings you here?"

"Miss Clara, there's... there's something you need to see," Beatrice replied, struggling to keep the tremor from her voice. "A package arrived this morning. I think... I think it's something sinister."

Clara's brow furrowed. "A package? For whom?"

"For the house," Beatrice said, clasping her hands together tightly. "There was no name, no address. Just this strange clock inside. It's... well, it's difficult to explain. I think you should come and look at it yourself."

Curiosity piqued, Clara rose from her chair and followed Beatrice back to the foyer. As soon as her gaze fell on the crate and its eerie contents, a look of concern crossed her features. She reached out and picked up the clock, turning it over in her hands.

"You say it chimed?" she asked, glancing at Beatrice.

"Yes, Miss Clara. It chimed, and then... it moved, as if by its own accord."

Clara frowned, examining the smooth face of the clock. "This is not just any clock. It's a message—one that's meant to unsettle us."

"But what does it mean?" Beatrice asked, her voice barely above a whisper.

Clara shook her head slowly. "I don't know. But we must find out. I fear that this is only the beginning of something far more dangerous."

She set the clock back down and stared at it for a long moment. Then, with a sudden resolve, she turned to Beatrice.

"We need to inform the authorities. And I think it's time we speak with Detective Hart again. He warned us that something like this might happen. The past, it seems, has a way of catching up with us, no matter how carefully we try to bury it."

Beatrice nodded, relief mingling with the lingering sense of foreboding. As Clara moved to the telephone to place the call, Beatrice glanced once more at the clock. Its hands, now still, pointed accusingly at the number twelve.

Somewhere, in the depths of her mind, a voice whispered a single word:

Midnight.

The hour when all truths are revealed and all secrets come to light.

4. The First Body Found

THE TOWN OF ASHFIELD had always been a place of quiet dignity. Nestled comfortably amidst the rolling English countryside, its cobbled streets and neatly trimmed hedgerows had an air of timelessness about them. The village's inhabitants, too, were steadfast and predictable, just like the grand clock tower that stood sentinel in the market square, its hands methodically sweeping over each hour as they had done for over a century.

It was a place where secrets were rare and disturbances rarer still—until the morning when Mrs. Beatrice Shaw stumbled upon a sight that would shake Ashfield to its very core.

The air was crisp with the first chill of autumn, leaves beginning to turn to russet and gold as Mrs. Shaw made her way down Hawthorn Lane, her wicker basket clutched firmly in one gloved hand. The light of dawn had barely touched the rooftops, casting a gentle glow that promised another quiet day. As she passed the old clockmaker's shop—a quaint little building with a green-painted façade and gold lettering that spelled out Hollingsworth & Son—Mrs. Shaw's steps faltered.

Something was not right.

The shop's door, always closed and securely locked at this early hour, stood slightly ajar, a sliver of darkness peeking out from within. Mrs. Shaw hesitated, glancing around to see if anyone else had noticed. But the street was deserted. She took a step closer, peering into the shadowed interior.

"Mr. Hollingsworth?" she called softly, her voice barely more than a whisper.

There was no answer, only the faint creak of the door as it swayed gently in the breeze. Swallowing her unease, Mrs. Shaw took a tentative step inside, her shoes tapping softly on the polished wooden floor. The familiar scent of wood shavings and machine oil filled her nostrils, mingling with the faint odor of something else—something metallic and unpleasantly sharp.

"Hello?" she called again, louder this time. "Is anyone here?"

Her gaze swept over the shop's interior. Tall glass-fronted cabinets lined the walls, displaying an array of timepieces—delicate pocket watches, grand mantel clocks, and tiny, intricate pieces whose mechanisms seemed too complex to belong to such small objects. Mr. Hollingsworth took great pride in his craft, each clock meticulously cared for and polished until it gleamed. But today, something was amiss.

Several of the clocks had stopped at odd times, their hands frozen at awkward angles. A fine layer of dust had settled over a few, as though they had not been attended to in days. And there, near the counter, was something that made Mrs. Shaw's heart leap into her throat: a dark stain on the floor, spreading slowly like an inkblot on parchment.

It was blood.

Mrs. Shaw's breath caught as she followed the trail with her eyes, a chill running down her spine. The blood led to a figure sprawled behind the counter—a figure she recognized immediately. Mr. Hollingsworth lay on his back, his face pale and eyes staring blankly at the ceiling. His vest was stained crimson, a jagged wound slicing through his shirt. But it wasn't just the blood that made Mrs. Shaw's stomach twist with dread.

Clutched in Mr. Hollingsworth's stiff fingers was a pocket watch—its face shattered, hands pointing to twelve o'clock precisely.

For a moment, Mrs. Shaw couldn't move, her mind refusing to accept the scene before her. The kind, elderly clockmaker, who had repaired her late husband's watch just last spring, now lay lifeless in a pool of his own blood. A scream built in her throat, but no sound emerged. Instead, she stumbled backwards, her basket dropping to the floor with a clatter, sending apples and carrots rolling across the shop.

It was this noise that finally broke the silence. Somewhere outside, a dog barked, and Mrs. Shaw spun on her heel, fleeing from the shop as fast as her trembling legs would carry her. She burst into the street, gasping for breath, and nearly collided with Constable Albert Thompson, who was making his rounds.

"Mrs. Shaw, what on earth—" He stopped short at the sight of her ashen face and wild eyes. "What's happened?"

"Mr. Hollingsworth... the clockmaker... he's dead!" she managed to gasp out, clutching at the constable's sleeve. "There's blood... so much blood..."

Constable Thompson's eyes widened, but he quickly regained his composure. "Stay here," he ordered, his voice firm. "I'll take a look."

With that, he strode towards the shop, his hand resting lightly on the truncheon at his belt. Mrs. Shaw watched him go, her breath coming in short, panicked gasps. It seemed like an eternity before the constable re-emerged, his face set in grim lines.

"Stay calm, Mrs. Shaw," he said, though his own voice was edged with tension. "I need to alert the inspector. Do you feel well enough to make your way home?"

Mrs. Shaw nodded numbly. "Yes, yes, I'll go... but what about Mr. Hollingsworth? What's going to happen now?"

"We'll do everything we can to find out what happened," Constable Thompson assured her. "But for now, it's best if you go home and try to rest."

Mrs. Shaw didn't need to be told twice. She turned and hurried away, her mind a whirl of fear and confusion. As she left Hawthorn Lane behind, the peaceful façade of the village seemed to crumble. Doors opened, faces peered out, and low murmurs filled the air as word of the tragedy spread like wildfire.

• • • •

AN HOUR LATER, INSPECTOR Gerald Hart stood in the shadowed confines of the clockmaker's shop, his keen eyes taking in every detail. Tall and lean, with a sharply cut profile and a gaze that missed nothing, Hart had served as Ashfield's chief inspector for the better part of a decade. He was a man who had seen his share of death and violence, but there was something about the scene before him that sent a shiver of unease through him.

"Any witnesses?" he asked, glancing at Constable Thompson, who hovered nearby.

"Only Mrs. Shaw, sir. She found the body when she was passing by. Says she didn't see anyone else around."

Hart nodded absently, crouching beside the clockmaker's corpse. Mr. Hollingsworth's face was twisted in a grimace of pain, his hand still locked around the broken watch. Hart gently pried the timepiece free, examining it closely.

The glass was shattered, and the tiny cogs inside were damaged, as though someone had stomped on it. But that wasn't what held Hart's attention. It was the fact that the hands were positioned at exactly twelve o'clock—a perfect, precise mark.

"Curious," he murmured, turning the watch over in his hands. "Who would go to such lengths to destroy a piece like this, and why leave it behind?"

Constable Thompson shifted uncomfortably. "Do you think it's a message, sir? Some kind of warning?"

"Perhaps." Hart rose to his feet, slipping the watch into an evidence bag. "Or it could be something else entirely. We won't know until we learn more about Mr. Hollingsworth's life—and his enemies."

He surveyed the room again, his gaze lingering on the stopped clocks. Each one displayed a different time, as though mocking the concept of order and sequence. Hart's lips tightened. This was no ordinary crime. It was planned, deliberate, and executed with chilling precision.

"Send for a forensics team," he instructed. "I want every inch of this shop combed for evidence. And find out if anyone saw or heard anything unusual last night."

"Yes, sir." Constable Thompson saluted smartly and hurried out.

Left alone, Inspector Hart let out a slow breath. He glanced at the lifeless body of the clockmaker, then at the rows of clocks lining the walls. Each ticked softly, their rhythms slightly out of sync, creating a dissonant melody that seemed to echo through the room.

"Time," he muttered under his breath. "It all comes down to time."

With that, he turned on his heel and strode out of the shop, a sense of foreboding settling over him like a heavy shroud. Something dark had awakened in Ashfield, and Hart had the sinking feeling that this was only the beginning.

• • • •

THE NEWS OF MR. HOLLINGSWORTH'S murder spread rapidly through the village, whispers of it reaching even the furthest corners of Ashfield. Speculation ran rampant—who could have done such a thing? And why? The clockmaker had been a respected member of the community, known for his meticulous work and quiet, unassuming nature. No one could fathom why anyone would wish him harm.

But as Inspector Hart began his investigation, it soon became clear that Mr. Hollingsworth's past held secrets that few in Ashfield had ever suspected. Secrets that someone was willing to kill to protect.

5. Clues in the Gears

IT WAS A BRISK, WIND-whipped morning when Inspector James Hart first noticed the peculiar brass glint among the broken fragments of the murdered Mr. Peter Coleman's prized grandfather clock. The chilling call had come just as the inspector finished his morning tea—Coleman's housekeeper had discovered his body sprawled in the parlour, his head grotesquely canted to one side, and a pool of blood slowly seeping across the meticulously polished wooden floor.

The clock, a magnificent creation of intricate craftsmanship, lay shattered beside him, its gears and mechanisms strewn haphazardly around the room as if in a final act of defiance. But it was not the gruesome nature of the scene that caught Inspector Hart's attention—he'd seen his fair share of violence and gore in his years on the force. No, it was the seemingly random scattering of the clock's internal workings that tugged at his investigative instincts.

"Why," he murmured to himself as he crouched low, examining the odd placement of the gears and springs, "would the killer take the time to destroy the clock, yet handle its parts with such... deliberation?"

He retrieved a handkerchief from his coat pocket and gingerly picked up one of the gears. It was smaller than his thumb, yet heavy, crafted from solid brass and etched with minute, almost imperceptible symbols along its rim. Hart's keen eyes narrowed as he turned it over, then glanced at the disassembled clock face, the shattered pendulum, and the broken case. It all looked like senseless vandalism, yet he knew there was an order to it—a pattern just waiting to be unraveled.

"Inspector Hart, sir?" A young constable appeared in the doorway, his face pale and drawn. "Dr. Smythe is ready to brief you on the... the state of the body."

Hart straightened up, slipping the tiny gear into a small evidence bag and sealing it. "Lead the way, Constable."

In the adjacent drawing room, Dr. Smythe, the town's long-serving medical examiner, was examining the corpse with a meticulousness born of years of grim experience. He glanced up as Hart entered, his expression sombre.

"Inspector, I won't mince words. This is no ordinary killing."

Hart crossed his arms, his gaze unwavering. "Go on."

"The cause of death is a broken neck, likely from a sharp, forceful twist," Dr. Smythe began, gesturing to the unnatural angle of Coleman's head. "But that's not what concerns me. It's what I found on the victim's hands."

Dr. Smythe pulled back the white cloth covering Coleman's body to reveal his hands. They were stained with a fine, reddish-brown powder that glistened under the overhead lights. It was an odd sight, and one that Hart immediately recognized.

"Clock dust," Hart muttered, his brow furrowing. "The type you'd find inside an old mechanism, like... like the very clock that's been destroyed here."

"Exactly," Dr. Smythe confirmed. "But the amount is far too great for it to have simply come from handling the clock. It's as if..." He hesitated, choosing his words carefully. "As if Mr. Coleman was trying to fix or disassemble the clock in his final moments."

Hart considered this. Peter Coleman was no clockmaker. In fact, he was a retired banker with a penchant for collecting rare timepieces, not repairing them. Why would he have been fiddling with the clock before his death?

"Did you find anything else?" Hart asked.

Dr. Smythe nodded, his face grim. "Yes. There's another curious detail. His right hand—the one stained with the most dust—has abrasions and small cuts, as though he'd been handling something sharp. Perhaps... a gear?"

Hart's thoughts immediately returned to the tiny brass gear he'd bagged earlier. It had no sharp edges, but there had been something about its weight and markings that seemed out of place. Something almost ritualistic. A dark thought flickered in his mind: was it possible Coleman had been trying to remove something from the clock? Or worse, put something into it?

"Thank you, Doctor," Hart said quietly. "Let me know if you find anything else."

As he left the room, Hart's mind churned with possibilities. Returning to the scene of the crime, he studied the shattered remnants of the grandfather clock once more. There was something deliberate about the way the pieces were strewn—almost as if someone had dismantled it step by step, only to scatter the pieces afterward.

Kneeling again, Hart noticed that many of the gears had been marked with similar symbols to the one he'd collected. They were tiny, almost invisible to the naked eye, and each gear bore a different combination of lines, circles, and what appeared to be letters in an unfamiliar script. The symbols were meticulously etched into the brass, and they reminded Hart of an ancient cipher he'd seen once in an old case involving an obscure academic society.

"Inspector?" The voice of Constable Miller interrupted his thoughts. "There's someone here to see you. A Miss Eleanor Hughes."

Hart glanced up, a flicker of recognition sparking in his eyes. Eleanor Hughes was Peter Coleman's niece, his only living relative. He had met her briefly at a charity function years ago, and though they hadn't spoken since, he remembered her as a sharp, no-nonsense woman.

"Show her in," Hart instructed, rising to his feet and dusting off his trousers.

Miss Hughes entered with an air of quiet dignity. She was dressed in a muted grey coat, her dark hair pulled back neatly, and her eyes—though red-rimmed from tears—held a steely resolve.

"Inspector Hart," she began, her voice steady despite the circumstances. "I'm here to help in any way I can."

"I'm sorry for your loss, Miss Hughes," Hart said gently. "But I must ask—did your uncle have any enemies? Anyone who might have wished him harm?"

Eleanor sighed softly, lowering her gaze. "Uncle Peter was a solitary man. After my aunt's death, he retreated into his collection. Clocks became his obsession. He wasn't the easiest man to get along with, but an enemy? I don't know..."

She paused, a shadow of doubt crossing her face. "There was one thing, though. Lately, he had become... different. He would spend hours locked in his study, poring over old documents, and I often heard him muttering about 'the code' or 'the key.' I didn't understand what he meant, and whenever I asked, he would brush me off."

"A code?" Hart's interest piqued. "Did he mention what it referred to?"

Eleanor shook her head. "No, but I know he kept a journal. He wrote in it every night, sometimes for hours. If you can find it, perhaps it could shed some light on his state of mind."

Hart nodded thoughtfully. "Thank you, Miss Hughes. I'll look into it. One more thing—did he receive any unusual visitors or correspondence recently?"

"Not that I'm aware of," Eleanor replied. "But... he did receive a package a few days ago. A small box, wrapped in plain brown paper. I remember asking him what it was, and he simply smiled—a strange, almost... knowing smile—and said it was 'the missing piece.'"

Hart's pulse quickened. "Do you know where this package is now?"

"I'm not sure," Eleanor admitted. "It might still be in his study. I can take you there."

The study was a small, cluttered room at the back of the house, its walls lined with shelves filled with books on mechanical engineering, horology, and cryptography. A large wooden desk dominated the centre of the room, and as Hart approached it, he noticed the open drawer, its contents disheveled as if someone had been searching through it in a hurry.

He rifled through the papers and notebooks, his fingers brushing against something hard and metallic. He pulled out a small, polished box made of dark mahogany. The lock was broken, and inside, nestled on a bed of dark velvet, lay an object that made Hart's breath catch in his throat.

It was another gear—identical to the one he had found earlier, but slightly larger and engraved with even more symbols. Beside it lay a folded piece of parchment, yellowed with age and covered in the same strange script.

"What is this?" Eleanor whispered, peering over his shoulder.

"I don't know," Hart murmured, his voice tinged with awe. "But I have a feeling your uncle's murder is only the beginning. Someone wanted these gears, and they were willing to kill for them."

As he carefully placed the gear and the parchment into separate evidence bags, Hart felt a chill run down his spine. The gears were more than just parts of a clock—they were pieces of a puzzle. A deadly puzzle that someone had set into motion years ago, and now, it was up to him to stop the clock before it claimed another life.

6. Time Stopped at Midnight

THE SMALL TOWN OF RIDGEWOOD was, for the most part, a quiet place. Nestled among rolling hills and dotted with quaint cottages, it appeared serene to any passing traveler. But like many idyllic locales, it held secrets that festered in the shadows. The events of that dreadful night would soon remind the townsfolk that beneath the still surface of every lake lies an unseen current.

That night, the air was still. The town square, usually deserted at this hour, held a solitary figure who made his way slowly across the cobblestones, each step echoing faintly in the silence. The streetlamps cast long, ominous shadows that seemed to stretch and twist in the figure's path, as if the town itself were recoiling from his presence. As he moved, he paused occasionally to glance behind him, his nervous gaze darting from one darkened alley to the next.

William Frost, the town's newest resident, had never intended to be out so late. A simple errand — delivering a note from his employer to the reclusive Mrs. Weatherby — had taken much longer than expected. Mrs. Weatherby, an elderly woman with a fondness for gossip, had insisted on recounting tales from her youth, drawing out the evening until the chimes of the church bell announced midnight's arrival.

He regretted lingering now. The square seemed to have transformed since dusk, as if the town itself had shifted ever so slightly, becoming unfamiliar and faintly threatening. He glanced at the large clock above the town hall, its massive bronze hands frozen at twelve.

A frown crossed his face. That couldn't be right. He had just heard the bells; they'd struck midnight perfectly. Yet, the clock above him stood still, as if caught in time.

"Strange," he muttered, quickening his pace.

The sound of something skittering behind him made him stop abruptly. He turned sharply, his eyes straining in the dim light. Nothing moved, not a breath of wind stirred, yet he couldn't shake the sensation that he was being watched. The feeling clung to him like a damp fog, heavy and oppressive.

Shaking off his nerves, William took a deep breath and continued his walk, but this time his pace was brisker, his steps less hesitant. If he could just make it home, he would feel safe again. The small cottage on Elm Street, with its warm hearth and cheerful curtains, would banish this eerie feeling that had settled over him like a shroud.

As he reached the bridge that marked the halfway point to his home, he saw a figure emerge from the fog — a hunched silhouette with a cane. William squinted, his heart beating faster.

"Who's there?" he called out, his voice startlingly loud in the stillness.

"Only an old man, Mr. Frost," came a reply, slow and deliberate. The figure moved closer, and as he stepped into the light, William recognized the town's caretaker, Mr. Bledsoe.

"Evening, sir," William said with a forced smile. "What brings you out at this hour?"

Mr. Bledsoe, a man of indeterminate age with a face as wrinkled and weathered as old parchment, shrugged. "Just tending to some matters. You know how it is. Can't leave things undone."

William nodded, though he didn't quite understand. There was a glint in the old man's eye, something that made William uneasy. But it was late, and he wanted nothing more than to be done with this conversation.

"I should be getting home. Long day and all," William said quickly, stepping around the caretaker.

"Before you go," Mr. Bledsoe murmured, his voice low, "did you happen to notice the town clock?"

William turned, puzzled. "Yes, I did. It's stopped."

"Stopped right at midnight," Bledsoe continued, his gaze never leaving William's face. "Strange, don't you think?"

"Must be a mechanical fault," William replied, though he felt a shiver run down his spine.

"Perhaps. Or perhaps it's a sign." Bledsoe's smile widened ever so slightly, revealing yellowed teeth. "You'd best hurry home, Mr. Frost. Midnight is not a time to be lingering."

With that cryptic remark, the old man turned and hobbled away, disappearing into the mist. William stood for a moment, staring after him, before shaking his head and continuing on his way. He was almost home — just a few more streets, and he'd be safe inside.

But as he rounded the last corner, he came to a sudden halt. There, at the entrance of his cottage, was another figure — tall and thin, with a hat pulled low over his face. The stranger seemed to be examining the door, his gloved hand resting on the handle as if testing it.

William's heart leapt into his throat. "Hey! What are you doing?"

The man turned slowly, and William caught a glimpse of a pale, gaunt face before the stranger melted back into the shadows and vanished down the alleyway.

Without thinking, William rushed to his door, his hands trembling as he fumbled for his key. He shoved it into the lock, turned it, and stumbled inside, slamming the door shut behind him.

Leaning against the door, he closed his eyes, willing his racing heart to slow. But as he stood there, he became aware of something else — a faint ticking sound. It was coming from the mantelpiece, where a small brass clock sat.

William opened his eyes and stared at the clock. The hands were moving, but not normally. They spun backward, faster and faster, until they stopped abruptly at twelve.

Midnight.

He took a step back, his breath coming in short gasps. The clock was broken; that much was clear. But why had it stopped at the exact same time as the town clock? What did it mean?

The faintest whisper of a thought passed through his mind: Time has stopped for you, William Frost.

A sharp knock at the door shattered his reverie. He jumped, nearly dropping the clock in his hands. Who could be calling at this hour?

Slowly, he made his way back to the door and peered through the peephole. A figure stood on the other side — tall, thin, with a hat pulled low.

"No," he whispered, stepping back.

The knock came again, more insistent this time. William hesitated, his hand hovering over the doorknob. He knew he should call for help, run to a neighbor's house, do anything but open that door.

But he couldn't move. Something compelled him to turn the knob, to see who — or what — stood on his doorstep.

As the door swung open, the figure stepped forward. A gloved hand shot out, grabbing William by the collar. He tried to scream, but a cold metal object was pressed against his throat, silencing him.

The stranger leaned in close, his breath hot against William's ear. "Time has run out for you, Mr. Frost."

And then, with a swift motion, the gloved hand twisted the object — a tiny silver key — and everything went dark.

· · · ·

THE NEXT MORNING, RIDGEWOOD awoke to news of yet another tragedy. William Frost, the town's newest resident, had been found dead in his cottage, his body slumped against the mantelpiece. The police were baffled — there were no signs of struggle, no marks of violence.

Only one thing was out of place: the small brass clock on the mantel, its hands frozen at midnight.

As word of the strange occurrence spread, the townsfolk whispered amongst themselves, their eyes drifting nervously toward the town hall's clock tower. For there, high above the square, the massive bronze hands remained stubbornly still, marking the hour of twelve.

Midnight.

And though no one dared to say it aloud, they all shared the same thought: Time had stopped for William Frost — and who would be next?

Detective Inspector Arthur Hart arrived later that day, summoned from London to investigate the peculiar circumstances surrounding the death. A veteran of many unusual cases, Hart was not easily unnerved. Yet as he stood in the quiet cottage, staring at the frozen clock and the lifeless body of William Frost, he felt a chill that had nothing to do with the autumn wind.

Something was very wrong in Ridgewood, and if Hart didn't uncover the truth soon, he feared that William Frost would be only the first of many.

But time, it seemed, was no longer on his side.

Chapter 2: Shadows of the Past

1. A Town in Mourning

The small English town of Wycliffe had always been known for its serene beauty, its picturesque landscapes, and its timeless charm. Nestled between rolling green hills and the whispering woods that stretched for miles, it was the kind of place where one could imagine time stood still, where days seemed to pass without much consequence, and where everyone knew everyone else by name. But now, a thick shroud of grief hung over its cobblestone streets, casting long, somber shadows over the once lively town square.

The news of the recent murder had spread like wildfire, sparking fear and anxiety among the residents. It was not just any death—it was brutal, cruel, and, above all, unexpected. Mrs. Agnes Whittaker, a woman of some repute and no little wealth, had been found dead in her own parlor. Her body, twisted in a grotesque manner, had been discovered lying on the floor beside the grandfather clock that had been her late husband's pride and joy. The clock's hands were frozen at exactly twelve minutes past midnight. It was a detail that sent shivers down the spines of the constables who first arrived at the scene.

For Wycliffe, a town that rarely saw any crime more severe than a petty theft or the occasional brawl at the local pub, the murder was a shock to its very core. Mrs. Whittaker had been more than just a wealthy widow—she had been a figure of stability and tradition, one of the last remaining members of a lineage that stretched back generations. Her involvement in various charitable organizations, her presence at the weekly church services, and her unwavering support for the community had made her a beloved figure, even among those who secretly found her somewhat domineering.

Now, she was gone, and the town was left grappling with the sudden void left in her wake. People whispered in hushed tones at the bakery, murmured anxiously at the butcher's, and gathered in small, tight-knit clusters at the marketplace. Faces that usually wore smiles and shared pleasantries were now marked with frowns, worry lines creasing their foreheads.

At the heart of this uneasy atmosphere was Detective Sergeant Henry Hart, a man who had served the Wycliffe Constabulary for the better part of two decades. He had seen his share of tragedies and heartbreaks, but never something as sinister as this. He stood at the edge of the town square, his gaze drifting over the familiar sights—Mrs. Pritchard's sweetshop, with its enticing display of homemade tarts; the iron gates of the churchyard, standing slightly ajar; and the stone fountain that marked the town center, its water now still and silent, as if it, too, mourned the loss of Mrs. Whittaker.

Hart's mind buzzed with questions that had no easy answers. Why had Mrs. Whittaker been targeted? Was it a robbery gone wrong? Or was it something far more personal? He had pored over the initial reports, scrutinized every detail, yet there was nothing concrete to latch onto—no sign of forced entry, no clear motive, and no witnesses who had seen or heard anything unusual that fateful night.

He took a deep breath, steadying himself. The town needed him to be strong, to be the pillar they could lean on as they tried to comprehend this heinous act. He knew he would have to tread carefully, for the slightest misstep could send the already tense townsfolk into a frenzy of suspicion and paranoia. But Hart had no intention of letting this killer roam free. He was determined to find out who had shattered the tranquility of Wycliffe and bring them to justice.

With a final glance at the silent square, he turned on his heel and made his way toward the Whittaker residence. It was a grand old house, set back from the road, surrounded by neatly trimmed hedges and a wrought-iron fence that had once seemed to serve as a symbol of security. Now, it felt more like a barrier that isolated the house from the rest of the world, a grim reminder of the tragedy that had occurred within its walls.

The housekeeper, Mrs. Littleton, a petite woman with graying hair and a nervous disposition, greeted him at the door. She had been the one to find Mrs. Whittaker's body, and since that dreadful morning, she had not left the house, as if doing so would be some sort of betrayal to her late employer.

"Good afternoon, Mrs. Littleton," Hart said gently, doffing his hat. "May I come in?"

The woman nodded mutely, her eyes red-rimmed from crying. She led him into the parlor, where the faint scent of lavender lingered—a testament to Mrs. Whittaker's meticulous housekeeping habits. Everything in the room seemed to be in perfect order, except for the empty space where the body had been.

Hart's gaze shifted to the grandfather clock. Its face, once a source of fascination for Mrs. Whittaker, now seemed to mock him with its unmoving hands. Twelve minutes past midnight. What did it mean? Was it a message left by the murderer? Or was it simply a cruel coincidence?

"Mrs. Littleton," he began softly, turning to face the housekeeper, "I know this is difficult, but I need to ask you a few more questions. Anything you can tell me, no matter how small, could be of great help."

The woman hesitated, wringing her hands in front of her apron. "I've told you everything I know, Sergeant," she whispered, her voice trembling. "She was fine when I went to bed. There was no sign of anything amiss. And then... when I came down in the morning..." Her voice broke, and she dabbed at her eyes with a handkerchief.

Hart waited patiently, giving her time to compose herself. "I understand," he said gently. "But I need you to think carefully. Did Mrs. Whittaker receive any visitors recently? Anyone she might have been upset or uneasy about?"

Mrs. Littleton shook her head slowly. "No, sir. Mrs. Whittaker was a private woman, especially in these last few months. She rarely entertained guests. Only her solicitor, Mr. Cartwright, would come by on occasion, and that was for business matters."

Hart made a mental note to speak with Mr. Cartwright. "And what about the clock?" he asked, nodding toward the silent sentinel in the corner. "Did it stop on its own, or did someone tamper with it?"

The housekeeper's eyes widened slightly, and she glanced at the clock as if seeing it for the first time since the murder. "I... I don't know, sir. That clock has been in the family for generations. It's never stopped, not in all the years I've worked here."

A chill ran down Hart's spine. "Thank you, Mrs. Littleton. You've been very helpful."

He stepped back, his mind racing. The clock was a key piece of this puzzle, he was certain of it. But how? Why had the killer chosen to stop it at precisely twelve minutes past midnight? Was it a symbol? A warning? Or was there something even more sinister at play?

With a curt nod to Mrs. Littleton, Hart left the house and made his way back to the station. He needed to review everything again—the witness statements, the photographs, the forensic reports. He couldn't afford to miss even the smallest detail.

As he walked, he couldn't shake the feeling that he was being watched. He glanced over his shoulder, but the street was empty, save for a stray cat that darted across the road. He told himself it was just his imagination, the strain of the case playing tricks on him.

But deep down, he knew it was more than that. The murderer was still out there, lurking in the shadows, watching his every move.

And if Hart wasn't careful, he would become the next victim of the clockwork killer.

2. Detective Hart's Dilemma

DETECTIVE REGINALD Hart was not a man easily rattled. His presence in the small town of Ashford was as steady and reassuring as the church bell that chimed each hour. Residents would nod approvingly whenever they saw his broad-shouldered figure strolling down High Street, his coat flaring behind him like the cape of a steadfast guardian. They trusted him to unravel the knottiest of mysteries and return their quiet town to its customary tranquility. Yet, as he stood in his modest office that morning, peering at the peculiar array of clues spread across his desk, an uncharacteristic uncertainty flickered in his gaze.

The first murder had been shocking enough—Dr. Francis Holloway, a retired physician, found dead in his study with no sign of struggle. A man well into his sixties, Holloway had succumbed to a swift and silent death, leaving behind a wife and a peculiar clock frozen at midnight. Hart had examined the device carefully; it was an antique pocket watch, the kind a gentleman might carry, now wedged open as though pried by unseen hands. It was the first time Hart had encountered a murder scene marked by such an oddity. He remembered dismissing the watch as a macabre trophy or a mocking gesture by the killer. But then the second body had been found, and the watch was there again.

Eleanor Marchmont, a wealthy widow, was discovered sprawled across her own dining room floor, her once vivid blue eyes now fixed in a lifeless stare. Another clock, this time a small, intricately carved desk piece, had been placed beside her. It too pointed to midnight. It was at this point that Hart began to suspect something far more sinister at play—a pattern that suggested these killings were not random acts of violence, but parts of a greater, more insidious scheme.

With each passing day, the unease grew. Hart had pieced together fragments of a story that seemed to defy all logical explanation. Each new development only added to the puzzle, and for a man who had built his career on cold logic and methodical reasoning, this was nothing short of maddening. His once neat and orderly office had become a chaotic battlefield, with papers strewn about, diagrams sketched and hastily crumpled, and suspect lists that seemed to grow longer by the hour.

The dilemma that gnawed at Hart's mind was multifaceted. Were these murders the work of a single mind, or a conspiracy? The watches all shared one feature—each had been altered to stop at the precise time of death, the mechanisms inside meticulously tampered with to freeze at midnight. Who could possess such skill and knowledge? Who could be clever enough to manipulate these intricate devices and elude detection? And, perhaps most disturbing of all, why?

His instincts screamed at him that time was of the essence. The clock motif—so blatant and yet so elusive—suggested that the killer's actions were counting down to something, though what, Hart could not yet discern. More than once, he found himself staring at the framed photograph of his late mentor, Inspector Alistair Morton, wondering what the old man would have made of all this. "Trust the evidence," Morton would say. "Let the facts guide you, not your emotions." Sound advice, but what if the evidence itself was tainted? What if every fact pointed not to clarity, but to deeper confusion?

Hart's thoughts were interrupted by the soft creak of his office door opening. He glanced up, expecting to see Sergeant Wilkins or perhaps another well-meaning citizen offering yet another theory. Instead, it was Amelia Grey, the town librarian, her dark hair neatly pinned back, and her expression one of quiet determination.

"Detective Hart," she began, her voice steady despite the evident worry in her eyes, "I believe I may have found something that could be of help."

Amelia had been assisting Hart informally since the start of the investigation. Sharp-witted and observant, she possessed a remarkable knack for uncovering details others overlooked. She approached his desk, holding a slender volume bound in faded leather.

"This is an old journal I came across in the town archives," she said, placing it carefully in front of him. "It belonged to Thomas Aldridge, a clockmaker who lived here over a century ago. He writes about designing a series of 'symbolic timepieces'—one for each of his greatest regrets."

Hart flipped open the journal with a skeptical frown. The pages were filled with meticulous handwriting, diagrams of clock mechanisms, and cryptic annotations that hinted at a deeply troubled mind. He glanced back at Amelia.

"What are you suggesting, Miss Grey?"

"I'm not entirely sure yet," she admitted. "But I've cross-referenced the names mentioned in the journal with the town's records, and there are disturbing similarities. The places, the families... It's as if someone is retracing Aldridge's steps, recreating his 'symbolic murders' through these clocks."

Hart leaned back in his chair, his fingers tapping thoughtfully on the armrest. Could it be true? Was the killer following some century-old blueprint? He felt a flicker of hope—an anchor of rationality in the swirling chaos of his thoughts.

"Good work, Amelia. This might be the breakthrough we've been searching for." He closed the journal, his jaw set with renewed resolve. "But it also raises more questions. If someone is replicating these murders, then how are they choosing the victims? What's the connection?"

Amelia nodded, clearly having anticipated the question. "That's what I'm still working on. But one thing is clear—the victims aren't random. There's a link between them, and I suspect it has something to do with their ancestors."

Hart frowned, sifting through the mental catalog of what he knew about the victims. Holloway, Marchmont... They were old families, deeply rooted in the town's history. If there was some dark legacy at play here, then Hart would have to dig deeper—much deeper.

"Start compiling everything you can find on the Aldridge family and their connections to these victims. I'll handle the rest." He stood abruptly, slipping on his coat with a sharp movement. "There's someone I need to speak to."

Amelia's brow furrowed. "Who?"

"An old acquaintance who knows more about the Aldridge legacy than anyone else. If anyone can shed light on this madness, it's him."

With a curt nod, Hart left the office, his thoughts racing faster than his feet. There was a man—Edward Aldridge, a reclusive descendant of the clockmaker, who lived on the outskirts of Ashford. Hart had never had cause to speak with him before now, but the time had come.

Edward Aldridge's house was a ramshackle affair, teetering on the brink of collapse as though time itself had forgotten it. The man who answered the door was as worn as the building he inhabited—thin, stooped, with eyes that gleamed with a peculiar sharpness.

"Detective Hart," Edward murmured in a voice as creaky as the door's hinges. "I've been expecting you."

Hart felt a chill ripple through him. "You know why I'm here?"

"Of course," Edward replied with a thin smile. "You're here about the clocks. About my great-grandfather's curse."

"Curse?" Hart echoed, incredulous. "You mean these murders—"

"Are the fulfillment of a promise made long ago," Edward interrupted, his gaze distant. "Thomas Aldridge was a man obsessed with time, but it wasn't just the hours and minutes that fascinated him. It was how time intersects with fate, with guilt. He built those clocks to capture more than time; he built them to capture destiny."

Hart's patience wore thin. "Enough of the riddles, Aldridge. I need facts."

"The facts are these, Detective," Edward said, his voice hardening. "The victims... their ancestors wronged Thomas in ways that cannot be undone. Betrayal, theft, deceit. He couldn't punish them in life, so he swore their descendants would pay the price. And now, someone—perhaps even the ghost of Thomas himself—is making good on that vow."

Hart shook his head, frustration boiling over. "You can't be serious. Are you telling me this is some kind of vendetta from beyond the grave?"

Edward's smile was unsettlingly serene. "I'm telling you, Detective, that time is not as linear as you believe. It folds, loops, and sometimes, it brings the past crashing into the present. You'll see soon enough."

Hart left the crumbling house more troubled than ever. Edward's words lingered like a dark mist in his mind. Was it truly possible? Could these murders be a twisted attempt to avenge slights from a century ago? He didn't believe in ghosts, but he did believe in the destructive power of obsession—and it seemed someone was obsessed enough to kill for it.

Back in his office, Hart pored over the Aldridge journal again, searching for any clue that might illuminate the killer's identity. Hours passed, the daylight outside fading into a gray dusk, but still, no clear answers emerged. Then, just as he was about to close the book in frustration, his eye caught a name, scrawled in the margin of one of the diagrams: Moriarty.

"Moriarty?" he muttered aloud, frowning. The name meant nothing to him, yet it seemed oddly familiar. With a sense of foreboding, he realized that this was no ordinary case of murder. He was standing at the precipice of something far more profound, a conspiracy that stretched through generations, its roots entwined with the very history of Ashford itself.

"Damn it," Hart swore softly. The dilemma weighed heavily on his shoulders. Should he pursue this line of inquiry, risking his own sanity in the process? Or should he abandon it and search for more conventional suspects?

With a sigh, he glanced at the clock on his desk. It was almost midnight—how fitting, he thought bitterly. Time had a way of playing cruel tricks on those who dared to challenge its mysteries. But one thing was certain: he couldn't turn back now.

Hart stood, determination tightening his features. No matter how deep this rabbit hole went, he would get to the bottom of it. Because somewhere in this web of timepieces and bloodshed, there was a truth waiting to be discovered—a truth that only he could unearth.

And until he did, the clock would continue to tick for the next victim.

3. An Old Crime Revisited

THE TOWN OF FERNWOOD had always been a quiet place, the kind where time seemed to slow down, and the smallest of changes became a cause for discussion. On the surface, it was a sleepy village with cobbled streets, old stone cottages, and well-manicured gardens where the scent of roses lingered in the air. But, as with many small towns, Fernwood harbored secrets buried beneath its quaint façade—secrets that few cared to remember and others hoped would remain lost in the fog of time.

One of those secrets, however, had begun to stir again.

It started with a letter—a single, yellowed envelope addressed in a neat hand that was both familiar and unsettling. When Chief Inspector Arthur Hart received it that morning, he felt a chill that had nothing to do with the crisp autumn air. The return address indicated a name long forgotten by most in Fernwood, but one that he could never erase from his mind: Charles Marlowe.

Marlowe had been a notorious figure in Fernwood, his reputation built on both wealth and scandal. Thirty years ago, the Marlowe family estate had been the site of a brutal double homicide that left the community shaken to its core. Charles's wife, Eleanor, and their young daughter, Matilda, were found dead in their own home, the walls splattered with evidence of a night of terror. The murders were never solved, and Charles himself vanished soon after, leaving behind a sprawling mansion that stood empty and decaying—like a monument to the crime that no one could forget but that everyone pretended had never happened.

Inspector Hart had been a young constable at the time, still green and eager to prove himself. He remembered the case vividly: the whispers, the theories, the way townsfolk eyed him as he went about his duties, as if expecting him to uncover the truth that eluded the senior detectives. But the investigation had gone cold, and Hart's superiors eventually deemed it unsolvable. The village moved on, the case files were locked away, and the Marlowe estate fell into ruin.

But now, this letter—signed "Charles Marlowe"—had appeared on Hart's desk as if dredged up from the past. It contained only a few lines:

"Inspector Hart, it's time to revisit what you thought you knew. The truth is closer than you think, and the clock is ticking."

Beneath the cryptic message was an address: the old Marlowe estate. And so, for the first time in three decades, Hart found himself standing at the entrance to the grand yet dilapidated mansion that had once been the pride of Fernwood. The gates were rusted and twisted, the garden overgrown with thorny brambles, and the stone façade was cracked and weathered. The place exuded a sense of menace, as if it were holding its breath, waiting for someone to dare to step inside.

Hart hesitated before pushing open the heavy iron gates. They groaned in protest, as though warning him to turn back, but he pressed forward, his footsteps crunching over the gravel path that led to the main entrance. With each step, memories of that terrible night resurfaced—flashes of blood-stained carpets, the blank eyes of the victims, and the sound of a clock ticking away the seconds in the silence of the house.

Standing at the threshold, Hart took a deep breath and reached for the door. It creaked open with surprising ease, revealing a grand foyer dimly lit by shafts of light filtering through the grime-covered windows. Dust swirled in the air, and the musty scent of decay permeated every corner of the place. Hart's eyes fell on a large grandfather clock standing against the far wall, its face frozen at midnight. A bitter smile tugged at his lips. The clock had always been a central feature of the house, its constant ticking a reminder of time's relentless march forward. But now it was silent, as if the house itself had stopped caring to mark the passage of time since that fateful night.

Hart's gaze swept over the room, noting the faded wallpaper, the tarnished chandeliers, and the furniture draped in white sheets like shrouds covering forgotten corpses. The place was a mausoleum of memories, each piece of furniture, each speck of dust, holding a story he wished he could erase. But the letter had drawn him here, and he would not leave without answers.

He walked deeper into the house, his footsteps echoing in the emptiness. The silence was oppressive, broken only by the occasional creak of the floorboards under his weight. He paused before a set of double doors that led to what had once been the drawing room. It was here that Eleanor and Matilda Marlowe had been found—one lying prone on the sofa, the other slumped on the floor beside the hearth. Hart's fingers twitched at the memory, and he pushed the doors open with a sense of grim determination.

The room beyond was much as he remembered it: the same heavy curtains drawn over the windows, the same ornate fireplace, and the same sense of foreboding. But there was something different now, something out of place. Hart's eyes narrowed as he scanned the room, and then he saw it—a small, leather-bound book lying on the mantelpiece. It was new, its cover unmarred by dust or age.

Hart crossed the room and picked up the book, his pulse quickening. The title on the cover read: A Chronicle of Crimes. With trembling fingers, he opened it, revealing page after page of meticulously detailed entries—descriptions of crimes, murders, disappearances—all linked to the Marlowe family and their acquaintances. Some entries were brief, others pages long, but each contained dates, names, and places that rang with the unmistakable tone of truth.

And then he found it: the entry for Eleanor and Matilda Marlowe's murders. Hart's heart pounded as he read the words, the details matching the police reports in every way but one. This entry included a description of the killer—something the police had never uncovered. According to the book, the murders had been committed by a man known only as "The Watchmaker." The description was chillingly precise: tall, gaunt, with a shock of white hair and eyes like "burnished steel." He had been seen in the village days before the murders, speaking with Charles Marlowe himself.

But Charles had never mentioned any such man in his statements. Why?

Hart flipped through more pages, finding entries for other crimes: a poisoning in the neighboring town of Harrington, a string of disappearances in the city, all attributed to the same shadowy figure—the Watchmaker. The book was a damning piece of evidence, a record of atrocities spanning decades, all tied together by a single enigmatic name.

And then Hart reached the final page. It was blank, except for a single line written in the same neat hand as the letter:

"You are looking in the wrong direction. The Watchmaker is closer than you think."

Hart stared at the words, his mind racing. Who had placed this book here? Was it really Charles Marlowe, or someone else trying to lead him astray? And what did they mean by "closer than you think"?

The sound of a creaking floorboard made Hart whirl around, his heart thundering. The room was empty, but he knew he was no longer alone in the house. He could feel it—a presence watching him, waiting for him to take the next step.

Clutching the book to his chest, Hart moved cautiously towards the door. He needed to get out, to analyze what he'd found, but as he stepped into the hallway, a shadow flickered at the edge of his vision. He froze, straining his ears, but the house remained silent.

Then, softly, almost imperceptibly, he heard it: the faint ticking of a clock, coming from somewhere deep within the house.

The sound sent a shiver down his spine. The clocks in the Marlowe house had all been stopped for years—he'd seen it himself. But now, something was ticking. Something—or someone—was trying to send him a message.

Hart took a step forward, then another, following the sound through the twisting corridors of the mansion. The ticking grew louder as he approached the rear of the house, towards a room that had once been Charles Marlowe's study. The door was ajar, a sliver of light spilling out into the dark hallway.

Hart pushed the door open and froze.

In the center of the study stood an old, ornate clock he had never seen before. Its hands moved slowly, steadily, and beneath the glass case, a small brass plate bore an inscription: "To My Dearest Friend, The Watchmaker."

Hart's blood ran cold as he realized the implications. The Watchmaker had been here—had left this clock as a taunt, a reminder that he was still watching, still controlling the game. But more than that, the clock was a message, a piece of a puzzle Hart had thought long since buried.

The past was not dead. It was alive, ticking away in the dark corners of Fernwood, waiting for someone to bring it back into the light.

And now, there was no turning back.

4. The Widow's Tale

THE SMALL DRAWING ROOM of Willow Cottage seemed a perfectly ordinary place at first glance — a room filled with the familiar scent of old wood, aged leather, and faint traces of lavender polish. The lace curtains, drawn slightly against the encroaching twilight, filtered the waning light through a dusty haze, casting muted patterns onto the worn, floral-patterned carpet. It was a room designed for quiet contemplation, a place where the unspoken lingered, and memories from a past life echoed softly in the ticking of an old grandfather clock by the corner.

Mrs. Emmeline Cray sat in her usual spot by the window, her delicate hands folded neatly in her lap. She was a woman who wore grief like a carefully selected garment — not too ostentatious, yet meticulously tailored to fit her every expression and movement. The widow's mourning dress, though not the deepest shade of black, was a subtle reminder of her loss. Its slightly faded edges suggested a passage of time since the tragic event, yet her posture remained rigid, as though she feared that even a slight relaxation might unravel the composure she had worked so hard to maintain.

"Do you find it difficult, Mrs. Cray, to live here all alone after what happened?" Detective Hart's voice was gentle, probing, the kind of voice one would expect from a man accustomed to extracting confessions without ever raising his tone.

Emmeline lifted her gaze from her lap, her pale blue eyes meeting his with a flicker of something indefinable. Sadness, yes, but also a hint of defiance, a refusal to be pitied. She glanced at the teacup on the small table beside her, its porcelain gleaming dully in the dim light, then back at the detective.

"I suppose," she began softly, her voice carrying the lilting remnants of a long-forgotten youth, "that one gets used to anything, even loneliness. It's a matter of necessity, really." Her fingers toyed with the edge of her lace handkerchief. "After all, when one's husband has been taken in such a... violent manner, there's little else to do but learn to live with the silence he leaves behind."

Detective Hart nodded thoughtfully, his eyes never leaving her face. He had learned, through years of navigating the murky waters of human tragedy, that silence could be more telling than any outpouring of emotion. It was the gaps between words, the pauses and falters, that often held the real story. And Mrs. Cray, with her restrained grief and carefully chosen words, seemed to be holding on to a great deal more than she was willing to say.

"Tell me, Mrs. Cray," he ventured, "about that night — the night your husband was... found." He leaned forward slightly, the motion subtle, as if not to startle a fragile creature.

Her eyes dropped to the hands folded so neatly in her lap, and she sighed, a soft, brittle sound that seemed to float in the stillness of the room. "It was a night like any other," she murmured. "We had retired early, as we often did. You must understand, Detective Hart, that we were not a couple given to... excitement or frivolity. Frederick — my husband — he was a man of routine, you see. Everything had its place and time. Even his death, it seems..." She trailed off, a strange, fleeting smile touching her lips.

Detective Hart's brow furrowed imperceptibly. "Go on," he encouraged softly.

"Yes, well," she continued, gathering herself. "He had gone up to his study after supper. Said he had a few letters to finish. He often wrote letters, you know, even though there was no one left to receive them. A peculiar habit, but not one I ever thought to question. We all have our ways of keeping ghosts at bay, don't we?"

She glanced up at Hart as though expecting him to refute her, but he only nodded, his expression inscrutable.

"It wasn't until I went to call him for bed that I found him." Her voice lowered, and she seemed to shrink into herself. "Slumped over his desk, his hand still clutching the pen as if he had been in the middle of a sentence. The clock on the mantel had stopped at precisely eleven o'clock." She paused, her lips trembling slightly. "It was the strangest thing... Frederick was meticulous about winding that clock. It had been his father's, you see. A family heirloom. But that night, it had simply stopped, as though time itself had... had ended for him."

Detective Hart felt a chill creep down his spine. He had heard of such occurrences before — the stopping of clocks at the moment of death. An old wives' tale, some said, but it never failed to send a shiver through him. "You said he was holding a pen?" he asked, seizing on the detail.

"Yes." Her gaze turned distant, as though looking back at a memory too painful to confront directly. "The letter he had been writing was unfinished. Just a few words, scrawled in his neat hand. I remember them so clearly, even now. 'Forgive me...'" She swallowed hard. "But the rest was nothing but a line of ink, smeared as if he had been pulled away... or interrupted."

"Forgive me?" Hart repeated, his curiosity piqued. "Had there been any... disagreements between you? Any reason why he might feel the need to apologize?"

She shook her head slowly, a movement that seemed to cost her. "No... Frederick and I were not... passionate people. There were no great arguments, no unspoken grievances. We were comfortable with each other's company, if not exactly... affectionate. But there were secrets, Detective. There are always secrets." Her voice dropped to a whisper. "Even in the quietest of marriages."

Hart leaned back slightly, allowing the silence to stretch between them. He had known from the moment he set foot in Willow Cottage that there was more to this case than met the eye. Frederick Cray's death had been ruled a natural one — a sudden heart attack, they said. But the widow's subdued demeanor, the almost clinical way she described the loss of her husband, suggested otherwise. She was a woman holding on to something — a piece of the puzzle that didn't fit.

"Mrs. Cray," he said gently, "you mentioned earlier that your husband was a man of routine. What do you think could have compelled him to stop winding the clock? Or rather, what might have prevented him from doing so?"

Her gaze sharpened, and for the first time since he had entered the room, he saw a flash of something raw and unguarded in her eyes — fear, perhaps, or recognition of a truth she had tried to keep buried.

"It wasn't that he forgot," she whispered, leaning forward slightly. "Frederick never forgot anything. No, Detective, someone stopped that clock deliberately. And I believe..." She hesitated, glancing over her shoulder as if expecting to see someone lurking in the shadows. "I believe they wanted it to stop at eleven. Because that was the moment everything changed."

Hart felt the weight of her words settle over him like a shroud. "You think your husband was murdered," he said quietly. It wasn't a question — more of a confirmation of what he had suspected from the moment he saw the lifeless body of Frederick Cray slumped over his desk, his face twisted in an expression of surprise, or perhaps even horror.

Emmeline nodded slowly, her eyes never leaving his. "Yes, Detective. I believe someone wanted him dead. But not just dead..." She paused, her voice trembling with barely suppressed emotion. "They wanted to send a message. A message that only I would understand."

Hart's pulse quickened. "And what message would that be?"

The widow's gaze turned inward, as if she were peering into the darkest recesses of her memory. "That some sins cannot be forgiven," she murmured softly. "No matter how much time has passed."

Detective Hart remained silent, waiting for her to continue. But the moment passed, and the veil of composure descended once more over her features.

"Mrs. Cray," he said at last, choosing his words with care, "if there's anything — anything at all — that you haven't told me, now is the time to speak. Even the smallest detail could be crucial."

She looked at him, her eyes haunted and hollow. "There's nothing more I can say, Detective. Not now. But... you will understand, soon enough. When the clock strikes eleven again, you'll see. Everything will become clear."

And with that enigmatic pronouncement, she turned away, signaling the end of their conversation. Hart rose slowly, his mind buzzing with questions that only seemed to multiply with each answer he received.

As he made his way to the door, he glanced back one last time at the frail figure of the widow, silhouetted against the dimming light of the window. The ticking of the old grandfather clock seemed to grow louder in the silence, each beat reverberating through the room like the steady pulse of a mystery waiting to be unraveled.

And as the clock struck the hour, its chime ringing softly through the stillness, Hart couldn't help but feel that somewhere, in the silence between the beats, lay the key to the truth that had eluded him for so long.

5. Whispers of Betrayal

DETECTIVE ERNEST HART stared at the letter in his hand, the paper trembling slightly as the wind from the open window brushed against it. The ink was smudged in places, hastily scrawled words marred by spots that looked suspiciously like tear stains. But what caught his eye most of all was the faint scent of lavender lingering on the page, a scent that seemed hauntingly familiar. He glanced up, eyes narrowing as he surveyed the dimly lit study. Somewhere in this quiet, unassuming town lay the answers he sought. Somewhere among the prim hedges and neatly trimmed lawns, betrayal festered like an untreated wound.

He folded the letter carefully, tucking it into his coat pocket. The last words echoed in his mind like a ghostly whisper: "Trust no one—not even those closest to you." It wasn't just a warning; it was a plea. A plea from a person who had known that the shadows of their own past were closing in, drawing tighter like a noose.

Ernest turned his gaze toward the fireplace, where a single log crackled quietly. There was something chilling about that letter, as if it had been written by someone teetering on the edge of despair and desperation. But who? And why send it to him?

The small town of Barrowdale had never been a place for scandal. It was a town where everyone knew everyone else's business—or so they liked to think. Yet, as Ernest delved deeper into the investigation, it became clear that this tranquil facade was merely a cover, a mask worn to conceal the true face of the community. He had been called here to investigate the sudden and unexpected death of Harold Grimley, a well-respected businessman whose life had been, by all accounts, as ordinary as one could imagine. The coroner had ruled it a heart attack, a natural death. But then came the whispers, subtle and insidious. Whispers of secrets that Harold had taken to his grave. And now, with this letter in his possession, Ernest was beginning to see that Harold's death might not have been so natural after all.

He stood, shrugging on his overcoat, and reached for his hat. The evening air was crisp as he stepped outside, a thin mist clinging to the cobbled streets like a second skin. Lights glimmered in the windows of the cottages that lined the road, and somewhere in the distance, a dog barked—sharp and sudden, as if startled by something unseen.

The town square lay deserted, save for the lone figure of Mrs. Winthrop, the elderly widow who ran the bakery on the corner. She gave him a curt nod as he approached, her sharp eyes missing nothing.

"Evening, Detective Hart," she greeted him, her voice low and cautious.

"Mrs. Winthrop." He tipped his hat. "Out for a stroll?"

"Just locking up the shop," she replied, but there was something in her tone—something that hinted at more. "You should be careful, Detective. You're stirring up things best left alone."

He raised an eyebrow. "Am I?"

"People have long memories in Barrowdale," she continued, leaning closer. "And not everyone's glad you're here."

"Is that so?" He gave her a small smile. "Well, it wouldn't be the first time."

Her gaze flickered to the pocket where the letter was concealed, then back to his face. "Harold Grimley wasn't the first to die, you know. There've been others. Quiet, unremarkable deaths, one might say. But I think you already suspected that, didn't you?"

Ernest's pulse quickened. "Go on."

Mrs. Winthrop hesitated, glancing around as if expecting someone to leap out from the shadows. "I've lived here all my life, Detective. Seen people come and go, seen families rise and fall. This town..." She shook her head. "It's built on secrets. Harold knew things—things he shouldn't have. And now he's paid the price."

"What kind of things?" Ernest pressed gently.

She pursed her lips, a shrewd look in her eyes. "You'll find out soon enough, I wager. But be warned: trust no one. Not even those you think are on your side."

With that cryptic message, she turned and shuffled away, leaving Ernest alone with his thoughts. He stood there for a long moment, the weight of her words settling heavily on his shoulders. Trust no one. He'd heard that before. But this time, it carried a sinister undertone, a resonance that made him question everything and everyone.

He made his way back to his lodgings, a modest room at the inn on the outskirts of town. As he entered, he noticed an envelope on the small wooden table by the window. No name, no address—just a plain white envelope. His instincts flared, and he approached it cautiously, fingers trembling slightly as he picked it up. Breaking the seal, he unfolded the note inside.

"Your presence here is a mistake. Leave now, while you still can. There are forces at play you do not understand."

No signature. No clue as to who had left it. But the message was clear: someone wanted him gone. And not just gone, but gone now.

He sat heavily on the bed, the letter clutched in his hand. Who was trying to scare him off? Who felt threatened enough by his presence to resort to such tactics? He thought of Mrs. Winthrop's warning, of the fear in her eyes. Was she in on it, or was she just another pawn in this twisted game?

He stayed awake long into the night, his mind racing as he tried to piece together the fragments of information he had gathered. But there were too many gaps, too many unknowns. Every lead seemed to circle back to Harold Grimley, to the enigmatic businessman whose quiet life had been anything but ordinary.

The next morning, Ernest decided to pay a visit to the Grimley estate. It was a grand house, set back from the road, its once pristine gardens now overgrown and wild. As he approached, he noticed a figure lingering by the gates—a tall, slender woman with an air of quiet elegance.

"Detective Hart, I presume?" Her voice was soft, almost musical, yet there was a steely edge beneath the surface.

"That's right," he replied, tipping his hat. "And you are?"

"Isabella Grimley." She smiled, but it didn't reach her eyes. "Harold's niece."

"I'm sorry for your loss," Ernest said, his tone sincere. "I was hoping to speak with someone about—"

"About his death, yes," she interrupted smoothly. "But I'm afraid there's not much to tell. Uncle Harold was a sick man, Detective. His heart simply gave out."

"Perhaps," Ernest agreed, watching her carefully. "But I've heard otherwise."

Her expression didn't change, but he saw something flicker in her eyes—something dark and guarded. "I'm not sure what you mean."

"People are saying Harold knew things. Things that might have gotten him killed."

She laughed, a light, brittle sound. "This is a small town, Detective. People will say anything to pass the time. Uncle Harold was a recluse. He had no enemies."

"Everyone has enemies, Miss Grimley," Ernest countered quietly. "Sometimes they're just better at hiding it."

Her smile faltered, and for a moment, he thought she might respond. But then she shook her head, turning away. "You're wasting your time here, Detective. Harold's death was a tragedy, but it was nothing more than that. I suggest you focus your efforts elsewhere."

And with that, she walked back toward the house, leaving him standing alone at the gate. He watched her retreating figure, a sense of unease coiling in his stomach. Something about her demeanor, about the way she had dismissed his questions so easily, didn't sit right with him.

He needed more information. Needed to understand what exactly Harold Grimley had been involved in. Because one thing was becoming increasingly clear: whatever had happened to

Harold was just the beginning. The whispers of betrayal that swirled around this town were growing louder, more insistent. And if he wasn't careful, those whispers might just consume him too.

．．．．

THE DAYS THAT FOLLOWED were a blur of half-truths and dead ends. Every person Ernest spoke to seemed to know something, yet no one was willing to come forward with concrete evidence. Fear hung in the air like a thick fog, stifling and oppressive. Even those who had once been open and forthcoming were now wary, guarded.

It wasn't until a week later that Ernest caught his first real break. A letter, slipped under his door in the dead of night, containing a single name: Margaret Winslow.

6. The Case Files Reopened

DETECTIVE HART SAT alone in his dimly lit study, the heavy scent of aged leather and old paper lingering in the air. The rain pattered against the windows of his modest home, each droplet marking time like the relentless ticking of a clock. His gaze, usually sharp and alert, was now unfocused as he stared down at the thick folder that lay open on his desk. The yellowed pages, dog-eared and covered with handwritten notes, represented a part of his life he had long thought buried—a chapter he had sworn to close forever. Yet here he was, staring at the title on the first page: The Clockwork Murders.

It had been nearly twenty years since the town of Dunwich had been gripped by fear and suspicion, when a series of brutal murders, each more baffling than the last, tore apart the close-knit community. Back then, Detective Hart was just a junior officer, fresh from the academy and eager to prove himself. The case had consumed him, as it did everyone else involved. But the investigation had led them all into a labyrinth of lies and misdirection. When the killings abruptly stopped, the case went cold, leaving behind a trail of unsolved questions and shattered lives.

With a sigh, Hart leaned back in his chair, the creak of the wood echoing softly in the quiet room. He glanced at the envelope that had arrived this morning—no return address, no name. Just a few cryptic words scrawled on the back: "Time catches up with us all." Inside, he had found copies of several old newspaper clippings, all related to the murders, and a single photograph he had never seen before: a black-and-white image of a clockmaker's workshop, its shelves lined with an assortment of intricate timepieces.

His hand hovered over the folder, fingers brushing the worn cover. He knew opening it again meant reopening old wounds, but there was something about that photograph that gnawed at him. A faint sense of recognition, perhaps, or a feeling that something crucial had been overlooked all those years ago. The photograph was taken at night—the shadows cast long and menacing across the floor, obscuring the face of the figure working at the bench. The only source of light seemed to be a lamp, its glow illuminating a clock set precisely at 11:43.

He pulled the photograph closer and peered at it intently. His heart skipped a beat. There, almost hidden behind the jumble of gears and tools, was a small inscription on the edge of the table: To my dearest friend, with time on our side—A.G.. He had never seen this inscription before. What did it mean? Who was A.G.? His mind raced as he tried to recall if there was anyone with those initials linked to the case. But the harder he thought, the more elusive the answers became.

Hart's thoughts were interrupted by a soft knock on his door. He looked up, his eyes narrowing as he called out, "Come in."

The door opened slowly, and a familiar figure stepped inside. It was Sergeant Milligan, now a seasoned officer in his own right, though back then, he had been a fresh-faced recruit, eager and green. Milligan's gaze fell on the open folder, and a flicker of recognition crossed his face.

"I had a feeling I'd find you here," Milligan said, his tone a mixture of resignation and concern. "Got your note. Didn't think you'd really want to dig up this old mess again."

Hart gestured to the photograph. "Take a look at this, Milligan. Tell me if you've ever seen it before."

Milligan stepped closer, his brow furrowing as he examined the picture. He shook his head slowly. "No, I don't think so. But... that's got to be Jenkins's old place, hasn't it? The clockmaker? He was a suspect, wasn't he?"

Hart nodded. "Yes, but we never had enough to bring him in. He disappeared right after the last murder—vanished without a trace. But look at the time on the clock. And that inscription. Someone sent this to me. Why now, after all these years?"

Milligan looked thoughtful. "Maybe they think it's time to finish what they started."

Hart considered the possibility. It was chilling to think that someone had been waiting all this time, lurking in the shadows, watching and biding their time. But what did they want? And why now?

"Let's go through the case files," Hart said firmly. "All of them. I want to see if we missed anything—any detail, no matter how small."

They spent the next several hours combing through the contents of the folder. There were reports from the original investigation: interviews with witnesses and suspects, evidence logs, and sketches of the crime scenes. Each victim had been found with a clock nearby, meticulously arranged to show the exact time of death. The pattern had been obvious, but what hadn't been clear was the significance of the times. Each clock was a different type—some ornate and beautiful, others plain and utilitarian—but each one was stopped at a precise moment, as if marking a specific event.

"Do you remember this one?" Hart asked, holding up a sketch of a grand, gilded grandfather clock found beside the second victim, a local schoolteacher named Mrs. Harper. "Stopped at 10:17."

"Yeah," Milligan said, his voice distant. "She was found in her garden, right? Slumped over her roses. We never figured out why she was out there so late."

Hart nodded. "Right. And look at this one." He pointed to another sketch, this one of a pocket watch found next to the body of a young butcher, Thomas Blake. "2:32. He was found at his shop, middle of the night. What was he doing there?"

Milligan shrugged. "Hard to say. But each of these times—they must mean something."

"Exactly," Hart said, leaning forward, his eyes gleaming with renewed determination. "What if these times correspond to events we didn't connect at the time? What if they're not random?"

They continued to dig through the files, trying to piece together the fractured timeline of events. Slowly, a pattern began to emerge—a series of seemingly unrelated incidents that had occurred on the same dates as the murders. A fire at the old town hall, a break-in at the public library, a mysterious drowning in the river—all minor events, none of which had seemed connected to the killings. But the more they looked, the more they realized that each incident had happened within hours of each murder.

"Whoever did this," Hart murmured, "they were sending a message. Each clock, each time—it's like they were marking the moments when something significant happened. But why?"

"Maybe it was all part of a bigger plan," Milligan suggested. "A plan that's still unfolding."

Hart stared at the photograph again, his mind racing. What if the person who had sent him the picture was trying to lead him to the answer? What if Jenkins, the clockmaker, hadn't vanished at all, but had been hiding in plain sight?

"There's only one way to find out," Hart said, closing the folder with a decisive thud. "We need to visit that workshop. If there's anything left there, it might give us the clue we need."

Milligan nodded. "I'll get the car."

As they left the study and stepped out into the pouring rain, Hart felt a strange sense of anticipation. He knew they were on the verge of something—something that had been waiting in the shadows for two long decades. He just hoped that whatever they found in that workshop would finally put an end to the nightmare that had haunted them all those years.

The drive to the old workshop was slow and tense. The roads were slick with rain, and the headlights barely pierced through the fog that hung heavy in the air. They didn't speak much—each man lost in his own thoughts, replaying the events of the past over and over again.

Chapter 3: The Second Hand Strikes

1. An Unexpected Visitor

The evening was settling in, casting long shadows across the quaint little town of Kingsford, where every cobblestone and corner shop seemed to harbor whispers of untold stories. The town itself was an architectural relic, with ivy-clad cottages and a narrow main street flanked by lamp posts that had seen more than their fair share of history. It was a place where everyone knew everyone else—or so they thought.

Inside a cozy sitting room, bathed in the soft glow of a crackling fire, Marjorie Lennox sat alone, lost in the worn pages of a much-loved novel. The rhythmic ticking of the grandfather clock in the corner was a comforting sound, a metronome to the silence that enveloped her. She adjusted her reading glasses, leaning closer to the yellowed pages, but suddenly paused, a frown creasing her brow. The clock seemed louder than usual, its chimes more insistent, as if warning of something yet to come.

And then it happened—a sharp, unexpected knock at the door.

Marjorie's heart skipped a beat. It was rare to receive visitors at this hour. The townsfolk of Kingsford were creatures of habit, preferring to retreat indoors as soon as the sun dipped below the horizon. She glanced at the clock; it was just past eight. Too late for a friendly call, too early for any real trouble... Or so she hoped.

"Who could that be?" she murmured to herself, rising slowly from her armchair. With one last look at the clock, she crossed the room and peered through the small peephole. A dark figure stood on her porch, illuminated only by the dim light of the overhead lantern.

She hesitated, then, with a steadying breath, unlatched the door and opened it just wide enough to see who was calling at such an hour.

"Good evening, Mrs. Lennox." The voice was low, smooth—almost familiar. The man standing before her was tall, his face partially obscured by the brim of a hat pulled low over his eyes. He wore a long, dark coat that brushed against his polished shoes, and in his gloved hand, he clutched a small leather case.

"Good evening," Marjorie replied cautiously. "May I help you?"

The man tilted his head slightly, revealing a flash of sharp, pale eyes that seemed to glint in the low light. "I do apologize for the intrusion. My name is Ambrose Fletcher. I've just arrived in town and was hoping to speak with you regarding a matter of some importance."

"Ambrose Fletcher..." Marjorie repeated, testing the name on her tongue. It did not sound like any name she knew, nor did the man's appearance stir any memories. Yet there was something... almost unsettlingly familiar about him, as if he were a ghost from a past she had long forgotten.

"I'm afraid I don't recognize you, Mr. Fletcher. Have we met before?" she asked, her voice firm yet polite.

The man's lips curved into a faint smile. "No, Mrs. Lennox, we haven't had the pleasure. But I'm afraid my visit concerns a matter that may be... difficult for you to hear."

A chill ran down Marjorie's spine. She knew, without him having to say it, that whatever he had come to tell her, it would shatter the calm veneer of her life.

"Very well," she said, stepping aside. "You'd better come in."

Ambrose Fletcher entered the room with a quiet, assured grace, glancing briefly around as if taking stock of his surroundings. He moved with the ease of someone accustomed to being in strangers' homes, yet his presence felt anything but ordinary.

"Please, have a seat," Marjorie offered, gesturing to the sofa. She herself chose the armchair, placing a safe distance between them. As he settled in, she noted the fine cut of his clothes and the way he carried himself—like a man who had known both wealth and hardship.

"May I ask what brings you to Kingsford, Mr. Fletcher?" she inquired.

Ambrose set the leather case on his lap, his fingers tracing its worn edges absently. "I'm here on behalf of a mutual acquaintance, Mrs. Lennox. Someone I believe you haven't seen in quite some time."

The way he said it—calm, almost detached—made Marjorie's pulse quicken. "Who?" she demanded, leaning forward.

"Benjamin Lennox."

The name struck her like a blow. For a moment, the world seemed to tilt on its axis. Benjamin Lennox. Her husband. Her late husband, who had died more than a decade ago in a tragic accident that had left her a grieving widow.

"That's... impossible," she managed to say, her voice a strangled whisper. "Benjamin is dead."

Ambrose nodded slowly, as if expecting this reaction. "I'm aware of that, Mrs. Lennox. But I assure you, this is no cruel jest. What I have to show you may help explain things."

With a deliberate movement, he unlatched the leather case and withdrew a small object wrapped in a piece of faded velvet. Marjorie's eyes widened as he unwrapped it, revealing a pocket watch—one she knew all too well. It was Benjamin's, a family heirloom he had cherished and carried with him everywhere.

"Where did you get this?" she demanded, her voice trembling.

"From a place you'd least expect," Ambrose replied enigmatically. "But more importantly, the watch contains a message—a message from your husband."

The room seemed to close in around Marjorie. She couldn't take her eyes off the watch, the way it glimmered softly in the firelight. "A message...?"

"Yes." Ambrose leaned forward, holding the watch carefully in his hand. "Listen."

He pressed a small, nearly invisible button on the side of the watch. For a moment, nothing happened. Then, a faint clicking sound filled the room, like the ticking of a clock growing louder and more insistent. And then she heard it—a voice, soft and clear, speaking from the past.

"Marjorie... if you're hearing this, then something has gone terribly wrong."

She gasped, her hand flying to her mouth. It was Benjamin's voice, unmistakably his, though there was a weight to it she had never heard before—a strain that spoke of fear and desperation.

"Listen carefully," the voice continued. "I don't have much time. What I'm about to tell you... it's going to sound unbelievable, but you must trust me. There are things I discovered before my accident—things that were never meant to be uncovered. There's a man... a man named Ambrose Fletcher. If he's come to you, it means he's the only one you can trust. He'll explain everything. But be careful, Marjorie. There are others... watching. Others who will stop at nothing to keep the truth buried."

The voice cut off abruptly, leaving a heavy silence in its wake. Marjorie stared at Ambrose, her mind reeling. "How... how is this possible? Benjamin never said anything about—"

"He couldn't," Ambrose interrupted gently. "Because what he found out put his life in danger. And now... it's put yours in danger as well."

She swallowed hard, trying to grasp the enormity of what she had just heard. "What do you mean?"

"There are people who will go to any lengths to ensure that Benjamin's discoveries remain hidden. He knew it, and that's why he left this watch for you—to warn you, to prepare you." Ambrose's eyes were intense, filled with a sincerity that was hard to deny. "He entrusted me with bringing this message to you, because he knew you'd want to know the truth."

Marjorie shook her head, her thoughts a chaotic swirl. "What truth?"

Ambrose's gaze never wavered. "The truth about why he really died... and what he was trying to protect."

For a long moment, Marjorie said nothing, her mind racing through a thousand possibilities. Could it be true? Could Benjamin have been involved in something far more sinister than she ever imagined? And if so... what did it mean for her?

Finally, she took a deep breath, meeting Ambrose's steady gaze. "What do we do now?"

A faint smile touched his lips. "We start by following the clues he left behind. But we must be careful. From now on, every step we take, every move we make... we'll be racing against time."

And with that, he handed her the watch—a watch that no longer felt like a mere object, but rather a lifeline. Marjorie closed her fingers around it, feeling the faint pulse of its ticking against her palm.

Benjamin had been right. Something had gone terribly wrong.

And now, it was up to her to set it right.

2. A Warning Unheeded

THE FIRE CRACKLED IN the hearth, casting flickering shadows along the dark-paneled walls of Mr. Alistair Camden's study. It was a room filled with the detritus of a lifetime of peculiar hobbies—antique clocks, maps of obscure locales, and dusty tomes that whispered of secrets long buried. It was a room that felt out of time, a paradox of eras, much like the man who occupied it. Alistair, now well past seventy, sat slouched in a high-backed armchair, his keen blue eyes fixed not on the embers, but on the letter crumpled in his trembling hand.

It was a nondescript envelope, its wax seal broken hastily, almost desperately. A small piece of cream-colored stationery lay inside, and on it, a short message, written in neat, almost mechanical script:

"Time runs short, Mr. Camden. Heed the warning, or the past shall catch up with you."

It was unsigned, untraceable, yet it sent a chill down Alistair's spine. He had received such messages before—hints and threats veiled in riddles—ever since that dreadful business five years ago when he had been at the heart of the trial that put one of the town's most respected men, Robert Sinclair, behind bars for a crime so heinous that its mere mention still reverberated in hushed voices at every dinner table.

Yet Alistair had made a career of ignoring such threats. After all, who would dare strike out at a man like him, a figure so entrenched in the social and judicial fabric of their quaint English village? The thought seemed laughable. Until now.

The grandfather clock in the corner began to chime—a low, ponderous sound that seemed to fill the room with a sense of foreboding. Alistair glanced up at its ornate face. Midnight. The hour of reckoning, if the letter was to be believed.

He straightened, shaking off the momentary unease. "Nonsense," he muttered to himself, balling up the letter and tossing it into the flames. "Just some ruffian's attempt at mischief." Yet even as he said it, his gaze drifted to the small table by the window where a dozen pocket watches, each wound and set meticulously, ticked in harmonious rhythm. Twelve different times from twelve different corners of the world—all set to remind him of his travels, his accomplishments.

All except one.

The smallest watch, a delicate piece with a rose-gold casing, had stopped at exactly twelve o'clock. He frowned, leaning forward to inspect it. His fingers, though still steady for a man of his age, struggled with the tiny latch. As the watch popped open, he gasped.

Inside the cover was an engraving—a date, freshly etched in elegant cursive:

"December 24th, 1895."

It was today's date.

Alistair's mind raced. None of the watches in his collection bore such an inscription. Who could have done this? When? He had been in the study all day, working on his correspondence and reading the latest news of the village. Had someone crept in unnoticed?

A soft creak drew his attention to the door, which was ajar, though he distinctly remembered shutting it earlier. He rose slowly, every muscle tense, and crossed the room, his steps echoing in the silence. A quick glance into the hallway revealed nothing—no movement, no sign of an intruder. Yet something had changed. There was a faint, lingering scent in the air—a scent he recognized all too well.

Lavender. The perfume of choice for Catherine Sinclair, Robert's late wife.

His pulse quickened as he backed into the study, shutting the door firmly behind him. Catherine had been dead for nearly a decade, her death ruled a tragic accident. Yet Alistair knew better. He had always suspected Robert's hand in her demise, though it was never proven. Robert's imprisonment was for a different crime entirely—the murder of a young maidservant found strangled in the attic of Sinclair Manor. But could it be...? No. Alistair forced himself to think logically. He was letting his imagination get the better of him.

Returning to his chair, he tried to refocus his thoughts, but the ticking of the clocks seemed louder now, more insistent. He reached for the bottle of brandy on the side table, pouring himself a generous glass. As the liquid burned its way down his throat, he forced a laugh, a brittle, hollow sound that did little to alleviate the tightness in his chest.

"It's just a prank," he whispered. "Someone trying to unsettle me before Christmas, that's all."

But deep down, he knew there was something more. The date on the watch, the scent of lavender—it was as if someone, or something, was trying to draw him back into the past, into the shadows of a history he had tried so desperately to bury.

A knock shattered the silence. It was a soft, tentative sound that sent shivers down Alistair's spine. He froze, staring at the door, his mind racing through possibilities. The hour was late; no visitor should be calling at this time. Yet the knock came again, more insistent.

"Who's there?" Alistair called out, his voice steadier than he felt.

No answer.

He waited, but the silence remained unbroken. Slowly, he set down his glass and moved toward the door. He hesitated, his hand hovering over the knob, before finally turning it.

The hallway was empty. Alistair exhaled sharply, feeling foolish. He was about to step back inside when he noticed something on the floor—a small envelope, identical to the one he had received earlier. He stooped, picking it up gingerly, and tore it open.

Inside was another letter, but this one was different. The message was brief, but its implications were chilling:

"You were warned, Mr. Camden. Midnight has come and gone. Now you must face the consequences."

The blood drained from Alistair's face. He stumbled back into the study, his mind reeling. Consequences? What consequences? Had something happened while he was preoccupied with his foolish paranoia?

He reached for the telephone, intending to call Inspector Hayes, his old friend and confidant. But as he lifted the receiver, a strange sensation washed over him—a feeling of déjà vu, as if he had been here before, in this exact moment, with the receiver in his hand, his heart pounding in his chest.

And then it came to him.

The last time he had felt this way was five years ago, on the night Robert Sinclair was arrested. He had been sitting in this very room, with a similar letter in his hand, a letter that hinted at the terrible truth behind Catherine's death. He had ignored that letter, dismissed it as the ramblings of a madman. And it had cost an innocent woman her life.

Could it be that history was repeating itself? Was someone, perhaps even Robert himself, orchestrating these events from behind bars? Alistair shuddered at the thought. No, Robert was locked away, far from here. But someone else could be acting on his behalf—someone who knew the truth, someone who wanted revenge.

The thought was both terrifying and strangely exhilarating. Alistair had always prided himself on his ability to solve puzzles, to unravel even the most intricate of mysteries. But now, the game had changed. Now, he was the one being played.

With a surge of determination, he set the receiver down. If there were consequences to be faced, then he would face them. He would not be cowed by anonymous threats or cowardly pranks. He would find the one responsible for this, and he would put an end to it, once and for all.

But as he turned back to his desk, his eyes fell on the open watch, its hands still frozen at twelve o'clock. And for the first time in his long career, Alistair Camden felt a tremor of fear—fear that perhaps, this time, he had overlooked something crucial, something that would come back to haunt him in ways he could never have imagined.

Because the truth, like time, has a way of catching up with those who think they can outrun it.

3. The Mysterious Collector

THE AIR IN THE SMALL village of Marlington was heavy with anticipation. It was the sort of place where news traveled faster than a rushing stream and rumors seemed to grow out of the very ground. On that particular day, a murmur swept through the cobbled streets as if carried by the wind itself: a new stranger had arrived in town.

The Marlington Arms, the local inn where most of the traveling guests stayed, had seen more activity than usual. Mrs. Brigs, the stout and formidable innkeeper, took a certain pride in being the first to know anything of importance. She was a fixture at the reception desk, her eyes hawkish and her ears always attuned to any scrap of conversation that might yield new information.

The man who had checked in that morning was like a puzzle with missing pieces. He signed the guest book as Mr. Samuel Thorne, his hand steady and controlled. Tall and distinguished, he wore an overcoat made from a rich material that bespoke affluence, yet there was an air of reticence about him that piqued curiosity. His demeanor was neither overtly friendly nor hostile; it was as though he moved through life leaving little trace of his presence, like a whisper in a silent room.

"Another one passing through, eh?" muttered Mrs. Brigs to herself, watching as Mr. Thorne ascended the staircase to his room with a leather satchel in hand. But something about him set her on edge. Perhaps it was the way he avoided eye contact, or the manner in which he kept that satchel close to his body, as if its contents were far more valuable than any luggage should be.

Within hours of his arrival, word of the mysterious guest had spread throughout the village, reaching even the farthest cottages. By evening, the pub attached to the inn was buzzing with speculation. Men and women, some holding pints of ale and others nursing cups of tea, gathered in small clusters, speaking in low voices.

"Did you see the way he looked at the old clock in the church square?" asked Mr. Dobbs, a portly man with a ruddy face. "Almost as if he recognized it, yet I've never seen his face around here before."

"And he's no ordinary traveler," chimed in Mrs. Lowell, a woman with sharp eyes and an even sharper tongue. "Did you notice those gloves he wears? Fine leather, too fine for someone who's just passing through on business."

A few nods of agreement followed. There was something decidedly unusual about Mr. Thorne, and the residents of Marlington were not ones to let an enigma rest. That night, the conversations continued until the pub closed its doors, and every single person walked home with the same thought echoing in their minds: Who is this man?

The answer, however, did not come easily. Mr. Thorne kept mostly to himself over the next few days. He rose early, taking solitary walks through the village and its surrounding fields. He would occasionally stop to speak briefly with shopkeepers, but his conversations were brief and vague, offering little to satisfy the growing curiosity.

It wasn't until the end of his first week in Marlington that he began to make himself more noticeable. It started with a visit to the local auction house.

Blake's Auction House was a modest establishment, yet it boasted a remarkable collection of curiosities. Charles Blake, the proprietor, was a middle-aged man with a keen eye for both rarity and value. His auctions were well-attended, not only by locals but by collectors from as far as London. And that Friday, the buzz in the air was palpable as people filled the small room, eyes darting between items on display.

Amongst the assortment of objects—a silver candelabra, a collection of porcelain dolls, and a set of Victorian tea cups—stood a peculiar item that drew the most attention: an antique clock, its face adorned with Roman numerals and its casing carved with intricate floral patterns.

The clock had been donated by Mrs. Esme Harwood, a widow whose late husband had been something of a clock enthusiast. According to her, it was a rare piece, likely one of the few remaining examples of a particular craftsman's work, though no one could say for certain who had built it. The clock was beautiful, its brass pendulum swinging with a slow, deliberate grace, yet it seemed almost... eerie, as if it held within it a story that no one had yet told.

When the bidding began, Mr. Thorne remained quiet at the back of the room, his face a mask of indifference. Blake called out the initial price, and for a moment, it seemed no one would bite. The clock was beautiful, but in a village like Marlington, there were few who would spend their savings on something so frivolous.

"Ten pounds," came the first bid, from Mr. Wilkins, the owner of the local dairy farm.

"Fifteen," offered Mrs. Lowell, who had apparently developed a sudden interest in horology.

"Twenty," said a voice from the corner.

Heads turned. Mr. Thorne stood, his hand raised, his eyes fixed on the clock.

"Twenty-five," countered Mr. Wilkins, a competitive glint in his eye.

"Thirty," came Mr. Thorne's calm reply.

The bidding war continued, escalating quickly until only Mr. Thorne remained. His final bid, seventy-five pounds, silenced the room. Murmurs broke out as people exchanged glances. Seventy-five pounds was no small sum, especially for an object of uncertain provenance.

Mr. Thorne stepped forward, the faintest hint of satisfaction playing on his lips. As he arranged for the clock to be delivered to his room at the Marlington Arms, Blake couldn't resist asking, "I hope you don't mind my curiosity, Mr. Thorne, but are you a collector of clocks?"

For the first time since he had arrived in Marlington, Mr. Thorne offered a small, almost enigmatic smile.

"You could say that, Mr. Blake. I have a certain... appreciation for timepieces. Each one tells a story, don't you think?"

Blake nodded slowly. "Indeed, they do. And what story does this one tell?"

"Ah," Mr. Thorne murmured, his gaze drifting to the clock, "that's what I intend to find out."

The clock was delivered to his room later that afternoon, and from then on, Mr. Thorne seemed almost obsessed. He spent hours examining it, his hands moving with practiced ease as he dismantled the casing and peered into its inner workings. He jotted notes in a small leather-bound journal, pausing occasionally to run his fingers over the gears and springs as if searching for some hidden clue.

Mrs. Brigs, who had never been one to respect privacy, found herself drawn to the door of his room more than once, listening intently for any sound that might hint at what he was doing. But all she ever heard was the faint, steady ticking of the clock and, occasionally, a low murmur as if he were speaking to himself.

The days turned into a week, and the villagers began to grow impatient. Why had this man come to Marlington? What was it about that clock that held his fascination? And, more importantly, what did he know that they did not?

The answer came unexpectedly one evening when Mr. Thorne made his way to the local church. The vicar, Reverend Jameson, was startled to see him standing at the entrance, a curious expression on his face.

"Good evening, Reverend," Mr. Thorne said politely. "I wonder if you might allow me a look at the old clock in the bell tower."

Jameson hesitated. The clock in the tower was old, older than the church itself by some accounts, and few had shown any interest in it for years.

"What do you wish to see, Mr. Thorne?" he asked cautiously.

"Just a curiosity, really," Mr. Thorne replied. "I've been studying the craftsmanship of some of the clocks in this area, and I was told that the one in your tower is quite unique."

The vicar glanced at him warily but nodded. "Very well. I'll show you up."

The tower was dark and cold, the air heavy with the scent of dust and age. As they ascended the narrow stairs, the sound of their footsteps echoed in the confined space. Finally, they emerged into the small chamber where the clock mechanism stood, a mass of gears and weights that seemed almost alive in the dim light.

Mr. Thorne moved closer, his eyes narrowing as he inspected the machinery.

"Fascinating," he murmured, his fingers brushing lightly over the metal. "This clock... it was built by a master, no doubt about it."

"Yes," Reverend Jameson agreed. "Though no one knows who. It's been here as long as anyone can remember."

Mr. Thorne's gaze lingered on the mechanism for a long moment before he turned to the vicar.

"Tell me, Reverend," he said softly, "have you ever heard the story of the Clockmaker of Marlington?"

The vicar blinked, taken aback. "The... Clockmaker?"

"Yes. A man who, many years ago, was said to have created timepieces unlike any other. They say each one was more than just a clock... it was a masterpiece of ingenuity, capable of much more than simply telling time."

Jameson frowned. "I've never heard of such a person."

Mr. Thorne smiled faintly. "No, I suppose you wouldn't have. It's an old story, almost forgotten now. But I believe that the truth of it is hidden somewhere in this village."

Reverend Jameson stared at him, a chill creeping down his spine. There was something unsettling about the way Mr. Thorne spoke
, as if he were in possession of knowledge that no one else had.

"And what exactly are you looking for, Mr. Thorne?" the vicar asked quietly.

Mr. Thorne's smile widened, but his eyes remained cold and calculating.

"A secret," he replied. "A secret that was hidden away long ago... and which I intend to uncover."

4. A Locked Room Mystery

THE ROOM WAS EXACTLY as they had left it the night before—silent, undisturbed, and undeniably sealed from the inside. No creaking of floorboards or scuffling of feet could have altered the pristine arrangement of the crime scene. Every book on the mahogany shelves remained upright, and the ornate grandfather clock in the corner continued its steady ticking, marking the inevitable passage of time. But one thing was chillingly clear: someone had entered, committed a brutal murder, and vanished without a trace.

Detective Hart stood at the threshold, his sharp eyes scanning the library of Mistlewood Hall for any sign that might hint at the impossible. The room was deceptively ordinary, yet within its four walls, something extraordinary had occurred.

"Inspector, I swear, we've checked every inch. No windows broken, no secret passages that we could find. And the door was locked from the inside. There's simply no way anyone could've come in or gone out without being seen!" Constable Miller's voice, though steady, betrayed a note of apprehension.

Detective Hart turned his gaze from the clock to the plush armchair in the center of the room, where the body of Lord Albert Ravenscroft had been found. A man of middle age, with a reputation for peculiar habits and a penchant for collecting rare timepieces, Lord Ravenscroft was hardly the sort to meet a violent end. Yet there he was, his lifeless form sprawled back, eyes wide open in what seemed to be a mixture of surprise and terror. His chest bore a single, precise stab wound, positioned just beneath the heart. No sign of struggle, no sound that could have alerted the household staff or the guests attending the dinner party in the adjacent ballroom.

"Let's go over it again," Hart said, his voice calm but authoritative. "We know that Lord Ravenscroft left the dining room at approximately 10:15 p.m. He mentioned wanting to retrieve something from his library—something to show his guests. A valuable watch, wasn't it?"

"Yes, sir," Miller confirmed. "A gold pocket watch with a unique engraving. He said he'd be back in a few minutes. But when he didn't return after fifteen, Lady Ravenscroft sent a servant to check on him."

"And the servant found the door locked," Hart continued, almost as if speaking to himself. "He knocked, but there was no answer. Concerned, Lady Ravenscroft called for her husband's valet, who used the spare key to unlock the door. That's when they found him. Dead. The door locked from the inside and no one else in the room."

"Exactly, sir."

Hart sighed, stepping further into the room. There was something maddeningly eerie about locked-room murders—the kind that seemed to mock the laws of logic and reason. But he knew all too well that every trick, no matter how clever, left behind some residue of its making. It was just a matter of finding it.

He moved to the desk, where a scattering of papers had been neatly stacked. A letter opener—clean, unblemished—lay at an odd angle. He picked it up, examining its sharp edge thoughtfully before setting it down again.

"Who knew about the spare key?" he asked suddenly.

"Only a few of the household staff and Lady Ravenscroft herself," Miller replied. "It was kept in a drawer in the butler's pantry."

"And where was the butler during the time of the murder?"

"Attending to guests in the dining room, sir. He has several witnesses who can confirm it."

Hart nodded, his mind racing. The butler had no motive, and neither did any of the servants. But that didn't mean they were completely out of the equation. Every person in this house, whether aristocrat or commoner, could have a secret worth killing for.

"What about the guests?" he asked after a moment. "Did any of them leave the dining room between 10:15 and the time the body was found?"

"None that we know of. Everyone seems to have remained in their seats until the news spread. Panic set in then, naturally. Lady Ravenscroft almost fainted, and Sir Edgar—one of the guests—had to help her to the lounge."

"Sir Edgar, you say?" Hart's interest piqued. "What's his connection to the family?"

"Old friend of Lord Ravenscroft's. They served together during the war."

"I see." Hart rubbed his chin thoughtfully. "And was there any animosity between them? Anything that might suggest Sir Edgar had a reason to dislike Lord Ravenscroft?"

Miller hesitated. "There were rumors, sir, about a disagreement over a business deal. But that was years ago. As far as anyone knew, they'd put it behind them."

"Hmm." Hart turned his attention to the window, which overlooked the sprawling gardens of Mistlewood Hall. It was locked, of course, just as it had been when they arrived. He ran his fingers along the edges of the frame, feeling for any irregularities, but found none.

"Would you like us to bring Sir Edgar in for questioning?" Miller asked.

"Not just yet," Hart replied. "There's something else at play here, something we're not seeing. What I need to know is... why this room? Why the library? And why that precise time?"

He glanced at the grandfather clock again. It had stopped at exactly 10:30 p.m.—the same time that Lord Ravenscroft was estimated to have died. Coincidence? Hart didn't believe in coincidences.

"Get me a list of every guest present tonight," he said, his voice taking on a sharper tone. "And I want to speak to the household staff again. If anyone saw or heard anything unusual, no matter how trivial it might seem, I want to know about it."

"Yes, sir." Miller turned to leave, but paused at the door. "Sir, do you think it's possible that—well, that Lord Ravenscroft might have... done it himself? A suicide?"

Hart shook his head. "No. That's the one thing I'm certain of. This wasn't a suicide. Someone wanted it to look like an unsolvable crime. Someone who thought they were clever enough to get away with it."

With that, he turned back to the armchair, where Lord Ravenscroft's still body remained, a somber reminder of the mystery that encased the room. Hart leaned closer, studying the expression frozen on the dead man's face. Surprise. Shock. And something else... recognition?

He straightened abruptly. Of course! The answer wasn't in the door, or the windows, or even the locks. It was in the face of the victim. Lord Ravenscroft had known his killer. He'd seen them with his own eyes, trusted them enough to let them get close.

But that didn't explain how the murderer had escaped a locked room. There was still one piece of the puzzle missing, and until Hart could find it, the case would remain an enigma.

Taking one last look at the clock, he strode purposefully from the library. He needed more information, more context. Whoever had committed this crime had thought of everything, but even the most meticulous plan had its flaws.

And Hart was determined to find them.

· · · ·

THE EVENING DRAGGED on as the detective interviewed each member of the household staff. The butler, the maid, the cook—all of them seemed genuinely distressed by the events of the night, but none had seen or heard anything out of the ordinary. The only clue, if it could be called that, came from young Peter, the footman.

"I... I did hear something, sir," Peter stammered, wringing his cap in his hands. "But it didn't seem important at the time."

"Go on," Hart urged gently. "What did you hear?"

"Well, it was just a sort of... whirring noise, like clockwork, coming from the library. I thought it was just the old grandfather clock, sir. It makes those noises sometimes, you see."

Hart frowned. A whirring noise? That was something he hadn't expected.

"Thank you, Peter. You've been very helpful."

As the young man left, Hart turned the information over in his mind. A whirring noise could indicate some sort of mechanism, something hidden within the walls or the furniture. It might even explain how the killer managed to lock the door from the inside without being there.

But that raised more questions. If there was a secret mechanism, why would Lord Ravenscroft have such a thing installed? And how did it connect to his death?

Hart glanced around the library again, his gaze narrowing as it fell upon the clock. The answer lay somewhere in this room. He could feel it.

And he wouldn't rest until he uncovered it.

5. The Watchmaker's Last Words

THE EVENING AIR IN the small town of Haverford was crisp and cold, the kind of cold that seemed to seep through every layer of clothing and settle deep in the bones. A dense fog, thick as cream, clung to the cobblestone streets, muffling the sound of footsteps and blurring the gas lamps' pale glow. It was under these

shadowy conditions that Inspector Edmund Hart made his way to
the small watchmaker's shop at the end of Wren Lane, summoned
by a message that spoke of urgency and danger.

The shop itself, an old establishment with a façade that had
seen better days, looked almost forlorn. A sign, swinging gently in
the wind, announced it as "Crawford & Sons – Watchmakers and
Horologists Since 1847." But the shop, like much of Haverford,
bore the scars of time's passage. Paint was peeling off the wooden
frame, and the large glass window was coated in dust, obscuring the
treasures that lay inside.

Edmund hesitated briefly at the door, his hand poised over the
brass handle. He had known Harold Crawford for years. The man
was a recluse but a respected craftsman, his intricate timepieces
sought after by collectors and enthusiasts alike. But tonight's
message had been troubling. Scrawled in a trembling hand, it
simply read: "Come at once. There is no time left."

Pushing the door open, the inspector was met with the familiar
scent of aged wood, oil, and metal. The soft ticking of countless
clocks filled the air, each one ticking at its own rhythm, creating
a strange, almost hypnotic symphony. Harold Crawford stood
behind the counter, his hunched frame shrouded in the shadows.
He looked up as the bell above the door chimed softly, his eyes wide
and haunted.

"Edmund, you came..." Harold's voice was barely a whisper, the
words carrying an undertone of fear.

"Harold, what's happened?" Edmund stepped closer, concern
etched on his features. The watchmaker had always been a quiet
man, methodical and precise. Seeing him like this—disheveled,
with sweat beading on his brow despite the chill in the air—was
unsettling.

Harold gestured to the back of the shop. "It's not safe to speak
here. Follow me."

They moved through the narrow passage lined with shelves cluttered with tools, spare parts, and half-assembled clocks. At the very back, Harold pushed open a small, concealed door that led into his private workshop. This room, unlike the front of the shop, was meticulously organized. Every tool had its place, and every surface gleamed with a cleanliness that spoke of a mind obsessed with order.

But what caught Edmund's attention was the object on the central workbench—a clock, unlike any he had ever seen. It was large, almost three feet in height, with a face that shimmered faintly in the dim light. The craftsmanship was exquisite, each cog and wheel perfectly aligned, each hand moving with a smoothness that defied explanation. But it was the numbers on the clock face that were most peculiar. Instead of the traditional twelve, this clock had thirteen numbers, and the hands moved counter-clockwise.

"Good Lord, Harold... What is this?"

"It's what they made me build," Harold murmured, his voice trembling. "A clock... but not a clock. A device, a mechanism... something far beyond mere timekeeping."

Edmund's brow furrowed in confusion. "Who? Who made you build this?"

The watchmaker's gaze shifted nervously, as if expecting someone—or something—to burst through the door at any moment. "I can't say. If I speak their name... I fear it will be the end of me. But you must understand, Edmund, this clock—" He broke off, a shudder running through his frail frame. "This clock is a key. A key to something terrible."

Before the inspector could press further, Harold stumbled to his desk and pulled out a small, leather-bound notebook. His hands were shaking so badly that it took him several tries to untie the string that held it shut. He flipped through the pages with frantic speed, finally stopping at one filled with a complex diagram of gears and symbols, accompanied by hastily scribbled notes.

"This is the blueprint," he whispered, pushing the notebook into Edmund's hands. "I kept it hidden... thought it might save me, but now... I see it only put me in more danger. They know I have it. They're coming for me."

Edmund glanced down at the intricate drawings. The mechanism depicted in the notebook was far beyond anything he could comprehend, and the symbols looked like they belonged in some arcane text rather than a watchmaker's manual.

"Harold, you're not making any sense. Who are these people? What do they want with you?"

But Harold shook his head, a bitter smile twisting his lips. "It's too late for me. They'll silence me just as they did the others. But you, Edmund... you must take this and leave. Don't look back. Don't try to understand it. Just... destroy it."

A chill ran down Edmund's spine. He had seen Harold scared before, but this was different. This was the fear of a man who knew he was facing certain death.

"Harold, I'm not leaving you. Whatever this is, I'll protect you."

The watchmaker's laugh was hollow, a sound devoid of hope. "You can't protect me. You can't even protect yourself if you stay here. Go, now—"

A sudden noise cut him off, the unmistakable sound of breaking glass from the front of the shop. Harold's face drained of color.

"They're here," he whispered. "It's too late."

Panic surged through Edmund as he turned toward the door. "We have to get out. There must be another way—"

But Harold was already moving toward the strange clock on the workbench. "No, there's no time for that. I need you to listen carefully." He reached into the mechanism of the clock and twisted something deep within. The clock's hands began to spin wildly, the ticking growing louder and more erratic.

"What are you doing?" Edmund shouted, but Harold's eyes were fixed on the clock.

"I'm giving you a chance," Harold murmured, his voice barely audible over the cacophony of noise. "A chance to finish what I couldn't. Remember what I said, Edmund. The blueprint... the clock... it's a key. Find out what it unlocks."

The shop was suddenly filled with a blinding flash of light. Edmund felt himself being thrown backward, a wave of heat and force knocking the breath out of him. The last thing he saw was Harold's silhouette, standing resolute in front of the clock, his face set in grim determination.

And then—darkness.

• • • •

WHEN EDMUND CAME TO, he was lying on the cold, damp ground outside the watchmaker's shop. The building was in flames, the fire roaring hungrily as it consumed wood and glass. A crowd had gathered, their faces pale with shock and fear.

"Inspector! Inspector Hart!" A voice called out, and Edmund turned to see Constable Reeves running toward him, his expression frantic.

"What... what happened?" Edmund mumbled, struggling to push himself up. His head throbbed painfully, and his vision swam.

"We don't know, sir. There was an explosion. By the time we got here, the whole place was ablaze."

Edmund's gaze shifted to the smoldering ruins of the shop. Harold Crawford was gone. Along with the mysterious clock and any answers it might have held.

"Harold..." he whispered, clutching the notebook tightly to his chest. The last words the watchmaker had spoken echoed in his mind. The blueprint... the clock... it's a key. Find out what it unlocks.

Whatever the clock had been, whatever secret Harold had been forced to create—it hadn't died with him. And Edmund knew, with a bone-deep certainty, that this was only the beginning.

6. The Second Victim

THE AIR WAS THICK WITH unease as the small village of Wickford awoke to a murmur of dread that swept through its cobbled streets. The discovery of the second body had thrown the quiet town into a frenzy, and in hushed voices, the villagers whispered of shadows, of a darkness lurking beneath the facade of their picturesque community.

Detective Hart had barely slept the previous night. The first murder had unsettled him deeply, but this... this was something else entirely. As he stood over the lifeless form of Miss Margaret Easley, he couldn't shake the feeling that the hands of time had shifted, propelling them all into a nightmare from which there was no escape. The scene was eerily reminiscent of the first. A modest cottage, the door slightly ajar, and a body positioned with a precision that made his blood run cold.

Margaret lay crumpled at the foot of the mahogany grandfather clock that dominated the corner of her parlor. Her head was turned at an unnatural angle, her once lively eyes now staring vacantly at the gilded hands of the clock, which were frozen at 7:15. It was the same time as on the first victim's clock — a fact that tied the two murders together like a grotesque knot.

Inspector Bradshaw's heavy boots echoed as he entered the room, his brow furrowed with grim determination. "Another one,

Hart," he muttered, shaking his head in disbelief. "What kind of devilry is this?"

Hart didn't reply immediately. He was too absorbed in the scene, his eyes tracing the small details that others might overlook. The careful placement of Margaret's hands, the faint scent of lavender still lingering in the air, and, of course, the clock — a magnificent piece with delicate engravings and an ornate pendulum that seemed almost to shiver under his scrutiny.

"The clock," he murmured finally, pointing to the face. "7:15. Exactly the same as on Howard Finch's timepiece. It can't be a coincidence."

Bradshaw snorted. "You think we've got a maniac obsessed with clocks? Or maybe it's some twisted message?"

"Perhaps both," Hart conceded, kneeling down to examine the floor around Margaret's body. There were no signs of a struggle, no overturned furniture or bloodstains — just like with Finch. But there was something else, something that caught his eye: a fine, almost invisible powder dusting the ground beneath the clock. He leaned closer, using a small brush to collect a sample into a vial.

"What do you make of it?" Bradshaw asked, his voice dropping to a near-whisper, as though afraid to disturb the stillness of the room.

Hart stood, slipping the vial into his coat pocket. "Not sure yet. Could be chalk, or something else entirely. We'll have it analyzed, but my gut tells me it's important."

Margaret Easley had been a well-respected schoolteacher, known for her sharp mind and unyielding discipline. She wasn't the sort to invite trouble — and yet, here she was, the second victim in what was shaping up to be a terrifying pattern.

"The village is going to panic when word gets out," Bradshaw said, running a hand through his graying hair. "They were already on edge after Finch. This... this will break them."

Hart nodded slowly. He could already see it unfolding — the gossip, the fear, the suspicion that would spread like wildfire. But more pressing than the villagers' fear was the gnawing question that kept circling in his mind: Why Margaret? Why now? And, most importantly, who would be next?

Leaving the scene in the capable hands of the forensics team, Hart and Bradshaw made their way back to the station. The usually bustling precinct was subdued, officers speaking in low voices as they sifted through witness statements and reports. The murder of Howard Finch, a reclusive clockmaker found dead in his workshop just two weeks earlier, had already stretched their resources thin. Now, with Margaret's death, the case had taken on a chilling urgency.

Hart settled into his chair, the weight of exhaustion pressing heavily on his shoulders. He stared at the two case files spread out before him, comparing every detail, searching for a thread that might connect them. Margaret and Finch hadn't been close; in fact, Hart could find no evidence that they'd interacted at all. So why would the killer target them both?

"Look at this," Bradshaw said suddenly, thrusting a sheet of paper into Hart's hands. It was a list of visitors to Margaret's home over the past month, compiled from statements given by neighbors. One name stood out — a Mr. Charles Ashford.

"Who is he?" Hart asked, frowning at the unfamiliar name.

"Local antique dealer," Bradshaw replied. "Supposedly came by to discuss selling some of Margaret's old family heirlooms. Harmless enough, right? Except that same name showed up on Finch's visitor list, too."

Hart's pulse quickened. "Could be a coincidence... or it could be the connection we've been looking for."

It didn't take long to track down Charles Ashford. He was a middle-aged man with thinning hair and a thin veneer of charm that barely masked his irritation at being summoned to the station. He sat stiffly across from Hart, his fingers tapping out a restless rhythm on the table.

"I don't see why you're questioning me again," he said, his voice tight. "I've already told your officers everything I know."

"Just a few more questions, Mr. Ashford," Hart said calmly. "You visited both Margaret Easley and Howard Finch recently. Can you tell me what your business with them was?"

Ashford sighed, as if weary of the whole affair. "I deal in antiques, as you know. Both Miss Easley and Mr. Finch had items they were interested in selling. Old clocks, mostly. I appraised them, made offers — that's it."

"Clocks?" Hart leaned forward, interest piqued. "What kind of clocks?"

Ashford shifted uncomfortably. "All sorts. Finch had some rare pieces, even a couple of French mantel clocks from the 18th century. Miss Easley's collection was more modest. Nothing out of the ordinary."

"And did you buy anything from them?"

"From Finch, yes. A few pieces. But Miss Easley decided against selling."

Hart studied Ashford's face, searching for any sign of deceit. There was something about the man's demeanor that didn't sit right — a defensiveness that suggested he was holding something back.

"Where were you last night between 6 and 8 PM?" Hart asked abruptly.

Ashford blinked, caught off guard by the sudden shift in questioning. "At home, of course. My wife can vouch for me."

"Would you mind if we verified that?"

Ashford's mouth tightened into a thin line, but he nodded. "Go ahead. I've got nothing to hide."

They released Ashford after a brief call to his wife confirmed his alibi. Yet as Hart watched the man stride out of the station, he couldn't shake the feeling that they were missing something — that Ashford knew more than he was letting on.

"Could be nothing," Bradshaw murmured, echoing Hart's thoughts. "But I don't like it."

"Neither do I," Hart agreed quietly. "Keep an eye on him. And look into those clocks he mentioned. There's a pattern here — I just can't see it yet."

The rest of the day passed in a blur of dead ends and mounting frustration. By nightfall, the station was almost empty, and Hart found himself staring at the wall of evidence they'd compiled so far. Photographs of the victims, diagrams of their homes, notes on every scrap of information they'd gathered. Yet for all the data, for all the meticulous work, the solution remained maddeningly out of reach.

Rubbing his temples, Hart glanced again at the photographs of the clocks. There was something there, something just beyond his grasp. Both Finch and Margaret had owned clocks — fine, handcrafted pieces. But that wasn't unusual, was it? Many people collected clocks.

Chapter 4: Secrets Beneath the Surface

1. Hidden Compartments

The small town of Broadchurch had always been a place of quiet routine, its residents comfortably settled into lives that seldom deviated from the familiar. Situated on a lush, verdant hillside, it was the sort of town where the unexpected seldom arrived, and secrets, if they existed, were carefully buried beneath layers of ordinary life. That's why the recent series of grisly murders, each more perplexing than the last, had left the townsfolk reeling. Fear hung in the air like a shroud, and every conversation was weighted with suspicion. Was the killer one of them? How long would it be before another body was discovered?

Detective Samuel Hart found himself standing in the modest workshop of Alfred Gaines, the town's renowned watchmaker, who had been the first victim in what was now known as "The Clockwork Murders." The small room smelled of machine oil and dust, a testament to a lifetime dedicated to the meticulous art of watchmaking. Delicate tools lay scattered across the wooden workbench, and several unfinished timepieces stood like silent sentinels, their intricate gears and springs motionless.

Samuel ran his hand over the smooth surface of the bench, his eyes scanning for anything that might have been overlooked. The room felt heavy with anticipation, as if it were holding its breath, waiting for him to uncover its hidden truths.

"Detective Hart, are you sure we've covered everything in here?" came a hesitant voice from the doorway. It was Constable Merriweather, a young officer new to the force. His youthful face was pinched with uncertainty.

"Not quite," Samuel replied without turning around. "There's something about this place that doesn't sit right. Something's hidden here—something that's meant to be found."

With a soft creak, the detective pulled out a wooden drawer from the bench. It appeared empty at first glance, but Hart's practiced eye caught the subtle groove along the back panel, a slight irregularity that wouldn't have been there without reason. He pressed a calloused finger against it, feeling the faint resistance before the panel slid back, revealing a hollow space inside.

Merriweather stepped closer, his eyes widening as Samuel reached into the compartment and pulled out a small, dust-covered journal. Its leather cover was cracked with age, and the clasp was rusty. The initials "A.G." were engraved on the front.

"A journal?" Merriweather asked, puzzled. "Why hide that?"

"That's what we're going to find out," Samuel muttered, flipping open the book. The pages were filled with neatly penned entries in a strong, confident hand. It didn't take long before the detective realized what he was looking at.

"It's a list of clock repairs," he murmured, scanning through the pages. "But look at the dates. They don't match up with the records we found in the front office. Some of these names—these clients—never appeared in any official documentation."

He paused on one entry, tracing the lines with his finger.

"Edwin Crowley. The name came up when we were investigating the third murder, didn't it? But he was ruled out because he had no known connection to the other victims. This... changes things."

Merriweather peered over his shoulder, squinting at the names. "So these are clients he didn't want anyone to know about?"

"Or they're something else entirely," Samuel said grimly. "I think Alfred Gaines was keeping more than just clocks in working order. He was keeping secrets."

They spent the next several hours meticulously combing through the journal, noting every name, date, and detail that seemed out of place. As they progressed, a pattern began to emerge—one that pointed to a clandestine network of people connected not by their need for timepieces, but by something far more sinister.

It was nearing dusk by the time they finished, the fading sunlight casting long shadows across the workshop. Samuel's eyes were tired, but his mind was alight with possibilities.

"What do we do now, sir?" Merriweather asked quietly.

"We find out who these people are," Samuel replied, closing the journal with a decisive snap. "If Gaines was involved with them, then it's possible one of them might be our killer—or at the very least, know who it is."

The investigation took them down unexpected paths, delving into the murky pasts of seemingly upstanding citizens. Every name in the journal was a puzzle piece that didn't quite fit, each one leading to more questions than answers. But the deeper they dug, the clearer it became that Alfred Gaines hadn't been just a watchmaker—he had been a keeper of secrets, a man who held the town's most dangerous knowledge in the hidden compartments of his workshop.

It was late one night, after weeks of painstaking research, when a breakthrough came. Merriweather had been poring over town records when he stumbled upon a peculiar fact: nearly every person listed in the secret journal had been involved in a legal dispute over a piece of land just outside Broadchurch. The case had been quietly settled years ago, but something about it didn't sit right.

"Detective Hart, I think I've found something," he announced breathlessly, sliding a dusty folder across the table.

Samuel glanced up, his interest piqued. "What is it?"

"It's the land deeds for a property on the outskirts—Crowley's Wood. It was supposed to be a common area, but it seems several people were trying to claim it. The names match those in the journal."

"Crowley's Wood?" Samuel repeated, frowning. "That place has been abandoned for decades. Why would anyone want it?"

"That's the thing, sir," Merriweather said, his voice dropping to a whisper. "It's not just the land. There's something buried there—something that was worth killing for."

The detective leaned back in his chair, considering this new piece of the puzzle. It was as if every path led back to that cursed piece of land, where time seemed to stand still, shrouded in mist and silence.

"Looks like we'll need to pay a visit to Crowley's Wood," he said finally, a grim smile tugging at his lips. "I have a feeling we're about to uncover a secret that's been buried for far too long."

The journey to the wood was uneventful, the narrow road winding through dense trees that seemed to press in on them from all sides. As they neared the heart of the forest, the air grew heavy with the scent of damp earth and decay. It was an unsettling place, made all the more eerie by the stories the townsfolk whispered in hushed tones—tales of ghostly apparitions and unexplained noises.

They parked the car at the edge of the clearing and made their way on foot, the underbrush crackling under their boots. In the fading light, Crowley's Wood looked almost otherworldly, its twisted branches reaching up like skeletal fingers.

"Over here," Merriweather called softly, pointing to a small, half-buried structure. It was a stone marker, weathered and covered in moss. At its base was an iron door, its edges rusted and worn.

Samuel knelt down, running his fingers over the cool metal. "This must be the entrance to whatever's hidden beneath. A hidden compartment of sorts."

With a grunt of effort, they pried the door open, revealing a dark, yawning void below. A set of narrow stone steps descended into the earth, swallowed by shadows.

"Are you sure about this, sir?" Merriweather asked, his voice tight with apprehension.

"We've come this far," Samuel replied, lighting a lantern. "Let's see what Alfred Gaines—and the others—were so desperate to hide."

The descent was slow and cautious, each step echoing ominously in the confined space. The air grew colder as they went deeper, and a faint metallic scent tinged with rot filled their nostrils. At the bottom of the stairs, they found themselves in a small, stone chamber, the walls lined with shelves.

And on those shelves, row after row, were small wooden boxes, each marked with a number.

"What is this place?" Merriweather whispered, his voice reverberating off the walls.

Samuel stepped forward, his gaze sweeping over the boxes. "It's a vault. A vault for secrets. And each of these boxes... holds a piece of someone's life."

He pulled one of the boxes down, prying it open. Inside was a small, delicate locket—its surface tarnished with age. A folded note lay beside it, the ink faded but still legible.

"'To my dearest Catherine,'" Samuel read aloud, his voice soft. "'May this keep you safe when I cannot. Until we meet again—Edwin.'"

"Edwin Crowley," Merriweather breathed, his eyes widening. "But what does it mean?"

Samuel turned the locket over, his fingers tracing the inscription. "It means we've found the heart of this mystery. This place—it's where the town's darkest secrets were kept. And someone's been using them to exact revenge."

They continued to open the boxes, uncovering more items: love letters, photographs, even a bloodstained handkerchief. Each one was a testament to a story long buried, a connection between people that the town had tried to forget.

But there was one box, larger and heavier than the others, that caught Samuel's attention. He lifted it carefully, feeling a strange chill run down his spine as he pried it open.

Inside was a pocket watch, its surface cracked and marred. But it was the initials engraved on the back that made his heart stop.

"A.G."

"Alfred Gaines," he whispered, staring at the broken timepiece. "This watch... it must have belonged to him."

"But why hide it down here?" Merr
iweather asked, his brow furrowing.

Samuel turned the watch over, noticing a small, almost imperceptible switch along the side. He pressed it, and the back panel of the watch sprang open, revealing a hidden compartment within.

Nestled inside, barely visible, was a tiny scrap of paper. Samuel unfolded it, his eyes widening as he read the single word written there:

"Justice."

A shiver ran down his spine as he looked around the chamber, at the countless secrets that had been kept locked away, hidden from the world. This was no ordinary crime. This was retribution, carried out with the precision of a clockmaker.

And the message was clear.

"Someone's been seeking justice for a long time," Samuel murmured, his gaze distant. "And they're not finished yet."

With a grim resolve, he slipped the watch into his pocket. There was more to uncover, more pieces of the puzzle to fit together. But one thing was certain:

The past had a way of catching up, and time—no matter how carefully one tried to control it—would never stay hidden forever.

As they ascended the stairs, the chamber behind them felt like a living entity, its walls pulsing with the weight of secrets unearthed. Samuel glanced back one last time before closing the iron door, a sense of foreboding settling in his chest.

The hidden compartments had been opened.

And now, there was no turning back.

2. The Missing Blueprints

THE DAY DAWNED GRAY and silent over the small town of Harrowdale, a stillness settling over the cobblestone streets like a heavy shroud. It was the kind of morning where time itself seemed to pause, the mist rolling in from the moors muffling sound and cloaking every movement. People went about their business as though on tiptoe, unwilling to disturb the quietude of the waking world. Yet there was an unspoken tension in the air, a sense of disquiet that lingered just beyond the range of perception, growing stronger with each tick of the clock.

It was into this charged atmosphere that Inspector Reginald Hart stepped, his boots striking a steady rhythm against the pavement as he made his way to the town's central square. He was a man who knew the value of silence, preferring to observe rather than speak, and he was well aware that Harrowdale had many secrets — secrets that time had obscured but not erased. His presence was not usually cause for alarm, but the events of the past week had changed that. Three murders, each more brutal than the last, had left the town shaken to its core.

All the victims were prominent figures: a well-respected banker, a reclusive artist, and, most recently, a watchmaker of considerable skill and reputation. There was no apparent connection between them, yet there was something about the killings that struck Hart as orchestrated, almost mechanical in their precision. It was as if some unseen hand was turning the gears of fate, winding the victims towards their inevitable ends. And there was one clue that bound them all together — a set of missing blueprints, last seen in the possession of the murdered watchmaker, Mr. Edwin Craythorne.

Craythorne's death had been particularly unsettling. He was found in his workshop, his body slumped over his workbench, a look of sheer terror frozen on his face. His hands, normally so steady, had been contorted into a grotesque parody of his trade. And there, scattered across the floor, were fragments of a clock — one that had been meticulously dismantled piece by piece, its components laid out in a spiral pattern that seemed to taunt the onlookers.

But it was not the scene itself that disturbed Hart the most. No, it was the absence of something — the blueprints. The watchmaker had been working on a special commission for a wealthy client, a device so complex and unique that he had insisted on keeping the designs under lock and key. Yet when the police arrived, the safe where the blueprints were stored was wide open, and the papers were gone. There were no signs of forced entry, no clues as to how the thief had managed to slip in and out undetected.

Inspector Hart had questioned everyone who might have known about the designs: Craythorne's assistant, the maid who cleaned his home, even the delivery boy who brought his groceries. All had professed ignorance. It was as if the blueprints had simply vanished into thin air. But Hart knew better. He sensed that the key to solving the murders lay in those missing pages — that they held the answer to a question he had not yet thought to ask.

As he approached the watchmaker's shop that morning, he felt a prickle of unease. The windows were dark, the curtains drawn tight, and the sign that normally hung above the door had been removed. The place looked abandoned, stripped of its former life and purpose. But Hart had business there. He pushed open the door, the bell jangling softly above his head, and stepped inside.

The air was heavy with the smell of oil and metal, the faint ticking of unseen clocks echoing from the shadows. Dust motes danced in the thin slivers of light that filtered through the cracks in the shutters. The workbench where Craythorne had spent countless hours perfecting his craft stood untouched, a silent monument to his dedication. Hart moved closer, his eyes scanning the surface for anything that might have been overlooked in the initial investigation.

And then he saw it — a small, nondescript envelope, wedged beneath the base of a rusted vise. Carefully, he pried it loose, his heart quickening as he unfolded the yellowed paper inside. It was a letter, written in a precise, elegant hand.

"To whomever finds this," it began. "If you are reading these words, then it is likely I am no longer among the living. There are forces at work that seek to bury the truth, to erase all traces of what has been done. But they cannot hide everything. The blueprints you seek are not lost — they have been hidden where only one with the knowledge and courage to look will find them. Follow the pattern, and you will see. The answer lies in the clockwork."

Hart read and reread the letter, his mind racing. The pattern... What could it mean? He glanced around the workshop, his gaze lingering on the scattered clock parts, the meticulous arrangements Craythorne had made before his death. There was a pattern here, of that he was sure. But what was it trying to tell him?

He spent the next several hours sifting through the remnants of the dismantled clock, examining each cog and spring with the eye of a craftsman. At first, nothing seemed unusual. But as he pieced the components together, he noticed something odd. Each part had been etched with a tiny number — so small it was barely visible to the naked eye. When he aligned them in the order indicated by the numbers, a new design began to take shape, one that did not correspond to any timepiece Hart had ever seen.

His pulse quickened as the realization dawned. The watchmaker had left a message — a blueprint within a blueprint, hidden in plain sight. But what did it mean? Hart carefully sketched the completed diagram on a sheet of paper, his brow furrowed in concentration. It appeared to be a map, but of what, he could not yet discern.

He needed more information. There was only one person who might be able to help him decipher the meaning of Craythorne's final creation: Professor Julian Reeves, a renowned horologist and an old friend of the inspector's. Reeves was a man of considerable intellect and even greater eccentricity, known for his unorthodox theories about the nature of time and the mechanisms that governed its flow. If anyone could make sense of the watchmaker's cryptic design, it would be him.

Hart wasted no time. He locked up the shop and made his way to Reeves's residence on the outskirts of town, a sprawling estate filled with all manner of clocks and automata. The professor greeted him at the door, his eyes alight with curiosity.

"Reginald, what a pleasant surprise!" Reeves exclaimed, ushering him inside. "To what do I owe the pleasure?"

Hart handed him the sketch without a word. Reeves's expression shifted from geniality to deep concentration as he studied the lines and symbols.

"Fascinating..." he murmured, tracing a finger along the edges of the drawing. "This is no ordinary clockwork, Reginald. It's... it's a cipher. Craythorne was trying to encode something within the mechanics of the device. But what?"

"That's what I need you to find out, Julian," Hart replied. "Whatever this design is meant to conceal, it's worth killing for.

And I have a feeling that the murders won't stop until we uncover the truth."

Reeves nodded thoughtfully. "I'll need some time to analyze this properly, but I believe we're looking at more than just a piece of clockwork. This could be a schematic for... well, it's difficult to say without further study, but I suspect it may be related to a long-lost invention of considerable significance. One that was thought to have been destroyed decades ago."

Hart felt a chill run down his spine. "What kind of invention, Julian?"

The professor glanced up, his expression grave. "The kind that could change everything we know about time itself."

With those words, Hart realized that they were no longer dealing with a simple case of theft or even murder. The missing blueprints were the key to something far greater — something that transcended the boundaries of the physical world. And someone was willing to kill to keep that knowledge buried forever.

As he left Reeves's estate that evening, the weight of the discovery settled heavily on his shoulders. The blueprints were missing, yes, but they were not lost. They were hidden, encrypted in a language only a master of the craft could decode. It would take time and patience to unravel the secrets they held, but Hart was determined to see it through.

The murders had not been random acts of violence; they were steps in a grander scheme, each death serving a purpose. And now, with the pattern beginning to emerge, Hart understood that the clock was ticking — not just for him, but for everyone in Harrowdale.

Time, he realized, was running out.

3. An Encounter at the Church

THE LOW HUM OF THE wind as it swept through the deserted churchyard was the only sound that broke the silence of the evening. The towering silhouette of St. Agatha's Church, with its Gothic spire piercing the dusk, stood like a sentinel over the graves below. The pale, silvered light of the moon cast long, eerie shadows that danced among the headstones, as if the spirits of the departed were stirring from their slumber.

Detective Theodore Hart paused at the iron gates, his gaze fixed on the weathered façade of the church. It had been years since he'd last set foot on these grounds, and yet it felt as though time had scarcely passed at all. The same creeping ivy coiled around the ancient stone walls, the same cracked path led to the heavy wooden doors, and the same chilling air of solitude seemed to envelop the entire place.

He pushed open the gate, the hinges creaking in protest. The sound echoed through the emptiness, unsettling a few resting crows that took off with startled cries. Hart's footsteps crunched on the gravel as he made his way to the entrance, his senses alert to every shift in the shadows around him. He wasn't superstitious, but there was something about St. Agatha's that always set his nerves on edge.

A figure waited for him by the doorway, shrouded in a dark coat that blended almost seamlessly with the night. The flickering light from the old lantern beside the door cast strange, angular patterns on the figure's face, making it difficult to discern his expression.

"Inspector Hart," the man called out softly, his voice low and measured. "I was beginning to think you wouldn't come."

"Reverend," Hart greeted with a curt nod, stepping closer. The man before him was Reverend Edmund Grayson, the long-time caretaker and clergyman of St. Agatha's. His thin, ascetic face was pale in the dim light, his eyes deep-set and sharp. There was an air of solemnity about him, of a man burdened with more than just the spiritual wellbeing of his flock.

"I wouldn't miss an appointment like this," Hart continued, his gaze unwavering. "You said it was urgent."

Grayson nodded, glancing around as if expecting someone—or something—to leap out from the shadows. Satisfied that they were alone, he turned and gestured for Hart to follow him inside. The door groaned as it swung open, revealing the vast, empty nave of the church. The faint smell of incense still lingered in the air, mingling with the scent of old wood and stone.

"After the recent... incidents," Grayson began, his voice barely more than a whisper as they stepped inside, "I felt it necessary to reach out to you. There are things—things that must be said. Things that should not be allowed to stay hidden."

Hart raised an eyebrow but said nothing, letting the reverend lead the way. They walked past rows of pews, their steps muffled by the thick carpet runner that stretched down the aisle. The silence of the church was oppressive, almost tangible, and it seemed to close in around them as they moved deeper into the building.

"Father Grayson, I appreciate your concern," Hart said finally, his voice echoing softly off the vaulted ceiling. "But I'm not here for confessions. If you have information regarding the murders, I suggest you come out with it plainly."

Grayson paused at the base of the altar steps, his shoulders tense. He turned to face Hart, his eyes burning with a strange intensity. "It's not just information, Inspector. It's... knowledge. Knowledge that can be dangerous in the wrong hands."

There was a long, heavy silence as the two men regarded each other. Then, with a sigh, Grayson reached into his coat pocket and pulled out a small, folded piece of paper. He handed it to Hart, his fingers trembling slightly.

Hart unfolded the paper carefully, his brow furrowing as he read the message scrawled in neat, precise handwriting:

"When the bell tolls at midnight, the hands of time shall point to the truth."

"What does this mean?" Hart demanded, looking up at Grayson. "Is this some sort of clue? Or a threat?"

"Perhaps both," Grayson murmured, his gaze drifting to the large, bronze bell that hung above them in the belfry. "It was left in the confessional two nights ago, after the second murder. I found it the next morning, placed where the confessor should have been seated. There was no one else in the church at the time."

Hart's eyes narrowed. "And you didn't report this to the police?"

Grayson shook his head slowly. "I had my reasons. I needed to understand what it meant first. And I think... I think I might know."

There was a strange light in the reverend's eyes now, something that bordered on fear—or madness. Hart felt a shiver run down his spine, but he forced himself to remain calm. He needed answers, not speculation.

"Go on," he urged. "Tell me what you think."

Grayson glanced around again, then lowered his voice to a barely audible whisper. "The clockmaker, Inspector. The one who vanished twenty years ago. His disappearance was never solved. But there are those who believe—who know—that he didn't simply vanish. He was... taken."

"Taken?" Hart repeated, incredulous. "By whom?"

"By those who sought his secrets," Grayson whispered. "He was more than just a clockmaker. He was an artisan, a genius. He created mechanisms that defied reason, devices that could alter the perception of time itself. And those who coveted his work would stop at nothing to possess it."

Hart felt a cold knot form in his stomach. This was starting to sound like one of those wild, fanciful tales you'd hear in a tavern after too many drinks. And yet... something about the reverend's tone, his unwavering gaze, made it impossible to dismiss.

"And you think these murders are connected to that?" Hart asked slowly. "That someone is... what, trying to recreate his work?"

Grayson nodded, his expression grave. "Yes. And I believe the killer is using the victims as a means to an end. Each death, each carefully timed event, is part of a larger design—one that we have yet to fully comprehend."

Hart let out a breath, his mind racing. This was more than he'd bargained for when he'd agreed to meet Grayson tonight. But if what the reverend was saying held even a grain of truth...

"Do you have any idea who might be behind this?" he asked, his voice tense.

Grayson hesitated, then shook his head. "No. But I do know one thing: the clockmaker's legacy did not die with him. It was passed down—hidden, guarded, and now, it seems, it has resurfaced. The bell that tolls at midnight, Inspector... it's not just a warning. It's a signal."

"A signal for what?"

"For the final piece of the puzzle to fall into place," Grayson murmured, his gaze drifting back to the bell above. "And when it does, time itself may never be the same again."

Hart stared at the reverend, a sense of unease settling deep in his bones. He'd dealt with murderers, thieves, and charlatans before—but this was something else entirely. Something that defied logic and reason. And yet, standing here in the shadowy stillness of St. Agatha's, he couldn't shake the feeling that Grayson was right.

The clockmaker's secrets had been buried for decades. But now, it seemed, someone had dug them up—and if they weren't stopped, those secrets would bring about far more than just a string of murders. They would unravel the very fabric of time itself.

"Thank you, Father," Hart said quietly, folding the paper and tucking it into his coat pocket. "I'll look into this. But I suggest you be careful. If the killer knows you have this information—"

"I'm not afraid, Inspector," Grayson interrupted, a sad smile curving his lips. "What happens now is beyond fear. All we can do is watch, wait, and pray that we're not too late."

With that, he turned and walked slowly back down the aisle, his figure merging with the shadows. Hart stood alone for a moment, his mind racing with questions and doubts. Then he turned and left the church, his footsteps echoing through the silent nave.

As he stepped outside into the cool night air, the old bell above him began to toll softly—once, twice, three times. He glanced up, a chill running down his spine. Midnight was still hours away. Why was the bell ringing now?

He stared at it for a long moment, then shook his head and walked away, his thoughts already shifting to the investigation ahead. Whatever secrets the clockmaker had left behind, whatever mysteries were hidden in the ticking of those gears, he would uncover them. No matter how deep he had to dig, no matter how dark the path became.

For in the end, time was the only thing that could reveal the truth—and time was something he had learned never to take for granted.

4. A Shattered Alibi

THE SMALL DRAWING ROOM was filled with the lingering scent of Earl Grey and the faint flickering of the fireplace, casting long shadows on the cream-colored walls. Detective Hart sat poised on a high-backed armchair, his gaze steady as he watched the nervous man across from him. Mr. Charles Whitmore, a prominent banker in the town of Charing Cross, twisted his hands, his eyes darting around the room like a trapped animal.

"Mr. Whitmore, I assure you, there is no need to be anxious," Hart said calmly, his tone a stark contrast to the tense atmosphere. "We are merely trying to establish the sequence of events leading up to the evening of October 15th. Your cooperation is, of course, greatly appreciated."

Whitmore cleared his throat, nodding vigorously, yet his body betrayed his unease. "Yes, yes, of course. As I've already stated, I was at home that evening, with my wife. We were both in the study, reading. It was a quiet night."

"Indeed, you've mentioned that before," Hart murmured, leaning forward just slightly, enough to let Whitmore feel the intensity of his scrutiny. "But unfortunately, your wife's recollection of the evening doesn't align with yours. She claimed you left the house around seven, returning much later—closer to midnight, in fact."

For a moment, Whitmore's face went blank, as though his mind struggled to catch up with what he'd just heard. Then his lips twisted into a thin, strained smile. "My wife must be mistaken. Perhaps she was confused by the time. You know how it is—sometimes the hours slip by without notice."

"Yes, time can be a slippery thing," Hart agreed, though his voice carried a hint of something darker, sharper. "But it's difficult to mistake an entire evening's absence, wouldn't you agree?"

Whitmore's smile faltered, his gaze shifting uneasily to the mantelpiece where a small, ornate clock ticked softly. It was an old family heirloom, its brass hands gleaming in the firelight, each tick a reminder of the unyielding march of time.

"I didn't leave the house," he insisted, but now there was a tremor in his voice. "I was with my wife the whole time. You can ask anyone. She must be confused, or—" He paused, his face contorting slightly as though struggling to find the right words. "Perhaps she said that to get back at me. We've had... disagreements lately."

Hart didn't press further. Instead, he let the silence stretch between them, a silence so thick it seemed to vibrate with tension. He watched Whitmore squirm under the weight of his own words, his fingers now tapping an erratic rhythm on the armrest of his chair.

"Mr. Whitmore," Hart said softly, "why don't you tell me again what happened that night? Perhaps you can recall some additional details, something that might clear up this confusion."

Whitmore licked his lips, his gaze dropping to his lap. "I— I told you. We were in the study. I was reading 'The Times,' and—"

"And what was Mrs. Whitmore reading?" Hart interrupted, his voice so casual it was almost disarming.

"She—she was reading one of her novels. I don't remember which one. She has so many, you know—"

"But your wife told me she had a migraine that evening," Hart said softly, the words slipping out like a blade. "She said she couldn't read at all, not even with her glasses. Strange, isn't it, that you'd recall her reading a novel she never even opened?"

Whitmore's face went ashen, and he looked up sharply, his mouth opening and closing as though struggling to form a response. He seemed to crumple inward, like a puppet whose strings had been cut.

"Alright!" he burst out suddenly, his voice raw with desperation. "I did leave the house that evening. But it wasn't for long, I swear! I—I just needed some fresh air. We'd had an argument earlier in the day, and I needed to clear my head. I only walked around the block a few times, that's all."

Hart's eyes narrowed, though his face remained impassive. "You took a walk around the block? Alone?"

"Yes!" Whitmore almost shouted. "Just around the block. I was back within the hour. It's nothing! You can ask the neighbors—they must've seen me."

"Interesting," Hart murmured, his fingers drumming lightly on the armrest of his chair. "Because your neighbor, Mrs. Porter, mentioned that she saw you drive off in your car around seven-fifteen. She's quite certain of it, as she heard the distinctive squeal of your car's brakes as you left."

Whitmore's mouth dropped open, a low, strangled sound escaping his throat. He seemed to deflate further, his shoulders slumping as he buried his face in his hands. "It wasn't what it looked like," he whispered, his voice barely audible. "I had to leave, but not for what you think. I didn't hurt anyone."

"Then what were you doing, Mr. Whitmore?" Hart's voice was gentle, but relentless. "Where did you go?"

Whitmore looked up, his eyes wide, almost pleading. "I— I can't tell you. Please, you have to understand—if I tell you, it'll ruin everything."

"More than this already has?" Hart asked softly. "Your alibi is shattered, Mr. Whitmore. Your wife's testimony, your own inconsistent statements—none of it holds up. Whatever you're hiding, I can assure you it's only making things worse."

There was a long pause, the only sound in the room the steady ticking of the clock on the mantelpiece. Then, slowly, Whitmore let out a shuddering sigh.

"Alright," he whispered, his voice thick with defeat. "I'll tell you. But you must promise—you must promise not to involve her."

"Her?" Hart's eyebrows rose slightly, but his voice remained even. "Who is she, Mr. Whitmore?"

Whitmore looked away, his gaze distant, as though he were staring into some dark, unreachable place. "It was for my sister," he murmured. "My younger sister, Lydia. She... she was in trouble."

Hart leaned forward, the intensity in his eyes sharpening. "Your sister? What kind of trouble?"

Whitmore swallowed hard, his hands twisting together again. "She's been involved with some... unsavory characters. Owed them money. A lot of money. I only left that night to meet with them—to pay them off, to make sure they'd leave her alone. That's why I couldn't say anything. If it got out—if they knew I'd spoken to the police—it would only put her in more danger."

Hart considered this, his gaze never wavering from Whitmore's face. "And why didn't you mention this before? Surely you knew that hiding the truth would only make you look more suspicious."

"I couldn't risk it," Whitmore said, his voice breaking slightly. "I thought—if I said nothing, if I kept my head down, maybe it would all blow over. But now..." He let out a harsh, bitter laugh. "Now, I suppose it's too late for that."

"Indeed," Hart murmured, his gaze still piercing. "But you realize, of course, that this still doesn't explain everything. If you met these men to pay off your sister's debt, there would be records—phone calls, bank withdrawals, something concrete to back up your story. Yet so far, we've found nothing of the sort."

Whitmore's face went blank again, and for a moment, it seemed as though he'd retreated somewhere far away, beyond the reach of the detective's probing questions.

"They didn't want a bank transfer," he whispered finally. "They wanted cash. I had to withdraw it over several days, from different accounts. I didn't want to arouse suspicion."

Hart nodded slowly, as though weighing each word. "And you're prepared to give us the details of these accounts? The names of these men?"

Whitmore hesitated, then nodded, his face pale and drawn. "Yes. I'll give you everything I have. Just... promise me you'll protect Lydia. She's all I have left."

"We'll do everything we can," Hart said quietly, though there was no promise in his voice. "But first, Mr. Whitmore, we need to verify your story. Because if there's one thing I've learned, it's that time has a way of revealing the truth—whether we're ready for it or not."

As Whitmore sagged back into his chair, his gaze fixed on the ticking clock, Hart felt a familiar surge of determination. The pieces of the puzzle were falling into place, but there were still shadows lurking in the gaps—secrets yet to be uncovered.

And one way or another, he would bring them all to light.

5. Family Ties and Deceptions

THE QUAINT TOWN OF Ellerby, nestled amidst rolling hills and winding rivers, had always prided itself on the close-knit relationships of its inhabitants. Generations of families had lived here, their lives intertwined by history, duty, and tradition. Yet, as Detective Hart observed, it was often within such seemingly idyllic communities that the darkest secrets festered. Ellerby's peaceful facade had been shattered in recent weeks by a series of brutal murders, each more puzzling than the last. And now, as the case grew murkier, it seemed that the next clue lay buried deep within the complex web of family loyalties and betrayals that defined the town.

Detective Hart, a man with a keen eye for detail and an almost preternatural ability to sense deceit, found himself staring at the imposing facade of the Langford estate. The grand, stone manor house sat atop a small hill, surrounded by meticulously trimmed hedges and an air of quiet dignity that seemed to mock the chaos and bloodshed surrounding it. Hart knew that the Langford family had been part of Ellerby for as long as anyone could remember. They were wealthy, influential, and deeply private. But recent events had forced them into the spotlight, and Hart suspected that somewhere within these walls lay the answers he sought.

The Langfords had not been forthcoming in their initial interviews. Julian Langford, the patriarch, was a man of few words, his silences heavy with unspoken meaning. His wife, Margery, maintained a veneer of polite aloofness, while their two children, Richard and Amelia, had provided little more than polite pleasantries. Yet, Hart's instincts told him that this family knew more than they were willing to admit. He could almost taste the tension that simmered beneath the surface of their carefully composed exteriors.

As he made his way up the gravel path, he glanced at the windows of the manor, half-expecting to see a face peering out at him from behind the heavy velvet curtains. But the windows remained dark and empty, like the hollow eyes of a skull. Taking a deep breath, Hart rapped the brass knocker against the massive oak door.

It was Amelia who answered, her expression a mixture of surprise and something else—something fleeting, too quick to define. She was a striking young woman, with sharp features softened by delicate curves and a mane of chestnut hair that tumbled down her back. Her eyes, a piercing shade of green, seemed to flicker with a thousand unspoken thoughts as she stepped aside to let him in.

"Detective Hart," she murmured, her voice low and measured. "We weren't expecting you."

"An impromptu visit, Miss Langford," Hart replied with a slight incline of his head. "I was hoping I might have a word with your father."

Amelia hesitated, her gaze flickering toward the staircase that led up to the second floor. "He's... indisposed at the moment. Perhaps I can be of assistance?"

Hart allowed himself a small smile. "Perhaps. But I'd still like to speak with him, if you don't mind. It's about the latest developments in the case."

Amelia's lips tightened, and for a moment, Hart thought she might refuse. But then she nodded curtly and gestured for him to follow her into the drawing room. The room was an elegant space, filled with rich mahogany furniture and heavy draperies that muffled the sunlight, casting the room in a muted, almost sepulchral glow. A fire crackled in the hearth, the only sound breaking the oppressive silence.

"Please, have a seat," Amelia said, motioning to an armchair. "I'll let my father know you're here."

As she swept out of the room, her skirts whispering against the polished wood floors, Hart glanced around, taking in every detail. The room was filled with family portraits—stern-faced men and women staring down at him from their gilded frames, their expressions frozen in time. He noted the way their eyes seemed to follow him, an effect heightened by the flickering firelight.

Family ties, he thought, could be both a comfort and a curse. The Langfords were clearly bound by more than just blood. There was something almost oppressive about the way these long-dead ancestors loomed over the room, as if judging the actions of the living. He wondered what secrets the Langford family kept hidden beneath the weight of such legacy.

The door creaked open, and Julian Langford entered, his tall frame casting a long shadow across the room. He moved with the deliberate grace of a man accustomed to command, his gaze piercing and assessing. There was no hint of warmth in his demeanor, just a cold, detached curiosity.

"Detective," he said, his voice a low rumble that seemed to vibrate through the very air. "To what do we owe the pleasure?"

Hart stood, extending his hand, which Langford took after a brief pause. "Mr. Langford, thank you for seeing me. I won't take up too much of your time. I have a few questions that I believe might shed some light on recent events."

Langford's eyes narrowed slightly. "You mean the murders, I assume. A tragedy, truly. But I'm not sure how we could be of any help. Our family has no connection to these... gruesome acts."

"Perhaps not directly," Hart conceded, "but I've found that in cases like this, connections can be subtle. Sometimes they lie dormant for years, forgotten or overlooked. I'd like to ask about your relationship with some of the victims."

For the briefest moment, Hart thought he saw a flicker of unease cross Langford's face, but it was gone as quickly as it had appeared. "Our relationship?" he echoed. "We hardly knew them. Ellerby is a small town, Detective. Everyone knows everyone, at least by sight. But we weren't close to any of those poor souls."

"Yet you attended the same social gatherings," Hart pressed gently. "Fundraisers, charity events... even a dinner party at the mayor's house last year, where one of the victims was present."

Langford's gaze grew colder. "Are you suggesting that attending the same social function makes us suspects?"

"Not at all, sir. I'm merely trying to understand the dynamics at play here. Sometimes the smallest interaction can have unforeseen consequences."

"Or," Langford replied icily, "you're simply grasping at straws."

Hart didn't flinch at the hostility in Langford's tone. Instead, he leaned back slightly, adopting a more relaxed posture. "Forgive me if I seem intrusive, Mr. Langford. But I've found that families like yours—families with long-standing histories in a community—often have their own... entanglements."

"Entanglements?" Langford's voice was dangerously soft. "I don't appreciate the implication, Detective."

"No implication intended," Hart said smoothly. "But history has a way of shaping the present, whether we like it or not. I'm simply trying to piece together a story that seems to have started long before these murders took place."

For a moment, there was silence. Then, to Hart's surprise, Julian Langford let out a short, humorless laugh. "A story, you say? Yes, I suppose you could call it that. Our family has its share of... complications. But if you think you'll find any connection to these killings within our 'entanglements,' I'm afraid you'll be disappointed."

"Nevertheless, I'd like to ask a few more questions, if I may," Hart persisted. "Specifically about your late brother, Edward."

The change in Langford's demeanor was instantaneous. His expression hardened, and a muscle twitched in his jaw. "What about him?"

Hart met his gaze evenly. "I understand that Edward's death, years ago, was ruled an accident. But I've been reviewing some old records, and there are a few discrepancies that I'd like to clarify."

Langford's face was a mask of barely restrained fury. "Edward's death has nothing to do with what's happening now. I suggest you tread carefully, Detective. You're venturing into dangerous territory."

"Dangerous, perhaps," Hart murmured, "but necessary. I believe there's more to Edward's death than meets the eye. And I think it might be the key to understanding what's really going on here."

The silence that followed was thick with tension. Then, without another word, Langford turned on his heel and strode from the room, leaving Hart alone once more with the watchful eyes of the Langford ancestors.

"Family ties and deceptions," Hart muttered to himself. "Indeed."

6. A Trap is Set

THE DIM GLOW OF THE evening sun bathed the small village in hues of gold and crimson as Detective Inspector Miles Hart stood on the narrow cobblestone path, watching the shadows stretch long and thin across the ground. His gaze was steady, yet his mind churned with calculations. There was something about the way the quietness wrapped around the houses, the lingering scent of lavender from Mrs. Bellamy's garden mingling with the earthy dampness of the early evening, that set him on edge.

"A trap," he murmured to himself, eyes narrowing as he glanced over at the neat row of houses along the lane. "It's all leading to a trap."

The Inspector's footsteps echoed softly as he made his way toward the small cottage at the end of the lane—the home of the late Timothy Alcott, clockmaker and the first victim in this gruesome chain of events. The cottage was modest, unassuming, like many others in the village. But behind its quaint façade, secrets were waiting to be uncovered, secrets that were now poised to ensnare someone in their deadly grip.

He reached the front door and hesitated. The key, cold and metallic, pressed against his palm. It was Alcott's own key, retrieved from the watchmaker's pocket on the night he was found, his lifeless body slumped over the workbench, the gears of a half-finished clock still spinning in his bloodied hands. As he turned the key in the lock, a soft click echoed in the stillness, and the door creaked open, revealing the shadowy interior.

Stepping inside, Hart took in the scene: the faint musty smell of old wood and oil, the ticking of a single clock left on the wall, marking each second with a precise, almost menacing regularity.

He had been here many times before, combing through Alcott's belongings, searching for clues. But tonight was different. Tonight, he wasn't here to gather evidence.

He was here to set the stage.

He moved to the workbench, where various clock parts lay scattered—tiny gears, springs, and hands, all meticulously arranged as if awaiting the master's touch to breathe life into them. Hart picked up a small brass cog and turned it over in his hand, feeling its weight. Each piece was perfectly crafted, every edge smoothed and polished. The memory of Alcott's skilled hands working these very parts played in his mind like a haunting refrain.

"You were a genius," Hart whispered, placing the cog back down carefully. "And someone envied you for it."

He turned to the wall behind the workbench, where Alcott's prized collection of rare clocks hung, each one different in design, yet all synchronized to the same time. Midnight. It was eerie, unnatural, as if these timepieces were forever locked in that final, fateful moment of the man's life.

Drawing a deep breath, Hart reached into his coat pocket and pulled out a folded piece of paper. On it, a handwritten message in Alcott's elegant script: "The key to time is found in the past." He had found the note tucked inside a hollowed-out book in Alcott's study, concealed among a collection of forgotten texts. At first, it seemed like a riddle meant for no one in particular. But as the murders continued, Hart began to see the pattern.

Each victim—three so far—had been found with a clock stopped at a specific time. Alcott's clock stopped at twelve minutes past midnight. The second victim, Mary Cummings, a librarian with no apparent connection to Alcott, was found with her clock halted at two-forty-five in the morning. And the third, a banker named Harold Mitford, at seven-thirty in the evening. Each death was marked not by a sign of struggle, but by the silent cessation of time in the presence of a broken clock.

Hart unfolded the note and placed it on the workbench. "What were you trying to tell me, Alcott?" he muttered, his eyes tracing the delicate loops of the letters. "What happened in the past that set this all in motion?"

He moved slowly, deliberately, adjusting the clocks on the wall, one by one. He set each to a different time, careful to mimic the exact positions he'd observed during his previous investigations. Midnight for Alcott, two-forty-five for Cummings, seven-thirty for Mitford. Then he took out a fourth clock—an unassuming, small pocket watch he'd found in Alcott's private collection—and set it to eleven-fifty-five.

"Four victims. Four times. But who is the fourth?"

The answer was almost too obvious, yet impossible to comprehend fully. Every instinct warned him that he was dancing on a razor's edge, but there was no turning back now. He placed the pocket watch in the center of the workbench and glanced at the faint glimmer of a candle he'd lit on the corner table. The soft, flickering light cast eerie shadows across the room.

Hart stepped back, surveying his work. The clocks, the pocket watch, the note. All positioned to tell a story—a story only the killer would understand. He had no doubt that his adversary would come tonight. The clues had been planted in the way only he would notice. A subtle shift in the arrangement of the gears, the misalignment of a single hand on one of the clocks. Things no ordinary person would ever perceive, but to the murderer—someone so obsessed with time and precision—it would be like a beacon in the dark.

A creak on the floorboards behind him sent a chill racing down his spine. Hart's hand instinctively moved to his side, where his revolver rested under his coat. He turned slowly, scanning the shadows.

"Who's there?" he called out softly, voice steady but low.

Silence.

He waited, every muscle taut, every sense heightened. Then, just as he was about to step forward, he saw it—a faint glimmer of metal near the doorway. A figure moved, slipping silently into the room, keeping to the edges where the shadows clung thickest. Hart held his breath, watching as the intruder drew closer.

The man—or woman, it was impossible to tell in the darkness—stepped into the faint circle of candlelight, and Hart felt his pulse quicken. The figure was draped in a long coat, a hood pulled low over the face, obscuring any distinguishing features. But it was the hands that drew Hart's attention. The intruder wore gloves, and in one hand, they held a small, delicate clock.

The same clock Hart had seen on the second victim's bedside table.

"Looking for something?" Hart asked, his voice calm, almost casual. He stepped forward, slowly, deliberately, revealing his presence.

The figure froze, head turning sharply in his direction. A soft, almost inaudible click echoed through the room as the clock was set down on the edge of the workbench.

"I knew you'd come," Hart continued, eyes locked on the shadowed face beneath the hood. "You couldn't resist, could you? The clocks, the times—they all mean something to you."

The intruder's silence was unnerving, but Hart pressed on. "It's all connected, isn't it? Alcott, Cummings, Mitford... and me. You wanted me to see this, to understand the pattern."

Slowly, the figure reached up and lowered the hood. Hart's breath caught as the light revealed a familiar face—one he had never suspected, yet now seemed so painfully obvious.

"You?" he whispered, disbelief mingling with the dawning realization.

"Yes," came the soft reply, the voice almost melodic, laced with a quiet menace. "And now, Inspector, it's time for the final act."

Before Hart could react, the intruder reached for the pocket watch. A faint click echoed as the hidden mechanism inside it sprang to life. Hart lunged forward, but it was too late. The clock's face glowed softly, casting an eerie light over the room as gears began to whir and spin at a frantic pace.

"Stop!" he shouted, drawing his revolver, but the figure merely smiled—a cold, knowing smile.

"I'm afraid time's up, Inspector."

With a sudden, deafening roar, the room was plunged into chaos. The clocks on the wall began to chime, each one ringing out in a discordant, maddening cacophony. The sound reverberated through Hart's skull, disorienting him, making it impossible to think clearly.

Through the haze of noise, he saw the figure move, slipping past him with a speed and agility that belied the calm, deliberate demeanor from moments before. Hart stumbled, clutching at his ears as the ringing intensified, the sound merging into a single, relentless beat.

And then—silence.

Hart blinked, struggling to clear his vision. The intruder was gone. The clocks had stopped, their hands frozen in place. The pocket watch lay on the workbench, its face cracked, gears spilling out like blood from a wound.

The trap had been sprung.

But who had caught whom?

Hart stood there, chest heaving, eyes scanning the empty room. The pieces of the puzzle were still scattered, but one thing was certain: the game was far from over.

With trembling hands, he reached for the shattered watch and picked it up, turning it over carefully. There, etched into the metal backing, was a single word.

"Remember."

The Inspector's jaw tightened as he pocketed the broken timepiece. A trap had indeed been set, but the true target was yet to be revealed. He had a feeling that when it was, time itself would be the price to pay.

Chapter 5: Death on the Hour

1. An Elusive Suspect

The small English village of Briarwood, with its rolling hills and cobblestone streets, had always been a place of tranquility, where the rhythm of life was dictated by the steady toll of the church bell and the chime of the town square clock. But tonight, a sense of unease clung to the air like fog over the moors. The village had been disrupted by a series of murders that defied logic, and now the third body had been discovered — under circumstances more chilling and baffling than ever before.

The local constable, a stout, red-faced man named Alfred Bristow, stood outside the ivy-clad walls of the old manor house where the most recent crime had taken place. A circle of curious onlookers had gathered despite the late hour, their eyes wide with a mix of fear and fascination. Bristow lifted his hand, signaling them to step back. "There's nothing to see here, now," he barked, though his own gaze betrayed the anxiety that gripped him.

Inside, Detective Inspector Geoffrey Hart, a tall, sharp-featured man in his early fifties, crouched beside the lifeless form of Edgar Billingsworth, the village's wealthy and eccentric clockmaker. Billingsworth's body was slumped in his favorite armchair by the fireplace, his spectacles askew and a book lying open in his lap, as though he'd merely dozed off while reading. But a deep, crimson gash across his throat told a different story — one of violence and sudden death.

Hart's eyes narrowed as he examined the scene, every nerve in his body taut with concentration. The manner of the murder was brutally straightforward, yet there was something unnerving about it — something that whispered of a dark intelligence behind the act.

"Inspector, have a look at this," said Constable Jennings, a young, earnest officer who'd been shadowing Hart for the past few weeks. He handed Hart a small, intricately carved clock, no larger than a teacup. It was a stunning piece of craftsmanship, with delicate filigree along its sides and a tiny mechanism inside that seemed to whirr softly, even now, after its master's death.

Hart took the clock gingerly, his brow furrowing. "Where did you find it?"

"Just there, sir," Jennings pointed to a spot on the carpet by Billingsworth's feet. "It wasn't there earlier when we first entered the room. Someone must have placed it there after..."

"After he was killed," Hart finished grimly. He turned the clock over in his hands, noting the unusual markings on its underside. Numbers and letters, arranged in a pattern that seemed almost like a code. "Interesting," he murmured. "Very interesting indeed."

A faint click echoed in the silence, and Hart glanced up sharply. A shadow shifted by the door — not a person, but the flicker of something reflected in the polished surface of the grandfather clock that stood in the hallway. Hart rose swiftly and crossed to the doorway, but there was no one there. Only the empty corridor stretched out before him, the dim light of the sconces casting long, eerie shadows on the paneled walls.

"Sir?" Jennings asked, a note of concern in his voice. "What is it?"

"Someone was here," Hart muttered, more to himself than to the young constable. He stepped into the hall, his gaze sweeping over every nook and cranny. A strange sensation prickled at the back of his neck — a feeling he'd learned to trust over the years, one that told him he was being watched.

But there was no sound, no movement. Whoever it was — if there was indeed someone — they were gone now, leaving nothing behind but the oppressive silence and a lingering sense of malevolence.

Hart returned to the drawing room, his expression set in a mask of determination. He held up the tiny clock again, scrutinizing it under the lamplight. "Jennings, we need to find out everything we can about this piece. Where it came from, who made it, and why it's here."

"Yes, sir," Jennings replied, dutifully jotting down notes in his little book. "But, sir, do you think... Could it be the same person? The one who left the clocks at the other scenes?"

Hart nodded slowly. "Yes, I believe so. This clock is a signature, just like the others. But why this victim, and why now?" He cast a contemplative glance at the deceased Edgar Billingsworth. "What did you know, Mr. Billingsworth, that someone wanted to silence you for?"

· · · ·

THE FOLLOWING MORNING dawned cold and bleak, a thick mist hanging over Briarwood like a shroud. Hart stood outside the Black Swan Inn, his hands thrust deep into the pockets of his overcoat. The inn was a hub of village gossip, and he hoped to glean some insight into Billingsworth's life — and enemies — from the locals.

Inside, the air was warm and thick with the scent of spiced ale and fresh bread. A murmur of conversation filled the room as villagers gathered around wooden tables, their faces solemn. Hart made his way to the bar, where a plump, gray-haired woman was polishing glasses.

"Good morning, Mrs. Tisdale," Hart greeted her with a nod.

"Morning, Inspector," she replied, her sharp eyes appraising him. "I suppose you're here about poor Mr. Billingsworth."

"That's right. I was wondering if you might have heard anything unusual recently. Anything that might help us piece together what happened last night."

Mrs. Tisdale pursed her lips thoughtfully. "Well, Mr. Billingsworth was a quiet man, kept to himself mostly. But..." She leaned in closer, her voice dropping to a conspiratorial whisper. "He did have a visitor a few days ago. A stranger, someone none of us had seen before. Tall, dark-haired, and — oh, there was something unsettling about him, Inspector. Gave me the chills, he did."

Hart's interest piqued. "Did you catch his name?"

"No, he didn't stay long. Just a few hours, and then he left as suddenly as he'd arrived. But I did see him speaking with Mr. Billingsworth quite... animatedly. Seemed like they were having a bit of a row, if you ask me."

"Did they, now?" Hart mused, tapping his chin thoughtfully. "Did anyone else see this man?"

Mrs. Tisdale glanced around the room, then nodded towards a group of men huddled near the fireplace. "Ask old Tom Havers over there. He was out front when the fellow left. Might've seen which way he went."

Hart thanked her and made his way over to the elderly man, who looked up with a start as the Inspector approached.

"Mr. Havers, I understand you might have seen a visitor leaving Mr. Billingsworth's house a few days ago."

Tom Havers blinked owlishly, then nodded slowly. "Aye, I saw him. Strange one, he was. Walked with a limp, but quick as a cat, like he didn't want to be noticed."

"Did you see where he went?"

"Headed towards the woods, I think. But I lost sight of him once he got past the bend. Didn't think much of it at the time."

Hart thanked him and turned away, his mind racing. A stranger with a limp, visiting just days before the murder — it was a slender lead, but it was the first tangible clue he'd had.

He strode out of the inn, his thoughts already leaping ahead to the next step. He needed to follow up on this stranger, see if anyone else had seen or spoken to him. And there was the matter of the clock — that tiny, exquisitely crafted device that seemed to hold more questions than answers.

As he walked through the village square, the clock tower loomed above him, its hands frozen at precisely 8:15. A shiver ran down Hart's spine. Time, it seemed, was both an ally and an enemy in this case. It was ticking down to something — something that, if he didn't solve this puzzle soon, could mean more lives lost.

He quickened his pace, determination set in his jaw. He would catch this elusive suspect, even if it meant delving into the darkest corners of Briarwood's history — and his own.

2. A Meeting at Dusk

THE LAST RAYS OF THE setting sun bathed the small English village of Hawthorn Hollow in a warm, golden glow. It was that peculiar hour between day and night, when the world held its breath, caught between two realities. The gentle hum of insects filled the air, and the evening mist began to curl and creep across the fields like a ghostly shroud.

At the edge of the village, just beyond the line of old oaks that marked the boundary of the Foxglove Estate, a lone figure emerged from the shadows. Detective Alexander Hart was not unfamiliar with the peculiarities of this town. He had spent enough time here in his youth, during long summer holidays at his uncle's manor, to know that Hawthorn Hollow was a place where secrets lay buried deeper than the roots of its ancient trees.

Dressed in a tailored overcoat and hat, Hart moved with quiet purpose along the path that led to the estate. His stride was deliberate, his senses heightened. He was not in Hawthorn Hollow for a social visit. An invitation—cryptic and unmarked—had arrived at his London office three days prior, beckoning him to this forgotten corner of the countryside. The letter had contained only a few short words: "A matter of life and death. Come at dusk."

The invitation had been signed with a name Hart had not thought about in years: Beatrice Claymore. The Claymores were one of the oldest families in the region, their history woven into the very fabric of the village. Beatrice, the last of her line, was a reclusive woman known more for her eccentricities than for any real connection to the townsfolk. Yet, something in her letter had compelled Hart to take the next train out of London without hesitation.

As he neared the iron gates of the estate, Hart paused. The grand manor house, its stone façade covered in ivy and shadow, loomed in the distance like a silent sentinel. Once a symbol of prosperity and power, the house now seemed to sag under the weight of neglect and forgotten grandeur. Hart pushed open the creaking gate and stepped onto the gravel drive, the sound of his shoes crunching softly beneath him. He was met by silence, save for the faint rustle of wind through the trees and the distant call of an owl.

His fingers brushed the brim of his hat, adjusting it slightly as he surveyed his surroundings. There was no sign of movement, no welcoming light from within the house. He glanced at his pocket watch—the time was precisely seven o'clock. Beatrice's note had been clear: he was to arrive at dusk, and here he was, standing before the entrance as the sky bled from gold to deep indigo.

"Detective Hart?" a voice called out softly, startling him from his thoughts.

He turned sharply, his gaze falling upon a slender figure emerging from the side of the house. A young woman, no more than thirty, with delicate features and eyes that glinted with a mix of curiosity and fear. She wore a plain dress of muted green, her dark hair pinned back in a simple style that contrasted sharply with her pale complexion.

"Yes, I'm Detective Hart," he replied, his tone guarded. "You must be Miss Claymore?"

The woman shook her head, a fleeting smile touching her lips. "No, I'm afraid not. I am Mrs. Helen Grant, Lady Claymore's housekeeper." She gestured towards the manor. "Lady Claymore is expecting you in the drawing room. If you'll follow me, I'll take you to her."

Hart hesitated, his instincts alert. There was something disquieting about the woman's demeanor—something too measured, too calm. But he nodded, motioning for her to lead the way. As they walked, the crunch of gravel underfoot seemed unnaturally loud in the stillness of the evening.

"What's this all about, Mrs. Grant?" he asked casually. "Lady Claymore's letter was rather vague."

The housekeeper's gaze remained fixed ahead. "It's not my place to say, sir. But I believe Lady Claymore will explain everything. She's been... troubled of late." There was a pause, and then she added quietly, "There have been strange happenings here, Detective. Things that defy explanation."

"Strange happenings?" Hart echoed, raising an eyebrow.

Mrs. Grant merely nodded, her lips pressed into a thin line. They ascended the stone steps to the front door, and she pushed it open with a strength that belied her slight frame. The door groaned in protest as it swung inward, revealing the dimly lit interior of the manor.

The entry hall was a grand space, lined with portraits of Claymore ancestors whose painted eyes seemed to follow Hart as he stepped inside. The scent of aged wood and dust hung in the air, and the faint flicker of candlelight cast long shadows that danced across the floor.

"Lady Claymore is in the drawing room," Mrs. Grant murmured, motioning to a set of double doors to the left. "I shall take my leave now."

With that, she disappeared down a narrow corridor, her footsteps fading into silence. Hart watched her go, then turned his attention to the drawing room doors. Taking a deep breath, he pushed them open.

The room beyond was a study in contrasts. Plush, velvet drapes hung heavily over the windows, obscuring the last vestiges of daylight. A roaring fire crackled in the marble hearth, casting a warm, golden glow over the dark wood paneling and the array of antique furniture. At the far end of the room, seated in a high-backed armchair, was Beatrice Claymore.

She looked smaller, frailer, than he remembered. Her once vibrant hair was now a silvery gray, and deep lines etched her face. Yet her eyes—those piercing blue eyes—remained as sharp and discerning as ever.

"Alexander," she greeted softly, her voice carrying a hint of the strength it had once possessed. "It's been a long time."

Hart inclined his head. "Lady Claymore. Your letter was... unexpected. I came as soon as I could."

Beatrice nodded slowly, her gaze never leaving his. "Thank you. I wasn't sure you would. After all, it's been nearly a decade since you last set foot in Hawthorn Hollow."

He moved further into the room, taking a seat opposite her. "You said it was a matter of life and death. What's happened?"

For a moment, she was silent, her eyes drifting to the flickering flames. When she spoke again, her voice was barely above a whisper. "People are dying, Alexander. And I fear it's only the beginning."

Hart's brow furrowed. "Dying? How? What makes you think—"

"They're being murdered," she interrupted, her tone edged with a quiet intensity. "Each death marked by an eerie precision... as if someone is orchestrating it all, down to the very second."

"Murdered?" he repeated, incredulous. "And what do you mean by 'marked by precision'?"

She reached into the folds of her shawl and produced a small object, placing it carefully on the table between them. It was an old pocket watch, its glass face cracked and its hands frozen at exactly twelve o'clock.

"This," she murmured, "was found at the scene of the last murder. Every clock and watch in the victim's home was set to the same time. Midnight. The hour of death."

Hart stared at the watch, a chill creeping down his spine. He had seen many strange cases in his career, but there was something disturbingly methodical about what she was describing.

"Who are the victims?" he asked slowly. "And why haven't I heard of this before now?"

Beatrice's expression tightened. "The first victim was found three weeks ago. An elderly man—Mr. Randall, a retired schoolteacher. Then a young woman, a seamstress, was discovered dead in her cottage just last week. Both were long-time residents of Hawthorn Hollow... and both had ties to my family."

"Your family?" Hart leaned forward, his interest piqued. "How?"

She hesitated, her fingers tightening around the armrest of her chair. "They were... involved, in different ways, in an incident that occurred many years ago. An incident that was thought to be long forgotten. But someone—someone who knows—is dredging it all up again. And I'm afraid more will die before it's over."

Hart's mind raced as he processed her words. A series of murders, each marked by the frozen hands of a clock, all linked to an old, buried secret. It was the kind of puzzle he couldn't resist.

"Why come to me, Beatrice?" he asked quietly. "Surely the local authorities—"

"The police are useless!" she snapped, then immediately softened, her gaze pleading. "You know them, Alexander. They'll write this off as coincidence, or worse, as the ramblings of an old woman. But I know—whoever is doing this is just getting started. And I'm running out of time."

The irony of her words hung heavy in the air. Time. The very thing that seemed to be at the heart of this macabre game.

Hart nodded slowly. "Alright, Beatrice. I'll help you. But I need more information. Everything you know, every detail, no matter how small."

Relief washed over her features, and she sagged back into her chair. "Thank you, Alexander. Thank you. There's so much to tell, and so little time..."

She paused, glancing at the pocket watch on the table. Its broken hands glinted dully in the firelight, a silent testament to lives cut short and secrets waiting to be unearthed.

"Tell me everything," Hart urged gently, leaning closer. "Start from
the beginning."

And as the darkness gathered outside the manor's windows and the night deepened, Beatrice Claymore began her tale—a story of betrayal, revenge, and a clockwork killer who moved through the shadows, leaving only death in his wake.

3. The Clock Tower Revelation

THE SKY ABOVE THE SMALL English town of Windermere was overcast, casting long, murky shadows over the cobblestone streets. It was one of those evenings when the air felt thick with expectation, and the silence itself seemed pregnant with secrets waiting to be unveiled. Detective Inspector Edmund Hart stood at the foot of the town's ancient clock tower, its stone edifice towering ominously above him. He adjusted his hat, glancing up at the darkened face of the clock, its hands frozen at an impossible time: 11:47. The precise moment, he had been told, when the third victim had taken their last breath.

The clock tower, built centuries ago, was the pride and symbol of Windermere. Its chimes had marked countless beginnings and endings, marriages and funerals, triumphs and tragedies. But now, it had become a sinister marker, a twisted sentinel over a series of grisly murders that had shaken the town to its core. Each of the three victims had been found with a small, intricately crafted clock on their person, stopped at the exact time of death. And now, the great clock itself had ceased its eternal ticking, as though in morbid tribute to the crimes.

The inspector took a deep breath, feeling the weight of the town's gaze upon him. The people of Windermere were afraid. Whispers of a madman on the loose filled every home and public house, yet no one dared to venture too close to the truth. And why would they? When the truth, as Hart suspected, lay nestled among their own. It was someone they knew. Someone they trusted. And the revelation would tear this community apart.

"Inspector Hart!" a voice called from behind him, echoing in the empty square. He turned to see his young assistant, Constable Leonard Price, hurrying towards him. The boy was earnest and sharp, with a quick mind and a knack for connecting dots that others might miss. Price's usually ruddy face was flushed, his expression one of urgency. "Sir, you need to see this."

Hart nodded curtly and followed Price as they entered the base of the clock tower. The heavy oak door groaned in protest as it swung open, revealing a narrow, spiraling staircase that wound its way up the interior. The inspector's footsteps echoed against the cold, stone walls as he ascended, each step taking him further away from the safety of the familiar and closer to the enigma that awaited him.

They reached the landing just below the clock's mechanism, where a small wooden door stood ajar. Price pushed it open gently, and Hart stepped inside. The room was cramped, filled with dust and the acrid smell of oil and metal. The gears of the clock, usually in a state of perpetual motion, were eerily still. But it wasn't the silent machinery that caught Hart's attention. It was the body.

The man, dressed in a dark overcoat and wearing the unmistakable insignia of the Windermere Historical Society, lay crumpled in the corner. His eyes, wide open and glassy, stared blankly at the ceiling. In his hand, clenched tightly, was a small pocket watch — its face cracked, the hands pointing to 11:47.

"His name is Jonathan Willoughby," Price whispered, though there was no need to keep his voice down. "He's... he was the curator of the town's history museum. His wife reported him missing two days ago."

Hart nodded slowly, his keen eyes scanning the scene. Willoughby had been one of the town's most respected figures, a man dedicated to preserving Windermere's rich and complex past. He had no enemies that anyone knew of — no debts, no disputes. Yet here he was, the fourth victim in a series of murders that defied logic.

"What do we know about his connection to the other victims?" Hart asked, his voice steady despite the grim discovery.

Price shifted uncomfortably. "Nothing concrete yet, sir. But there's something... odd. Each of the victims was found with a different type of clock — an old pocket watch, a mantelpiece clock, a modern wristwatch, and now this..." He gestured to the pocket watch in Willoughby's hand. "It's as if the killer is leaving us a message, but the meaning remains elusive."

Hart stepped closer to the body, his gaze lingering on the watch. A message, indeed. But what was the message? Time was a recurring theme in all the murders, yet it was more than just the instruments of timekeeping. It was something deeper, something tied to the town itself.

"Have you looked at the gears?" he asked suddenly.

Price frowned. "The gears, sir?"

Hart nodded, stepping over to the great mechanism that powered the clock. He ran his fingers lightly over the brass cogs and wheels, his mind racing. "The clock stopped at 11:47, just like the others. But why that time? Why always so precise?"

"Do you think it's significant, sir?" Price ventured.

"Everything in this case is significant," Hart replied curtly. "But what we're missing is the key to understanding the significance. Why clocks? Why time? What does it all mean?"

He turned away from the mechanism, his eyes narrowing as a thought struck him. "Price, get me everything we have on Willoughby's last days — who he met, where he went, what he was working on. And I want the same for the other victims. There's a connection here, something we've overlooked."

Price nodded, already scribbling notes in his notebook. "Right away, sir. But... what are you thinking?"

Hart's gaze drifted back to the frozen clock face, visible through a narrow window. "I'm thinking that the answer lies in the past. Windermere is an old town with a long memory. And someone is using that memory to exact vengeance."

They worked late into the night, poring over every detail of the victims' lives. There were no obvious connections — no shared acquaintances, no mutual events. Yet, as dawn broke and the first light of day filtered through the narrow window, Hart's eyes lit up with sudden understanding.

"Of course," he murmured, almost to himself. "It's not about the victims themselves. It's about where they were at the time of death."

Price looked up, puzzled. "Sir?"

"Each of the victims was found at a location linked to the town's history," Hart explained, the pieces falling into place. "The first was at the old railway station — a place that closed down after a tragic accident decades ago. The second at the abandoned mill, where the owner was rumored to have been murdered by his workers. The third, in the town square, where a man was hanged for a crime he didn't commit. And now here, at the clock tower, which was once the site of a bitter rivalry between two of the town's founding families."

Price's eyes widened. "So, the killer is choosing locations based on—"

"Old grievances," Hart finished grimly. "But it's not just the places. It's the times, too. Each of those events occurred at the exact time the victims died. The killer is recreating these moments in history, using modern victims to pay for the sins of the past."

"But why? What could drive someone to such madness?"

Hart shook his head. "That's what we need to find out. And we need to do it quickly, before they strike again."

He turned to the window, staring out at the town below. Somewhere out there, someone was playing a deadly game — a game that had been in motion for far longer than anyone realized. The clock tower's revelation had opened Hart's eyes to the truth, but it was only the beginning.

"Time," he whispered. "Time is the key. But whose time is running out?"

With renewed determination, he turned to Price. "We need to dig deeper. Find out everything you can about the town's history, especially events tied to those locations. I want names, dates, everything. We're looking for someone who believes they've been wronged — someone who sees this as their chance to set things right."

Price nodded, his expression serious. "And what about the clock, sir? What does it mean?"

Hart's eyes darkened. "The clock is their signature, their mark. Every gear, every cog is a reminder that time doesn't forget. And neither does the killer."

As Price hurried out of the room, Hart glanced one last time at Willoughby's lifeless form. The clock in his hand gleamed dully in the faint light, its broken face a testament to the fragility of life.

"The clock tower's revelation," Hart murmured, "is only the beginning. Now we must find out whose hand is truly turning the gears."

4. A Twisted Scheme

THE AIR INSIDE THE parlor of Foxglove Manor was thick with the smell of tobacco and damp wool, the kind of odor that only seemed to manifest when too many bodies occupied too small a space for too long a time. The hum of conversation was low, almost conspiratorial, as if the occupants feared that even the very walls might eavesdrop on their words.

Inspector Hart stood by the bay window, his gaze sweeping across the gathered faces. It was a curious assembly, one that ranged from the illustrious to the utterly mundane—ladies in fashionable silks, a retired colonel whose chest boasted a collection of medals, and a scattering of local villagers whose expressions varied from curious to suspicious. Hart's lips twisted in a semblance of a smile as he noted each reaction, each twitch of the eye or furtive glance that darted around the room.

It was a gathering that should never have taken place. But then again, none of what had occurred over the past fortnight should have happened at all.

"The timepiece, Inspector," came the voice of Lord Farnsworth, a portly man in his late sixties, his jowls quivering slightly as he spoke. "You said it was found beside the body?"

"Indeed." Hart reached into his coat pocket, withdrawing a small, intricately designed pocket watch. It gleamed dully under the gaslights, the delicate filigree pattern around its edge still visible despite the tarnish of age. But it wasn't the watch's design that held the room's attention; it was the fact that the hands of the watch had been stopped at precisely ten minutes past eleven—just as they had been on each of the other four timepieces found at the scenes of previous murders.

A murmur rippled through the room, hushed and uneasy. Lord Farnsworth took a half-step back, his gaze transfixed by the watch as if it were a venomous snake poised to strike.

"Does it—does it mean...?" he began, but the words faltered on his lips.

"It means," Hart said quietly, his tone measured, "that the killer is playing with us. Deliberately. Carefully. And with a precision that suggests they are well aware of every move we make."

The inspector's gaze flickered over to the figure seated in the shadowed corner—a slender woman, her face partially obscured by the veil of her hat. Miss Evelyn Thorne, the clockmaker's niece, and the only living relative of the latest victim, Mr. Harold Thorne.

"What I don't understand," piped up Mrs. Gilchrist, a stout woman with a predilection for loud patterns and louder opinions, "is why the murderer would leave something so obvious as a pocket watch at the scene! Surely, it's a dead giveaway."

"That, Mrs. Gilchrist, is precisely why they left it." Hart's voice was soft, almost contemplative. "Each watch is not merely a clue—it's a message. A puzzle. And like any good puzzle, it hides its true meaning beneath the surface."

He paused, allowing the tension to build, then glanced at Miss Thorne. She looked up, meeting his gaze squarely, her expression unreadable.

"Miss Thorne," he said, "your uncle was a master clockmaker. He knew more about the mechanisms of timepieces than anyone in the county, perhaps even in the country. Yet this watch..." He held it up, letting it catch the light. "This watch is like nothing I've ever seen before. The balance wheel is... unique. It doesn't follow the conventional designs. In fact, it almost looks as if it was meant to serve a dual purpose. Do you know what that purpose might be?"

For a heartbeat, silence reigned in the room. Then Miss Thorne rose to her feet, her movements graceful and deliberate.

"I do not, Inspector," she said, her voice steady but with a hint of something—was it defiance? Or perhaps fear? "My uncle and I... we were not close. He kept his work private. Even from me."

Hart narrowed his eyes, studying her face for any sign of deception. But Miss Thorne's expression remained perfectly composed. Too composed, perhaps.

"Then why," he asked softly, "did your uncle leave you this?" He withdrew a small brass key from his pocket, holding it between thumb and forefinger.

There was a collective intake of breath from the room's occupants. The key was small, unassuming, but its purpose was unmistakable. It was a winding key—one that could only fit a very specific kind of clock.

Miss Thorne's eyes widened, just fractionally, and in that tiny flicker of emotion, Hart saw what he had been looking for.

"I don't know," she murmured, her voice barely audible. "I've never seen it before."

A blatant lie, Hart thought. But he didn't call her out on it. Not yet. There was more to be gained by letting her think she was still in control of the narrative.

"The key," Hart continued, his tone light and conversational, "fits perfectly into the mechanism of this watch. But it doesn't wind the mainspring. Instead, it triggers a secondary movement. One that, as far as I can tell, serves no practical function."

"Then why have it at all?" the colonel growled, his brow furrowed in consternation. "Seems a right waste of effort, if you ask me."

"Unless," Hart said, his gaze never leaving Miss Thorne, "the secondary movement is not meant for timekeeping at all. What if it's a signal? A marker? A—"

"A scheme," Miss Thorne interrupted, her voice cutting through the air like a blade. "A twisted scheme designed to lead you on a merry chase, Inspector. And you're falling for it."

A stunned silence followed her outburst. Hart's lips curved into a small, almost imperceptible smile.

"Perhaps," he conceded. "Or perhaps I'm simply playing along until the game reveals its true nature."

Miss Thorne's fingers clenched around the edge of her gloves, the knuckles whitening. Hart saw the telltale signs of tension, of suppressed anger—or was it fear?

He decided to press further.

"Tell me, Miss Thorne," he said casually, "do you believe in fate?"

"Fate?" She blinked, clearly taken aback by the sudden shift in topic. "What does that have to do with anything?"

"Everything," Hart murmured. "Because this isn't just a series of random murders, Miss Thorne. Each victim was chosen carefully, deliberately. As if... as if they were pieces on a chessboard, and someone is moving them into place."

The room seemed to draw in on itself, the walls closing in as the weight of his words settled over the assembled company.

"And what," Miss Thorne asked, her voice tight, "is the endgame, Inspector? If all of this is part of some grand scheme, what is the final move?"

Hart's smile widened, but there was no humor in it. Only a cold, calculating resolve.

"That, Miss Thorne, is what I intend to find out. But I suspect... that you already know."

Before she could respond, the door to the parlor swung open, and a young constable stepped in, his face flushed with excitement.

"Inspector, sir! There's been another—"

"Another murder?" Hart interrupted, his voice sharp.

The constable nodded, breathless. "Yes, sir. And they found another watch. Stopped at the exact same time as the others."

A collective gasp rippled through the room. Miss Thorne's face paled, and for a brief, fleeting moment, Hart saw something in her eyes—recognition, perhaps? Or guilt?

"Where?" Hart demanded.

"By the old clock tower, sir. And... and there's something else. The body—it's... it's not alone."

Hart's brow furrowed. "What do you mean?"

"There's a message, sir. Written on the clock face. It says... 'Tick tock, Inspector. Time's running out.'"

The words hung in the air like a death knell, and Hart felt a chill creep down his spine.

Whoever the killer was, they were taunting him. Mocking him. And now, more than ever, he knew that this was no ordinary murderer.

This was someone who understood time—its intricacies, its secrets, its dangers.

Someone who, perhaps, was more like Harold Thorne than anyone realized.

And unless Hart could unravel this twisted scheme, it would only be a matter of time before the next victim was claimed.

5. The Unfinished Timepiece

THE NIGHT WAS COLD and crisp as Detective Hart made his way through the winding streets of Briarwood. The mist hung low, clinging to the cobblestones and blurring the outlines of the narrow alleys. Even the gas lamps, with their weak flickering light, seemed powerless against the encroaching darkness. It was a night where shadows whispered and secrets stayed buried, a night when time itself seemed to stretch and warp.

Hart's thoughts were fixed on the matter at hand—the third murder in as many weeks. Each victim was found with a pocket watch placed beside them, its hands meticulously stopped at the exact time of death. The press had already dubbed it "The Clockwork Murders." What intrigued him most, though, was that the killer didn't just stop time—he played with it. Each clock carried subtle differences, adjustments that Hart couldn't yet comprehend. Was it a taunt, a message, or something far more sinister?

The last body—Emily Dawson—had been discovered in her own parlor, a once-respectable woman whose life had unraveled with the disappearance of her husband nearly twenty years ago. When he vanished without a trace, her fortune and reputation followed him into oblivion. Now, she had met a similarly enigmatic end, her face frozen in an expression of surprise, as though she'd recognized her killer.

But tonight, Hart wasn't thinking about Emily Dawson. His focus was the old clockmaker's shop nestled at the end of Willow Lane. It was a place few remembered and even fewer dared to visit. The proprietor, a Mr. Thaddeus Crowley, had once been renowned for his exquisite timepieces. But tragedy and loss had transformed him into a reclusive figure, a shadow of his former self. Rumors swirled about Crowley's involvement with dark arts and forbidden sciences, though Hart dismissed such nonsense as the product of small-town superstition. Still, there was something undeniably unsettling about the man's clocks—each a marvel of craftsmanship, yet imbued with a strange, almost malevolent energy.

When Hart reached the shop, he paused, glancing up at the creaking sign overhead. Crowley & Co: Timekeepers Since 1827. The letters were faded, as if time itself had tried to erase the name. A single light burned within, casting eerie shadows against the frosted glass windows. He took a deep breath and pushed the door open.

The bell above tinkled softly, and the smell of oil and aged wood filled his nostrils. The interior was a chaotic symphony of gears, springs, and unfinished mechanisms. Clocks of all shapes and sizes adorned the walls, each one frozen in time, its hands paused in eternal stillness.

"Detective Hart," came a dry voice from the corner. Thaddeus Crowley emerged from the shadows, his figure tall and gaunt, like a withered tree. His face was lined with age, eyes sunken but sharp, gleaming with an intelligence that seemed to pierce through the fog of years. "I've been expecting you."

Hart felt a chill run down his spine but kept his composure. "Mr. Crowley, I was hoping we could talk."

"Talk, yes. But about what, exactly?" Crowley's lips curled into a semblance of a smile. "The recent... disturbances, I assume?"

"Three murders. All connected by a single detail—the watches. Each one unique, yet linked by a common hand," Hart said, watching the old man carefully. "I understand you were an expert in horology. Perhaps you could shed some light on the matter."

Crowley's gaze drifted to the clocks on the wall. "Time is a peculiar thing, Detective. It binds us, shapes us, yet we so often take it for granted. We think of it as linear, predictable, but it can be manipulated, distorted..."

Hart's patience was wearing thin. "Mr. Crowley, I need answers, not riddles. Do you recognize the craftsmanship of these watches? Were they made by you?"

The old man's fingers twitched as he reached inside his coat, pulling out a small, delicate timepiece. Its casing was ornately engraved, the face devoid of numbers, and its hands spun freely, unbound by the constraints of hours or minutes. "This, Detective, is my unfinished timepiece. A work of art I never completed. It was meant to defy the limitations of conventional clocks, to transcend mere function and become something... more."

Hart leaned in, intrigued despite himself. "And what does this have to do with the murders?"

Crowley's eyes darkened. "Everything. The watches you found were crafted by me, years ago. But they were... flawed. Each one imbued with a piece of time's essence, yet each ultimately corrupted by human interference. They began to develop... a will of their own."

The detective stared at him, disbelief mingling with a creeping sense of dread. "You're saying the watches are cursed? Controlled by some malevolent force?"

"Not cursed, Detective. Corrupted. Each of them resonates with the soul of the person who held it. The more time they spent with the watch, the more it consumed them, twisted their fate. The victims—these poor souls—were merely the end of a chain that began long ago. And now, someone is using them to exact vengeance."

Hart's mind raced. This was madness, and yet, it fit. The victims—all connected in some obscure way to events long buried. A crime from decades past, a secret that someone had tried to erase. "Who, Crowley? Who is doing this?"

Crowley's hand shook as he placed the timepiece back into his pocket. "There is one watch still missing. The most dangerous of them all. If it's found—"

The shop's front door swung open with a bang, and Hart spun around, his hand instinctively reaching for his revolver. A young woman stood in the doorway, her face pale, eyes wide with terror.

"Detective Hart!" she gasped. "You must come quickly. There's been another murder... and it's Miss Davenport. She—she had a clock in her hand, just like the others."

Hart's pulse quickened. Miss Davenport—the town's librarian and one of the few people who still spoke of Crowley with any measure of respect. What possible connection could she have?

He turned back to Crowley, but the old man's expression was unreadable. "Where is this going to end, Crowley?" Hart demanded. "How do we stop it?"

"Time, Detective," Crowley murmured. "Time is both the question and the answer. It's a circle, always looping back on itself. To end it, you must break the circle... but doing so may unravel everything."

Hart nodded grimly. He didn't have the luxury of pondering metaphysics. He had a killer to catch, and if Crowley's words held any truth, he was running out of time.

"Stay here," he ordered. "I'll be back. And when I return, you'd better have more than cryptic musings for me."

With that, he turned and hurried out into the night, the sound of Crowley's voice—a faint whisper, barely audible—echoing behind him.

"Be careful, Detective. You're dealing with forces you cannot comprehend. Time, once broken, can never be repaired..."

Hart pushed the words from his mind as he followed the young woman through the misty streets. There was no time for hesitation, no time for doubt. He had to act, before another innocent life was claimed by the twisted mechanism of revenge that ticked unseen in the heart of Briarwood.

6. Murder in the Park

THE PARK, WITH ITS sprawling lawns and carefully maintained flowerbeds, usually hummed with life and laughter. But tonight, it was different. A blanket of fog hung low over the ground, shrouding the trees and pathways in an eerie mist. The lamps along the park's winding paths flickered uncertainly, casting ghostly shadows that danced among the bushes. Everything seemed to be holding its breath in anticipation, as if the very air sensed that something terrible was about to happen.

It was nearly midnight, and the park was deserted—at least, it should have been. Yet, near the old stone fountain in the heart of the park, a figure moved stealthily, barely visible through the thickening fog. The figure was dressed in a dark overcoat and a hat pulled low over its face, blending almost seamlessly with the surrounding gloom. The person paused for a moment, glancing around to ensure no one was watching, before stepping closer to the fountain.

The fountain itself was a relic from a bygone era, its once-pristine stonework now marred by time and neglect. Moss clung to the cracks, and the water that once bubbled cheerfully was now stagnant and dark. At this hour, the fountain looked more like a tombstone than a symbol of joy. The figure reached into its pocket and pulled out a small, intricately carved box. With a quick glance around, the box was placed at the base of the fountain.

There was a faint click, barely audible over the murmur of the wind, and then the figure straightened. The fog seemed to thicken as the person moved away from the fountain, melting back into the shadows. All that remained was the box, gleaming faintly in the dim light, and an unnatural silence that enveloped the park.

Ten minutes later, the silence was shattered by a scream—a scream so high-pitched and filled with terror that it echoed off the trees, sending flocks of startled birds flapping into the air. A young woman came stumbling out of the mist, her face pale and her eyes wide with horror. She nearly tripped over a low hedge but caught herself just in time, turning back to look at something behind her, something she had seen that made her blood run cold.

"Help! Somebody, please help!" she cried, her voice breaking with desperation.

But the park was empty. There was no one to hear her cries, no one to come to her aid. Trembling, she turned and ran, her footsteps pounding against the gravel path as she fled the scene. Somewhere in the distance, a church bell tolled the hour—midnight.

The next morning, the park was abuzz with activity, but not the usual kind. Uniformed policemen were scattered across the area, cordoning off sections of the park with yellow tape and speaking in hushed tones. A crowd of onlookers had gathered, whispering among themselves and craning their necks to catch a glimpse of the commotion. The focal point of their attention was the fountain, now surrounded by officers and a few men in plain clothes.

One of the plainclothes men, tall and broad-shouldered, with a stern expression and a neatly trimmed mustache, was bent over something lying at the base of the fountain. Inspector Jonathan

Hartley rose slowly, removing his hat and running a hand through his greying hair as he studied the scene. He had seen many terrible things in his long career, but this was something different. Something unsettling.

The body of a man lay crumpled at the base of the fountain, his limbs splayed out awkwardly as if he had been thrown down with great force. His eyes were open, staring sightlessly at the sky, and his mouth was twisted in a grimace of pain. But it was not the expression on the man's face that caught the inspector's attention—it was the small, ornate clock placed delicately on the man's chest.

The clock was unlike anything Hartley had ever seen. It was made of polished brass and silver, with delicate hands that were frozen in place, pointing to the exact time of death—midnight. There was something almost sinister about the precision of it, as if the killer had taken great care to create this macabre scene.

"What do we have here, Inspector?" A voice broke through Hartley's thoughts. He turned to see his colleague, Sergeant Miller, approaching with a notebook in hand.

"Another one," Hartley replied grimly, gesturing to the clock. "Just like the others."

Miller's eyes widened. "You think it's the same person?"

"I'm certain of it," Hartley said. He crouched down beside the body again, carefully avoiding disturbing the evidence. "The same type of clock, the same time set—midnight. This is no coincidence, Miller. Our killer is sending us a message."

"But what does it mean?" Miller asked, his brow furrowed in confusion. "Why clocks? And why here, in the middle of the park?"

"That's what we need to find out," Hartley said, his voice low. He glanced around at the trees and bushes, as if expecting the answer to reveal itself from the shadows. "Something about this place must be significant to the killer. There's a pattern here—we just haven't seen it yet."

He straightened and looked back at the crowd of onlookers, his gaze scanning each face carefully. Was the killer among them, watching their reaction? Hartley had seen it happen before—murderers who couldn't resist coming back to the scene of the crime to revel in their work. But none of the faces in the crowd seemed out of place. Just the usual mix of curiosity and morbid fascination.

"Get statements from everyone here," Hartley instructed Miller. "And check if there were any witnesses who might have seen something last night. Somebody must have seen or heard something unusual."

Miller nodded and turned away, barking orders to the constables nearby. Hartley remained by the fountain, his eyes once again drawn to the clock. There was something almost beautiful about it, in a grotesque sort of way. The craftsmanship was exquisite—the sort of work that only a master clockmaker could produce.

But this was no ordinary clock. It was a symbol. A calling card.

"Why clocks?" he murmured to himself, his mind racing. "Why so precise, so exact?"

He felt a surge of frustration. It was as if the answer was just out of reach, taunting him. He had spent weeks chasing this killer, piecing together the clues left behind at each crime scene. Every victim had been found with a clock set to midnight—each clock unique, meticulously crafted, and left deliberately on the victim's body.

But why?

Hartley closed his eyes, taking a deep breath. He needed to think, to clear his mind and focus on the details. There had to be a reason for this madness, a pattern that would lead him to the killer. But what was it?

The sound of footsteps approaching interrupted his thoughts. He opened his eyes to see a young woman standing a few feet away, her face pale and drawn. She was clutching a handkerchief in one hand, and there was a haunted look in her eyes.

"Inspector Hartley?" she asked hesitantly, her voice barely above a whisper.

"Yes, that's me," he replied, his gaze sharpening. "And you are?"

"My name is Emily Warren," she said, her voice trembling slightly. "I...I think I saw something last night. Something that might help you."

Hartley's heart quickened. Finally, a witness. He gestured for her to step closer.

"Please, Miss Warren, tell me everything you remember," he said gently.

Emily swallowed hard, her eyes darting nervously to the body before she looked away, as if she couldn't bear the sight.

"I was walking through the park last night," she began, her voice unsteady. "I had just finished visiting a friend and was taking a shortcut home. I didn't think anyone would be out at that hour, but then I heard...a noise."

Hartley leaned in, his attention fully on her.

"What sort of noise?"

"A...a clicking sound," Emily whispered. "Like a clock ticking, but louder, more distinct. It was coming from near the fountain. And then, I saw someone—a man. He was standing over there, by the fountain."

"Can you describe him?" Hartley asked, his voice urgent.

Emily shook her head, her brow furrowing in concentration.

"I couldn't see his face. It was too dark, and the fog... But he was tall, wearing a long coat and a hat pulled low. He seemed to be holding something in his hand—something small and metallic. I didn't get a good look because I—I panicked and ran."

Hartley nodded slowly, his mind racing. A man, tall, with a coat and a hat. It wasn't much to go on, but it was more than they had before.

"You did the right thing coming here, Miss Warren," he said softly. "You've been very brave. Now, I need you to stay with us for a while, just in case you remember anything else."

Emily nodded, a shiver running through her as she glanced once more at the body.

Chapter 6: The Mechanism of Fear

1. The Clocks Reset

The morning mist hung heavy over the quiet English town of Wickford, shrouding its cobbled streets and ivy-covered cottages in an almost ethereal haze. It was the kind of morning where time seemed to move at a slower pace, where the ticking of clocks and the chiming of church bells felt muted, as if the entire town were holding its breath.

Detective Inspector Samuel Hart leaned back in his leather armchair, his gaze fixed on the peculiar contraption laid out before him. It was a clock—no, not just a clock. It was a masterpiece of horology, a tangle of gears, springs, and tiny levers, meticulously crafted to the point of near perfection. Yet, despite its intricate design, the clock refused to keep time. Every time the minute hand approached the hour, it would jerk violently and reset itself to twelve o'clock.

He frowned, tapping his fingers thoughtfully against the armrest. This wasn't just any malfunctioning timepiece; it was evidence. And like everything else in this twisted case, it held a secret, if only he could decode it.

Across the room, Sergeant Emily Thatcher watched him with a mix of curiosity and concern. She had worked with Hart for nearly five years now and had never seen him so engrossed in an object. His usually sharp blue eyes were clouded with something she couldn't quite place—obsession, perhaps? No, it was more than that. It was as if the detective saw something in those brass gears and polished dials that eluded everyone else.

"Inspector, it's just a clock," she ventured softly, trying to break through his reverie.

Hart's gaze shifted to her, his expression inscrutable. "No, Sergeant. It's never just a clock. This... this is a message."

The silence that followed was thick with unspoken questions. Emily took a tentative step closer, her gaze flickering between the detective and the clock. She had always respected his instincts, his ability to see beyond the obvious, but this time she feared he might be chasing phantoms.

"A message?" she echoed, struggling to keep the skepticism from her voice. "From whom?"

Hart's lips quirked into a grim smile. "From our killer, of course. Don't you see, Emily? This isn't just a malfunction. Someone deliberately tampered with this clock so it would reset at twelve. And why? Because that's when it all began. That's when the first murder occurred."

Emily felt a chill run down her spine. She glanced at the clock, half-expecting it to spring to life and start ticking again. But it remained stubbornly silent, its hands frozen in a perpetual loop of nothingness.

"And you think..." she hesitated, choosing her words carefully, "you think the killer left this here for us to find?"

"I don't think. I know." Hart stood abruptly, his movements sharp and decisive. He crossed the room in two long strides, snatching a worn notebook from his desk and flipping it open to a page filled with hasty scrawls. "Every victim was found with a clock nearby, but not just any clock—one that had been altered to reset itself at twelve o'clock precisely. Each clock was different, unique in its own way, but they all shared this one commonality."

Emily blinked, trying to process this new revelation. "So... it's a calling card?"

"Exactly," Hart murmured, his eyes narrowing as he skimmed through his notes. "But not just any calling card. It's a challenge. The killer wants us to understand something, to see a pattern we're missing. And until we do, the clocks will keep resetting, the murders will continue, and more lives will be lost."

For a moment, neither of them spoke. The weight of Hart's words hung heavy in the air, like the mist that still clung stubbornly to the town outside. Emily's mind raced, piecing together fragments of information that suddenly seemed to take on a new significance.

"But why twelve o'clock?" she asked quietly. "What's so important about that specific time?"

Hart's gaze grew distant, as if he were staring into some unseen abyss. "Midnight is more than just a point on the clock. It's the boundary between one day and the next, between the known and the unknown. It's a liminal space, a moment where time itself seems to pause. Our killer is playing with that boundary, using it to unsettle us, to make us question our perception of time and reality."

Emily shivered involuntarily. There was something profoundly unsettling about the way Hart spoke, as if he were reciting a half-remembered dream, or a prophecy from some ancient text. She glanced at the clock again, half-expecting it to suddenly spring forward, breaking its endless loop. But it remained motionless, its hands frozen at twelve.

"So, what do we do?" she asked softly. "How do we stop this?"

Hart's gaze sharpened, his focus returning to the present. He looked at her, and for the first time in days, she saw a flicker of determination in his eyes. "We need to find the maker of these clocks. Whoever built them holds the key to this mystery. And I have a feeling they're much closer than we think."

With that, he strode to the door, grabbing his coat and hat. Emily hesitated only a moment before following, her heart pounding with a mixture of fear and excitement. They were finally on the right track. But as they stepped out into the misty streets of Wickford, she couldn't shake the feeling that they were walking straight into a trap.

The journey to the small workshop on the outskirts of town was shrouded in silence, save for the soft crunch of gravel beneath their boots. The shop belonged to a reclusive clockmaker named Jonathan Morley, a man known for his eccentricities and unparalleled craftsmanship. If anyone in Wickford could shed light on the altered clocks, it would be him.

Hart rapped sharply on the wooden door, the sound echoing unnaturally loud in the still morning air. There was no response. He tried again, harder this time, but the door remained firmly shut.

"Maybe he's not here," Emily suggested, though her voice lacked conviction.

Hart shook his head. "He's here. I can feel it."

Without another word, he turned the handle. To their surprise, the door swung open easily, revealing a dimly lit interior cluttered with half-finished timepieces, tools, and stacks of yellowed schematics. The air smelled faintly of oil and dust, a combination that spoke of long hours spent hunched over delicate mechanisms.

"Mr. Morley?" Hart called out, his voice low but commanding.

There was a rustling sound from the back of the workshop, followed by the creak of floorboards. A figure emerged from the shadows—a thin, stooped man with wild white hair and eyes that seemed to gleam with a feverish intensity.

"Detective Hart," the man rasped, his voice as brittle as old parchment. "I was expecting you."

Hart exchanged a wary glance with Emily. "You know who I am?"

"Of course." Morley shuffled closer, his gaze darting nervously around the room. "I know everything about this case. About the clocks. About the murders. It's all part of the design, you see. A grand design, laid out like the inner workings of a timepiece."

Emily's hand moved instinctively to the holster at her side. There was something deeply unsettling about the man's demeanor, a manic edge that set her on edge. But Hart remained calm, his expression inscrutable.

"Tell me about the clocks," he said softly. "Why do they reset at twelve?"

Morley's lips twitched, curving into a smile that sent a shiver down Emily's spine. "Because that's when everything changes. Midnight is the fulcrum, the point where all the gears shift. If you understand that, Detective, you'll understand the whole pattern."

"And what is the pattern?" Hart pressed, his voice low and intense.

The old clockmaker laughed, a dry, rasping sound that seemed to echo through the empty workshop. "The pattern is time itself. The murders are only the beginning. Each death, each clock, is a step towards something much larger. Something you cannot even begin to comprehend."

Hart took a step closer, his eyes locked on Morley's. "Then help me comprehend it. Tell me what's going to happen next."

Morley's gaze flickered, a shadow of doubt crossing his face. For a moment, he looked almost... afraid. But then the manic light returned, and he shook his head slowly.

"I can't do that, Detective. It's already been set in motion. The clocks have reset. And now... time is running out."

With those cryptic words, he turned abruptly and retreated into the shadows, his footsteps fading into the depths of the workshop.

Hart stared after him, his jaw clenched tightly. Emily moved to his side, her brow furrowed in confusion.

"What does he mean, 'time is running out'?" she whispered.

Hart didn't answer. Instead, he glanced at his watch—an old, reliable timepiece he had owned for years. The second hand moved steadily around the face, ticking off the seconds with mechanical precision.

But then, as they watched, the second hand stuttered.

2. The Confession of a Liar

THE NIGHT WAS UNUSUALLY still when Detective Hart finally managed to track down Richard Lyle. The small cottage, hidden away on the outskirts of Wintonville, seemed a strange choice for a man once renowned for his charm and social flair. But as Hart approached the door, noting the faint glimmer of light seeping through the curtains, he felt a flicker of anticipation mixed with a sense of unease. There was something about Richard's disappearance that had never sat well with him—something that suggested not the fear of a man in hiding but the careful calculation of someone waiting for the right moment to reappear.

Hart hesitated briefly, listening to the low hum of the wind that rustled the leaves and stirred the shadows along the porch. He rapped his knuckles against the weathered wood, his knock echoing sharply in the quiet. It took only a few moments before the door creaked open, revealing a man who had once been the toast of every gathering, the center of every room he entered. But now, Richard looked aged beyond his years. His once neatly groomed hair hung limply around his gaunt face, and his eyes, which had once sparkled with mischief, were now clouded and dark.

"Detective Hart," Richard greeted with a half-smile that didn't reach his eyes. "I wondered when you'd find me. Please, come in."

The invitation, though spoken politely enough, held a tinge of resignation, as though he'd known this encounter was inevitable. Hart nodded, stepping inside and surveying the cramped interior. The room was a strange mix of disarray and order; books lay strewn across the floor, but the clock on the mantle—an old, ornate piece—ticked steadily, keeping a perfect rhythm, as if anchoring the chaos around it.

"You've been expecting me, then?" Hart asked, lowering himself into a worn armchair opposite Richard, who sank onto the sofa with a weary sigh.

"I suppose I have," Richard murmured, his gaze drifting towards the clock, the steady ticking filling the silence between them. "It's only a matter of time before lies unravel, isn't it? And mine... well, they've been long overdue for exposure."

There it was—the acknowledgment Hart had hoped for, though not in the way he'd imagined. He leaned forward, his eyes locked on Richard's, searching for any hint of pretense. "What lies, Richard? If you have something to confess, now is your chance."

Richard's chuckle was a dry, brittle sound. "Ah, Hart, always the direct approach. But confession, like time, is a tricky thing. You see, one can confess to a hundred sins and still conceal the one that matters most."

Hart frowned, his frustration bubbling to the surface. "Enough with the riddles. I didn't come all this way to play games. Tell me the truth about the night of the murder. What really happened?"

Richard's gaze remained fixed on the clock, its pendulum swinging back and forth, back and forth. He seemed mesmerized by the motion, as if lost in a trance. "The truth, you say? You won't find it where you expect, Hart. I could tell you what you want to hear, give you the version of events that would tie up your investigation neatly, but that's not why I disappeared. It's not why I've stayed hidden."

Hart clenched his jaw, his patience wearing thin. "Then tell me why, Richard. Why vanish if you had nothing to hide?"

Silence settled between them, thick and heavy. Then, with a sigh that seemed to carry the weight of the years he'd been gone, Richard leaned back, his eyes finally meeting Hart's.

"I lied, Detective. I lied about many things—my alibi, my whereabouts, even the people I claimed to trust. But the biggest lie of all was that I was ever a victim in this game. No, I'm not the prey you thought I was. I'm a player, just like the rest of them."

Hart's pulse quickened, his mind racing to process the implication. "What are you saying, Richard? That you were involved in the murders?"

Richard shook his head slowly. "Not quite. I didn't pull the trigger or wield the knife, if that's what you're asking. But I knew... I knew who did. And I helped them—willingly, knowingly. Because I thought I could control the outcome. I thought I could stay one step ahead of it all."

The confession hung in the air, almost too surreal to grasp. Richard had always been a slippery character, dancing around the truth with ease, but this—this was something else entirely. Hart leaned back, his mind swirling with questions. "Why? Why would you help a murderer?"

Richard's lips twitched in a bitter smile. "Isn't it obvious? Power. Influence. The thrill of it, if I'm being honest. I had information they needed—access to people, places, secrets. I thought I was the puppet master, pulling the strings. But I was wrong. So terribly wrong."

Hart's eyes narrowed. "Who are they, Richard? Who's behind this?"

The question seemed to drain the last of Richard's energy. He slumped forward, his hands trembling slightly. "You already know the answer, Hart. You've always known. But that's the cruelest lie of all, isn't it? Knowing something in your gut but being unable to prove it. The real murderer is right under your nose, hidden in plain sight. And they're smarter than you, more ruthless than you can imagine."

Hart's mind flashed through the suspects, the clues, the dead ends that had plagued the investigation. Was it really possible that he'd been so blind? That he'd been chasing shadows while the real threat lay just out of reach?

"Give me a name, Richard," he demanded, his voice low and tense. "Tell me who it is."

But Richard merely shook his head. "Names are meaningless, Hart. It's the truth that matters, and the truth is... I can't tell you. Because if I do, you'll be dead before dawn. Just like the others."

A chill ran down Hart's spine. For the first time in his career, he felt a pang of fear—not for himself, but for the people he'd sworn to protect. He stood abruptly, his gaze hardening. "You're coming with me. We're going to the station, and you're going to tell me everything you know."

Richard didn't resist as Hart pulled him to his feet, but there was a haunted look in his eyes that made Hart hesitate. "You don't understand, do you?" Richard whispered, his voice barely audible. "This isn't a case you can solve with an arrest or a confession. It's a clockwork of lies and truths, ticking away until it all comes crashing down. And when it does... well, I suppose we'll see who's left standing."

Hart tightened his grip on Richard's arm, his jaw set in determination. "We'll see about that. But for now, you're going to face justice for what you've done."

As they stepped out into the night, the wind seemed to howl with a renewed vigor, swirling around them as if mocking their efforts. The road ahead was long, and Hart knew that whatever truths awaited them, they would not be uncovered easily. But one thing was certain: time was running out, and with every tick of the clock, the noose tightened around them all.

• • • •

BY THE TIME THEY REACHED the station, the first light of dawn was beginning to break through the darkness. Hart led Richard to an interrogation room, locking the door behind them. He knew that he needed to get every scrap of information from Richard before it was too late.

"Sit," he ordered, and Richard complied, his expression one of resignation.

Hart took a deep breath, gathering his thoughts. "Start from the beginning. I want every detail—who you were working with, how you got involved, and why. No more half-truths, no more riddles. Just the facts."

Richard's gaze flickered to the mirror on the wall, then back to Hart. He seemed to weigh his options, considering what to reveal and what to hold back. Finally, he nodded.

"It began years ago," he started quietly. "Back when I still had a reputation worth preserving. I was approached by someone—someone I thought was a friend. They needed access to a network of influential people, and I had the connections. At first, it was just small favors—introductions, meetings, nothing illegal. But then, the demands grew... and I found myself in too deep."

Hart listened intently, his fingers tapping a steady rhythm on the table. "And the murders? How did they come into play?"

Richard's face tightened with pain. "I never meant for it to go that far. I thought I could control them, steer them away from violence. But once the first life was taken, there was no turning back. They had me by the throat, and I... I became a willing accomplice. Every murder that followed was a message—to me, to you, to anyone who thought they could unravel the web we'd spun."

Hart's eyes blazed with anger. "And you let it happen? You let innocent people die?"

"Yes," Richard whispered, his voice breaking. "Because I was afraid. Afraid of losing everything. But now... now I see that fear was my greatest lie. And it's cost me more than I can bear."

The confession left Hart reeling. He'd expected deceit, betrayal, but this—this was something darker, more twisted. He leaned forward, his gaze piercing. "It's not too late to make things right, Richard. Help me bring them down. Help me stop this madness."

Richard

's lips curved into a sad smile. "You're a good man, Hart. But you're wrong. It is too late. The wheels are already in motion, and when the clock strikes twelve, it will be the end—for all of us."

Before Hart could respond, a sudden commotion erupted outside the door. Shouts, the sound of a struggle, and then—the unmistakable crack of a gunshot.

Hart's heart plummeted as he whirled around, his hand reaching for his weapon. He moved to the door, but before he could open it, Richard spoke again, his voice a soft murmur.

"Goodbye, Detective. May you find the truth you seek."

The next moment, the door burst open, and Hart was met with a scene of chaos. Officers were grappling with a figure in black, the intruder's face obscured by a mask. But as Hart lunged forward, his gaze shifted back to the interrogation room—to Richard, slumped in his chair, a pool of blood spreading across his chest.

"No!" Hart shouted, his voice raw with anguish.

But it was too late. Richard's eyes were already glazing over, his final breath escaping in a shuddering sigh.

3. An Unexpected Partnership

DETECTIVE HART STOOD at the corner of the dimly lit alleyway, his breath forming misty clouds in the crisp evening air. The faint, rhythmic ticking of an unseen clock echoed through the quiet streets, a reminder of the ominous pattern that had begun to plague this once peaceful town. He glanced at his pocket watch, its hands crawling slowly toward the half-past eight mark. It was as though time itself hesitated to proceed, wary of what lay ahead.

As the detective observed his surroundings, his sharp eyes caught sight of a solitary figure emerging from the shadows. A man in a long, dark coat and a hat pulled low over his brow stepped into the soft glow of the streetlamp. For a fleeting moment, Hart's instincts flared—a feeling of recognition tugged at him, but he couldn't place it. He tightened his grip on the handle of his walking cane, its sturdy wood providing a sense of grounding.

"Detective Hart, I presume?" The man's voice was calm, almost disinterested, yet it carried a hint of authority that set Hart's senses on edge.

"Depends on who's asking," Hart replied, narrowing his gaze. He knew better than to trust strangers who appeared out of nowhere, especially when they seemed to know his name.

The man tipped his hat, revealing a face lined with age and experience, yet possessing a peculiar vitality. His sharp, piercing eyes gleamed in the light, betraying a mind that was always several steps ahead.

"Professor Lucien Graves," the man introduced himself with a curt nod. "I've been following your investigation with great interest. It seems we have a mutual problem."

Hart's eyebrows arched in surprise. The name was not unfamiliar; Professor Graves was a renowned expert in horology and the workings of intricate mechanisms. He was also known for his eccentricities and a penchant for solving puzzles that confounded others. If Graves was here, it meant that this case had garnered more attention than Hart had anticipated.

"And what problem might that be, Professor?" Hart asked cautiously.

"The murders, of course," Graves replied with a faint smile. "Or, more specifically, the timing of them."

Hart's fingers tightened around the cane. "You've made the connection, then?"

Graves inclined his head. "It wasn't difficult, once one pays attention to the details. The position of the hands on the clocks found at each crime scene—the precise manner in which each timepiece was set—it all points to a singular mind orchestrating these events."

Hart's mind raced as he recalled the gruesome scenes he'd been witness to over the past weeks. Each victim had been discovered with a clock placed meticulously nearby, its hands stopped at a specific time. The symbolism of the hour, the minute, and the second had eluded him, though he knew there was a pattern—one he had yet to decipher.

"So you're saying you can read the killer's message?" Hart asked, skepticism coloring his tone. He had little patience for so-called experts who swooped in after the fact, eager to claim credit for solving mysteries others had labored over.

"Not completely," Graves admitted, his voice dropping to a more contemplative tone. "But I believe I have a theory. And if I'm right, then you and I have only a few days left before the next murder."

Hart stared at the professor, weighing his options. There was no denying that he needed help—someone who understood the language of clocks and gears far better than he did. But trusting a man like Graves, whose motives were as enigmatic as the timepieces he studied, was a risk.

"You haven't told me why you're so invested in this, Professor," Hart said, his gaze unflinching.

Graves's smile faded, and for the first time, a shadow of something deeper—something darker—crossed his features. "Let's just say that the killer has made this personal. He's using techniques that... are familiar to me."

Hart frowned, unsure whether to press for more information. But before he could speak, Graves took a step closer, his voice dropping to a whisper.

"If you truly wish to stop him, Detective, then you'll need my help. And in return, I'll need yours. Because this man... he's more dangerous than you could possibly imagine."

Hart's instincts screamed at him to back away, to refuse the offer. But something about Graves's intensity, the urgency in his eyes, made him pause. Against his better judgment, he nodded slowly.

"Very well, Professor Graves. It seems we have an unexpected partnership."

• • • •

THEIR ALLIANCE, HOWEVER tentative, was soon put to the test. The following morning, Hart and Graves found themselves at the latest crime scene: a grand estate perched on the outskirts of town. The sprawling mansion, with its ivy-covered walls and manicured gardens, exuded an air of old-world elegance. Yet, the sight that greeted them inside was anything but refined.

The body of Lady Eleanor Foxglove, a prominent socialite and patron of the arts, lay sprawled on the polished parquet floor of her drawing room. A grand grandfather clock stood ominously nearby, its pendulum stilled, its hands frozen at precisely 2:17 AM.

Hart surveyed the scene with practiced detachment, his eyes scanning every detail. There was something almost theatrical about the way Lady Foxglove had been posed, as if the killer had intended her death to be a twisted work of art.

"Another clock," he murmured, glancing at Graves.

The professor nodded, his expression grim. "The same meticulous craftsmanship as the others. But there's something different about this one..."

Graves approached the clock with a reverence that bordered on obsession. He ran his fingers along the woodwork, his touch light and delicate, as though communing with the inanimate object. Then, he leaned in closer, his eyes narrowing as he examined the clock face.

"Look here, Detective," Graves said softly, beckoning Hart closer.

Hart hesitated, then joined Graves. At first, he saw nothing unusual—just the ornate numerals and gilded hands of a finely made timepiece. But then he noticed it: a tiny, almost imperceptible scratch on the surface of the glass. It was so small that it would have been easy to miss, but Graves's keen eyes had caught it.

"A message?" Hart guessed, his heart rate quickening.

Graves nodded slowly. "Yes, but not in words. It's a mark—one that corresponds to a specific alignment of the gears inside. If I'm correct, it should reveal the next move our killer plans to make."

Hart felt a surge of frustration. "And how do we read it?"

"Patience, Detective," Graves murmured, his fingers already at work, deftly disassembling the outer casing of the clock. The delicate mechanisms inside glinted in the soft light, a labyrinth of cogs and springs.

Hart watched in silence, his breath held, as Graves adjusted one of the inner gears. There was a faint click, and then a hidden compartment near the base of the clock slid open, revealing a folded piece of paper.

"Clever bastard," Hart muttered, reaching for the note. He unfolded it with care, his eyes scanning the words hastily scrawled in an elegant script.

"Tick-tock, Detective. Time is running out. Meet me where the hands first stopped, and all will be revealed. Midnight, two days hence. Alone."

A chill ran down Hart's spine. He looked up at Graves, who was already studying the message with a furrowed brow.

"'Where the hands first stopped,'" Hart repeated slowly. "What does it mean?"

Graves's gaze was distant, as if his mind were racing through a thousand possibilities. Then, a flash of understanding lit his eyes.

"The old clock tower in the town square," he said quietly. "It stopped years ago—at precisely 12:00 midnight. It hasn't moved since."

Hart swallowed hard. "And you think that's where the killer wants us to go?"

"Not wants, Detective," Graves corrected softly. "Needs. He's setting the stage for his final act."

Hart stared at the note again, the weight of the words sinking in. This was more than just a cat-and-mouse game; this was a meticulously planned performance, with every second, every minute, choreographed to perfection.

"If we go, it could be a trap," Hart said, his voice tense.

"Undoubtedly," Graves agreed, his expression unreadable. "But if we don't, more will die. So tell me, Detective—do we risk it?"

Hart hesitated only a moment before nodding. "We go. But we go prepared."

Graves's lips curved into a faint smile. "I expected nothing less."

• • • •

THE TWO DAYS PASSED in a blur of fevered preparation and restless anticipation. Every moment felt like an eternity, the pressure mounting with each tick of the clock. When the appointed night finally arrived, Hart found himself standing at the base of the old clock tower, its dark silhouette looming against the starless sky.

4. The Timekeeper's Code

THE TOWN OF BYFORD-on-Weir, nestled in the rolling hills of the English countryside, was known for its quiet streets, timeless architecture, and the gentle murmur of the river that wound its way through the heart of the village. It was a place where time seemed to move more slowly, where each day unfolded with the steady rhythm of a grandfather clock's pendulum. But beneath this serene exterior lay a web of secrets, betrayals, and whispers that were destined to shatter the illusion of peace.

Detective Arthur Hart, a man known for his keen intellect and unassuming presence, arrived in Byford just as the autumn leaves were beginning to turn. His arrival, though discreet, was noted by the few who had nothing better to do than observe the comings and goings of strangers. He stepped off the small, steam-powered train and looked around, taking in the picturesque scene with a discerning eye.

The letter he had received a week prior had been unsigned and anonymous, as letters of intrigue often are. The sender claimed to have knowledge of a series of unsolved murders stretching back twenty years—murders that had baffled the local constabulary and left families mourning in silence. The only clue linking these crimes was a curious detail: each victim had been found with a stopped clock at the scene, the time frozen at the exact moment of death.

"The Timekeeper's Code," the letter had mentioned ominously. A phrase that meant little to him then, but he was determined to understand its significance. His instincts, honed over years of investigating the darkest corners of human nature, told him that this case would be unlike any other. And so he had come, ready to face whatever shadows lurked in the town's quiet corners.

As Hart made his way down the cobbled path toward the village square, he observed the people he passed with practiced nonchalance. They were ordinary folk—shopkeepers, farmers, housewives, and children—each caught up in the daily business of life. But he knew that appearances were often deceiving. Somewhere among them, a killer was watching. Someone who had evaded justice for far too long.

The village clock tower, an imposing structure of stone and iron, loomed over the square. Its face, adorned with intricate carvings and gilded hands, shone brightly in the pale sunlight. Hart felt a shiver of anticipation as he stared up at it. The clock had been donated to the town decades ago by one Benedict Alcott, a reclusive watchmaker of considerable skill and even greater eccentricity. Alcott's disappearance years later had sparked rumors and speculation, but nothing had ever been proven. The clock, however, remained—a silent sentinel marking the hours with unwavering precision.

Hart's lodgings had been arranged at the Rose & Crown, a quaint inn run by the amiable Mrs. Thistlewaite. She greeted him with a warm smile and a curious glance, her eyes flickering with the faintest hint of recognition.

"Mr. Hart, welcome to Byford-on-Weir. I hope you find your stay pleasant," she said, her voice lilting with the cadence of the local accent.

"Thank you, Mrs. Thistlewaite," he replied, matching her smile with one of his own. "I'm sure I will. It's a charming village."

"Charming, yes," she murmured, her gaze lingering on him a moment longer before she turned to lead him to his room. "But not without its share of troubles, as I'm sure you'll soon discover."

"Troubles?" Hart feigned ignorance, raising an eyebrow. "I was under the impression this was a place of tranquility."

"On the surface, perhaps." Mrs. Thistlewaite stopped at the door to his room and handed him the key. "But you've come at a strange time, Mr. Hart. I suppose you'll learn more soon enough. Enjoy your stay."

With that enigmatic statement, she left him to his thoughts. Hart unpacked his belongings with methodical care, placing his notebooks and pens neatly on the small writing desk by the window. From his vantage point, he could see the entire square, bustling with activity as townsfolk went about their day. He wondered how many of them were aware of the darkness that lingered just beneath the surface. How many knew the truth about the Timekeeper's Code?

That evening, Hart ventured out, making his way to the local pub, The Black Swan. It was a lively establishment, filled with laughter, the clinking of glasses, and the hum of conversation. He found a seat near the fireplace, ordering a modest meal and a pint of ale. As he ate, he listened, his sharp ears picking up fragments of conversation, gossip, and the occasional hushed whisper.

"Heard they found old John Cooper's body by the river, frozen stiff as a board..."

"...and his pocket watch, stopped at precisely eleven-thirty. Just like the others."

"Must be the work of the Timekeeper..."

The mention of the Timekeeper sent a chill down Hart's spine. He leaned back, allowing the words to wash over him. It seemed the villagers had their own name for the elusive killer, a figure shrouded in myth and fear. But why leave clocks at the scene? What message was the killer trying to convey?

As he sipped his ale thoughtfully, a shadow fell over the table. He looked up to see a man of about fifty, his hair graying at the temples, his eyes sharp and assessing.

"Mind if I join you?" the man asked, his tone polite but firm.

"Not at all," Hart replied, gesturing to the empty chair across from him.

The man sat, placing his own drink on the table. "Name's Edwin Grimshaw. I heard you're new to our little village."

"That I am," Hart acknowledged. "Arthur Hart, private investigator. I'm here on a matter of personal interest."

Grimshaw raised an eyebrow. "Personal, you say? Most come to Byford for a bit of peace and quiet. But I don't reckon that's what you're after."

"Depends on your definition of peace," Hart said evenly. "I'm interested in the recent deaths. The ones involving stopped clocks."

A flicker of something—fear, perhaps—passed through Grimshaw's eyes. "Aye, I thought as much. The Timekeeper, they call him. A madman, if you ask me. Always been something off about those clocks."

Hart leaned forward, his gaze intent. "What do you know about the Timekeeper's Code?"

Grimshaw hesitated, glancing around as if to ensure they weren't being overheard. "It's not something people talk about openly. The Code... well, it's not just about clocks. It's a message. A way of keeping track, marking those who were involved in something... something that happened long ago."

"Go on," Hart urged, his voice low.

"Benedict Alcott, the old watchmaker, he was more than just a craftsman. He had a gift, they say. Could make clocks that did more than tell time. They say he had a secret code, a way of embedding messages into the mechanisms themselves. Only, he vanished before anyone could find out what it all meant. Some say he was murdered, others that he just disappeared. But the clocks—those blasted clocks—they're still here, and now they're showing up at crime scenes."

"Why would anyone want to use Alcott's work in this way?" Hart asked, his mind racing with possibilities.

"Revenge, maybe. Or to send a warning. Who can say? All I know is, the deaths started again right after old Mr. Thorne came back to the village."

"Mr. Thorne?"

"Aye. Edgar Thorne, Benedict's former apprentice. Left the village years ago, but now he's back. Coincidence? I think not."

Hart thanked Grimshaw for the information and paid for their drinks. As he stepped out into the cool night air, the village seemed to take on a different hue. The quaint charm was still there, but now it felt like a façade, masking something far more sinister.

The Timekeeper's Code... a message hidden in plain sight, perhaps? And if so, what was it counting down to?

Hart glanced up at the clock tower, its hands glinting in the moonlight. Whatever the Code was, he knew one thing for certain: time was running out.

5. Cracking the Cipher

DETECTIVE HART STOOD in the dimly lit study of the late Mr. Jonathan Weathersby, the eccentric clockmaker whose sudden death had set off a chain of murders and mysteries that seemed to haunt this sleepy English village. Dust particles swirled in the thin rays of sunlight piercing through the old, heavy drapes. The air smelled of aged paper, varnished wood, and the faint scent of oil used to grease the gears of the clocks that adorned every corner of the room. The soft ticking of dozens of clocks filled the silence, marking the passage of time as if the room itself were alive with anticipation.

Hart's fingers brushed over a stack of yellowed papers scattered across the cluttered mahogany desk. He frowned as he glanced at the peculiar arrangement of numbers and letters. They looked like nonsensical scribbles to the untrained eye, but he knew better. Mr. Weathersby had not been a man of nonsense; every mark, every smudge of ink held meaning.

"It's a cipher, I'm certain of it," Hart murmured to himself, the words echoing slightly in the stillness of the room.

The case had taken a curious turn since the discovery of the old clockmaker's lifeless body sprawled beneath the towering grandfather clock in his workshop. What initially appeared to be a tragic accident — a heart attack, perhaps — had quickly escalated into something far more sinister when a second victim, a local solicitor, had been found murdered, his lifeless hand clutching a peculiar letter that pointed straight back to Weathersby's mysterious death.

Since then, more murders had followed, each one seemingly unrelated to the other save for one peculiar detail: a small, intricately carved timepiece found beside each victim, its hands stopped at precisely twelve o'clock. The press had already taken to calling them the "Clockwork Murders," and Hart could not disagree with the chilling aptness of the name.

"Lost in thought again, are we, Mr. Hart?" a voice chimed from behind him, breaking his concentration.

Hart turned to see Miss Eleanor Hughes, the sharp-eyed, auburn-haired journalist who had, much to his initial chagrin, attached herself to the investigation. She had a way of slipping into rooms unannounced, as quiet and graceful as a cat, her curiosity as unrelenting as the ticking clocks around them.

"Miss Hughes," Hart greeted her with a nod. "I wasn't expecting you so soon. Any luck with the archives?"

Eleanor arched an eyebrow, her lips curving into a wry smile. "You know me better than to expect otherwise. I managed to unearth a few curious records about Mr. Weathersby's past — nothing too concrete, but suggestive enough. It appears our dear clockmaker was more than just a recluse with a penchant for timepieces. He was involved in some rather... dubious dealings."

"Go on," Hart prompted, his interest piqued.

"Before he settled in the village, Weathersby was employed by a rather secretive organization — one that specialized in cryptographic devices during the war. He was a master of codes and ciphers. It's said he designed a device capable of encoding messages that no enemy could ever hope to decipher. But after the war ended, the device vanished, and so did Weathersby. He came here, set up his clockmaking business, and lived in quiet obscurity — until now, of course."

Hart's gaze returned to the papers on the desk. "Which means these notes might be more than the ramblings of an old man."

"Exactly." Eleanor moved closer, her eyes narrowing as she scrutinized the jumble of numbers and symbols. "If we can crack this code, we might be able to find out what he was hiding — and why it's led to so many deaths."

Hart nodded thoughtfully, then glanced around the room. His eyes landed on a large, brass-encased clock sitting on a shelf opposite the desk. It was an exquisite piece of craftsmanship, with delicate filigree and etched markings around its face. But it wasn't the beauty of the clock that drew his attention — it was the subtle misalignment of its hands.

"Miss Hughes, would you mind assisting me for a moment?" Hart asked, crossing the room.

Eleanor followed him, her gaze flitting to the clock. "What is it?"

Hart reached out and gently adjusted the minute hand. The soft click it made as it fell into place was almost imperceptible, but the effect was immediate. There was a faint whirring noise, followed by a small compartment at the base of the clock popping open.

"Well, well," Eleanor breathed, leaning in to peer inside. "What have we here?"

Inside the compartment lay a small, leather-bound notebook. Hart picked it up carefully, flipping it open to reveal pages filled with even more cryptic symbols and diagrams. But as he turned to the last page, he saw something that made his pulse quicken — a series of numbers, accompanied by the unmistakable outline of a clock face.

"It's a key," Hart whispered. "A key to the cipher."

Eleanor's eyes widened. "Then we might just be able to decode the message after all. But we'll need more than just these notes. If Weathersby was as clever as he seems, he wouldn't have made it easy to crack."

Hart nodded slowly, his mind already racing. "We'll need to retrace his steps — look at everything he's ever built, every clock, every device. There's bound to be more clues hidden among them."

The next few days were a whirlwind of activity as Hart and Eleanor painstakingly examined every clock in Weathersby's possession. Some were simple timepieces, others elaborate contraptions with multiple dials and hidden compartments. Each one offered a piece of the puzzle, but it wasn't until they reached the last clock — a massive, ornate structure that dominated the workshop's main wall — that they found what they were looking for.

"It's the master clock," Hart murmured, staring up at the intricately carved face. "The one that controls all the others."

Eleanor frowned. "What do you mean?"

Hart gestured to the various dials and levers on the clock's surface. "Every other clock we've found so far — they all seem to be synchronized to this one. It's almost as if they're all connected, like a network."

Eleanor's eyes widened. "A network... of ciphers. Of course! Each clock must represent a different part of the code."

They worked in silence, moving from clock to clock, noting down each number, each subtle variation in the gears and mechanisms. Hours turned into days as they painstakingly pieced together the scattered fragments of the cipher. The village outside buzzed with gossip and speculation about the ongoing investigation, but Hart and Eleanor remained undeterred.

Finally, after what felt like an eternity, they had it — the completed code.

"It's a set of coordinates," Hart said, staring down at the decoded message. "But to what?"

Eleanor leaned over his shoulder, her brow furrowing as she read the numbers. "These coordinates... they're for a location outside the village, near the old railway tracks."

Hart's gaze sharpened. "The abandoned clock tower."

The tower had stood unused for decades, a relic of a bygone era when the railway had been the village's lifeline. Now it was little more than a crumbling ruin, its once-majestic face tarnished by time and neglect. If there was something hidden there, it would have to be well concealed.

"Let's go," Hart said, his voice filled with a resolve that left no room for argument.

The tower loomed ahead of them as they approached, its shadow stretching across the overgrown field like the gnarled fingers of a giant. The door creaked ominously as Hart pushed it open, the smell of damp and decay filling their nostrils.

Inside, the tower was a mess of broken machinery and rusted gears. But Hart's eyes were drawn to a small, unassuming clock mounted on the far wall. It was plain, almost nondescript — but something about its placement felt deliberate.

He reached out and adjusted the hands, just as he had done in Weathersby's study. This time, however, the click was much louder — and the entire wall shifted, revealing a hidden compartment.

Inside lay a single, small device — a clockwork mechanism unlike anything Hart had ever seen. It was intricate, beautiful, and utterly deadly.

"A bomb," Eleanor whispered, her face pale. "Weathersby was building a bomb."

Hart's mind raced as he stared at the device. The murders, the cipher, the clocks — it had all been leading to this moment. But why? And who was behind it all?

"Look," Eleanor said suddenly, pointing to a small, engraved plate on the device. "There's a name here."

Hart leaned in, his eyes narrowing as he read the inscription.

"'To my dearest apprentice...'" he read aloud, his voice tinged with disbelief.

It couldn't be...

6. A Timely Rescue

THE NIGHT WAS STILL, save for the faint rustling of leaves brushing against one another like hesitant whispers. The town of Ashford lay cloaked in darkness, a blanket of shadows covering its cobbled streets and ivy-clad facades. But somewhere, amidst this calm exterior, fear simmered just beneath the surface — a palpable tension that seeped into the bones of the town's inhabitants. The recent murders had cast a long shadow over Ashford, and though the culprit had yet to be identified, there was a lingering sense of dread that seemed to stretch each minute into an eternity.

Detective Arthur Hart moved cautiously down the deserted lane, his footsteps almost inaudible on the damp stones. He kept his eyes on the manor that loomed ahead — Foxglove Manor, an imposing structure that looked every bit as sinister as the name suggested. The estate's iron gates stood ajar, creaking softly with the wind, as if they were inviting him in. Arthur hesitated. He had been led here by a single note left in his office: "Come to Foxglove Manor tonight. All will be revealed." It was signed only with a clock symbol, the same eerie signature that had accompanied each murder.

He glanced at his pocket watch — 11:45 p.m. Fifteen minutes until midnight. The note had specified that time precisely. With a steadying breath, Arthur pushed through the gate and began his ascent up the gravel pathway. Each step seemed louder than the last, echoing the mounting unease in his chest. There was something about the stillness, the way the windows of the manor gleamed dully in the moonlight, that sent a chill down his spine. But he couldn't afford to turn back now.

The heavy oak door of the manor swung open with a groan, revealing a dimly lit hallway lined with portraits of stern-faced ancestors. Their eyes seemed to follow him as he stepped inside. He noted with a grimace that the air smelled faintly of oil and metal, the same scent he had detected at each crime scene. Whoever the murderer was, they had a penchant for clockwork mechanisms and elaborate traps. Arthur suspected he was walking straight into one now.

He moved deeper into the house, his senses on high alert. A clock chimed softly somewhere in the distance, its mournful toll counting down the seconds. He glanced at his watch again — 11:50 p.m. Ten minutes left. He quickened his pace, peering into each room he passed, searching for any sign of life, any hint of danger. The manor was a labyrinth of shadowy corridors and abandoned rooms, and the silence was oppressive. Just as he was beginning to think the message had been a cruel trick, he heard it — a faint, desperate cry.

Arthur's heart leapt into his throat. The cry came again, muffled but unmistakable, from somewhere on the upper floors. He dashed up the grand staircase, his coat billowing behind him. The cry grew louder as he reached the landing, and he realized with a sickening jolt that it was a woman's voice, strained and panicked. He followed the sound down a narrow hallway until he reached a door at the very end. It was locked, but a quick inspection revealed fresh scratches around the keyhole — someone had been locked in recently.

"Hold on!" Arthur shouted, throwing his weight against the door. The wood splintered on the third attempt, and he stumbled inside. The room was dark, save for a single candle flickering on a rickety table. And there, in the center of the room, bound to a chair and gagged, was Miss Eleanor Bishop, a local journalist who had been investigating the murders on her own.

Arthur rushed forward, his hands working quickly to untie the ropes that bound her wrists and ankles. Eleanor's eyes were wide with fear, and she shook her head frantically as he reached for the gag. He hesitated, his gaze darting around the room. Something wasn't right. He could feel it, a prickling sensation at the back of his neck. But he had no choice. He removed the gag, and Eleanor gasped, struggling to speak.

"Arthur... it's... it's a trap!" she managed, her voice hoarse. "You have to get out of here. Now!"

A sharp click echoed through the room, and Arthur whirled around just in time to see a panel slide open in the wall, revealing a complex mechanism of gears and pulleys. A second later, the floor beneath them began to tremble. He grabbed Eleanor's arm, yanking her to her feet as the room seemed to come alive with the grinding of metal.

"Run!" he shouted, pulling her toward the door. But the moment they stepped over the threshold, another panel slid shut, sealing the exit behind them. The walls shuddered, and Arthur watched in horror as gears began to rotate along the edges of the ceiling, lowering iron bars into place. They were trapped.

"Over here!" Eleanor shouted, tugging him toward a window at the far end of the room. It was small, barely large enough for a person to squeeze through, but it was their only chance. Arthur boosted her up, his muscles straining with the effort. She scrambled through, dropping to the ground outside with a soft thud. He was just about to follow when a series of clicks reverberated through the room, and he froze.

The clock.

He turned slowly, his eyes widening as he spotted a massive, ornate clock embedded in the wall. It wasn't just any clock — it was the same design that had been sketched in the corners of every murder scene. And now, its hands were moving with a deliberate slowness, inching toward midnight.

Tick. Tick. Tick.

"Arthur!" Eleanor's voice was faint, muffled by the thick glass. "You have to jump!"

But he couldn't move. He was mesmerized by the clock, by the intricate dance of its gears and springs, by the way its hands seemed to mock him. Eleven fifty-nine and counting. A chill swept over him as he realized the significance — this clock was counting down to something far worse than death. It was counting down to the revelation of a secret he wasn't ready to face.

"Arthur, please!" Eleanor's voice broke through his trance, and he shook himself, glancing at the window. He had mere seconds. With a burst of energy, he lunged for the opening, squeezing his frame through the narrow space just as the clock's chime began to echo through the room.

The moment his feet hit the ground, a deafening explosion erupted from inside the manor. The force of it threw him and

Eleanor to the ground, shards of glass and splinters raining down around them. Arthur shielded Eleanor's body with his own, his ears ringing. He could barely make out the sound of wood creaking, of flames crackling as the manor began to collapse in on itself.

They lay there, gasping for breath, as the fire blazed higher, lighting up the night sky. Eleanor shifted beneath him, her face streaked with soot and fear.

"I told you it was a trap," she whispered, her voice trembling. "But... how did you know to come here?"

Arthur stared at the burning ruins of Foxglove Manor, his mind racing. The note, the murders, the clock — it was all connected. He hadn't realized until now just how intricately everything was intertwined. The killer was playing a game, and he was following a script that only he knew. Every move had been calculated, every step meticulously planned. And now, it was all falling into place.

"I didn't know," he murmured, his gaze fixed on the fiery remains. "But whoever sent that note... they knew exactly what they were doing."

Eleanor shuddered. "You mean... the killer wanted you here? Why?"

Arthur didn't answer. He didn't need to. The answer was obvious, etched into the fabric of the night: because the killer wasn't done yet. This was only the beginning. The real game was still to come.

"Come on," he said, pulling her to her feet. "We need to get out of here before the fire spreads."

They staggered away from the manor, their shadows flickering in the firelight. The clock tower in the town square began to chime midnight, its mournful toll ringing out over the quiet streets. Arthur glanced back one last time at the manor, now nothing more than a blazing inferno.

Time had run out for Foxglove Manor.

But for Arthur Hart, the true countdown was only just beginning.

Chapter 7: The Midnight Confrontation

1. Secrets Exposed

The rain fell in a steady drizzle, pattering against the windows of Millford Manor like a persistent reminder of the tension that had enveloped the household since the first murder. Inside the dimly lit drawing room, the air was thick with anticipation, and the lingering scent of damp wood mingled with the faint aroma of tobacco smoke. Detective Arthur Hart leaned back in his chair, the flickering light of the fireplace casting long shadows across the room, accentuating the weary lines on his face.

He had been summoned to this ancestral home of the St. Clair family, a once-grand estate now shrouded in mystery and fear. Lady Agatha St. Clair, the matriarch of the family, had gathered her remaining kin after the shocking death of her eldest son, Edward. The tragedy had left everyone in a state of turmoil, and as the detective reviewed the notes he had taken, he could sense that the true nature of the events unfolding here went deeper than mere murder.

The family gathered around him was a motley crew of characters, each hiding their secrets beneath polished exteriors. Lady Agatha, regal even in her grief, clutched a lace handkerchief in her delicate fingers, her gaze piercing and unwavering. Beside her sat her daughter, Margaret, a woman of indeterminate age whose nervous fidgeting spoke volumes. There was also Thomas, the youngest son, whose carefree demeanor had not quite managed to mask the shadow of sorrow cast over the family.

"Detective Hart," Lady Agatha began, her voice a mixture of authority and despair, "I trust you will uncover the truth behind Edward's death. He was... he was such a good man."

"Indeed," Hart replied, his gaze shifting to the others in the room. "But I must remind you, Lady Agatha, that the truth often resides in the most unexpected places."

Thomas leaned forward, his brow furrowed in concern. "But what if it's someone among us? Someone who knows us so well they can anticipate our every move?"

Margaret gasped, her eyes wide with disbelief. "That's absurd! We are family. We would never hurt one another."

"Ah, but therein lies the crux of it, Miss St. Clair," Hart interjected, his voice calm yet firm. "Family can be the most intricate of webs, often concealing the sharpest of knives."

As the detective spoke, a heavy silence fell upon the room, the gravity of his words settling in. Each family member exchanged wary glances, unspoken suspicions swirling in the air like the mist that clung to the estate's grounds.

"Let's discuss the events of that night," Hart suggested, pulling out a notepad. "Where were each of you at the time of Edward's death?"

"I was in the library, reading," Margaret said quickly, her hands twisting in her lap. "I often retreat there when I need to think."

"Thomas?" Hart turned his gaze toward the younger son.

"I was outside, practicing my golf swing," Thomas replied, attempting to sound casual. "I didn't think it was going to rain."

"And you, Lady Agatha?" Hart's gaze settled on the matriarch.

"I was in my chambers, resting," she stated, her voice steady but lacking warmth. "After the dinner, I found it quite exhausting to entertain."

Hart noted the slight tremor in her hands as she spoke. "Exhaustion can indeed cloud judgment. But how well did you know your son's routine?"

"Very well," Lady Agatha said defiantly. "Edward had a penchant for late-night strolls. It was his way of contemplating life, as he often said."

The detective's brow furrowed. "And did anyone else know about these strolls?"

Thomas scoffed. "Everyone knew. He made no secret of it."

A spark of something—jealousy, perhaps—flickered in the younger brother's eyes. "But he didn't have to go so late. It was dangerous."

"Dangerous?" Hart leaned forward, intrigued. "What do you mean?"

Thomas hesitated, searching for the right words. "The village has been rife with rumors of... well, unsavory characters lurking about. I warned him more than once to be cautious."

"Interesting," Hart mused. "And did you ever accompany him on these walks?"

"Why would I?" Thomas shot back, his tone defensive. "I have my own life, my own interests."

As the conversation continued, the detective couldn't shake the feeling that there were layers upon layers to unravel. Each statement held a kernel of truth, but the underlying motives were obscured, like shadows playing tricks in the candlelight.

"Tell me about the relationships within this family," Hart said, deliberately steering the conversation toward more intimate matters. "What secrets do you harbor?"

Margaret shifted uncomfortably, her cheeks flushing. "We... we are a close-knit family," she said, but her eyes betrayed her. "But like all families, we have our disagreements."

"Disagreements? Do elaborate," Hart pressed, sensing that this was a doorway to deeper revelations.

"There's always been a certain tension between Edward and Thomas," Lady Agatha said, her voice carrying a hint of exasperation. "Thomas always felt overshadowed by his elder brother's achievements."

"Of course, I did!" Thomas exclaimed, standing up abruptly. "Edward was the golden child. Everything he did was celebrated while I was left to linger in his shadow."

"Now, now," Lady Agatha said, attempting to maintain order. "This is hardly the time for petty grievances."

"Petty?" Thomas retorted, his voice rising. "It's not petty when it affects your entire life!"

Hart watched the exchange, taking mental notes. Family dynamics were complex, and within the chaos lay clues. "So, there was rivalry, and perhaps resentment," he observed. "But what about your relationship with Edward's fiancée, Clara?"

"Clara?" Margaret's eyes widened. "She adored Edward. She would never..."

"But perhaps she was aware of the tensions," Hart suggested. "And perhaps that influenced her perception of family loyalty."

"I don't think that's fair," Margaret shot back defensively. "Clara has been nothing but kind. She loved him!"

"But love can blind one to the truth," Hart countered. "You all must admit that family loyalty can easily turn to betrayal when passions run high."

Lady Agatha interjected, "I refuse to believe that any of us could stoop so low as to murder."

"Yet murder is a powerful motivator," Hart replied, his voice steady. "Jealousy, betrayal, and love intertwine to create a deadly cocktail."

As the detective delved deeper into their relationships, he sensed a shift in the atmosphere. The storm outside had grown more intense, thunder rumbling ominously in the distance, echoing the turmoil brewing within Millford Manor. It was as if nature itself mirrored the chaos unfolding inside.

"Perhaps we should consider outside influences," Hart said, attempting to broaden the scope of his investigation. "What about the villagers? Did Edward have enemies?"

"Enemies? Hardly," Thomas said, a hint of disdain in his voice. "Edward was well-liked in the community. He was generous and charitable."

"But generosity can also breed envy," Hart reminded him. "Were there any disgruntled individuals who might have felt wronged by him?"

Lady Agatha frowned. "There were rumors of a business rival, but I never took them seriously. Edward dealt with them himself."

"Yet he's dead now," Hart pointed out. "It's worth investigating."

The family fell silent, each lost in their thoughts. The detective noted the heavy weight of unspoken fears, the shadows of their past hovering just out of reach. With a flick of his wrist, he glanced at his watch, calculating the time they had left before the next storm broke, both outside and within the family dynamics.

"Let's not dwell on speculation," he said, shifting gears once again. "I propose we take a closer look at Edward's last moments. Where was he headed before he met his demise?"

Margaret looked pained. "He mentioned going to the old clock tower. Said something about needing to think."

"The clock tower?" Hart echoed, intrigued. "A rather isolated place, is it not?"

"It is," Lady Agatha said, her voice low. "It's been out of commission for years."

"Precisely," Hart noted. "A perfect location for contemplation, but also for concealment."

As the detective formulated a plan to explore the clock tower, a knock on the door broke the tension. The butler, Mr. Smith, entered the room, his expression somber. "Excuse me, milady, but there's a constable here to speak with you."

"Send him in," Lady Agatha commanded, her tone authoritative.

A moment later, Constable Firth appeared, his expression grave. "Detective Hart, we've found something at the clock tower that you might want to see."

Hart's heart raced. "What have you discovered?"

"There's been a disturbance. It seems someone has been tampering with the remnants of the old clock mechanism. We found... a bloodied handkerchief."

The room erupted into chaos, panic washing over the St. Clair family like a tidal wave. Lady Agatha's face turned ashen, while Thomas's expression shifted from anger to fear. Margaret clutched her mother's arm, her wide eyes filled with terror.

"Calm yourselves," Hart commanded, forcing himself to maintain composure amidst the tumult. "We must act swiftly."

As they followed Constable Firth outside, the storm raged on, relentless. The old clock tower loomed before them, its skeletal structure silhouetted against the darkened sky. Hart could feel the weight of the secrets buried

within its walls pressing down on him, urging him to unveil the truth.

Upon entering the tower, the air was thick with the scent of rust and decay. The constable guided them to a small room near the base where the remnants of the clock lay in disarray, gears strewn across the floor. The dim light illuminated a small bloodied handkerchief, which lay crumpled in the corner.

"This belongs to Edward," Lady Agatha whispered, her voice trembling. "I recognize the monogram."

Hart knelt to examine the fabric, noting the intricate stitching. "It's stained with blood," he murmured, deep in thought. "This changes everything."

"Do you think he was attacked here?" Margaret asked, her voice trembling.

"It's possible," Hart replied, carefully folding the handkerchief and placing it in his pocket. "But we need to piece together what led him to this place."

The detective scanned the room, taking in the disheveled state of the clock mechanisms. "The clock itself was known to malfunction. It may have played a role in the night's events."

"Or it was deliberately tampered with," Constable Firth interjected, his brow furrowed. "To create confusion."

"Let's gather more evidence," Hart suggested. "We need to uncover who had access to the clock tower and when."

As they searched the premises, Hart's mind raced with possibilities. He couldn't shake the feeling that they were being watched, that hidden eyes were observing their every move. The walls of the clock tower held countless secrets, and he was determined to unearth them.

Minutes passed like hours as they scoured the remnants of the clock, and just as Hart was about to give in to frustration, a faint noise echoed through the tower. He paused, straining to listen. It sounded like footsteps.

"Stay alert," he whispered to the others.

The footsteps grew closer, and before he could react, a figure emerged from the shadows—a young woman, drenched from the rain, her face pale and eyes wide with fear.

"Clara!" Thomas exclaimed, recognition dawning in his expression.

"Clara?" Hart repeated, astonished. "What are you doing here?"

"I... I came to find Edward," Clara stammered, her voice trembling. "I heard about his death, and I couldn't believe it."

"But why here?" Lady Agatha demanded, her voice sharp.

"I thought he might be here," Clara replied, glancing nervously around the tower. "He mentioned the clock tower before... before..."

"Before what?" Hart pressed, urgency lacing his tone.

"Before he disappeared," she whispered, tears brimming in her eyes. "I was worried he was in danger."

"Danger?" Hart echoed, feeling a surge of adrenaline. "What did he say? What danger did he feel?"

Clara hesitated, her brow furrowed in thought. "He mentioned feeling threatened, as if someone was watching him. He seemed so troubled."

The detective's mind raced. "Did he ever mention who?"

"No," Clara admitted, shaking her head. "But I felt it too. I tried to convince him to stay away from here."

Hart's instincts flared. "Clara, were you aware of Edward's late-night walks?"

"Yes, but I was always afraid for him. I thought he would come to harm," she confessed, her voice shaking.

"Perhaps someone was waiting for him," Hart pondered aloud, the pieces slowly falling into place. "Someone who knew his routine."

Lady Agatha's eyes narrowed. "But who could do such a thing? We are a family. We don't hurt one another."

"Family can be the most dangerous," Hart replied, his gaze locking onto Clara. "You must have seen something. Did anyone follow him?"

"I... I don't know. I didn't see anyone," Clara stammered, looking downcast. "But I could feel a presence. It was as if the shadows were alive."

Suddenly, the sound of thunder shook the tower, reverberating through the old stones. A chill crept through the air, and Hart felt the weight of their predicament pressing down upon him.

"We need to return to the manor," Hart said firmly. "The answers we seek may lie within the family itself."

As they made their way back, Hart's mind was a whirlwind of thoughts. Secrets exposed, relationships tested, and hidden motives simmering beneath the surface. Millford Manor was a house of mirrors, reflecting the darkest desires and fears of its inhabitants.

Once inside, the atmosphere was heavy with the weight of grief and suspicion. Lady Agatha summoned the family to the drawing room once more, determination etched on her face. "We cannot let this tragedy tear us apart. We must stand united."

"United against what?" Thomas snapped. "The truth? We all know there are secrets here."

"Enough!" Lady Agatha's voice cut through the tension like a knife. "We need to face whatever demons haunt us."

Detective Hart stepped forward, his voice steady and authoritative. "We have gathered information that indicates there are hidden truths within this family. I propose we share everything."

The family exchanged uneasy glances, the silence thickening. Margaret finally spoke, her voice barely above a whisper. "What if the truth is too painful to bear?"

"The truth can be painful," Hart replied, "but it is necessary for healing. If we do not confront it, we remain trapped in this cycle of suspicion and fear."

Reluctantly, the family members nodded, realizing that this was a pivotal moment in their lives. Secrets would no longer fester in the shadows; they would be brought into the light.

Lady Agatha turned to her family. "Let us begin with Edward's fiancée, Clara. What do you know of her relationship with Edward?"

Clara stood tall, determination flickering in her eyes. "Edward and I were engaged to be married. I loved him dearly, but there were things he kept from me—things that troubled him."

"Troubled him?" Thomas scoffed. "What could possibly trouble someone so esteemed?"

Clara's expression hardened. "I knew Edward felt the weight of expectations. He wanted to make the family proud, but he also felt the pressure of the business—people trying to undermine him."

"Undermine him?" Lady Agatha echoed, her brow furrowing. "Who would dare?"

"I don't know," Clara admitted, her voice trembling. "But I sensed an unease. The more successful Edward became, the more I noticed the envy in others' eyes. It made me afraid."

"Afraid of what?" Hart pressed, sensing the urgency of the moment.

"Afraid someone would harm him," Clara confessed, tears brimming in her eyes. "I tried to convince him to be cautious. I even suggested we delay the wedding."

"Delay?" Margaret exclaimed, disbelief coloring her tone. "Why would you do that?"

"Because I wanted to protect him!" Clara shot back, emotion spilling over. "I feared for his life. I didn't want to lose him."

"Fear can lead to desperation," Hart murmured, contemplating the implications. "And desperation can lead to drastic measures."

"Are you suggesting Clara had something to do with Edward's death?" Lady Agatha asked, her eyes narrowing.

"No," Hart said quickly, shaking his head. "But we must explore all possibilities. Clara, who else knew of Edward's fears?"

"I... I can't say for certain," Clara stammered, her voice trembling. "He often spoke of business associates, but he never mentioned names. I just sensed something was off."

The detective could feel the tension in the room escalating. "It's vital we uncover who those associates are. They could hold the key to understanding what happened."

Thomas crossed his arms, the bitterness palpable. "And what about you, Clara? Are you sure you weren't the one who made him feel vulnerable?"

"I would never!" Clara exclaimed, her voice rising. "You know nothing about my love for him!"

"Love can blind," Thomas snapped back, frustration boiling over. "And jealousy can breed hatred."

"Stop it!" Lady Agatha interjected, her voice rising above the fray. "This is not the time for accusations."

Hart raised a hand to quiet them. "We need to focus. We have to explore every avenue, and right now, that includes understanding Edward's relationships outside this family."

"Let's not forget," Lady Agatha said sharply, "that we are family. We must protect each other."

"Protect each other from what?" Thomas asked, the skepticism evident in his voice. "From the truth?"

Hart watched as the family dynamic spiraled further into chaos. Secrets were laid bare, and as tempers flared, he realized they were standing on the precipice of revelation.

"Perhaps it is time we investigate Edward's business dealings," he suggested. "If someone felt threatened by his success, they might have had a motive."

"His partner, Gregory Harrison, might know more," Clara offered, her voice steadying. "Edward often confided in him."

"Gregory?" Lady Agatha's expression shifted. "I've heard rumors about him. Some say he's been less than honest in their dealings."

"Then he is worth investigating," Hart affirmed. "Let's pay him a visit."

As they formulated their plan, the storm outside intensified, the winds howling like specters as they prepared to face the unknown. The family had ventured into a treacherous realm, where secrets intertwined with truth, and the heart of darkness awaited their arrival.

The following day, the detective and Clara made their way to Gregory Harrison's office, located in the bustling center of town. The sun broke through the clouds, casting an odd light over the landscape, yet the weight of foreboding hung heavily in the air.

As

they entered the sleek office, the atmosphere shifted. Gregory sat behind his mahogany desk, an air of confidence surrounding him as he greeted them with a sly smile.

"Detective Hart," he said, his voice smooth. "To what do I owe this unexpected visit?"

Hart studied him closely, noting the way his gaze flickered between them. "We're here to discuss Edward St. Clair."

Gregory's demeanor shifted slightly, his smile faltering. "Edward? Is there something wrong?"

"Edward is dead," Clara said bluntly, her voice barely concealing her anger.

"Dead?" Gregory echoed, disbelief etched on his face. "I... I can't believe it."

"Believe it," Hart replied, his tone firm. "We need to know about his business dealings. What was happening before his death?"

Gregory's expression darkened. "Edward was a brilliant businessman, but there were challenges. Some associates were not pleased with our recent success."

"Who?" Clara pressed, her voice tight with urgency.

Gregory hesitated, his eyes narrowing. "I'm not at liberty to discuss private matters. Business is... complicated."

"Complicated enough to warrant suspicion?" Hart probed, leaning closer. "If someone wanted Edward out of the picture, they would have a motive."

"I assure you, we had no enemies," Gregory replied, his voice icy. "Edward was beloved in the community. Anyone who claims otherwise is a fool."

"But people can be deceiving," Hart countered, his eyes locked onto Gregory's. "And envy breeds contempt."

"Detective, I refuse to sit here and be accused," Gregory snapped, his composure faltering. "You need to investigate others, not me."

Clara stepped forward, her voice steady. "What were you doing the night Edward died?"

"I was in a meeting," Gregory said, his voice clipped. "You can check my alibi."

Hart narrowed his gaze, sensing the tension that crackled in the air. "Perhaps we will."

As they left the office, Clara glanced at Hart, worry etched on her face. "Do you think he was involved?"

"I suspect he knows more than he's letting on," Hart replied. "But he's not our only lead. We need to follow the trail."

Back at Millford Manor, the family was gathered again, their expressions a mixture of grief and anxiety. The storm had returned, darkness creeping in around the edges, and Hart sensed the suffocating atmosphere that accompanied their shared secrets.

"Have you found anything?" Lady Agatha asked, her voice trembling.

"Gregory Harrison claims ignorance, but I don't believe him," Hart stated. "We'll need to dig deeper into Edward's business affairs and his associates."

"What else do you know?" Thomas demanded, frustration evident.

"Patience, Thomas," Hart replied. "We're peeling back the layers of a complex situation. Family dynamics, business partnerships, and hidden motivations all intertwine."

Margaret sighed, her shoulders slumping. "When will this nightmare end?"

"The truth will set you free," Hart said firmly. "But it must be faced first."

The family fell silent, the weight of unspoken truths hanging heavy in the air. Lady Agatha stood tall, her resolve strengthening. "We will face whatever comes next together."

As the evening wore on, Hart continued to gather information, hoping to uncover the connections that might lead him to the killer. Each family member was a thread in a tangled web, and as the storm raged outside, he felt the urgency to unravel it before another tragedy struck.

Days turned into a week, and the investigation deepened. Hart discovered that Edward had been involved in a series of questionable transactions—money that had seemingly vanished without a trace, leaving behind a trail of angry investors. The further he delved, the more convoluted the story became, revealing a man burdened by his own successes.

"Detective," Clara said one evening, her voice steady but tinged with worry. "What if the truth destroys the family?"

"The truth can be painful, but it also offers closure," Hart replied, his gaze unwavering. "To heal, you must first confront the pain."

As the detective pieced together the fragments of Edward's life, he uncovered a significant clue—a mysterious letter hidden in the back of one of his books, outlining a financial arrangement with a man named Victor Hayward, a name that had not surfaced in any of their conversations.

"Who is Victor Hayward?" Hart pondered aloud, sensing a new lead emerging.

"I've heard whispers about him," Clara replied, her brow furrowing. "He was known for his aggressive business tactics."

"Perhaps he had something to gain from Edward's downfall," Hart suggested. "We need to find out where he is."

Hours later, Hart and Clara found themselves at a dingy pub on the outskirts of town, the kind of place where secrets thrived amidst the shadows. As they entered, the air was thick with smoke and murmurs, patrons deep in their own worlds.

"Victor Hayward," Hart called, scanning the room. "I'm looking for Victor Hayward."

A man in the corner raised his head, his expression a mix of indifference and curiosity. "What do you want?"

Hart approached, Clara close behind him. "We need to talk."

"About what?" Victor asked, his tone dismissive.

"About Edward St. Clair," Hart replied. "I hear you had dealings with him."

Victor leaned back in his chair, a smirk playing at the corners of his lips. "And what's it to you?"

"His death," Hart stated bluntly. "Did you have a motive?"

Victor's eyes narrowed, and he chuckled softly. "Motive? Edward was a fool. But I had no reason to harm him."

"Then why did you reach out to him?" Clara pressed, her voice firm. "There were financial dealings at play."

"I reached out because I wanted what was owed to me," Victor snapped, his voice rising. "Edward had made promises. He was a man of his word... until he wasn't."

"Promises can be broken," Hart said, gauging Victor's reaction. "But breaking a promise doesn't lead to murder."

"Maybe not," Victor replied, his voice low. "But desperation can lead to poor choices."

As they left the pub, Hart couldn't shake the feeling that Victor was hiding something. "We need to find out more about his relationship with Edward. It could provide the final pieces of the puzzle."

Days turned into nights as they continued to piece together the intricate web of deceit, lies, and half-truths. Each revelation pushed them closer to the heart of darkness, and the tension within Millford Manor escalated.

As they prepared for the final confrontation, Hart sensed that the family was on the brink of collapse. Unspoken truths had become tangible, and the air was electric with anticipation.

On the night of their final meeting, they gathered in the drawing room, the atmosphere tense. Lady Agatha stood at the head of the table, her expression resolute.

"We cannot let fear divide us any longer," she declared, her voice steady. "We must confront the truth."

Hart nodded, his heart racing. "The truth is this: Edward's death was no accident. It was a carefully orchestrated event, driven by jealousy and desperation."

"What do you mean?" Margaret gasped, her face pale.

"I mean that each of you had a motive," Hart stated, his gaze sweeping the room. "The rivalry, the secrets, and the hidden truths intertwined to create a dangerous environment. But the person behind it all is someone you least suspect."

"Who?" Lady Agatha demanded, her voice firm.

"Clara," Hart said, his voice unwavering. "You loved Edward, but you feared losing him to a world that would consume him. You knew of the dangers he faced, and in your desperation to protect him, you pushed him toward the very shadows he sought to escape."

Gasps filled the room, the air thick with disbelief. Clara's eyes widened, her voice trembling. "That's not true! I would never!"

"But you did," Hart countered. "You wanted to keep him safe, and in doing so, you inadvertently drove him into danger."

Lady Agatha shook her head, tears streaming down her face. "No! This cannot be true!"

"Your family secrets are a labyrinth, each twist leading to darker corners," Hart continued. "You must face the truth, or risk losing everything."

As the tension reached a boiling point, Clara's expression shifted from shock to despair. "I never wanted this! I loved him too much to let him go!"

"Love can be a double-edged sword," Hart murmured. "And in this case, it cut deep."

The storm outside raged on, the winds howling like the anguished cries of the past. In that moment, the truth hung heavily in the air, waiting to be embraced. Secrets exposed, relationships shattered, and the echoes of betrayal reverberated through the halls of Millford Manor.

But as the family faced the darkest chapter of their lives, they stood on the brink of a new beginning—a chance to rebuild, to confront their fears, and to emerge from the shadows of the past. Only then would they find solace and healing in the aftermath of the clockwork murders that had forever changed their lives.

2. The Man in the Shadows

UNDER THE PALLID GLOW of the crescent moon, the shadows stretched long and thin across the cobblestone streets of Ashford. The night was still, save for the occasional rustle of leaves and the distant hoot of an owl. It was the perfect backdrop for secrets to unfold, a fitting stage for the events that were about to transpire.

Detective Eliza Hart stood outside the dilapidated manor, the crumbling walls of Ravenswood looming over her like a sentient being. This place had a reputation, whispered about in hushed tones by the locals. They spoke of the clockmaker who had vanished without a trace, and of the peculiar happenings that followed. A sense of foreboding wrapped around her, yet she couldn't help but feel a thrill of excitement. This was a case that promised not only intrigue but perhaps a glimpse into the darker corners of human nature.

As she adjusted her collar against the night's chill, Eliza recalled the day she had received the enigmatic letter that led her to this forsaken abode. The handwriting was elegant yet rushed, conveying an urgency that set her instincts ablaze. "The truth lies hidden, and the clock is ticking," it had read. It ended with an ominous postscript: "Beware the man in the shadows."

With a steadying breath, she pushed open the creaking gate and stepped into the overgrown garden. Weeds crawled like vines, reclaiming the space that had once flourished with life. The air was thick with the scent of damp earth and something else—something metallic, like rusted gears in a forgotten machine.

As she approached the entrance, the large oak door swung open with a groan, revealing a dimly lit foyer. Dust motes danced in the beams of moonlight filtering through the cracked windows. The interior was adorned with remnants of a grander time: faded portraits of stern-faced ancestors stared down at her, their eyes seemingly following her every move. She felt an unsettling chill creep up her spine as she entered.

"Detective Hart," a voice broke the silence, smooth yet laced with an undercurrent of tension.

Eliza turned sharply to see a figure emerging from the shadows near the staircase. He was tall, clad in a dark overcoat that obscured his frame, and his face was partially hidden beneath the brim of a felt hat.

"Who are you?" she demanded, her heart racing.

The figure chuckled softly, the sound echoing in the vast emptiness of the manor. "Names are a triviality, don't you think? What matters is why you are here."

Eliza's instincts flared. She recognized the danger that dripped from his words. "I'm investigating the recent murders linked to this place," she replied cautiously. "You know more than you're letting on."

He stepped forward, revealing a gaunt face, the sharpness of his features illuminated by the soft light. "And what do you hope to find, Detective? A tidy resolution? Justice for the dead? Or perhaps merely a thrill?"

"I seek the truth," she declared, her resolve hardening. "The clock is ticking, and I intend to uncover it, even if it leads to the shadows."

He smiled, a curious mixture of admiration and disdain. "Ah, the truth. Such a slippery concept. Tell me, do you believe that those who dwell in the shadows can ever be brought to light?"

Eliza didn't flinch. "I believe that every shadow has its source. I will find that source, and when I do, the truth will emerge."

He regarded her for a moment, his eyes narrowing as if assessing her worth. "Then you are braver than most. But heed my warning: the deeper you delve, the darker it becomes. The man in the shadows is not to be trifled with."

"Who is he?" she pressed, refusing to be intimidated.

"An enigma, a specter of this town's dark history. Many have tried to uncover his identity, and all have failed." He took a step back, retreating into the darkness. "But you, Detective, you might just succeed. Or perhaps you will join the others who vanished into the night."

With that, he melted away into the shadows, leaving Eliza alone in the vast emptiness of Ravenswood. She felt a mix of anger and frustration; she had come too far to turn back now.

Determined to uncover the truth, she began her investigation in earnest. She searched the manor from top to bottom, rifling through old furniture draped in sheets, examining every crevice and corner for clues. The echoes of her footsteps reverberated off the walls, filling the silence with the weight of her resolve.

As she moved deeper into the heart of the manor, she stumbled upon a hidden study, its door almost concealed behind an ornate bookshelf. Inside, the air was thick with dust, and the scent of old paper filled her nostrils. Eliza's eyes fell upon a massive oak desk littered with papers and mechanical parts. It was here that the clockmaker had toiled before his disappearance.

She carefully sifted through the documents, most of which were technical drawings of intricate clock mechanisms. Among them, one sketch stood out—a design for a unique clock that appeared to incorporate elements of a music box. Beneath it, an inscription read: "To create time is to possess it."

Eliza felt a shiver run down her spine. Was this clock the key to unlocking the mystery? She knew she had to find out more about the clockmaker's final creation.

As she left the study, she noticed a glimmer on the floor. Bending down, she discovered a small brass key, intricately designed. It was heavy in her palm, the cool metal comforting against her skin. But what did it unlock?

Just then, a loud thud echoed from the upper floors, startling her. Heart racing, she crept back towards the staircase, the shadows seeming to swallow her whole. She listened intently, straining to hear any sound above.

There it was again—footsteps, deliberate and slow, as if someone was testing the creaking boards. Eliza's instincts kicked in, and she stealthily ascended the staircase, clutching the brass key tightly.

At the top, she paused, scanning the dim corridor lined with closed doors. The footsteps had ceased, and an unsettling silence enveloped her. She approached the first door on her right and placed her ear against it, but heard nothing. The next door was slightly ajar, and a sliver of light peeked through.

Taking a deep breath, she pushed the door open and stepped inside. The room was empty, save for a single window draped with heavy curtains. The air felt thick, charged with anticipation. Eliza closed the door behind her and turned to explore the space, her gaze drawn to the large antique wardrobe against the wall.

As she approached, the wood creaked softly under her weight. Curious, she opened the doors and peered inside, only to find it filled with moth-eaten garments. A flash of movement caught her eye in the corner of the room.

Before she could react, the man from the shadows emerged from behind the door, a smug smile on his lips. "You're tenacious, Detective, I'll give you that," he said, stepping forward. "But your curiosity may cost you more than you bargained for."

"What do you want?" Eliza demanded, her heart pounding.

"Only to help you," he replied, his tone disarmingly smooth. "You are chasing ghosts in a house of horrors, and I can guide you through it. You need to understand the man in the shadows before it's too late."

Eliza narrowed her eyes, skepticism flooding her mind. "And why should I trust you?"

"Because I know things, things that could save your life. The clock is ticking, and soon the truth will not be the only thing that will surface." He leaned closer, his voice dropping to a whisper. "The clockmaker's final creation is not merely a machine—it is a weapon."

"Against whom?" she asked, feeling a chill run through her.

"Against the darkness that has consumed this town for far too long. Join me, and we can uncover the truth together."

Eliza hesitated. His words were both tempting and terrifying. She knew she was treading dangerous waters, but her instincts urged her to push forward.

"Fine," she said, meeting his gaze with determination. "But know this: I'm not afraid of the shadows."

With a satisfied grin, he extended his hand. "Then let us begin our descent into the depths of this mystery. We shall find the clockmaker, unveil the man in the shadows, and perhaps, finally bring justice to the victims of Ravenswood."

As Eliza took his hand, a sense of trepidation settled in her gut. But she was committed now. Together, they would navigate the labyrinth of secrets and lies that lay ahead, each tick of the clock reminding them that time was of the essence.

As they left the room, the weight of their pact lingered in the air, a promise forged in uncertainty. The man in the shadows had revealed himself, but Eliza was determined to uncover his true intentions. In the twisted tapestry of Ravenswood's history, every thread was connected, and every secret whispered of betrayal.

Outside, the night deepened, wrapping the manor in its embrace. With every step they took, the darkness threatened to swallow them whole, yet Eliza's resolve burned brighter than ever. The clock was ticking, and the truth awaited, shrouded in shadows.

Thus began their journey, one filled with danger, deception, and the promise of revelation. The man in the shadows would not easily yield his secrets, but Eliza Hart was ready to confront whatever horrors lay ahead. The game was
afoot, and time was running out.

3. The Broken Clock

IN THE SMALL, PICTURESQUE village of Ashbourne, where the streets twisted and turned like a well-worn tapestry, time seemed to have an almost magical hold over its residents. Here, in the heart of the village, stood a quaint clockmaker's shop, its wooden sign creaking gently in the breeze. "Harrison's Timepieces" it read, a name synonymous with quality and craftsmanship, revered by the townsfolk. The soft chime of clocks echoed through the air, each tick-tock a reminder of the delicate nature of time itself.

Old Samuel Harrison, the clockmaker, was a fixture of the village, much like the ancient oak tree that graced the town square. He had spent decades meticulously crafting and repairing clocks, filling the air with the soothing rhythm of gears meshing and pendulums swinging. But today, something felt different.

As Samuel adjusted a particularly intricate pocket watch, his brow furrowed in concentration. He had been feeling unwell for the past few days, an unfamiliar heaviness settling in his bones. His hands trembled slightly as he delicately polished the watch face, a movement he had performed countless times before.

"Mr. Harrison," called a voice from the door, snapping him from his reverie. It was Eleanor Fogg, a lively young woman who frequented the shop, eager to learn the art of clockmaking. Her wide brown eyes sparkled with enthusiasm, and her chestnut hair danced around her shoulders as she entered the shop, brushing off the chill of the autumn air.

"Ah, Eleanor!" Samuel smiled, though it didn't quite reach his eyes. "What brings you here today?"

"I was hoping to help you with that grandfather clock you mentioned," she replied, her voice bubbling with energy. "I've been thinking about how to restore it to its former glory."

Samuel's heart warmed at her enthusiasm. "It's a beautiful piece, indeed. But I must confess, I'm not at my best today."

Eleanor frowned, concern etching her features. "You really should take care of yourself, Mr. Harrison. You've worked too hard. Let me help you."

As they began their work, the sun dipped lower in the sky, casting a golden glow through the shop window. Samuel's gaze drifted to the wall clock, its hands frozen at precisely three-thirty. It had been that way for weeks, a testament to the mysteries of time.

"What's the story behind that clock?" Eleanor asked, her curiosity piqued as she followed his gaze.

Samuel hesitated. "It belonged to my late wife, Margaret. She loved that clock more than anything. When she passed, I could never bring myself to fix it."

Eleanor's heart sank. She had often heard Samuel speak of Margaret with such fondness, but the pain in his voice was palpable. "Perhaps it's time to give it another chance?"

A heavy silence filled the room as Samuel considered her words. Could he face the memories associated with that clock?

As the days turned into weeks, Samuel found solace in Eleanor's company. Her laughter echoed through the shop, filling the void left by Margaret's absence. Together, they worked tirelessly, restoring the grandfather clock, dismantling its intricate gears, and polishing the wooden casing.

Yet, as they toiled, a series of strange events began to unfold in the village. Clocks started to malfunction inexplicably, their hands spinning wildly as if possessed by some unseen force. Townsfolk whispered about the eerie occurrences, attributing them to bad luck or perhaps the spirits of the long-dead clockmakers.

One evening, as the sun set behind the hills, painting the sky in hues of orange and purple, Eleanor entered the shop to find Samuel deep in thought, his brow furrowed as he studied the grandfather clock.

"Is something wrong?" she asked, her voice barely above a whisper.

He sighed, running a hand through his thinning hair. "I've noticed some strange things happening with the clocks around town. It's as if they're... alive."

"Alive?" Eleanor echoed, intrigued.

"Yes. Last night, I heard a clock chime at midnight when it wasn't supposed to. And earlier today, I found a pocket watch that had stopped at precisely the same moment."

Eleanor's eyes widened in disbelief. "That's odd. Do you think it's connected to the broken clock?"

Samuel considered her question, feeling a chill run down his spine. "Perhaps. The past has a way of creeping into the present. Maybe it's trying to tell us something."

Determined to uncover the truth, Eleanor proposed a plan. "Let's investigate the other clocks in town. There must be a pattern."

With a shared sense of purpose, they set out the next morning, visiting homes and businesses, their hearts racing with anticipation. Each clock they examined told a different story, yet they all shared one common thread: they were all broken or malfunctioning in peculiar ways.

As they gathered information, an unsettling realization dawned on them: every clock that had stopped or malfunctioned was linked to a tragedy that had befallen its owner. The baker's clock had stopped the day his wife left him; the innkeeper's clock had frozen on the anniversary of his son's death.

"It's as if the clocks are marking moments of grief," Eleanor murmured, her voice filled with awe.

Samuel nodded gravely. "Time can be a cruel reminder of what we've lost."

Returning to the shop, the air was thick with anticipation. They were on the verge of unraveling a mystery that had entwined the villagers for years.

Suddenly, a loud crash shattered the silence. They rushed to the source of the noise, only to find the grandfather clock had toppled over, its wooden frame splintered and broken.

"Samuel!" Eleanor gasped, her hands trembling as she surveyed the damage. "What happened?"

He stared at the fallen clock in shock. "I don't know! It was standing just fine!"

As they assessed the wreckage, they discovered something remarkable. Amidst the shattered wood and scattered gears lay a small, ornate key, gleaming in the dim light.

"What's this?" Eleanor picked it up, her eyes wide with wonder.

"I've never seen that before," Samuel admitted, his curiosity piqued. "It must have been hidden inside the clock."

Eleanor turned the key over in her hands, feeling the weight of its history. "Do you think it unlocks something?"

Samuel's eyes sparkled with excitement. "There's an old clock tower at the edge of the village. It hasn't worked in years, but I've always suspected there was something special about it."

With renewed determination, they set off towards the clock tower, their hearts pounding with anticipation. The tower loomed before them, its stone façade weathered by time.

Inside, they found an array of dusty gears and tarnished clock faces, remnants of a bygone era. As Samuel inserted the key into an ornate lock hidden beneath a layer of dust, the gears creaked to life, resonating with a deep, echoing sound.

With a gentle turn of the key, the clock began to chime, a rich melody filling the air as the hands moved for the first time in years.

"It's beautiful!" Eleanor exclaimed, her eyes shining with awe.

As the clock struck midnight, a series of images flashed through Samuel's mind—memories long buried, intertwined with the village's history. Each chime seemed to reveal a secret, a truth hidden within the echoes of time.

Suddenly, the chimes ceased, and a soft whisper filled the air. "Restore what was broken."

Eleanor looked at Samuel, bewildered. "Did you hear that?"

He nodded, a deep sense of understanding washing over him. "The clocks are urging us to remember, to heal the wounds of the past."

Returning to the village, they shared their discoveries with the townsfolk. Inspired by Samuel's stories and Eleanor's enthusiasm, the villagers began to restore their clocks, each repair symbolizing a step towards healing.

In the following weeks, laughter filled the air as families came together to celebrate the memories of their loved ones, allowing time to weave its magic once more.

Samuel, too, found solace in the process. The grandfather clock, though damaged, became a symbol of hope—a reminder that even broken things could be mended. With Eleanor's guidance, he began to heal the wounds left by Margaret's passing, embracing the memories without letting them consume him.

One crisp morning, as autumn leaves danced in the wind, Samuel stood in his shop, watching the townsfolk bustling about. The sound of ticking clocks filled the air, a melody of life that resonated with the essence of time.

Eleanor entered, a bright smile illuminating her face. "The village is alive again, isn't it?"

Samuel nodded, his heart swelling with gratitude. "Indeed. We've learned to cherish both the past and the present."

As they resumed their work on the grandfather clock, they felt a sense of purpose guiding them. The broken clock had led them on a journey of discovery, reminding them that time, while relentless, could also be a source of healing and renewal.

And so, in the small village of Ashbourne, time continued to flow, each tick echoing the stories of love, loss, and the enduring power of memories—a testament to the resilience of the human spirit.

With every chime of the restored clock, Samuel and Eleanor felt a connection to the past, an acknowledgment of the beauty that could arise from the broken pieces. As they stood side by side, the future felt brighter, promising new beginnings forged from the lessons learned in the hands of time.

4. A Fight for Life

AS THE PALE MORNING light crept through the curtains of the dimly lit room, a sense of foreboding hung in the air. The silence was thick, almost palpable, broken only by the distant chirping of birds outside. It was a day that promised tension, a day when shadows of the past would claw their way into the present.

Detective Samuel Hart sat at the edge of the small, rickety table, his fingers tracing the outline of an ancient clock that had been left behind in the room. The ticking of the clock seemed to mock him, a rhythmic reminder that time was not on his side. He glanced at the wall, adorned with sepia-toned photographs of a time long gone—smiling faces frozen in a moment of happiness, now tainted by the sorrow that had since unfolded.

Last night's revelations weighed heavily on his mind. The discovery of the second body had sent shockwaves through the small town of Ashbourne. The first victim, Geraldine Parker, had been found lifeless in her study, surrounded by an array of intricately designed clocks, each more elaborate than the last. But it was the second body—David McKinley, the town's reclusive clockmaker—that had turned the investigation on its head.

Both had been connected to the enigmatic clockmaker, Leonard Ashworth, whose dark past was slowly unfurling before him. Hart recalled the look of fear in Leonard's eyes as they had spoken the previous evening. It was a fear that hinted at something much deeper than mere coincidence.

Suddenly, the sound of footsteps echoed in the corridor outside, jolting Hart from his reverie. The door creaked open, revealing Leonard, his face pale and drawn. He stepped inside, closing the door behind him as if to shut out the world beyond.

"Detective Hart," he began, his voice trembling. "I don't know how much longer I can endure this. The clock... it's cursed!"

Hart raised an eyebrow, intrigued yet skeptical. "Cursed? Do you truly believe that?"

Leonard nodded vigorously, his eyes wide with desperation. "I've worked with clocks all my life, yet I've never encountered anything like it. The designs... they hold secrets, terrible secrets! Those who possess them meet untimely ends."

"You believe that's what happened to Geraldine and David?" Hart pressed, leaning forward in his chair.

Leonard hesitated, his gaze dropping to the floor. "Geraldine... she was the last to acquire one of my special clocks. It was beautiful, intricate, but I warned her not to take it. I feared its power."

Hart felt a chill run down his spine. "What power?"

"The power to manipulate time," Leonard whispered. "I thought it was just a myth—a tale spun by the old masters—but

I've seen it for myself. When the clock strikes, time shifts. It reveals truths, but it also exacts a price."

The detective was silent for a moment, contemplating the implications of Leonard's words. "And what do you propose we do now?"

"We must find the clock," Leonard replied, his eyes burning with intensity. "Before it claims another victim."

A shiver coursed through Hart. Time was indeed a relentless force, and it was clear that the clock was more than just a mechanism; it was a harbinger of doom.

The two men stepped out into the streets of Ashbourne, the morning sun casting long shadows across the cobblestones. The town seemed eerily quiet, as if holding its breath in anticipation of the unfolding drama.

Their first stop was Geraldine's house, now draped in a somber shroud of police tape. Hart led the way, his instincts sharp as he approached the entrance. Inside, the atmosphere was thick with memories and secrets. Dust motes danced in the shafts of light that broke through the windows, illuminating the stillness.

Leonard moved cautiously through the house, his fingers brushing against the walls, as if searching for something hidden. "The clock must be here somewhere," he murmured.

Hart's eyes roamed the room, taking in the chaos of books scattered on the floor, the overturned chair, and the ominous presence of the remaining clocks—each one seemingly ticking in synchrony.

"Look!" Leonard suddenly exclaimed, pointing to a dusty shelf in the corner. There, amongst the clutter, stood an elegant clock, its face intricately adorned with symbols and gears that gleamed even in the dim light.

As Hart approached the clock, he felt a strange sensation wash over him, a tingling at the back of his neck. It was as if the clock were alive, pulsating with an energy all its own.

"Is this it?" Hart asked, his voice barely a whisper.

Leonard nodded gravely. "Yes, that's the one. I can feel it."

The detective reached out, hesitating for a moment before lifting the clock from its perch. It felt heavier than it looked, as if it carried the weight of the souls it had claimed. He turned it over, inspecting the base, where intricate engravings told stories long forgotten.

"What do we do now?" Hart inquired, feeling a mixture of curiosity and dread.

"We must destroy it," Leonard said with finality. "Before it can do any more harm."

As the two men left Geraldine's house, a sense of urgency propelled them forward. They made their way to Leonard's workshop, a quaint building tucked away at the edge of town. Inside, the walls were lined with tools and machinery, a veritable sanctuary for clockmakers.

Leonard began rummaging through drawers, searching for the tools he needed. "We can dismantle it here," he explained. "In a controlled environment."

But just as Leonard had found what he was looking for, a loud crash echoed outside, followed by a commotion. Hart and Leonard exchanged worried glances before rushing outside.

What they saw sent a chill down their spines. A crowd had gathered around a figure lying motionless on the ground, surrounded by a pool of crimson.

"It's Arthur," someone whispered, pointing to the fallen man. "The postmaster!"

Hart's heart raced as he pushed through the throng, kneeling beside the body. Arthur's eyes were wide open, frozen in terror.

The detective quickly examined the scene, noting the splintered remains of a nearby clock tower that had toppled over during the commotion.

"Was he killed by the clock?" Leonard asked, horror written across his face.

"No, I don't believe so," Hart replied, his mind racing. "This looks deliberate."

As the paramedics arrived, Hart's instincts kicked into high gear. This wasn't just a town plagued by cursed clocks; it was a town unraveling at the seams. The death of Arthur seemed like a clear message—one that transcended the mysteries of time.

"Who would want to silence him?" Hart pondered aloud.

"I don't know," Leonard replied, his brow furrowed. "But I fear we're running out of time."

The sun hung low in the sky as Hart and Leonard returned to the workshop, the weight of impending doom pressing heavily on their shoulders. They worked quickly, determined to dismantle the clock before it could claim another victim.

As Leonard deftly removed the screws, the clock's gears began to whir ominously. Hart watched, transfixed, as the internal mechanisms revealed a labyrinth of complexities, each tick resonating like a heartbeat.

Suddenly, the workshop door burst open, and a figure stumbled in, breathless and pale. It was Eliza, a local journalist known for her tenacity and keen insights.

"Detective! You must come quickly!" she gasped. "There's been another murder!"

Hart's heart sank as he exchanged a glance with Leonard. Time was slipping through their fingers like sand, and the clock was still ticking.

Without a word, they followed Eliza out into the fading light, the urgency of the situation propelling them forward. As they reached the town square, the sight that greeted them was one of utter chaos.

The crowd had gathered around the fountain, where the lifeless body of a young woman lay, draped in a white dress that now appeared stained with blood.

"Who is she?" Hart asked, his voice barely audible over the cacophony.

"Margaret," someone whispered, their voice trembling. "She was just married last week."

Hart's heart sank deeper. This was no longer just a string of murders; it was a calculated campaign of terror, one that threatened to consume the entire town.

As the sun dipped below the horizon, casting long shadows across the square, Hart felt a surge of determination. They had to stop this madness before it was too late.

With Leonard and Eliza by his side, he returned to the workshop, where the dismantled clock lay in pieces. The gears glimmered ominously in the dim light, and Hart felt an inexplicable connection to the mechanism.

"We must find out who is behind this," he stated firmly, addressing both Leonard and Eliza. "And we must do it quickly."

Leonard nodded, his eyes filled with a mixture of fear and resolve. "I will do everything I can to help," he promised.

As the night wore on, the three of them delved deeper into the mystery, piecing together clues that had begun to surface. They learned of hidden relationships, clandestine meetings, and betrayals that ran deeper than anyone had anticipated.

With each revelation, the atmosphere grew heavier, charged with an urgency that crackled like electricity in the air. The ticking of time became a haunting reminder of the lives that hung in the balance, and they knew they had to race against it.

Days turned into a blur as they pursued leads, interrogated suspects, and sought the truth that lay hidden beneath layers of deception. The townsfolk whispered about the clock

, about the power it held, and Hart couldn't shake the feeling that they were merely pawns in a game far greater than they could comprehend.

But just when they thought they were making progress, a twist sent them spiraling back into uncertainty. A shadowy figure had been watching their every move, slipping through the cracks like a ghost. Hart and his team found themselves on the precipice of a revelation that would change everything they thought they knew.

The final confrontation loomed closer, the stakes higher than ever. With time slipping away, Hart understood that they would have to face not only the murderer but the very essence of what it meant to manipulate time itself.

As they gathered one last time in Leonard's workshop, the clock lay in pieces before them, a haunting reminder of the chaos it had wrought. They were running out of time, and the clock had become a ticking time bomb, ready to explode at any moment.

"This ends now," Hart declared, steeling himself for the inevitable showdown. "We will uncover the truth, and we will stop this once and for all."

With resolve in their hearts, they stepped into the shadows of the night, determined to fight for life, for justice, and for the souls that had been lost. The clock's ticking echoed in their minds, a relentless reminder that the hour of reckoning was at hand.

And as they moved forward, ready to confront the darkness that loomed ahead, they knew that the battle for time—and for their lives—had only just begun.

5. The Hidden Passage

THE FLICKERING GAS lamps cast a dim glow in the narrow corridor of Ashcombe Manor, their light wavering as a soft breeze whispered through the old stones. As evening descended, the manor, with its grand architecture and lingering scents of aged wood and leather, held an air of timeless elegance and a hint of foreboding. Detective Eliza Hart moved cautiously, her footsteps muffled against the richly woven carpet, a stark contrast to the echoing silence that enveloped her.

She had come to Ashcombe at the behest of Lady Margaret Pendleton, the manor's current occupant and widow of the late Lord Pendleton, who had recently met an untimely demise under suspicious circumstances. Eliza had always been drawn to the curious case, intrigued by the enigmatic nature of both the manor and its residents. There were whispers in the village, tales of secrets buried within the walls, and Lady Pendleton had hinted at a concealed passage—an ancient relic of the manor's past, long forgotten by its inhabitants.

As she approached the library, Eliza's keen eye caught sight of an ornate bookshelf, its wood polished to a shine. The books, lined up in perfect order, seemed to guard the mysteries that lay beyond. She had spent countless hours poring over the dusty volumes of Ashcombe's archives, searching for clues that might unravel the enigma of Lord Pendleton's death. Rumors suggested he had been involved in illicit dealings, entangled with individuals whose motives were as murky as the shadows that danced upon the walls.

With a practiced hand, Eliza brushed her fingers along the spines of the leather-bound tomes, feeling the weight of history beneath her touch. A particular volume caught her attention: a thick, leather-bound book titled The History of Ashcombe. Curiosity piqued, she pulled it from the shelf. To her surprise, the entire shelf shuddered slightly, and she felt a small catch release.

The wall behind the bookshelf groaned as it slowly shifted, revealing a narrow passage that had been concealed for decades.

Her heart raced with anticipation as she stepped into the darkness of the hidden passage, the air cool and damp against her skin. The sound of her footsteps echoed ominously in the confined space, creating an eerie symphony of solitude. The passage was dimly lit by occasional shafts of light filtering through cracks in the stone, casting haunting shadows that seemed to reach out for her.

Eliza advanced cautiously, her senses heightened. She was acutely aware that she was stepping into the unknown, into the depths of Ashcombe's secrets. What she might find here could unravel the fabric of the case, shedding light on the dark corners of Lord Pendleton's life that had led to his untimely death.

As she progressed deeper into the passage, she found remnants of the past: old wooden beams overhead, cobwebs adorning the corners like ghostly lace, and the scent of damp earth filling the air. The passage twisted and turned, and Eliza felt as though she was wandering through time, moving between the present and a long-forgotten era. She wondered what had compelled the original architects of Ashcombe to create such a space. Was it merely for concealment, or did it serve a darker purpose?

Suddenly, a glimmer caught her eye. She paused, squinting into the shadows. In the flickering light, she discerned the outline of an old trunk, its leather cracked and worn with age. Heart racing, she knelt beside it, carefully lifting the lid. Inside lay a trove of letters, each tied with a faded ribbon, their edges yellowed with age. They bore the initials of Lord Pendleton, and a sense of foreboding washed over her.

With trembling hands, Eliza began to sift through the letters, her heart racing as the contents revealed the intricate web of relationships surrounding Lord Pendleton. There were missives from various correspondents—some familiar, others obscure—discussing matters of business and personal affairs, hints of scandal and intrigue woven into the fabric of each message. The most striking was a letter dated just days before his death, expressing fear for his life, a shadow lurking just out of sight.

"I cannot trust anyone. The walls have ears, and even those closest to me may harbor ill intentions," the letter read, the ink smudged as if the writer had hurriedly penned the words in a fit of panic. Eliza felt a chill run down her spine. Who could he have been referring to? As she continued to read, the name Lydia surfaced frequently, and Eliza's mind raced—could this be the Lydia she had encountered during her investigation, the housekeeper with a reputation for meddling?

The sound of footsteps reverberated through the passage, snapping Eliza back to reality. Panic surged through her. She quickly tucked the letters back into the trunk and closed it silently. The last thing she needed was to be discovered here, in a place that was meant to remain shrouded in secrecy. She pressed her back against the cool stone wall, holding her breath as she strained to hear the approaching footsteps.

They stopped just outside the entrance to the passage, the faint glow of a lantern illuminating the doorway. A familiar voice echoed through the darkness—Lady Margaret Pendleton.

"Eliza, are you in there?" her voice called, a hint of urgency lacing her tone.

Eliza hesitated but knew she had to respond. "Yes, Lady Margaret. I've discovered something... something important."

The lantern light flickered as Lady Margaret stepped into the passage, her expression a mixture of relief and concern. "I was afraid you'd gotten lost. This place can be disorienting."

Eliza nodded, brushing away the dust that clung to her dress. "It's more than that, my lady. I found a trunk filled with letters... they belong to your late husband."

The color drained from Lady Margaret's face as she took a step closer, her eyes widening in fear. "Letters? What did they say?"

Eliza hesitated for a moment, weighing the impact of her words. "They speak of fear, of betrayal, and a name that recurs: Lydia."

A flicker of recognition crossed Lady Margaret's features, and she took a deep breath, steadying herself against the wall. "Lydia has been with us for years. I always trusted her, but now..." Her voice trailed off, uncertainty clouding her eyes.

Eliza sensed the tension between them, the weight of unspoken truths lingering in the air. "We need to confront her, my lady. There are pieces of this puzzle that don't fit, and I believe Lydia holds the key."

With renewed purpose, Eliza led Lady Margaret out of the hidden passage and back into the library. As they stepped into the light, the air felt charged, thick with unspoken fears and long-buried secrets. They needed to gather the others—Lydia, the housekeeper, and the rest of the staff—to confront the growing shadows that loomed over Ashcombe Manor.

As they prepared to call for Lydia, Eliza couldn't shake the feeling that they were venturing deeper into a web of deception, one that could ensnare them if they weren't careful. But she knew one thing for certain: the hidden passage had revealed more than just dusty relics of the past; it had unmasked the very essence of the mystery that enveloped Lord Pendleton's death.

Together, they stepped into the uncertain light of truth, knowing that the darkness had not yet relinquished its hold over Ashcombe Manor. The secrets of the hidden passage were but the first step in a labyrinthine journey that would lead them closer to the heart of the mystery—and perhaps even to danger itself.

Little did they know that Lydia had already begun to unravel the threads they thought they had secured. As they gathered the courage to confront her, the very walls of Ashcombe seemed to hold their breath, waiting for the inevitable clash that would expose not only the murderer but the hidden truths that had long been buried within its depths.

• • • •

AS THE DAY FADED INTO dusk, and the shadows lengthened, Eliza felt a sense of foreboding settle upon her. Time was slipping away, and with it, the chance to unravel the sinister plot that had unfolded within the hallowed halls of Ashcombe Manor. The hidden passage had opened a door, but now it was up to her to ensure that it did not close again before the truth was revealed.

6. Time Slips Away

AS THE CLOCK STRUCK eleven in the quaint little town of Elderswood, a chill crept into the night air, wrapping around the cobbled streets like a shroud. The faint, rhythmic ticking of the town's old clock tower echoed, mingling with the rustling leaves that danced gently in the wind. In the distance, the dimly lit windows of The Clock and Dagger, a local tavern, flickered invitingly, promising warmth and companionship.

Inside, the atmosphere was one of joviality. Laughter echoed off the wooden beams, and the scent of roasted lamb and fresh-baked bread filled the air. At a corner table sat Inspector Harold Finch, a man of middle years with a penchant for tweed jackets and a nose that twitched like a rabbit's when he was deep in thought. Across from him sat Mrs. Agatha Wilkins, the town's well-regarded historian, her spectacles perched precariously on the bridge of her nose.

"Have you ever noticed how time has a peculiar way of slipping away, Inspector?" Agatha mused, swirling the remnants of her wine in the glass, her eyes distant. "It's as if it flows like a stream, smooth and continuous, until suddenly, you find yourself marooned on a rocky shore of memories."

Harold looked at her, intrigued. "Indeed, Mrs. Wilkins. Time often has a way of eluding us, doesn't it? One moment you're young and full of promise, and before you know it, the sands have slipped through your fingers."

She smiled wistfully, then continued, "It is in those slips of time that secrets often lie buried. Like the town's old clock tower. Have you ever wondered about its history? It has stood there, ticking away, a silent witness to the lives and dramas that unfold beneath its gaze."

The inspector raised an eyebrow. "I cannot say I have given it much thought. But, as you suggest, perhaps there are stories hidden in its gears."

Just as Mrs. Wilkins was about to respond, a loud crash resonated through the tavern, drawing the attention of the patrons. The heavy oak door swung open, and in stumbled Edgar Lacey, the town's clockmaker, his face pale and eyes wide with panic.

"Inspector! You must come at once!" he gasped, breathless. "There's been a... a tragedy at the workshop! Someone has died!"

Harold's heart raced, and he rose from his seat, signaling for Agatha to follow. "Lead the way, Mr. Lacey."

They hurried through the streets, the chill of the night now a biting wind that whipped around them. Edgar spoke rapidly, detailing the scene. "I was working late on a new mechanism, you see. I heard a noise, and when I went to check... I found Henry Green, the local historian, sprawled on the floor, his body cold and lifeless, with the clock on the wall stopped at exactly ten twenty-five."

Arriving at the workshop, they were met with an unsettling sight. The room was filled with the scent of oil and wood shavings, the walls lined with clocks of all shapes and sizes. But it was the body of Henry Green that dominated the scene, lying ominously amidst the scattered gears and pendulums.

Inspector Finch knelt beside the body, examining the surroundings carefully. Henry was well-known in Elderswood for his extensive knowledge of local lore and history. His lifeless form was surrounded by an assortment of broken clock parts, yet there was something unusual about the scene.

"Edgar," Finch called out, glancing at the clock that hung prominently on the wall. "What can you tell me about Henry's last visit?"

Edgar swallowed hard. "He came by earlier to discuss some old town records. He was excited about a discovery he'd made regarding the clock tower's origins."

"And you didn't think to mention this before?" Agatha interjected, her voice sharp. "This could be important!"

"I... I was so flustered," Edgar stammered. "I never thought—"

"Thoughtless men rarely do," she snapped, a frown deepening on her brow.

"Inspector," Agatha said suddenly, "look at this." She pointed to the clock that had stopped at ten twenty-five. "If it was stopped at the time of death, it may hold the key to understanding what happened."

Harold nodded, his brow furrowing. "We need to investigate this further. Edgar, do you have any idea who might have wanted to harm Henry?"

"I can't imagine anyone would," Edgar replied, wringing his hands. "He was beloved by all."

"Beloved by all?" Agatha echoed, her tone skeptical. "That's often a façade, is it not? Perhaps we should start by speaking with some of his acquaintances."

As they pieced together the fragments of Henry's last hours, they learned that he had been researching something unusual about the clock tower—an ancient legend that suggested it was built on cursed ground, a place where time itself was said to have folded.

"There's a tale," Agatha began, her voice low and conspiratorial, "about a clockmaker who, centuries ago, attempted to stop time itself. They say he vanished, leaving behind a legacy of misfortune for those who dare to tinker with the natural order."

"An interesting tale," Harold said thoughtfully, "but how does this relate to Henry's death?"

"Perhaps he uncovered something—something someone wanted to keep hidden," she suggested.

As dawn approached, casting a pale light over the workshop, the inspector felt a growing sense of urgency. Each clue they discovered hinted at a deeper mystery, one entwined with the very fabric of Elderswood's history.

The investigation unfolded over the next several days, a tangled web of relationships and secrets among the townsfolk. They interviewed the local baker, who had a rivalry with Henry over the best pastries; the librarian, who seemed to know more about Henry's research than she let on; and even the mayor, whose shady dealings with the clockmaker were beginning to surface.

All the while, the clock tower loomed in the background, its hands moving steadily forward, indifferent to the chaos below. With each tick, the pressure mounted, revealing layers of deceit and betrayal that pulsed just beneath the town's charming exterior.

As the pieces fell into place, Inspector Finch became increasingly aware that time was of the essence. The clues led them to a hidden room beneath the clock tower itself, a place where shadows danced and secrets festered.

In that dimly lit chamber, they discovered Henry's notes scattered about—his frantic scrawls detailed an ongoing investigation into the town's founding families, suggesting that the curse of the clockmaker might be linked to their ancestry. There, amidst the old mechanisms and gears, lay the truth: a hidden ledger that tied the deaths of several townsfolk over the years to a singular family—the Lacey lineage.

"Edgar, your family…" Harold began, shock dawning upon him.

"My family?" Edgar's voice trembled. "But they were never implicated in anything sinister!"

"Not yet," Agatha interjected, "but the evidence is clear. If Henry was close to revealing this truth, then you might have been next on the list."

Panic surged within Edgar as he paced the room. "I had no idea! We were always told our ancestors were upstanding citizens."

"Sometimes the truth is obscured by the very clockwork of history," Harold stated, steely resolve in his eyes. "But we can unravel it—together."

Just as they began to formulate a plan, the room erupted in chaos as a loud crash echoed from above. A figure emerged from the shadows, their face obscured but their intentions clear.

"Leave it alone!" the figure shouted, advancing towards them. "You have no idea what you're meddling with!"

Fear gripped Edgar, but Agatha stood her ground, her voice steady. "And you have no idea what we've uncovered."

The confrontation escalated, the tension palpable as the truth hung like a pendulum in the air. But as the clock struck twelve, time itself seemed to pause, leaving the room suspended in an uncertain balance between revelation and destruction.

"Who are you?" Finch demanded, voice commanding. "What do you know about Henry's death?"

As the figure hesitated, the flickering light of the old gas lamps illuminated their face—a face etched with both familiarity and fear.

"I'm the one who warned him," they confessed, voice trembling. "I tried to stop him from digging too deep... but he wouldn't listen."

Harold's heart raced as recognition dawned. "You're—"

"Lacey," the figure admitted, a haunting sadness in their eyes. "A descendant of the clockmaker. I couldn't let history repeat itself."

With a heavy silence, they all stood at the precipice of understanding. The clock tower, once merely a relic of time, had transformed into a symbol of the dark secrets buried within Elderswood.

Time slipped away as they pieced together the final fragments of the mystery, a revelation unfolding that would forever change the town. Each moment counted, the past and present intertwining like the gears of a clock, driving them toward a conclusion both terrifying and inevitable.

As the sun set, casting long shadows across the workshop, the inspector knew that some secrets, once uncovered, could never be forgotten. The clockwork of life continued to turn, each tick a reminder that time was relentless, and in its wake lay the shadows of the choices made, lives lost, and the haunting echo of a curse that would linger for generations to come.

With the case resolved, Elderswood could begin to heal, but the memories of that fateful night would be etched in the hearts of those who had dared to confront the truth

. Time, after all, had a way of slipping away, but its lessons remained forever.

And so, as the clock tower chimed once more, a new chapter in Elderswood's history began, forever marked by the shadow of the clockmaker's curse.

Chapter 8: Unmasking the Puppet Master

1. Pieces of the Puzzle

The morning sun filtered softly through the grimy windows of Detective Arthur Hart's office, casting a gentle glow over the scattered papers and half-empty coffee cups that cluttered his desk. The air was thick with the scent of stale coffee and the lingering unease that had accompanied him since the first murder was discovered. As he glanced at the clock on the wall—its hands inching ever closer to the hour—his mind raced with the fragments of the case that lay before him.

It had all begun a fortnight ago in the quaint village of Windermere, a place that had once been known for its serene landscapes and tranquil lifestyle. That peace was shattered when Richard Cromwell, the town's beloved clockmaker, was found dead in his workshop, the telltale marks of foul play evident upon his lifeless body. The murder had sent shockwaves through the community, and each new day seemed to bring more questions than answers.

As Hart pondered the gravity of the situation, a sudden knock at the door jolted him from his reverie. It was Inspector Helen Fitzroy, a formidable presence in the local constabulary known for her sharp wit and unwavering determination. She stepped into the office, her expression betraying the weight of the investigation they shared.

"Arthur, we need to talk," she said, her voice steady yet urgent. "There's been another murder."

Hart's heart sank. "Who is it this time?"

"Margaret Lacey," she replied, crossing her arms tightly across her chest as if to shield herself from the grim news. "She was found in her garden, surrounded by the very clocks Richard had crafted. The way she died—it's all too similar to his murder."

Hart's mind raced as he recalled the details of Richard's death. The clockmaker had been discovered sprawled on the floor of his workshop, his life snuffed out just as he had been working on a peculiar timepiece. A clock, its face adorned with intricate gears, now sat atop the mantle in Hart's office, a grim reminder of the mysteries that needed unraveling.

"Margaret was Richard's closest friend, wasn't she?" he asked, the gears of his mind clicking into place. "She stood to inherit his shop, didn't she?"

"Yes, but there's more," Fitzroy continued, her brow furrowing in thought. "Margaret had been acting strangely for weeks before her death. Neighbors reported seeing her talking to herself, pacing around her garden at odd hours. It's as if she was consumed by something—perhaps even the clock itself."

"Did anyone see anything unusual?" Hart inquired, his curiosity piqued.

"Only that she was seen arguing with a man in the village a few nights before her death. A stranger who arrived just after Richard was killed," she explained. "His name is Thomas Wells, and I've spoken to him. He claims he was just passing through, but there's something about him that feels... off."

As they exchanged information, the two detectives began piecing together the events that had unfolded in Windermere. It was as if they were assembling a jigsaw puzzle, with each piece representing a suspect or clue that had emerged since the investigation began.

"There's a pattern forming, isn't there?" Hart murmured, scratching his chin thoughtfully. "Both victims had connections to that clockmaker's shop, and both were taken from us in brutal fashion."

Fitzroy nodded. "It's clear someone has a vendetta against anyone tied to Richard. We must determine what that vendetta stems from, and quickly."

Hart rose from his chair, the determination settling in his gut like a heavy stone. "Let's visit Margaret's garden. There may be something there that connects these murders."

The two detectives made their way to Margaret's home, their footsteps echoing on the cobblestone streets of Windermere. The village was unusually quiet, the inhabitants seemingly paralyzed by fear in the wake of the recent tragedies. As they approached the Lacey residence, Hart couldn't shake the feeling that the answer to the mystery lay hidden among the petals and soil of the garden.

Margaret's garden was a chaotic tapestry of wildflowers and unruly bushes, a stark contrast to the pristine order that Hart expected. The vibrant blooms danced in the gentle breeze, their colors almost too bright against the somber reality of death that loomed over them.

"What a beautiful place," Fitzroy remarked as she surveyed the scene, "yet it feels haunted, doesn't it?"

Hart nodded, stepping carefully around the garden's edge as he approached the spot where Margaret had been found. "Let's look for anything that might have been overlooked."

As they combed through the garden, Hart noticed an odd arrangement of flowers near the base of a large clock that stood sentinel-like in the corner. It was a peculiar sight, as if the clock had been intentionally placed there—its face cracked, its hands forever frozen at a quarter past five.

"Fitzroy," he called, gesturing to the clock. "Come see this."

She joined him, kneeling beside the odd fixture. "What do you make of it?"

"I don't know yet," he replied, inspecting the base of the clock where dirt was freshly disturbed. "It looks like someone has been digging here recently."

Together, they began to unearth the soil, the scent of damp earth filling their nostrils. As they scraped away the dirt, Hart's heart raced at the possibility of what they might find. With each handful, the anticipation grew, and finally, they uncovered a small, metal box—rusted and weathered but unmistakably distinct.

"This could be it," Fitzroy said, her voice barely above a whisper as she brushed off the dirt.

Hart carefully pried the box open, revealing a collection of intricate clock gears, each one carefully arranged and marked with faint notations. "These must belong to Richard's designs," he deduced, "but why were they hidden here?"

"Perhaps they were removed from his workshop after the murder. Someone wanted to keep them out of sight," Fitzroy speculated, her brow furrowing as she examined the contents.

As they sifted through the gears, a small piece of parchment slipped from the box, fluttering to the ground like a fallen leaf. Hart picked it up, his eyes scanning the words hastily scribbled on the page.

"To the one who seeks to understand time, the answer lies in the past—where love and betrayal entwine," he read aloud, his voice laced with intrigue.

"What could it mean?" Fitzroy pondered, her expression thoughtful.

"Love and betrayal," Hart repeated, turning the phrase over in his mind. "This isn't just about clocks or murder; it's deeply personal. We need to find out more about Richard and Margaret's past relationships."

"Agreed," she said, standing up with renewed determination. "Let's speak to those who knew them best. Perhaps the pieces of the puzzle will fall into place."

Their next stop was the local tavern, a rustic establishment known as The Clock and Key. It was the heart of the village, where secrets were exchanged over pints of ale and laughter echoed against the timbered walls.

As they entered, the noise of conversation hushed momentarily, eyes turning toward the two detectives. Hart could feel the tension in the air, the weight of unspoken words that lingered on the lips of the patrons.

"Good evening, Detective Hart," the bartender greeted them, wiping his hands on a rag. "What brings you here?"

"We're looking for information regarding Richard Cromwell and Margaret Lacey," Hart replied, scanning the room for familiar faces. "Any stories or memories you might share could be invaluable."

The bartender frowned, glancing around as if gauging the reactions of the patrons. "Well, Richard was well-liked, but he had his fair share of enemies. And Margaret? She was his devoted friend, but she'd changed in the weeks leading up to her death. Seemed a bit... unhinged, if you know what I mean."

"Unhinged?" Fitzroy asked, leaning forward. "What do you mean?"

"Some said she'd taken to talking to herself. Others thought she was trying to communicate with Richard, even after he was gone. It was odd, I tell you," the bartender said, shaking his head. "Then there was the argument she had with that Wells fella. He's a bit of a drifter, if you ask me. Not much good can come from someone like that."

"Where can we find him?" Hart pressed, eager for more information.

"I saw him last at the old railway station," the bartender replied, nodding toward the door. "But I wouldn't be surprised if he's moved on. Best be careful; he's not the kind of man you want to cross."

With this new lead, Hart and Fitzroy made their way to the railway station, their footsteps echoing against the cobblestones as the sun dipped below the horizon. The air turned cooler, the shadows lengthening as night encroached upon the village.

Upon arriving at the station, they found it dimly lit and nearly deserted, save for a few scattered travelers waiting for trains. Hart approached the station master, a weary man with tired eyes.

"Excuse me, we're looking for Thomas Wells. Has he been here recently?" Hart inquired.

The station master scratched his beard, contemplating. "Wells? Aye, he passed through a few days back. Left on the evening train, but I heard he might be back again soon."

"Do you know where he was headed?" Fitzroy asked, frustration creeping into her voice.

"Not a clue," the man shrugged. "But he mentioned something about heading to London, or so he claimed."

"Great," Hart muttered, running a hand through his hair. "We'll have to stake out the station for his return. He might just hold the key to unraveling this mystery."

As they settled into a nearby café, waiting for the flicker of a train's light in the distance, Hart's thoughts raced with the pieces they had collected thus far. They were mere fragments, hints at a larger truth that lay hidden beneath layers of deceit and betrayal.

Hours passed, and the night grew heavy with expectation. Just as Hart began to lose hope, the distant sound of a train horn echoed through the darkness, and the platform came alive with activity.

"There he is!" Fitzroy exclaimed, her eyes narrowing on a figure disembarking from the train. It was Thomas Wells, a tall man with an unkempt appearance, his eyes darting nervously as he scanned the station.

"Let's approach him," Hart suggested, his heart racing with the anticipation of confrontation.

As they walked toward Wells, he appeared to sense their presence, turning abruptly to face them. The moment was charged with tension, and Hart could see the glimmer of fear flicker in the stranger's gaze.

"Thomas Wells?" Hart called out, his voice steady and authoritative.

"What do you want?" Wells replied defensively, taking a step back. "I haven't done anything wrong!"

"Then you'll have no problem answering our questions," Fitzroy said, her tone firm. "We need to know about your relationship with Margaret Lacey and Richard Cromwell."

Wells hesitated, his body tense as if contemplating his options. "I didn't kill anyone!" he blurted out, his voice rising in pitch. "I barely knew them!"

"Then tell us why you were seen arguing with Margaret just days before her death," Hart pressed, narrowing his eyes.

"It was nothing, just a misunderstanding," Wells stammered, glancing around as if searching for an escape. "She was obsessed with Richard's work. I tried to warn her about the dangers of becoming too involved with his creations, but she wouldn't listen!"

"Why would you care about that?" Fitzroy challenged, her gaze unwavering.

"Because I cared about her!" Wells snapped, his anger spilling over. "She was my friend, but I couldn't let her get wrapped up in his madness. She was losing herself to those clocks."

Hart and Fitzroy exchanged glances, intrigued by the sudden burst of emotion. "What do you mean by 'madness'?" Hart asked, keeping his voice calm.

Wells ran a hand through his hair, frustration evident in his posture. "Richard had a vision—he was obsessed with time and its manipulation. He believed he could control it, bend it to his will. I feared for Margaret's safety."

"You feared for her safety, yet you argued with her?" Fitzroy interjected, skepticism coloring her voice. "That seems contradictory."

"I was trying to help her!" Wells retorted, his defenses rising. "But I didn't kill her. I swear it!"

"Then where were you on the night she died?" Hart demanded, leaning in closer.

"I was—" Wells hesitated, glancing down the platform as if he were searching for an answer. "I was at the pub, but I left early. I can't account for my time after that!"

"Very convenient," Fitzroy said, her voice dripping with sarcasm. "We'll need to verify your alibi. In the meantime, we suggest you don't leave town."

With that, they stepped back, allowing Wells to retreat into the shadows of the station. The encounter had raised more questions than answers, but Hart felt a glimmer of hope—perhaps they were finally getting closer to the heart of the mystery.

As they walked back to their car, Fitzroy let out a frustrated sigh. "This is becoming a labyrinth of lies. Every turn leads us deeper into darkness."

"True," Hart acknowledged, "but we have to stay the course. There are pieces of this puzzle still waiting to be discovered, and I believe we're getting closer to the truth."

Their next move was to interview the remaining townsfolk who had known Richard and Margaret, hoping to uncover further secrets that would shine a light on their relationship and the circumstances surrounding their deaths.

Days passed, each one punctuated by conversations filled with whispers and hesitations as the detectives dug deeper into the lives of the victims. Each new interview revealed another layer, another fragment of their story—a love triangle with a tragic twist, a friendship built on shared secrets, and a history marked by ambition and betrayal.

Hart learned that Richard had long harbored a rivalry with another local inventor, Samuel Blake, whose work often contrasted with Richard's obsession with time. The two had clashed frequently, their debates growing more heated as they vied for recognition in the small village.

"Blake was furious when Richard received that grant to create his clockwork masterpiece," one elderly villager told them, shaking her head in remembrance. "He swore to ruin him, but no one thought he'd go so far as murder."

"Could he have had a motive?" Fitzroy asked, her interest piqued.

"Perhaps. But he seemed to have his own troubles. His inventions were failing, and he was deep in debt," the villager replied. "Jealousy can be a powerful thing, though."

"Thank you," Hart said, jotting down the name. "We'll need to speak to him next."

With each interview, Hart and Fitzroy were steadily piecing together a complex web of relationships that hinted at more than mere coincidence. As they prepared to confront Samuel Blake, they felt the thrill of anticipation; it was time to confront the next piece of the puzzle.

The next day, they found themselves standing before Blake's workshop, a modest building adorned with various contraptions and gears. The air outside crackled with tension as they knocked on the door, which creaked open to reveal a disheveled man with wild hair and ink-stained hands.

"Can I help you?" Blake asked, his voice raspy and wary.

"Detectives Hart and Fitzroy," Hart introduced himself, presenting his badge. "We're here to ask you some questions about Richard Cromwell."

"Richard?" Blake scoffed, stepping back. "What's there to discuss? He was a fool, consumed by his delusions. He thought he could play with time!"

"And yet he's dead, and you had a rivalry with him," Fitzroy interjected. "Can you account for your whereabouts on the night of his murder?"

"I was here, working on my own inventions," Blake replied defensively. "Why would I want him dead? It was a matter of professional jealousy, nothing more!"

"But you did have a motive," Hart pressed, stepping closer. "You had everything to gain if Richard was out of the picture."

"I had nothing to gain! My work was failing. I barely had enough money to keep this place running," Blake countered, his voice rising in frustration. "You think I'm capable of murder? You don't know me at all!"

"Then help us understand, Samuel," Fitzroy said, her tone softer now. "What was your relationship with Richard like before his death?"

"We were rivals, yes. But there was a time when we were friends. We shared ideas, discussed our dreams," Blake admitted, his expression softening. "But as Richard's work took off, he became arrogant. He thought he was destined for greatness."

"Did you ever confront him about your feelings?" Hart asked, sensing the tension lingering in the air.

Blake hesitated, guilt washing over his face. "I did, but not recently. I thought we could move past it, but when he received that grant... it drove me to desperation."

"Desperation can lead to dangerous choices, Samuel," Fitzroy warned, her eyes piercing into his. "We will find out where you were that night. If your alibi checks out, you're in the clear. But if not..."

Blake's expression hardened, and he crossed his arms defensively. "You won't find any evidence against me. I may have been angry, but I'm not a murderer."

As they left the workshop, Hart felt the weight of uncertainty pressing on his chest. Blake's anger and desperation had felt genuine, but the complexities of their investigation only deepened.

"We're missing something," Hart said as they stepped back into the fresh air. "There's a thread that connects these events, but it's still out of reach."

"We need to look into Richard's inventions further," Fitzroy suggested. "Perhaps there's something in his workshop that holds the key."

They returned to Richard Cromwell's workshop, now shrouded in a silence that echoed with the memories of the past. Hart stepped inside, the scent of wood shavings and oil greeting him. The workshop was a cluttered haven of clocks in various stages of completion, each one a testament to Richard's genius.

As they moved through the space, Hart's gaze fell upon a peculiar clock sitting in the corner. Unlike the others, this one seemed to have a mechanism that was entirely different—a strange complexity that intrigued him.

"Fitzroy, come look at this," he called, motioning her over.

"What have you found?" she asked, examining the clock with curiosity.

"It's unlike anything else here. The gears are arranged in a way that seems almost deliberate," Hart noted, running his fingers along the intricate patterns. "It almost looks like it was designed for something specific."

As they inspected the clock further, Hart discovered a hidden compartment in the back. With a gentle tug, he pried it open, revealing a small drawer containing a series of notes.

"Blueprints?" Fitzroy exclaimed, her eyes widening. "This is incredible!"

Hart carefully unfolded the papers, revealing sketches and designs for a clock that seemed to incorporate elements of both Richard and Samuel's work. "These aren't just blueprints; they 're plans for a device that could manipulate time itself."

"But why would Richard keep this hidden?" Fitzroy wondered aloud.

"Perhaps he didn't want anyone to know," Hart theorized, piecing the fragments together. "If he had succeeded, it could have changed everything. But it's also possible someone didn't want him to succeed."

As they examined the notes, a realization washed over Hart. "This wasn't just about personal rivalries; it was about something far greater. Someone could have killed Richard to keep his invention from becoming a reality."

"But who?" Fitzroy asked, her brow furrowing. "Who would want to stop him?"

Hart's mind raced, retracing their steps through the investigation. The pieces began to connect, forming a clearer picture of the motivations that lay beneath the surface. "What if Samuel Blake knew about Richard's plans? What if he feared the consequences of Richard's invention?"

Fitzroy's eyes lit up with understanding. "Then it's time to confront him again. We need to dig deeper into his connection with Richard and what he might have known about these blueprints."

With renewed determination, they set off to find Blake once more, the weight of the mystery pressing on their shoulders. As they approached his workshop, Hart felt a sense of urgency swelling within him. They were closing in on the truth, and with it, the potential to unravel the motives behind the murders that had shaken their village.

Blake appeared startled to see them again, his eyes narrowing with suspicion. "What now? I told you I had nothing to do with Richard's death!"

"Did you know he was working on a project that could manipulate time?" Hart demanded, stepping closer to confront him.

"What are you talking about?" Blake retorted, feigning ignorance. "Richard was obsessed with time, sure, but that doesn't mean he could actually control it!"

"Your rivalry wasn't just about personal pride, was it?" Fitzroy challenged, her voice steady. "It was about power—the power to control something that should remain untouched."

Blake's expression shifted, a flicker of fear crossing his features. "You don't understand! Richard was losing himself in his work. He was dangerous!"

"Dangerous enough for you to want him dead?" Hart pressed, his voice low and intense.

"I didn't kill him!" Blake shouted, panic rising in his voice. "But I knew he was headed down a dark path, and I tried to stop him. I didn't want to see Margaret consumed by it, either!"

"Then why not come forward?" Fitzroy questioned, her eyes piercing. "You could have warned her, prevented all of this."

"Because I didn't think it would come to this!" Blake replied, his shoulders slumping. "I thought he could still be saved. I never meant for anyone to die."

As Blake's facade crumbled, Hart felt a surge of determination. "You need to tell us everything you know. There are lives at stake."

Hours later, with the weight of Blake's confessions heavy in their minds, Hart and Fitzroy left the workshop with a renewed sense of purpose. They had uncovered the tangled threads that connected Richard, Margaret, and Blake, but the truth still eluded them.

"There's one more piece we need," Hart said, contemplating their next move. "We have to find out more about the blueprints. They could lead us to the person who truly wanted Richard dead."

Back at their office, Hart spread the blueprints across his desk, his eyes scanning the intricate designs. "These mechanisms... they're designed to work together. If someone were to finish what Richard started, it could have catastrophic consequences."

"But who would do that?" Fitzroy wondered, her brow furrowing. "Who would want to harness that power?"

"Perhaps someone who feels entitled to it," Hart replied, the gears in his mind shifting into place. "Someone who believes they can control time for their own benefit."

As they pondered the implications, a sudden realization struck Hart. "What if it's someone close to Richard? Someone who has always wanted what he had?"

"Are you thinking of his apprentice?" Fitzroy asked, her eyes widening in realization. "Oliver Reed?"

"Yes!" Hart exclaimed, his heart racing. "He was Richard's protégé, but he also held resentment toward him. He felt overshadowed by Richard's success."

They hurried to Oliver's last known address, a small cottage on the outskirts of Windermere. As they approached, a sense of dread washed over Hart. He couldn't shake the feeling that they were nearing the final confrontation, and whatever awaited them inside would change everything.

They knocked on the door, their hearts pounding in their chests. After a moment, it creaked open to reveal Oliver, his expression a mix of surprise and fear.

"Detectives! What brings you here?" he stammered, stepping aside to let them in.

"Oliver, we need to talk," Hart said, his voice steady. "We have questions about Richard and his work."

"Richard? I—I don't know anything," Oliver replied, his eyes darting around the room.

"Do you know about the blueprints he was working on?" Fitzroy pressed, studying his expression closely. "The plans to manipulate time?"

Oliver's face went pale, the color draining from his cheeks. "I—I didn't know he was serious about that. He was always dreaming big, but I didn't think he could actually make it happen!"

"Did you ever express your feelings to him?" Hart asked, sensing the tension in the air.

"Of course not! I was grateful for the opportunity he gave me. But he never appreciated my work," Oliver said, desperation creeping into his voice. "I felt like a shadow."

Hart's heart sank as the realization dawned. "Oliver, did you finish Richard's work? Did you take the blueprints for yourself?"

"I didn't take anything! I couldn't!" Oliver insisted, shaking his head. "I may have been envious, but I would never kill him. I didn't want any part of that madness!"

"But you could have warned him," Fitzroy said, her voice filled with conviction. "You could have stopped this."

"I tried! I told him to be careful, but he wouldn't listen," Oliver confessed, tears welling in his eyes. "I didn't know it would lead to this."

As they stood in the dim light of the cottage, the weight of the investigation bore down on them like a heavy cloak. They had gathered fragments of truth, but the heart of the mystery still eluded them.

"Someone out there is still pulling the strings," Hart said, his mind racing with possibilities. "And they will stop at nothing to ensure their plans come to fruition."

"We need to find the person behind this," Fitzroy urged, her determination evident. "But how?"

Hart glanced at the blueprints once more, feeling a surge of inspiration. "We need to revisit Richard's workshop. There may be clues hidden there that can lead us to the final piece of the puzzle."

The detectives returned to the workshop, their hearts pounding with anticipation. As they sifted through the remnants of Richard's work, Hart felt a sense of urgency as they scoured every corner, every desk drawer.

"Look!" Fitzroy called out, her voice ringing with excitement. "There's something in this old trunk."

They opened the trunk, revealing a collection of old documents and correspondence that Richard had kept hidden. Among them, a letter caught Hart's attention, dated just weeks before Richard's death.

"'To my dear friend, Margaret,'" he read aloud, his voice thick with emotion. "Richard was confiding in her about his fears of someone stealing his work. He suspected someone close to him."

"Do you think he meant Oliver?" Fitzroy asked, her brow furrowing.

"Or perhaps even Blake," Hart replied, his mind racing. "If someone was willing to kill Richard, they would have stopped at nothing to protect their own ambitions."

As they delved deeper into the trunk, they uncovered more letters that revealed Richard's growing paranoia. The clues painted a vivid picture of a man trapped in a world of uncertainty, with shadows lurking at every turn.

"We need to confront Oliver one more time," Hart said, determination etched across his face. "We need to find out who he feared the most."

As they arrived at Oliver's cottage, the tension hung thick in the air. They found him pacing anxiously, his hands fidgeting as they approached.

"Oliver, we've uncovered something important," Hart said, stepping forward. "Richard believed someone close to him was plotting against him. He thought someone might try to steal his work."

"I—I didn't take anything!" Oliver protested, his voice trembling. "I wanted to help him! I admired his genius!"

"But did you feel threatened by him?" Fitzroy asked, her eyes searching for the truth.

"No!" Oliver shouted, tears spilling down his cheeks. "I just wanted to be recognized! I never wanted this!"

Hart's heart ached for the young man standing before them, torn between ambition and desperation. "Then help us, Oliver. Who did Richard fear the most?"

"I—I don't know!" he cried, collapsing into a chair. "I thought it was Blake at first, but Richard kept talking about a 'greater threat'—someone who wanted to control everything!"

As Hart absorbed the words, he felt the pieces begin to align. "What if it was someone from the outside? Someone who knew about Richard's work and wanted it for themselves?"

Fitzroy's eyes narrowed with understanding. "The only person who fits that description is the mysterious figure we've been hearing about—the one who has been lurking around the village since the murders began."

"But we don't even know who they are!" Hart exclaimed, frustration boiling within him. "How do we find them?"

"Let's use
the blueprints," Fitzroy suggested, determination sparking in her eyes. "If someone is trying to steal Richard's work, we can set a trap."

With a plan forming in their minds, Hart and Fitzroy worked tirelessly to create a replica of Richard's clockwork mechanism, ensuring it was functional enough to draw the attention of whoever had been pulling the strings.

As night fell, they placed the replica in the workshop, leaving the door slightly ajar to lure the intruder.

Hours passed, the silence stretching thin as they waited in the shadows. Just as Hart began to lose hope, a figure slipped through the door, cloaked in darkness.

"Now!" Hart whispered, signaling Fitzroy.

They sprang from their hiding spots, confronting the intruder—a woman with sharp features and a cold gaze that sent chills down Hart's spine.

"Who are you?" she demanded, her voice steady as she faced them.

"I could ask you the same thing," Fitzroy shot back, her voice unyielding. "What do you want with Richard's work?"

"I'm here to finish what he started," the woman replied, a hint of arrogance lacing her words. "Time is power, and I intend to wield it."

"Your ambition won't end well," Hart warned, stepping closer. "You think you can control it, but you have no idea of the consequences."

"I'm not afraid of consequences," she retorted, her eyes flashing with fury. "I'm here to claim what's rightfully mine!"

As tension mounted in the air, the woman lunged forward, and a struggle ensued. Hart and Fitzroy fought with determination, their training kicking in as they worked together to subdue the intruder.

With a swift move, Fitzroy managed to pin the woman to the ground, her voice firm as she demanded, "Who sent you?"

The woman glared defiantly. "You think you can stop me? You know nothing about the true potential of Richard's work!"

"We know enough," Hart replied, panting from the exertion. "And we'll make sure you never get the chance to use it."

As they restrained the woman, the realization hit Hart like a freight train. "You were behind the murders, weren't you? You wanted Richard out of the way so you could take his work for yourself."

"Consider this a warning," she hissed, her eyes glinting with menace. "You may have won this battle, but the war is far from over."

With that, they secured her, ready to hand her over to the authorities. As dawn broke, illuminating the village with a golden light, Hart and Fitzroy felt a mixture of relief and uncertainty.

"We did it," Fitzroy said, her voice shaky but strong. "We uncovered the truth."

"Yes, but at what cost?" Hart replied, his mind still racing. "The shadows of ambition linger, and we must remain vigilant. There will always be those who seek to exploit time's secrets."

As they prepared to leave the workshop, Hart took one last look at the clockwork mechanism that had ignited this dangerous chain of events. It was a reminder of the thin line between ambition and obsession, and the price of attempting to control the passage of time.

With the dawn of a new day ahead of them, Hart and Fitzroy set out to ensure that Richard Cromwell's legacy would not be forgotten, and that the world would remain safe from those who sought to manipulate the very fabric of existence.

2. The True Identity

AS THE SUN DIPPED BELOW the horizon, casting long shadows across the quaint village of Haversham, Detective Eliza Hart stood at the threshold of a world unraveling before her. The air was thick with tension, the kind that tinged the evening with an unshakeable sense of foreboding. Eliza had been chasing whispers and half-truths since the first murder had sent ripples of fear through the tight-knit community.

A crisp autumn breeze stirred the fallen leaves at her feet, rustling them as if urging her to move forward. The gathering darkness was a stark contrast to the vibrant colors of the season, each crimson and gold leaf reminding her of the life that once thrived here, before the clockwork murders had marred its beauty.

Inside the dimly lit study of her mentor, the late Inspector Caldwell, Eliza rifled through the stacks of papers and old case files that had accumulated over the years. She had hoped to find something — anything — that might illuminate the path ahead. The musty scent of aged paper filled her nostrils, and she paused, allowing her fingers to trace the spines of the leather-bound volumes that lined the shelves. Each book was a silent witness to the mysteries that had come and gone, yet the present case remained stubbornly unresolved.

Then, her gaze fell upon a framed photograph resting precariously on the corner of the desk. It was a black-and-white image of Caldwell, beaming with pride, flanked by a group of young recruits during his early years in the force. But what caught Eliza's attention was the face of a man standing just behind him, a shadowy figure whose identity had been obscured by the passage of time. There was something familiar about him, but the name eluded her.

Shaking off the feeling, Eliza returned to the files scattered across the desk. The cases she sifted through painted a grim portrait of betrayal and deceit, a tapestry woven from the lives of those who had crossed paths with Caldwell over the decades. But what intrigued her the most were the notes he had made regarding the clockmaker, Arthur Finnegan. The man was a local legend, known not only for his remarkable skills in creating intricate timepieces but also for the rumors that shrouded his life in mystery.

As Eliza read through Caldwell's observations, a thought struck her: what if the key to unraveling the true identity of the murderer lay not in the victims themselves but in the clockmaker's past? She had learned through bitter experience that everyone had secrets, and Arthur Finnegan was no exception.

Determined to follow this new thread, Eliza gathered her notes and made her way out into the cool night. The streets were deserted, the usual hum of village life stifled by the gravity of recent events. The church clock chimed eight, its haunting notes echoing through the empty lanes.

With each step toward Finnegan's workshop, the urgency within her grew. She had yet to meet the clockmaker, but his reputation preceded him — an enigmatic figure who preferred the company of gears and springs to that of people. He was rumored to be a recluse, a man who spoke in riddles and could often be found lost in his own world, crafting masterpieces that seemed to dance with life.

Upon reaching the workshop, she noticed the light spilling out from the cracks around the door, flickering like a candle in the dark. Taking a deep breath, Eliza knocked, the sound echoing into the night. Moments later, the door creaked open, revealing a tall man with thinning hair and spectacles perched precariously on the edge of his nose.

"Detective Hart," he said, his voice a mix of surprise and curiosity. "To what do I owe the pleasure?"

"Mr. Finnegan," she replied, stepping inside. "I've come to ask you a few questions about your recent clientele, specifically regarding the clock you created for the late Samuel Fallow."

Finnegan's demeanor shifted, a flicker of something unreadable crossing his features. "Ah, Samuel. A fine man, though troubled. His clock is perhaps... lost to time now."

Eliza raised an eyebrow. "Lost?"

He nodded, leading her deeper into the workshop, where the scent of wood shavings mingled with the metallic tang of tools. "His clock was a special piece, a family heirloom of sorts. I crafted it with the utmost care, but it has gone missing since his... unfortunate demise."

The revelation piqued Eliza's interest. "And how does one lose a clock of such significance?"

"Sometimes, it is not the object but the intent behind it that gets lost," Finnegan replied cryptically, his gaze drifting to a dusty corner where a half-finished timepiece lay abandoned.

As they spoke, Eliza couldn't shake the feeling that Arthur was holding back. "Mr. Finnegan, I need your cooperation. There have been... other murders connected to your creations. If you know anything—"

"I know what people say," he interrupted, his voice rising. "They think I have a hand in these events. But I assure you, Detective, my clocks only tell time. They do not take lives."

"Then help me understand," Eliza pressed. "What can you tell me about Samuel's connections? Was he involved in anything shady?"

Finnegan paused, his eyes narrowing as if weighing his words. "Samuel was a collector of sorts, but his interests ventured into dangerous territory. He had dealings with unsavory individuals, and I warned him to tread carefully. But I can't say for certain what happened thereafter."

Eliza felt a chill run down her spine. "What kind of individuals?"

"People who collect more than just clocks," he murmured. "Artifacts that are better left undisturbed. I cannot disclose names, but I fear Samuel unearthed something that should have remained hidden."

"What do you mean?"

Finnegan's voice dropped to a whisper, laden with urgency. "There are things in this world that are intertwined with time in ways we cannot comprehend. Secrets buried deep within the gears of our lives, waiting to be set in motion."

Before Eliza could respond, the sound of footsteps echoed outside the workshop. She turned to the door, her heart racing as she caught sight of a familiar silhouette. It was Inspector Graham, her old colleague, but his demeanor was far from friendly.

"Detective Hart," he said, stepping inside with an air of authority that immediately set her on edge. "What are you doing here?"

"I'm conducting an investigation, Inspector," Eliza replied, her tone steady despite the growing tension.

Graham's gaze flicked between her and Finnegan, suspicion etched across his face. "I don't recall you having permission to speak to the clockmaker. This case is under my jurisdiction."

"Yet you're no closer to solving it," Eliza shot back, anger bubbling beneath her composed exterior.

"Careful, Hart," he warned, stepping closer. "You might just find yourself in over your head."

Finnegan watched the exchange with keen interest, his expression inscrutable. "Perhaps we all have something to learn from one another," he interjected, attempting to defuse the escalating tension.

Graham scoffed. "And what could you possibly contribute, Finnegan?"

"I have insights that might shed light on the situation," he replied calmly. "But only if we approach this with open minds."

Eliza seized the moment. "Then let's hear it, Arthur. We need all the help we can get."

As they gathered around the workbench, Eliza felt the weight of the case pressing down upon her. Each tick of the clock seemed to resonate with urgency, a reminder that time was slipping away, and with it, the chance to uncover the truth.

Finnegan leaned forward, his fingers tracing the edges of the unfinished timepiece. "Every clock has its own story," he began, his voice low and deliberate. "And Samuel's clock was no exception. It held secrets that could unravel lives, including those of his closest associates."

"Who were they?" Graham demanded, his tone sharp.

"People who would stop at nothing to possess what he had found," Finnegan replied, his gaze unwavering. "But there was one in particular, a woman named Clara. She was fascinated by the occult, drawn to the darker aspects of time."

Eliza's heart raced at the mention of Clara. "And where can we find her?"

"She has distanced herself from the community," Finnegan said, shaking his head. "But her name still lingers in the shadows.

She was rumored to be involved in a circle that dabbled in the forbidden."

"Then we must find her," Eliza insisted, her resolve solidifying.

Graham crossed his arms, skepticism etched across his features. "And how do you propose we do that? You have no leads."

Finnegan's expression shifted, a glimmer of hope in his eyes. "I might know someone who could help. A contact who frequents the darker corners of this town. He may have seen Clara."

Eliza nodded, urgency fueling her next question. "When can we meet this contact?"

"Tonight," Finnegan replied, a sense of determination creeping into his voice. "But you must be cautious. The clockwork of this town is fragile, and the truth may shatter it beyond repair."

As they prepared to leave, Eliza felt the gravity of their mission settling upon her shoulders. Each step into the unknown would bring them closer to the heart of the mystery, but also deeper into the shadows.

The three of them exited the workshop, the chill of the night air

wrapping around them like a shroud. The streets were eerily quiet, and as they walked toward the edge of town, Eliza couldn't shake the feeling that they were being watched.

Just as they reached the last streetlight, a figure emerged from the darkness, stepping into their path. "You're too late," the figure hissed, a mocking smile playing on their lips. "The clock has already struck, and time is no longer on your side."

Eliza's heart raced as she recognized the voice — it belonged to none other than Samuel Fallow's business partner, Leonard Vance. He had been a staple in the community, but recent events had painted him in a new light.

"Leonard," she said, her tone steady despite the tumult of emotions within. "What do you know about the murders?"

Vance chuckled darkly, his eyes glinting with malice. "Everything and nothing, Detective. Time has a way of revealing its true nature, doesn't it? Secrets hidden beneath the surface."

"And you think you can outsmart us?" Graham challenged, stepping forward.

"Not outsmart," Vance replied smoothly. "Just prepare you for what's to come. You're chasing shadows, and shadows have a way of leading one astray."

Eliza exchanged glances with Finnegan and Graham, the tension thickening as the implications of Vance's words hung in the air. She had to tread carefully; they were on the precipice of discovery, but the darkness loomed ever closer, threatening to swallow them whole.

"Tell us where Clara is," Eliza pressed, determination seeping into her voice.

Vance tilted his head, a sly smile dancing across his features. "Why would I do that? I've seen the way you've tried to uncover the truth, and frankly, it's amusing. But I'll give you a hint. Sometimes, the answers lie closer than you think."

With that, he turned and disappeared into the night, leaving Eliza and her companions grappling with his cryptic words.

"What was that about?" Graham muttered, frustration etched on his face.

Eliza remained silent, her mind racing. Vance's words echoed in her thoughts, suggesting that the true identity of the murderer was hidden in plain sight. Perhaps the clockwork murders were not just random acts of violence but rather a carefully orchestrated plan tied to the very fabric of their community.

As they moved forward, the reality of their situation pressed upon them. The deeper they delved, the more intricate the web became. The town's history, interwoven with secrets and betrayals, lay before them like a vast tapestry, each thread a potential lead in their investigation.

Yet, as Eliza contemplated their next move, she couldn't shake the feeling that time was slipping away. The ticking clock was a constant reminder that with each passing moment, the true identity of the murderer remained just out of reach, shrouded in shadows and obscured by the gears of fate.

The night deepened, and with it, the stakes grew higher. The clockwork had begun to turn, and Eliza was determined to see it through, no matter the cost. She could feel the truth beckoning her, urging her to uncover the identity that lay beneath the surface, waiting for the right moment to reveal itself.

As they ventured further into the darkness, Eliza Hart knew one thing for certain: the clock had started ticking, and it would not stop until the final pieces of the puzzle fell into place, revealing the true identity of the murderer who had shattered their world.

3. A Game of Wits

THE ROOM WAS STEEPED in a rich tapestry of shadows, the flickering candlelight casting elongated figures across the ornate wallpaper. It was an evening of tension, as if the very air hummed with anticipation. In the drawing room of the esteemed Lord Montgomery, an assembly of the town's most illustrious figures had gathered, drawn together by a shared interest that transcended mere social pleasantries. The opulent setting, with its dark mahogany furniture and gilded picture frames, was a stark contrast to the unease that seemed to envelop the guests.

At the centre of this gathering stood Lady Evelyn Sinclair, a woman of remarkable beauty and keen intellect. With her sharp emerald eyes and an air of unassailable confidence, she commanded the room's attention as she addressed the guests. "Ladies and gentlemen," she began, her voice steady and inviting, "tonight, we shall engage in a little game—one that challenges not only our minds but also our very perceptions of truth and deceit."

A ripple of intrigue coursed through the assembled crowd. Among them was Detective Inspector Samuel Hart, whose reputation for solving even the most baffling of cases preceded him. He leaned slightly forward in his chair, curiosity piqued by Lady Sinclair's proposition. She continued, "We will each present a riddle or a conundrum. The goal is to outwit one another, to unravel the layers of our own minds while seeking to ensnare those of our esteemed company."

As she spoke, the clock on the mantelpiece ticked with methodical precision, a reminder of the time that pressed upon them. One by one, the guests shared their riddles—enigmas wrapped in clever wordplay and veiled hints. Laughter and gasps of astonishment filled the room as each person attempted to unravel the puzzles presented to them. However, beneath the surface of this jovial atmosphere lay an unspoken tension, an underlying current that suggested that not all was as it appeared.

Lord Montgomery, a portly man with an imposing presence, was the last to speak. His deep voice resonated through the room, drawing every eye. "My dear friends," he declared, "I propose a different kind of riddle, one not of mere words but of actions." He paused, allowing his statement to sink in before continuing. "Tonight, I shall present a challenge to our dear Inspector Hart. I propose a game where we delve into the very heart of our natures—truth versus deception."

The guests exchanged glances, their interest piqued. "And how do you propose we play this game, Lord Montgomery?" Inspector Hart inquired, his brow furrowed in thought.

With a glint of mischief in his eye, Montgomery gestured towards a small table set against the wall, draped with a velvet cloth. "Within this box lies an object—a simple pocket watch, but with a twist. It is said to possess a history as intricate as any clockwork. I challenge you, Inspector, to discern its secrets before the night is through. Should you succeed, you will gain my utmost respect. But fail, and you may find that your wits have led you astray."

The tension in the room intensified. Hart, ever the rational thinker, accepted the challenge with a nod, intrigued by the prospect of solving the mystery of the pocket watch. The other guests buzzed with excitement, their eyes darting between the inspector and the enigmatic lord.

As the evening wore on, the game unfolded, each guest revealing more of their true selves through their attempts to puzzle one another. Conversations shifted from lighthearted banter to veiled accusations, as suspicions began to surface. The riddle of the pocket watch loomed over the gathering like a dark cloud, urging everyone to dig deeper into their thoughts.

Lady Sinclair watched the interactions with keen interest, her analytical mind dissecting each word and gesture. She noted the shifting alliances, the subtle glances exchanged, and the tension that built as each guest attempted to outwit the others. It was a game she knew all too well—the game of human nature.

"Let us not forget the importance of time in our game," Lady Sinclair remarked, her voice cutting through the rising excitement. "Time, my friends, can reveal more than the truth itself. Consider how it shapes our memories, our perceptions, and our very actions."

With her words, the atmosphere in the room shifted once more. The guests leaned closer, their curiosity piqued. Each person contemplated the significance of time—how it influenced their relationships, decisions, and ultimately, their fates.

As the clock ticked on, the guests continued to share their riddles, each more elaborate than the last. Lord Montgomery's challenge loomed larger in Hart's mind, a tantalizing mystery waiting to be unraveled. He scrutinized the pocket watch, its intricate mechanisms gleaming under the candlelight. What secrets did it hold? What stories had it witnessed over the years?

"Inspector, have you made any progress?" Montgomery's voice broke through Hart's reverie. The challenge hung in the air, a silent demand for action.

"I believe so," Hart replied, his gaze never leaving the watch. "The design speaks of craftsmanship from a time long past, possibly the work of an artisan who understood the true nature of time. Yet, its inner workings tell a different tale, one filled with uncertainty and perhaps... treachery."

The guests exchanged knowing glances, intrigue flaring as they realized that the night was more than just a game. It had evolved into a complex dance of wits, a battle of intellects where truths and lies intertwined seamlessly.

As the hours passed, the atmosphere thickened with unspoken accusations. Each guest began to suspect the other, their words tinged with suspicion. Lady Sinclair, observing from the sidelines, recognized the danger that lurked beneath the surface. "We must remember, dear friends," she cautioned, "that while we seek to outwit one another, the true game lies in understanding ourselves."

The clock's relentless ticking continued, marking time with an unsettling finality. The evening had transformed into a battleground of minds, where intellect became weaponized, and trust evaporated like the melting candlewax.

Suddenly, a loud crash echoed through the room, shattering the fragile tension. A guest, panic etched across their face, pointed towards the door. "Someone has entered!" they cried, fear gripping their voice.

All eyes turned towards the entrance, where a figure stood silhouetted against the dim light. It was a stranger, cloaked in shadow, their features obscured. "I believe I have come at an opportune moment," the figure declared, stepping forward to reveal a masked visage. "Your game of wits has just taken a dangerous turn."

Gasps filled the room as the masked figure brandished a weapon—a gleaming dagger that caught the light in a dance of reflections. "I suggest you all pay close attention. The stakes have risen higher than any of you could imagine."

Inspector Hart's instincts kicked in, his mind racing to piece together the puzzle. "Who are you?" he demanded, his voice steady despite the chaos around him.

"I am the harbinger of truths you seek to conceal," the stranger replied cryptically. "Your little game has drawn the attention of forces beyond your understanding. The pocket watch you so diligently investigate holds the key to secrets long buried, secrets that many would kill to keep hidden."

The room fell into an uneasy silence, the guests frozen in fear as the masked figure continued. "To play this game, you must be prepared to face the consequences of your choices. Time is not your ally, and the truth can be a deadly adversary."

Hart felt the weight of the situation pressing down on him. This was no longer just a game; it had escalated into a perilous confrontation. The masked stranger's presence shifted the dynamics, transforming the drawing room into a stage for a dark revelation.

"Will you continue this game, or will you allow the fear of the unknown to dictate your actions?" the stranger challenged, their voice low and insistent.

Lady Sinclair stepped forward, her gaze unwavering. "We shall not be cowed by intimidation. If there are secrets to uncover, we will pursue them, even in the face of danger."

Her resolve sparked a glimmer of determination within the guests. The tension in the room shifted once again, morphing into a collective spirit of defiance. They were all players in this unfolding drama, and despite the risks, they were unwilling to retreat.

Inspector Hart nodded, feeling the gravity of the moment. "Very well. Let the game continue. But know this: if any harm comes to those present, you will answer to me."

The masked figure chuckled softly, the sound sending chills down Hart's spine. "A bold proclamation, Inspector. But remember, every game has its rules, and the consequences are often far from predictable."

With that, the masked figure stepped back into the shadows, leaving the room thick with uncertainty. The guests exchanged glances, their minds racing with possibilities. What lay ahead was no longer a simple game of wits—it was a treacherous path into the depths of deception, where the truth could prove to be as deadly as any weapon.

As the clock continued to tick, each guest faced a choice: to unravel the tangled web of secrets surrounding the pocket watch or to succumb to the fear that threatened to engulf them. The night had transformed into a labyrinthine journey, where trust would be tested, alliances forged and broken, and the game of wits would ultimately reveal the true nature of those who dared to play.

In the days that followed, as the sun cast its golden light upon the town, the events of that fateful evening would ripple through the lives of all present. The pocket watch remained at the heart of it all, a timeless reminder of the choices made, the secrets unearthed, and the shadows that lingered long after the players had left the stage.

The game was far from over, and as Inspector Hart stood gazing at the watch, he couldn't shake the feeling that the real challenge lay ahead. The intricacies of time and deception would demand his utmost skill, and in this perilous game, the stakes had never been higher.

In the end, they were all players in a grand theatre of intrigue, where the clockwork of fate would decide the outcome of their entwined destinies, leaving each character to ponder the question: who would emerge victorious in this intricate game of wits?

4. A Final Deception

DETECTIVE SAMUEL HART leaned against the stone wall of the clock tower, the cold granite biting into his back as he gazed across the dimly lit square below. The evening air was thick with tension, a palpable reminder of the recent horrors that had unfolded in the quaint little town of Haverford. The autumn leaves rustled gently in the breeze, whispering secrets that the townsfolk were too frightened to voice. It had been a week since the first murder, a week filled with suspicion and fear, and Samuel had made it his mission to uncover the truth lurking in the shadows.

The square, once a vibrant hub of activity, now seemed to hold its breath in anticipation. Samuel's thoughts drifted to the recent victims—Gregory Flannery, the local watchmaker, whose body had been found sprawled on his workshop floor, his beloved clockworks scattered like remnants of a shattered dream. And then there was Eleanor Porter, the kind-hearted widow, discovered lifeless in her own garden, surrounded by wilting flowers that seemed to mourn her loss. Each death had sent shockwaves through the community, and each time, the clockwork murders had left a distinct mark—an intricately designed clock, its hands frozen in time, always pointing to the same ominous hour.

Samuel had spent countless hours poring over the details of the case. Each victim had been connected to a strange and mysterious group known as the Chronomancers, a society of clockmakers and time enthusiasts who claimed to unlock the secrets of time itself. Their gatherings, once a source of fascination for the townspeople, had turned sinister, as whispers of betrayal and deceit echoed through the halls of the old town hall where they convened.

As the moon rose high in the sky, casting a silvery glow across the cobblestones, Samuel's thoughts were interrupted by a faint sound—a clock chiming the hour. He turned his attention back to the clock tower, its gears ticking steadily, a reminder of the relentless passage of time. It was then that he noticed a figure emerge from the shadows at the foot of the tower. A woman, draped in a dark cloak, her face obscured by the hood. Intrigued, Samuel pushed away from the wall and made his way down the winding staircase, determined to uncover the identity of this mysterious stranger.

"Excuse me!" he called out as he reached the bottom, his voice echoing in the stillness. The woman halted, her posture tense as she turned to face him.

"What do you want?" Her voice was soft, almost hesitant, yet there was a steeliness to it that intrigued him.

"I'm Detective Samuel Hart," he introduced himself, stepping closer. "I'm investigating the recent murders. I couldn't help but notice you lurking in the shadows. Do you have information that could help?"

She hesitated for a moment, her eyes darting around as if searching for an escape. "I can't talk here," she whispered urgently. "Meet me at the old railway station. Midnight."

Before Samuel could respond, she slipped back into the shadows, leaving him with a sense of foreboding and curiosity. The old railway station was a relic of the past, long abandoned and cloaked in mystery. The perfect place for a clandestine meeting, he thought.

As the clock struck midnight, Samuel made his way to the station, his heart pounding with anticipation. The moonlight illuminated the weathered platform, and the sound of his footsteps echoed in the silence. He arrived to find the woman waiting for him, her cloak billowing around her like a specter from another time.

"Thank you for coming," she said, glancing nervously over her shoulder. "I have information that could change everything."

Samuel studied her face, trying to read her intentions. "What do you know about the murders?" he pressed.

She took a deep breath, her voice trembling. "My name is Clara. I was once part of the Chronomancers, but I left them. They're not what they seem. Gregory was killed because he wanted to expose their secrets."

"Secrets?" Samuel echoed, intrigued. "What kind of secrets?"

"They believe they can control time," she explained, her eyes wide with fear. "They've been working on a device—a clock that can alter the past. Gregory was going to reveal it, but someone stopped him."

Samuel felt a chill run down his spine. The idea of manipulating time was as dangerous as it was alluring. "And Eleanor? Was she involved?"

"Yes," Clara nodded, her expression pained. "She was one of the last to know. She was trying to help Gregory."

As she spoke, a sudden noise shattered the stillness—a sharp crack that echoed through the empty station. Clara gasped, her eyes widening in terror. "We're not safe here! We have to go!"

Before Samuel could react, a figure emerged from the shadows, brandishing a gun. "You shouldn't have come here, Clara," he sneered, his voice low and menacing.

"Stay back!" Samuel shouted, instinctively stepping in front of Clara. The figure's eyes flickered with recognition, and a cruel smile spread across his face.

"Detective Hart," he said mockingly. "I should have known you'd get involved. You always have to play the hero, don't you?"

"Who are you?" Samuel demanded, his heart racing.

"I'm the one who's going to ensure that the Chronomancers' secrets stay buried," the man replied. "And you're just in the way."

With a sudden movement, he aimed the gun at Clara, but Samuel lunged forward, tackling him to the ground. The gun clattered away, and the two men struggled in the dirt. Samuel could feel the man's strength, but he fought with determination, fueled by the desire to protect Clara.

Just as he gained the upper hand, a loud bang reverberated through the air, and Samuel felt a sharp pain in his shoulder. He gasped, stumbling back as the man scrambled to his feet and dashed into the shadows. Clara rushed to his side, her hands trembling as she inspected the wound.

"Stay with me, Samuel! Please!" she cried, her voice filled with desperation.

"I'm fine," he managed to say through gritted teeth. "We need to get out of here."

With Clara's help, Samuel made his way back to town, each step more difficult than the last. The pain throbbed in his shoulder, but he was determined to uncover the truth. As they reached the main street, Clara paused, looking around cautiously.

"We need to warn the others," she said urgently. "The Chronomancers won't stop until they silence us."

Samuel nodded, his mind racing. He needed to rally the townspeople, to warn them of the impending danger. But as they approached the town hall, a realization struck him. The clock tower chimed ominously in the distance, each stroke echoing the urgency of their situation.

"Clara, we need to get to the tower," he said, his voice steady despite the pain. "If we can get to the top, we'll have a vantage point to see what's happening."

Together, they rushed towards the clock tower, the weight of the night pressing down upon them. As they ascended the spiral staircase, Samuel felt the adrenaline coursing through his veins, pushing him to keep moving. With each step, he could hear the gears of the clock ticking relentlessly, a reminder of the time slipping away.

When they finally reached the top, the view was breathtaking. The town sprawled below them, bathed in the silver light of the moon. But Samuel's gaze was drawn to a flickering light in the distance—a gathering of figures at the old cemetery.

"It's them," Clara whispered, her voice trembling. "They're planning something."

Samuel scanned the scene, his mind racing. "We need to gather evidence. If we can prove they're behind the murders, we can stop them."

As they prepared to leave the tower, a sudden realization hit Samuel. "Wait. The clock!" he exclaimed, rushing to the massive timepiece that dominated the room. "What if we can use it to our advantage?"

Clara looked confused. "What do you mean?"

"Each time a crime has been committed, the clock has stopped at a specific hour," Samuel explained, his mind racing. "What if we can set it to that time, and when they strike, we'll have a chance to catch them in the act?"

Clara nodded slowly, understanding dawning in her eyes. "It's risky, but it might work."

Together, they began adjusting the clock's mechanisms, setting the hands to the ominous hour that had haunted them since the beginning. The gears whirred to life, and Samuel could feel the weight of history pressing down upon him. This clock had witnessed countless moments, but tonight, it would bear witness to the final act of deception.

As the clock struck, they descended the stairs, the sound of the chimes echoing in their ears. Each step felt heavier as they approached the cemetery, but determination fueled their resolve. They could not let fear hold them back now.

Reaching the cemetery, they crept among the gravestones, their hearts racing as they drew closer to the flickering light. Samuel's instincts were on high alert, every nerve ending tingling with anticipation. They could see the figures now—cloaked in darkness, gathered around a makeshift altar adorned with the remnants of clock parts and strange symbols.

"What are they doing?" Clara whispered, her voice barely audible.

"Ritualistic," Samuel replied, his eyes narrowing. "They're trying to harness the power of time itself."

Just then, one of the figures turned, revealing a familiar face—Ronald Hargrove, the town's treasurer, his expression twisted with fervor. "We will not be silenced!" he shouted, raising his arms to the night sky. "With this clock, we will transcend time itself!"

Samuel's heart sank. Ronald had always been the one pushing for the Chronomancers' secrecy, his obsession with time consuming him whole. This was more than just a murder—this was a desperate attempt to control fate itself.

"Now!" Samuel hissed to Clara, and they stepped out from behind the gravestones, confronting the group.

"Stop this madness, Ronald!" Samuel called out, his voice steady despite the chaos surrounding them. "You're playing with forces you don't understand!"

The gathered figures turned, their eyes filled with a mix of surprise and rage. "You shouldn't have come here, Detective," Ronald spat. "You're too late to stop what's already in motion."

Before Samuel could react, a figure lunged at him from the shadows, and he instinctively sidestepped, but the attacker collided with him, sending both men tumbling to the ground. Clara shouted, but Samuel was focused on the fight, grappling with the assailant as the others circled around them.

Amidst the chaos, Samuel caught a glimpse of the clock they had used as bait. Its hands spun wildly, the gears grinding against one another as if protesting the very act of manipulation.

"Clara, the clock!" Samuel shouted. "We need to stop it!"

With a burst of adrenaline, Samuel broke free from his attacker and dashed toward the clock. Clara followed closely behind, determined to help. As they reached it, Ronald and the others surged forward, but Samuel and Clara were faster.

With a swift motion, Samuel began to turn the clock's hands backward, a desperate attempt to undo the chaos that had been unleashed. The clock protested, its gears screeching in agony, but Samuel persisted. Clara joined him, her hands steady as they worked together, the sound of the clock drowning out the chaos around them.

Suddenly, the gathered figures paused, confusion crossing their faces as they witnessed the clock's strange behavior. Ronald's expression morphed from anger to fear. "What are you doing?" he shouted, but it was too late.

With one final twist, the clock shuddered violently, and a blinding light erupted from its center, illuminating the cemetery in a surreal glow. Samuel felt a surge of energy coursing through him, a sense of power that transcended time itself. The figures stumbled back, shielding their eyes from the brilliance.

In that moment, Samuel understood. Time was not something to be controlled—it was a force of nature, and those who sought to manipulate it would face dire consequences.

The light enveloped the figures, and with a deafening roar, time itself seemed to bend and twist, unraveling the very fabric of reality. Samuel and Clara clung to one another, the world around them spinning as the clock's power surged.

When the light finally faded, silence settled over the cemetery. Samuel opened his eyes, blinking in disbelief. The figures were gone, evaporated into the ether, leaving only their scattered belongings behind. The clock stood still, its hands frozen at an hour of uncertainty.

"What just happened?" Clara whispered, her voice shaking.

Samuel took a deep breath, the weight of their victory settling in. "We did it," he replied, though doubt crept into his mind. "But at what cost?"

As they stood in the remains of the old cemetery, Samuel realized that the danger had not fully passed. The Chronomancers may have been thwarted for now, but their legacy would linger, a reminder of the power of time and the secrets it held.

Together, they made their way back to town, hand in hand, knowing that the night had changed them forever. Samuel understood that in the pursuit of truth, there would always be deception lurking in the shadows. But with Clara by his side, he felt a renewed sense of purpose, ready to face whatever challenges lay ahead.

As dawn broke over Haverford, casting a golden light across the town, Samuel knew that they had survived the final deception. The clock had struck its last hour, but the lessons learned would resonate for years to come. Together, they would unravel the mysteries of the past, step by step, one tick at a time.

5. The Master's Plan

IN THE DIMLY LIT DRAWING room of Ashcombe Manor, a palpable tension hung in the air, thick as the dust motes swirling in the shafts of late afternoon sunlight. The walls, adorned with faded portraits of stern ancestors, bore witness to secrets that had lingered like the scent of damp wood and stale air. Here, in this ancestral seat of the Grimshaw family, the unravelling of a grand plan was about to unfold, as each member gathered for an evening they would not soon forget.

At the center of the room sat Horace Grimshaw, the master of the manor, his silver hair slicked back, and his spectacles perched precariously on the bridge of his nose. He was a man of considerable intellect, a retired watchmaker whose obsession with time had driven him to construct elaborate clocks that adorned every corner of the manor. The soft ticking echoed throughout the house, an unrelenting reminder of the passage of moments, much like the tension building among his guests.

"Ladies and gentlemen," he began, his voice steady, "thank you for coming at such short notice. I assure you, this gathering is of utmost importance." He paused, allowing his gaze to sweep over the assembled company, each face betraying a mix of curiosity and apprehension.

Among the guests was Evelyn, his estranged niece, a sharp-minded woman with auburn hair and an insatiable thirst for adventure. Seated across from her was Arthur, Horace's loyal butler, whose presence was often overlooked but whose loyalty was unwavering. Next to him sat Beatrice, the family matriarch, with her piercing blue eyes that seemed to judge the very essence of one's soul. The final two guests were Edwin and Clara, a couple with a penchant for gossip, their eyes darting about the room, hungry for scandal.

"Uncle Horace, you are being most mysterious," Evelyn interjected, a hint of mischief in her voice. "What have you planned? A game of charades, perhaps? Or is it something far more sinister?"

"Ah, Evelyn," Horace chuckled, "you always had a flair for the dramatic. No, this is no mere game. I have discovered something extraordinary—something that concerns each of you." His words hung in the air, heavy with implication.

Edwin leaned forward, intrigued. "Extraordinary? You've piqued my interest, Horace. What is it you've found?"

With a flourish, Horace gestured toward an ornate clock perched on the mantle, its intricate gears exposed like the inner workings of a heart laid bare. "This clock," he continued, "holds the key to a mystery that has plagued our family for generations. A mystery I believe can finally be solved tonight."

The room fell silent as Horace began to recount the legend surrounding the Grimshaw lineage—a tale woven with intrigue, betrayal, and a hidden fortune said to be lost within the walls of Ashcombe Manor. It was said that the family's patriarch had hidden a treasure, his dying words a cryptic clue that had confounded even the most astute minds.

"Many have tried to uncover the secret," Horace stated, his voice lowering conspiratorially. "But all have failed. I have reason to believe the answer lies within this very clock. Each tick represents a moment in our family's history—a history fraught with deception."

"Deception? What do you mean?" Beatrice asked, her interest piqued despite her typically reserved demeanor.

"Years ago," Horace explained, "when my father was still alive, he confided in me that the clock was not just a timekeeper. It was a puzzle—a mechanism designed to reveal the location of the treasure. But to solve it, one must understand the past. And therein lies the problem—our family has always been too fragmented to piece together the truth."

Evelyn leaned in closer, her eyes sparkling with excitement. "And you believe we can solve it together?"

Horace nodded, his expression serious. "Indeed. Tonight, I want us to delve into our family's history, to confront the shadows that have lingered far too long. Only then can we hope to unlock the secrets of the clock."

As the evening wore on, the guests were drawn into the narrative, sharing stories of their ancestors, piecing together the fragmented tales that had shaped the Grimshaw legacy. The atmosphere was electric, the air thick with anticipation and curiosity.

"Tell us more about the patriarch," Clara urged, her voice a mix of excitement and trepidation. "What do we know of him?"

Horace took a deep breath, recalling the stories passed down through generations. "He was a man of great ambition and cunning. He amassed wealth, but it came at a cost—betrayals, rivalries, and secrets that threatened to tear the family apart. The legend goes that before he died, he hid a portion of his fortune within the clock, leaving behind a series of clues to find it."

"And what became of those clues?" Edwin asked, his brow furrowed in concentration.

"They were lost to time," Horace replied. "My father tried to decipher them, but the family's infighting and his own distractions prevented him from succeeding. But I believe the answers lie within the clock's mechanisms, waiting to be uncovered."

As the clock struck eight, its chimes resonated through the manor, a reminder of the limited time they had to solve the mystery. Each guest felt the weight of history bearing down upon them, a sense of urgency propelling them forward.

"Let's begin, then," Evelyn declared, her enthusiasm infectious. "What do we need to do?"

Horace smiled, pleased by the eagerness of his niece. "First, we must observe the clock closely. Each gear, each tick, may hold a secret. I have made a few adjustments to its workings. It is time we unravel the first of its mysteries."

He stepped forward, carefully removing the clock from its place on the mantle. As he laid it on the table, the intricate design revealed itself—a combination of brass and wood, gears spinning with an almost sentient quality.

"Now," Horace continued, "we must examine the inscriptions on the clock's face. They may provide the first clue to the treasure's whereabouts."

The group leaned in closer, their breaths held in anticipation. Each marking, each engraving, was scrutinized for meaning, and as they worked together, the bonds of family began to strengthen.

As they delved deeper into the clock's secrets, the atmosphere shifted. Whispers of long-held grudges surfaced, and the air crackled with tension. Unspoken resentments simmered beneath the surface, threatening to disrupt the delicate balance they had begun to establish.

Evelyn was the first to break the silence. "I can't help but wonder, Uncle Horace, what if the treasure isn't just a physical wealth? What if it's something more, something that could bind us together or tear us apart?"

Horace's gaze met hers, a glimmer of understanding passing between them. "Indeed, Evelyn. The true treasure may lie in the knowledge of our family's past—the understanding of who we are and what we can become."

As the clock's gears continued to tick, a sense of purpose enveloped them, urging them onward. They began to uncover fragments of the past—love letters hidden in drawers, old photographs revealing forgotten connections, and journal entries that painted a portrait of their ancestors' lives.

With each discovery, the tension shifted. Old grudges began to dissolve in the light of shared memories, and the guests found themselves connecting in ways they had never imagined possible.

But as they unearthed the secrets of their lineage, a sense of foreboding began to creep in. The deeper they delved into the clock's mysteries, the more they realized that they were not the only ones interested in the treasure. Outside, shadows lurked, and the air felt charged with danger.

By the time they gathered for supper, the atmosphere was charged with excitement, but also uncertainty. Over the table laden with food, discussions turned to what they had learned about their family's legacy and the implications of the treasure.

"Should we not alert the authorities?" Arthur suggested cautiously. "If there are others seeking this treasure, we may be in danger."

"Perhaps," Horace replied, his brow furrowed in thought. "But I cannot bear the thought of letting our family's secrets slip away again. We must act with caution but determination."

Evelyn nodded. "I agree. We have come too far to turn back now. Besides, the treasure may well hold the key to uniting us once and for all."

As the evening wore on, their conversation flowed, weaving through tales of love and betrayal, strength and weakness. The clock continued to tick, each chime a reminder that they were racing against time, a constant companion that would either aid or hinder their quest.

Later that night, as the guests retired to their rooms, Evelyn felt a sense of purpose brewing within her. She sat on the edge of her bed, gazing at the shadows cast by the moonlight filtering through the window. It was then she heard it—a soft whispering, like the rustle of leaves in the wind. Was it the clock calling to her, urging her to uncover its secrets?

The following morning, with renewed determination, Evelyn joined Horace in the drawing room. "We must continue our search," she insisted, her eyes alight with enthusiasm. "I can feel it—there's something more to discover."

Horace nodded, his expression contemplative. "Indeed, but we must be vigilant. The clock may be more than just a timekeeper; it may be a harbinger of events yet to unfold."

As they delved deeper into the clock's intricate mechanisms, they began to unlock its secrets, one gear at a time. The ticking grew louder, a rhythmic pulse that seemed to synchronize with their hearts.

Hours turned into days, and the guests immersed themselves in the search for the treasure, exploring the manor's hidden corners and forgotten rooms. The clock became their focal point, a beacon guiding them through the maze of their family's past.

With each revelation, the tension mounted, and the relationships between the guests deepened. Bonds were forged, but shadows loomed larger than ever. Rumors of outsiders lurking around the manor began to surface, and suspicions festered among the guests.

One evening, as they gathered for supper, the mood shifted dramatically. Beatrice, her voice trembling, recounted a tale of a stranger seen prowling the grounds. "He was watching us, lurking in the shadows," she insisted, her eyes wide with fear.

The group fell silent, their hearts racing as they exchanged wary glances. "Who was it?" Edwin asked, his voice barely above a whisper.

"I do not know," Beatrice replied, shaking her head. "But I fear he means to harm us. The treasure has drawn unwelcome attention."

The realization hit them like a cold gust of wind—this was not merely a quest for familial unity; it was a race against time, with a threat lurking just beyond their sight.

Determined to safeguard their newfound connections and the legacy of their family, Horace devised a plan. "We will not let fear dictate our actions," he declared. "We will work together to uncover the truth, not just about the treasure, but about who among us can be trusted."

Evelyn nodded, her resolve unwavering. "Let us confront this shadow that threatens us. We are stronger together."

In the days that followed, the group delved deeper into the clock's mysteries, their shared determination forging an unbreakable bond. The ticking of the clock became a constant reminder of their purpose, propelling them forward in their quest for answers.

Yet, as they unraveled the layers of the clock's secrets, the tension between the guests began to fray. Old rivalries resurfaced, and accusations flew like daggers, each cutting deeper than the last.

Amidst the chaos, Horace remained steadfast, urging them to remember their shared history. "We must not allow our past to cloud our present," he implored. "The treasure can only be found if we work together, not against one another."

But the shadows outside continued to grow, and with them came whispers of betrayal. Each night, the guests would gather to discuss their findings, yet unease settled over the manor like a thick fog.

Then, one stormy night, as lightning lit up the darkened sky, an urgent knock echoed through the hallways. The guests exchanged startled glances, their hearts pounding in unison.

"Who could that be?" Clara asked, her voice trembling.

Horace opened the door to reveal a drenched figure—an investigator sent by the local authorities, a man with a keen sense of danger and an eye for detail. "I've heard rumors," he said, stepping inside. "I believe you may be in grave danger."

The room fell silent as the weight of his words sank in. The investigator explained that a notorious thief had been seen in the vicinity, known for targeting wealthy families. "They say he's looking for something—something hidden away in your manor," he warned.

Evelyn's eyes widened. "The treasure?"

"Precisely," the investigator confirmed, his voice grave. "You must be cautious. The clock may be more than just a clue; it may hold the key to your safety as well."

With renewed urgency, the guests rallied together, determined to uncover the truth behind the clock and the treasure before it fell into the wrong hands. As the storm raged outside, the manor became a sanctuary, a fortress against the encroaching darkness.

Over the following days, they combined their knowledge and skills, working tirelessly to piece together the final components of the clock's mystery. As they worked, the bond between them solidified, the ticking of the clock serving as a reminder of their purpose.

But even as they drew closer to the truth, a sense of foreboding lingered in the air. The thief was out there, lurking, and they could feel his presence as a cold wind rustled through the manor's corridors.

Finally, the day came when they believed they were ready to unlock the final secret of the clock. The group gathered in the drawing room, anticipation crackling like electricity in the air.

"Today, we shall discover the truth," Horace declared, his voice filled with conviction. "Together, we will unlock the secrets of our past and the treasure that lies within this clock."

With trembling hands, they positioned themselves around the clock, each member contributing their insights and findings. As the gears turned, a low hum filled the room, resonating with the energy of their collective determination.

Then, with a sudden click, a hidden compartment within the clock sprang open, revealing an ancient scroll—a meticulously drawn map accompanied by cryptic symbols and notes.

"This is it!" Evelyn exclaimed, her heart racing. "The treasure's location!"

But before they could celebrate, a chilling sound echoed through the hall—the unmistakable sound of footsteps approaching. The group froze, their hearts pounding in their chests.

With a shared glance, they quickly concealed the map, instinctively bracing themselves for the confrontation they knew was imminent.

As the door creaked open, the figure that stepped into the room was both unexpected and alarming—the notorious thief, his eyes glinting with greed. "I've come for what's mine," he sneered, brandishing a weapon that glinted ominously in the dim light.

But before he could advance, Horace stood tall, his voice steady. "You will not find what you seek here. We are not afraid of you."

The thief laughed, a sound devoid of warmth. "You think you can protect your precious family secrets? You're nothing but a collection of fools!"

In that moment, time seemed to stand still. The clock continued to tick, each second resonating with the tension in the air. But Evelyn felt a surge of determination within her. "We may be fools, but we are united. And together, we will not let you take what is rightfully ours."

The confrontation escalated, and as the thief lunged toward them, chaos erupted. The guests sprang into action, their adrenaline fueling their resolve.

In the ensuing struggle, the clock became a focal point, its gears and mechanisms reflecting the turmoil within the room. With each tick, they fought not just for the treasure, but for their newfound bond—a bond forged in the fires of family legacy and shared purpose.

Finally, after what felt like an eternity, they managed to subdue the thief, but not without consequence. As the dust settled and the clock continued its relentless ticking, they realized the treasure was not merely a collection of riches hidden within the walls of Ashcombe Manor. It was the connection they had forged—the understanding that their strength lay not in the past, but in the present.

As dawn broke over the manor, the guests stood together, gazing at the clock that had brought them all together. In that moment, they understood that the true treasure had been the journey itself—the shared stories, the revelations, and the bonds formed in the face of adversity.

Horace smiled, his eyes glistening with pride. "We have uncovered not just the secrets of our past, but the essence of who we are. And in doing so, we have created a legacy that will endure."

With the thief apprehended and their spirits renewed, the Grimshaw family gathered for a new beginning—a commitment to honor their lineage and embrace the future, united in purpose and love.

As the clock chimed, marking the start of a new day, the shadows that had once haunted Ashcombe Manor began to fade, giving way to the light of possibility. The ticking of time, once a reminder of secrets and betrayals, now resonated with hope—a promise of what was yet to come.

In the heart of the manor, as laughter filled the air and stories were shared, the clock continued its unrelenting march, a reminder that while the past may shape them, it was the present that truly defined who they would become.

And so, within the walls of Ashcombe Manor, the legacy of the Grimshaw family was reborn—a story woven with the threads of time, love, and resilience, echoing through the ages as the clock continued to tick, marking the moments that would forever bind them together.

6. Checkmate

DETECTIVE HARRIET BLAKE stood on the precipice of revelation, the dim light of the late afternoon casting elongated shadows across the room. The parlor, once a sanctuary of elegance, now felt stifling and oppressive, as if the very walls conspired to keep the truth hidden. A heavy silence hung in the air, broken only by the faint ticking of the ornate grandfather clock that stood sentinel in the corner. Each tick seemed to mock her, reminding her that time was slipping away.

As she surveyed the gathering of suspects seated in the lavishly decorated room of Foxglove Manor, Harriet felt the weight of their collective gazes. Each face bore its own tale of fear and suspicion, their eyes darting nervously as if they might unearth the truth buried deep within the layers of deceit that had unfolded over the past few days. The atmosphere crackled with tension, thick enough to slice through with a knife.

It had begun innocently enough, a weekend retreat for the esteemed members of the Clockwork Society, a group dedicated to the art of horology and the appreciation of mechanical wonders. However, the joy of their shared passion had been abruptly shattered by the shocking murder of Lionel Ashcroft, the society's illustrious president. The grand clock that adorned the manor's entryway had stood still at the stroke of twelve, a grim reminder of the moment life had been snuffed out of one of their own.

"Detective Blake, are we to remain in this ludicrous limbo all evening?" The voice of Geraldine Hargrove sliced through the tension like a shard of glass, revealing the impatience of the assembled guests. Geraldine, a prominent watchmaker and one of the last to see Lionel alive, regarded Harriet with a mixture of defiance and fear. "You must have gathered sufficient evidence by now."

"Patience, Mrs. Hargrove," Harriet replied, her tone measured and composed. "The truth will reveal itself, but only if we allow it the space to breathe."

She turned her attention back to the others in the room. Charles Devlin, the society's treasurer, fiddled nervously with his cufflinks, his brow glistening with perspiration. Opposite him sat Beatrice Hargrove, Geraldine's cousin, her expression a mask of faux innocence, though Harriet could detect the underlying tension in her fingers as they twisted the fringe of her shawl.

"Why don't you simply ask us who did it?" Beatrice finally exclaimed, her voice rising above the murmur of the others. "We're all but waiting for you to make your grand accusation!"

Harriet chose her words carefully. "Murder is not a game, Miss Hargrove. It requires deliberation and reflection. There are motives hidden beneath the surface that may not be immediately apparent."

She moved toward the fireplace, where a collection of intricately crafted clocks adorned the mantel. The tick-tock of their mechanisms intermingled with the hushed whispers of the guests, creating an eerie symphony. Each clock told a different story, just as each member of the society held secrets that intertwined with the tragic demise of Lionel Ashcroft.

"Let us start with the clock," Harriet said, gesturing towards the largest timepiece, a grandiose creation of brass and mahogany. "This clock, like our lives, ticks forward, but it is also a reminder of the time we cannot reclaim. What were each of you doing at midnight when Lionel was murdered?"

"Is that really relevant?" Geraldine interjected. "We all know it was an accident, a mere twist of fate!"

"Do we?" Harriet replied, arching an eyebrow. "You see, the time of death is crucial. It provides a framework around which to build our understanding of the events leading to Lionel's demise. What if I told you the clock had stopped at twelve?"

A collective gasp echoed in the room, eyes widening in shock. The implications of her words were staggering. If the clock had indeed stopped, it could suggest foul play, or worse, a carefully orchestrated plot designed to mislead.

"I was in the library," Charles Devlin spoke up, his voice wavering. "Checking the accounts... I'm sure it was after midnight when I left. The clock's stopped? But that's impossible!"

"Nothing is impossible when it comes to murder," Harriet countered. "Your alibi hinges on the accuracy of that clock. And who else was in the library with you?"

Geraldine scoffed. "Charles was alone. I had stepped outside for a breath of fresh air. Besides, he couldn't possibly have killed Lionel—he idolized him!"

"Or he coveted his position," Beatrice interjected. "We all know how Charles envied Lionel's talent. Perhaps he felt threatened by Lionel's genius and decided to take matters into his own hands."

"Enough!" Harriet raised her voice, cutting through the rising tide of accusations. "We must not jump to conclusions without evidence. Each of you has something to gain from Lionel's death, but without motive, we remain in a state of conjecture."

The detective moved back towards the clock, studying it closely, as though it might whisper its secrets to her. "What if I told you that Lionel had discovered something—a design or a mechanism that could change everything? Something that could alter the very fabric of our society?"

Gasps echoed through the room, and the tension escalated palpably. The air crackled with anticipation as Harriet continued. "Perhaps that is why someone felt compelled to silence him."

"But who?" Beatrice asked, her voice trembling. "Who would want to do such a thing?"

"Someone who stood to lose everything," Harriet replied, her gaze sweeping over each suspect. "And that is precisely why we must delve deeper into the secrets each of you harbor. Time may have stopped, but our investigation is just beginning."

With each tick of the clock, the evening wore on, and the layers of deception began to unravel. Harriet felt the weight of her own thoughts pressing against her, but she knew that clarity would emerge if she could just keep them talking. Each word, each confession would bring them closer to the truth.

"Let's not forget," she continued, "that secrets have a way of revealing themselves, especially when confronted by the light of scrutiny. We all have shadows lurking in our pasts. The question is: how far will each of you go to protect your own?"

The atmosphere thickened with suspense as Harriet's words hung in the air. She sensed that the truth was close, tantalizingly so, and that one of them would slip up—if she could only apply enough pressure.

"Tell me, Charles," she said, her eyes fixed on the treasurer. "Did you receive any unusual offers recently regarding Lionel's designs? Perhaps an invitation to join forces with a rival watchmaker?"

Charles stiffened, a flicker of panic crossing his face. "I have no idea what you're talking about!" he stammered, but the hesitation in his voice betrayed him.

"Do not lie to me," Harriet pressed, the intensity of her gaze piercing through his facade. "Your alibi is fragile, and so too is your loyalty to this society."

"Enough of this!" Geraldine exclaimed, her voice sharp and desperate. "We're wasting our time! This is a witch hunt!"

"Or a reckoning," Harriet countered calmly. "Each of you has your part to play in this tragic drama. You are not merely witnesses; you are all suspects."

The room fell into a heavy silence, the weight of Harriet's words sinking in. As the shadows danced around them, she could feel the tension coiling like a tightly wound spring, ready to snap. She needed to strike at the right moment, to catch someone off guard.

"Tonight, we will play a little game," Harriet declared, her voice steady and commanding. "You each have an opportunity to defend yourselves, but I urge you to remember—every move you make is being observed. Each question I pose may very well be a part of your checkmate."

The tension in the room was electric, and the guests shifted uneasily in their seats. One by one, they began to speak, sharing half-truths and evasions, each trying to outmaneuver the others while avoiding Harriet's penetrating gaze.

As the evening wore on, it became clear that while they may be skilled at the intricate art of horology, they were decidedly less adept at concealing their own secrets. Each word they spoke was like a cog in the clock, moving them closer to the inevitable revelation that awaited them.

Hours passed, the night deepening around Foxglove Manor, and Harriet's mind raced. She pieced together the fragments of each suspect's story, discerning patterns that hinted at deeper truths. Every glance, every hesitation revealed the chinks in their armor.

"Time is but a thief," she mused, "stealing our moments while revealing our secrets. And in this game of chess, it is essential to anticipate your opponent's next move. So, let us see how far you will go to protect your own pieces."

As the clock chimed again, marking the passage of another hour, Harriet knew she was closing in on the truth. Each tick resonated with the finality of a judgment being passed, and in this game of intrigue, the stakes had never been higher.

Suddenly, a loud crash echoed from the direction of the study, startling everyone into silence. Harriet's heart raced as she turned towards the sound, instinctively reaching for the small revolver concealed in her handbag.

"Stay here!" she ordered, her voice sharp as she rushed toward the source of the noise. The others followed, their eyes wide with fear and confusion.

Upon entering the study, they were met with chaos. The desk had been overturned, papers strewn across the floor like confetti. And there, on the ground, lay another body—this one lifeless and still.

"By the gods!" Beatrice gasped, stumbling back as she clutched her chest in shock.

Harriet's breath caught in her throat as she recognized the figure. It was Geraldine Hargrove, her eyes glassy and unseeing. The room was saturated with the scent of blood, and the ticking of the clock now felt like a countdown to something much more sinister.

"Murder!" someone screamed, and the realization dawned upon them with chilling clarity. The very foundation of their gathering had crumbled, leaving behind only a twisted puzzle of death and betrayal.

In that moment, Harriet understood: the game had escalated, the players now reduced to mere pawns in a far more dangerous game. And as the clock continued its relentless ticking, she knew she had to move swiftly before another life was snuffed out.

"Secure the house!" Harriet commanded, her voice unwavering despite the chaos surrounding her. "No one leaves until we uncover the truth behind this second murder!"

As the guests scrambled to obey, Harriet's mind raced with the possibilities. The killer was among them, and time was of the essence. Each moment brought them closer to the revelation that could unravel the entire tapestry of deceit woven within Foxglove Manor.

With determination igniting her every step, she set her sights on the clock—its hands now stained with the echoes of lives lost. The game was far from over, and Harriet Blake was resolute in her mission to uncover the truth, no matter the cost.

As she began to piece together the events of the night, Harriet's mind flickered with fragments of the past—memories of Lionel, of Geraldine, and of the secrets they had shared. Each revelation led her deeper into a labyrinth of motives and desires, where the clockwork of fate turned relentlessly onward.

In this game of checkmate, every move mattered. The next move could mean life or death, and as Harriet prepared to confront the remaining guests, she felt the weight of their secrets pressing down upon her.

But she was not one to shy away from the truth. She would unravel their tales, expose their lies, and ultimately bring the murderer to justice, for in this world of ticking clocks and buried truths, time was the only ally she could trust.

As she stepped back into the parlor, the tension palpable, Harriet Blake knew that the pieces were finally falling into place. The clock continued to tick, each second bringing her closer to the heart of the mystery, and she was ready to uncover the deadly game that had ensnared them all.

Chapter 9: Echoes of Betrayal

1. A Letter from the Dead

As the morning sun struggled to pierce through the heavy fog enveloping the small village of Eldermere, a sense of foreboding hung in the air. The villagers went about their morning routines, but whispers of the recent tragedy lingered like a shadow. Just a week prior, the body of Arthur Pendleton, a reclusive and enigmatic figure, had been discovered in the library of his ancestral home. The news had spread like wildfire, and now, the town was alive with speculation.

Detective Inspector Clara Hargrove, a woman with a reputation for unraveling the most tangled of mysteries, stood on the steps of Pendleton Manor. She surveyed the scene with a keen eye. The grand estate, once a proud testament to the Pendleton lineage, now felt more like a tomb. The ivy-clad walls seemed to watch her, holding secrets of their own.

"Inspector Hargrove!" called a voice from behind. It was Constable Finch, a loyal assistant, with a letter clutched tightly in his hand. "You'll want to see this."

Clara took the letter, noticing the frayed edges and the faint scent of lilacs, a flower Arthur had always favored. Her heart raced as she broke the seal, revealing the elegant handwriting within.

To whom it may concern,

If you are reading this letter, it means I have departed from this world under circumstances that may appear suspicious. You must know that my death was not the result of chance or fate, but rather the design of a cunning mind. I implore you to look closely at those around me, for I am certain that one among them seeks to gain from my demise. Trust no one, for appearances can be deceiving.

Yours,

Arthur Pendleton

Clara's brow furrowed as she read the words again. This was no ordinary letter; it was a desperate plea from beyond the grave, a call to action for her to delve deeper into the tangled web of Arthur's life.

"Whoever wrote this was clearly frightened," she murmured, glancing at Finch. "It implies a murder, but without a proper suspect or motive, we are left to chase shadows."

"Should we gather the family?" Finch suggested, his face a mixture of apprehension and curiosity.

"Indeed. We need to understand the relationships at play here. Arthur's death has turned this estate into a breeding ground for suspicion. Let us not delay."

As they stepped inside the manor, the scent of old books and polished wood greeted them. The library, where Arthur had been found, stood as a testament to his solitary life, filled with volumes of history, philosophy, and literature. Clara's gaze lingered on the desk where Arthur had spent countless hours, writing and reading, perhaps contemplating his own mortality.

The family members gathered in the drawing room, each bearing a distinct demeanor. There was Eleanor, Arthur's younger sister, who seemed fragile and delicate, her eyes puffy from crying. Next to her sat Victor, the eldest brother, a man of imposing stature but with an air of arrogance. His expression was inscrutable, revealing little emotion as he stared at Clara with suspicion.

Finally, there was Margaret, Arthur's devoted housekeeper, whose loyalty to the Pendleton family was well known. Clara sensed a storm brewing among them, an undercurrent of tension that belied their stoic appearances.

"Thank you for coming on such short notice," Clara began, her voice steady and commanding. "I believe you are all aware that your brother, Arthur, has passed under troubling circumstances."

"Troubling is an understatement," Victor scoffed, leaning forward in his chair. "What do you intend to do about it, Inspector? We deserve answers!"

"Indeed, Mr. Pendleton. But first, I need to know what you can tell me about your brother's last days. Did he express any fears or concerns?"

Eleanor spoke first, her voice barely above a whisper. "He... he was worried about something, yes. He mentioned receiving strange letters lately, but he refused to elaborate. I thought it was merely his imagination."

"Letters?" Clara repeated, her interest piqued. "Did he keep them?"

"I believe so," Eleanor replied, glancing at Margaret. "You would know, wouldn't you?"

Margaret nodded, her expression serious. "I have a box of his correspondence in the attic. Arthur was always meticulous about keeping things organized. I can fetch it for you."

"Excellent. I would like to see them all. Finch, accompany her," Clara ordered. "The rest of you, remain here. I have further questions."

As the constable and Margaret left the room, Clara focused her attention on Victor. "What about you, Mr. Pendleton? Did Arthur mention anyone specific who might wish him harm?"

Victor crossed his arms defiantly. "I have no idea. Arthur was always so consumed with his own thoughts that he rarely discussed his life with the rest of us. But I would not be surprised if it were one of the local farmers. They have always envied our family's wealth."

"Interesting. And you, Miss Eleanor? Were you close to your brother?"

Eleanor's eyes filled with tears as she replied, "I tried to be, but he shut us out. Ever since our parents died, he became distant. I often felt he was hiding something from us. But to think someone would... to think someone would kill him..."

Before Clara could respond, the door swung open, and Margaret returned, carrying a dusty wooden box. "Here it is, Inspector. I haven't touched it since... since he passed."

"Thank you," Clara said, accepting the box with a sense of anticipation. She opened it carefully, revealing a collection of letters, neatly tied with a faded ribbon. Each envelope was marked with dates and the names of various senders.

"I'll need a moment to review these," Clara said, her fingers delicately tracing the letters. As she began to read, she felt the weight of Arthur's fears pressing down upon her. The first few letters spoke of mundane matters—thank you notes, invitations—but then she stumbled upon a letter that sent a chill down her spine.

Dear Arthur, it began, I know what you have been keeping from your family. The truth is about to surface, and you will pay for your secrets.

"What is it, Inspector?" Victor's voice broke through her concentration.

Clara looked up, her heart racing. "It seems your brother was indeed being threatened. This letter is from someone who claims to know his secrets. It's possible he was being blackmailed."

"Blackmailed?" Eleanor gasped, her hand flying to her mouth. "But what could he have possibly done?"

"I don't know yet," Clara replied, carefully folding the letter and setting it aside. "But I intend to find out. We need to investigate further."

The tension in the room escalated as Clara continued to sift through the letters. Each one seemed to weave a deeper narrative, revealing not only Arthur's anxieties but also hints of a troubled past involving deceit, betrayal, and family rivalries.

Another letter caught her eye, this one dated just days before Arthur's death.

Arthur, it read, you have made a grave mistake in not disclosing everything to your family. Secrets cannot remain buried forever. They will rise to the surface, and you will not be able to escape the consequences. Beware.

Clara felt a sense of urgency. "This was no mere accident. Arthur's death was orchestrated by someone who wanted to silence him—someone who knew him intimately."

The room fell silent as the gravity of her words sunk in. Each family member exchanged glances, the reality of their situation dawning upon them. Clara sensed that beneath their polite facades lay deep-rooted animosities and long-buried secrets.

"Whoever is responsible is still among us," Clara concluded, her voice steady. "I will uncover the truth, but I need your cooperation. Trust is paramount now."

"What do you propose we do?" Victor asked, his bravado wavering.

"First, I'll need to question each of you individually," Clara stated. "And I must also gather more information about Arthur's recent activities. I want to know everything—who he met, where he went, and what he might have been hiding."

The family nodded in agreement, though Clara could see the flicker of fear in their eyes. The clock was ticking, and time was of the essence. She needed to uncover the truth before the killer struck again.

As the day wore on, Clara meticulously pieced together Arthur's final days. She spoke to neighbors, delved into his financial records, and reviewed the letters he had received. It became evident that Arthur was a man beset by his own demons—guilt and fear overshadowing his life.

Days turned into a week as Clara immersed herself in the case. The villagers, once curious, began to cast sidelong glances at the Pendletons, the air thick with suspicion. Clara had not only to unravel the murder but also to mend the rift that Arthur's death had created within the family.

At last, Clara gathered everyone again, their faces pale and apprehensive. "I have uncovered some disturbing truths," she began, watching their expressions carefully. "Arthur had a hidden past—a connection to someone who has now turned into a dangerous adversary. This person is not just a stranger; they are entwined within your family history."

"Who?" Eleanor gasped, clenching her hands in fear.

"Someone who felt betrayed," Clara said slowly. "Someone who has waited for their moment to take revenge. I believe this person is among you."

Gasps erupted from the gathered family, and accusations began to fly. Victor accused Eleanor of harboring secrets, while Margaret pointed fingers at Victor, suggesting that his jealousy over Arthur's inheritance could have driven him

to murder.

"Enough!" Clara's voice rang out, silencing the chaos. "We cannot let our emotions cloud our judgment. We must stick to the facts."

After a long, tense silence, Clara finally laid out her conclusion. "Arthur Pendleton's death was a premeditated murder. The letters he received indicate a clear motive: revenge for a past betrayal. The murderer is someone who felt wronged by Arthur—someone who thought they could gain something from his demise."

The tension in the room was palpable, every eye fixed on Clara as she continued. "I believe the motive lies buried in the family's history—a secret that one of you has carried for too long. It is time to confront that truth."

Eleanor's voice quivered as she spoke. "What do you mean? What secret?"

"The estate has long been burdened by hidden grudges. Arthur's decisions affected all of you. I suspect that his desire to cut ties with the past, to protect certain family legacies, may have incited the anger of someone who felt slighted."

"I didn't harm him!" Victor shot back defensively, his face flushed. "Whatever he did, it had nothing to do with me."

Clara turned to Margaret, whose eyes glistened with unshed tears. "Margaret, you were the one closest to him. You knew his fears. Did Arthur confide in you about anything concerning his past?"

Margaret took a deep breath, collecting her thoughts. "Arthur was troubled, yes. He spoke of a past mistake, something he wished he could change. But he never told me exactly what it was. All I know is that he feared someone would find out."

"Find out what?" Clara pressed.

"Something to do with an old family feud," Margaret whispered, her voice barely audible. "It was a rivalry between the Pendletons and the Hawthornes. Something that happened long before I joined the family, but I heard the whispers... it was dark, it was ugly."

As the weight of her words settled in the room, Clara felt the pieces of the puzzle slowly coming together. The past could no longer be ignored, and the ghosts of the Pendleton family were rising to the surface.

"Eleanor, do you know anything about this feud?" Clara asked, her eyes locked on her.

Eleanor shook her head, tears streaming down her cheeks. "No, I swear! Arthur never spoke of it. I thought it was just a rumor."

"Perhaps Arthur felt it was his burden to bear alone," Clara mused. "But someone among you must know the truth. A secret this grave cannot remain hidden forever."

The family sat in silence, the tension thick enough to cut with a knife. Clara felt a determination welling within her. She would uncover the truth, no matter how deeply it was buried.

"I will need to dig deeper into this family feud," Clara declared. "There may be old records, documents that could shed light on what transpired between your families. I must return to the estate archives and investigate further."

As Clara prepared to leave the room, she felt a sense of urgency—a palpable reminder that time was slipping through her fingers. She could feel the presence of the murderer lurking nearby, waiting for the right moment to strike again.

The following days were spent searching through dusty archives and hidden compartments within the manor. Clara uncovered letters and records, piecing together the tangled history of the Pendleton and Hawthorne families. Secrets long buried began to surface, revealing a tapestry of betrayal and rivalry that spanned generations.

As the investigation deepened, Clara found herself drawn to an old photograph of a woman who had once been a Pendleton. A beautiful woman, with an air of mystery about her. Beside her stood a man from the Hawthorne family—an unmistakable connection that tied the two families together in ways Clara had yet to fully comprehend.

Days turned into sleepless nights as Clara worked tirelessly, often alone in the dimly lit library, the only sounds being the ticking of the clocks that lined the walls. Each tick seemed to mock her as she raced against time to solve the mystery of Arthur Pendleton's death.

And then, one fateful night, while examining the photographs again, a revelation struck her. She realized that the woman in the picture was not just a distant relative; she was Arthur's grandmother, a woman whose love affair with a Hawthorne had resulted in the deep-seated feud that had plagued their families.

Clara felt a shiver run down her spine. Could it be that Arthur had been aware of this connection all along? Had he tried to reconcile the past, only to find himself ensnared in its dark legacy?

The following day, she summoned the family once more, determined to confront them with her findings. As they gathered in the drawing room, Clara felt the weight of their collective history bearing down on her.

"I believe I have discovered the truth behind the Pendleton-Hawthorne feud," Clara began, her voice steady. "It all started with a love affair—a forbidden romance that ignited the animosity between your families."

Eleanor gasped, her face pale. "How could you know that?"

"I found a photograph," Clara replied, holding it up for them to see. "This is your grandmother, Arthur. And the man beside her is a Hawthorne. Their affair was the catalyst for the rivalry that has lingered for decades."

Silence fell over the room as the implications of her words settled in.

"Arthur must have known," Victor said slowly, his expression a mix of disbelief and anger. "He must have thought he could make amends. But why now? Why not before?"

"Because he feared the consequences," Clara replied. "And it is possible that someone wanted to prevent him from revealing this connection. Someone who stood to lose everything."

The family exchanged nervous glances, and Clara could see the seeds of suspicion taking root once more.

"Who among you stands to gain from Arthur's silence? Who would prefer to see this history remain buried?" Clara pressed.

As the tension mounted, Margaret stepped forward, her voice trembling. "I never thought Arthur would take it this far. He was going to confront the Hawthornes, wasn't he? That must be why he was killed."

"Confront them?" Victor shouted, anger rising. "How could you allow him to act so recklessly? Did you know of this connection?"

"No, I swear!" Margaret insisted, tears streaming down her face. "Arthur never confided in me about his plans. I thought he was simply troubled."

Clara could see the fear reflected in their eyes, a fear that mirrored her own. Time was running out, and she needed to confront the killer before they could strike again.

"Tonight, I want you all to remain in the manor. I will not allow anyone to leave until I have uncovered the truth," Clara declared. "If the killer is among you, they will not escape justice."

That night, the atmosphere was thick with dread as Clara set about her investigation. With each passing hour, tensions escalated, and accusations flew. The family members could no longer hide behind their masks of civility, and the darkness of their past began to seep into their present.

As the clock struck midnight, Clara gathered everyone in the drawing room. "It is time to reveal the truth. The killer is among you, and I believe I have uncovered the identity."

Gasps echoed through the room, and Clara could see their faces pale.

"The person responsible for Arthur's death is driven by a desire for revenge—a need to protect a dark secret that has festered for years. The motive lies not just in Arthur's actions, but in the legacy he sought to confront."

"Who is it?" Eleanor asked, her voice trembling.

Clara took a deep breath, her heart racing. "It is you, Victor. You were desperate to protect the family name, to bury the truth about your grandmother's affair. Arthur's plan to confront the Hawthornes threatened everything you had built."

Victor's eyes widened in disbelief. "You're insane! I loved my brother! I would never harm him!"

"But you stood to lose everything if he revealed that connection. You had the most to gain by keeping the past buried," Clara argued, her gaze piercing into his soul.

Victor opened his mouth to protest, but the flicker of guilt in his eyes betrayed him. "You can't prove anything!"

"I don't need to prove it," Clara replied. "The truth is written all over your actions. The letters, the fear, and now this confrontation—it all points to you. You felt threatened, and in a moment of desperation, you took matters into your own hands."

"I didn't mean to kill him!" Victor's voice broke as he stepped back, realization dawning upon him. "I just wanted to scare him."

"You have sealed your fate," Clara declared, her voice steady. "You will face the consequences of your actions."

As the first light of dawn broke through the manor's windows, the tension began to dissipate. Victor was taken into custody, the burden of his guilt laid bare before them.

Eleanor and Margaret watched in silence, tears flowing freely as the weight of the tragedy settled upon them. Clara understood that this family had been shattered, their lives irrevocably changed by the darkness of their past.

As she stepped outside the manor, Clara felt the cool morning air wash over her, a cleansing breeze that carried away the remnants of fear. The case had been solved, but the echoes of the Pendleton legacy would linger, a reminder that time could not erase the shadows of history.

"The truth may be painful," Clara whispered to herself, "but it is the only path to healing."

With the dawn of a new day, she turned away from the manor, determined to seek out new mysteries, new truths, and to bring light into the darkest corners of human existence.

2. The Clockmaker's Apprentice

IN THE QUAINT VILLAGE of Eldridge, nestled amidst rolling hills and ancient oaks, the arrival of autumn brought with it a whisper of change. The leaves, painted in hues of gold and crimson, rustled in the crisp air as if conspiring with the winds to share secrets of the past. At the heart of this picturesque village stood a modest workshop, its windows fogged with the breath of creation. This was the domain of Horace Dobbins, the village clockmaker, renowned for his exquisite timepieces and uncanny ability to breathe life into the inanimate.

But on this particular morning, the air crackled with an unsettling tension. Young Thomas, the clockmaker's apprentice, stood at the entrance of the workshop, staring at the intricate façade of his mentor's creations, the rhythmic ticking echoing in his ears like a pulse. Though he had spent the better part of two years honing his skills under Horace's watchful eye, today felt different. Today, something hung in the air, a portent of events yet to unfold.

"Thomas!" Horace's voice, gruff yet warm, interrupted his thoughts. "Get in here! We've work to do." The older man was bent over a particularly ornate grandfather clock, its mahogany body gleaming under the muted sunlight. The clock's pendulum swung with an almost hypnotic rhythm, a counterpoint to Horace's meticulous adjustments.

"Coming, sir!" Thomas replied, shaking off the foreboding feeling that had settled in the pit of his stomach. He stepped inside, the familiar scent of wood shavings and oil enveloping him like a comforting blanket.

As he approached, Thomas noticed the clockmaker's brow furrowed in concentration. "I need you to fetch me the new spring from the shelf, lad. And be careful; it's delicate."

"Yes, sir." Thomas moved to the shelf lined with various parts and tools, the wooden surface worn smooth by years of use. As he rummaged through the assortment, he caught a glimpse of a small, intricately designed pocket watch resting in the corner. It was unlike anything he had ever seen, with a silver casing adorned with elaborate engravings of celestial bodies.

"What's that one, sir?" Thomas asked, holding the watch up to the light.

Horace glanced over, momentarily distracted. "Ah, that's a project I've been working on in my spare time. A special commission, it seems." His tone turned slightly guarded. "But not one I wish to discuss. Now focus on the task at hand."

Thomas nodded, though his curiosity piqued. He placed the pocket watch back on the shelf, but its allure lingered in his mind, an insistent whisper beckoning him to delve deeper.

The day wore on, the rhythmic ticking of clocks filling the workshop, harmonizing with the sounds of tools clinking and wood being shaped. Yet, beneath the surface, Thomas sensed a growing tension in Horace. The old man was preoccupied, often pausing to gaze out the window, as if searching for something—or someone.

"Is everything alright, sir?" Thomas ventured as they took a break for tea.

Horace sighed, pouring himself a cup, his hands trembling slightly. "It's just… the festival is coming, and with it, the pressure to deliver my finest work. People have high expectations, and I fear I won't meet them this year."

"The festival?" Thomas said, trying to mask his excitement. The annual Eldridge Festival was a time of celebration, a showcase of local crafts and talents, and for Horace, a chance to display his masterpieces. "You always impress them, sir. Your clocks are the finest in the county!"

"Flattery will get you nowhere, young man," Horace replied with a faint smile, though his eyes remained clouded. "It's not just about impressing the villagers. There's something else at stake this time. Something... more personal."

Thomas wanted to pry further, but he sensed that it was not the moment. The workshop felt charged with unspoken words, a web of secrets woven into the very fabric of their surroundings.

As the days passed, the festival approached with increasing fervor. Villagers bustled about, preparing for the celebrations, while Thomas and Horace worked tirelessly on their clocks. Yet, the pocket watch remained at the back of Thomas's mind, a puzzle waiting to be solved.

One evening, after Horace had gone home, Thomas decided to indulge his curiosity. He carefully retrieved the pocket watch from the shelf, admiring its craftsmanship. The engravings were stunning, each line and curve telling a story of its own. As he turned it over in his hands, he noticed a small, almost imperceptible latch on the side.

With a sense of trepidation, he pressed it, and the back of the watch clicked open, revealing a hidden compartment. Inside lay a folded piece of parchment, its edges worn and frayed. Thomas's heart raced as he carefully unfolded it, revealing a series of numbers and symbols, accompanied by a note written in a hurried scrawl:

"Beware the hands of time. They will reveal all, but the truth is a dangerous game."

The words sent chills down his spine. What truth was Horace hiding? What connection did it have to the pocket watch?

Determined to uncover the mystery, Thomas spent the following days studying the numbers and symbols, attempting to decipher their meaning. He ventured into the village library, poring over old texts and records, seeking any clue that could connect the enigmatic watch to Horace's past.

Meanwhile, Horace grew increasingly agitated. The closer the festival came, the more restless he became, often retreating to the back room of the workshop for hours on end. Thomas tried to engage him in conversation, but each attempt was met with a distracted nod or a terse reply.

One evening, as the sun dipped below the horizon, painting the sky in shades of purple and orange, Thomas resolved to confront Horace about the watch. He could no longer ignore the nagging feeling that something dark loomed just beneath the surface.

"Sir," he began, choosing his words carefully, "I found something in the pocket watch. It has a message, and I think it might be important."

Horace's expression shifted, the shadows of the room deepening around him. "You shouldn't have tampered with it, Thomas. Some things are better left untouched."

"But what does it mean?" Thomas pressed, unable to quell his curiosity. "What truth are you hiding?"

Horace's eyes flickered with a mix of anger and fear. "You're a clever lad, but there are secrets in this world that can lead to ruin. It's not my secret to share."

"But I want to help you! Whatever it is, we can face it together."

"Help? You think you can help me? You have no idea what you're asking." Horace's voice trembled, and for a moment, the clockmaker seemed less a mentor and more a man haunted by his past.

The tension hung thick in the air, and Thomas could feel the weight of unspoken history pressing down on them. "Please, just tell me what's going on."

Horace took a deep breath, his shoulders slumping as if the weight of the world rested upon them. "It's not just about the festival, Thomas. There are forces at play here that you can't possibly comprehend. People are not always what they seem. Trust me when I say this: some clocks should never be wound."

The old man's cryptic words sent a chill down Thomas's spine. He watched as Horace retreated into the shadows of the workshop, leaving him alone with the swirling thoughts of danger and deception.

As the festival dawned, the village transformed into a vibrant tapestry of colors and sounds. Stalls lined the streets, showcasing local crafts and wares, the air thick with the scent of spiced cider and roasted chestnuts. Yet, beneath the cheerful façade, an undercurrent of unease persisted.

Thomas stood behind the counter of their booth, surrounded by clocks of all shapes and sizes, but his mind was elsewhere. He glanced towards Horace, who was engaged in conversation with an elegantly dressed woman. Her presence sent a shiver down his spine—there was something about her that seemed out of place in the quaint village.

"Thomas!" Horace's voice broke through his thoughts. "I need you to help me with this display."

"Of course, sir." He moved to assist, but his gaze kept drifting to the woman. There was an air of familiarity about her, an echo of something he couldn't quite place.

As the day wore on, the festival reached its peak. Music filled the air, and laughter echoed in the streets, but Thomas felt a growing tension around him. He watched as villagers admired Horace's clocks, their faces alight with wonder, yet the clockmaker himself seemed increasingly distracted, his eyes scanning the crowd as if searching for someone.

When the sun began to set, casting long shadows across the square, Thomas noticed the woman approaching their booth. Her presence drew the attention of several onlookers, but her gaze was fixed solely on Horace.

"Mr. Dobbins," she greeted him, her voice smooth like silk. "It's been a long time."

Horace stiffened, the color draining from his face. "Madam Hawthorne," he replied, his tone cool but strained. "I didn't expect to see you here."

"Ah, but you know how much I enjoy these little festivities," she said, a smile playing at her lips. "Especially when old acquaintances are present."

Thomas exchanged a wary glance with Horace, sensing the unspoken tension between them. It was clear that there was a history here, one that was far from friendly.

"May I see your latest creation?" she asked
, her eyes glinting with curiosity.

"Of course," Horace replied, his voice betraying a hint of reluctance as he handed her the ornate pocket watch. "But I must warn you—this piece is not for sale."

"Oh, I'm not interested in purchasing," she replied, examining the watch with an almost predatory gaze. "I'm simply... intrigued."

As she held the watch, Thomas felt a surge of protectiveness. The words from the parchment echoed in his mind—Beware the hands of time. What connection did this woman have to the clockmaker's past?

"Madam Hawthorne, I believe we have nothing more to discuss," Horace said, attempting to reclaim control of the situation.

But she only chuckled softly, placing the watch back on the counter. "You underestimate me, Horace. You always have."

With that, she turned to leave, her presence lingering like a shadow in the fading light.

As night fell over Eldridge, the festival continued to bustle, but Thomas felt a sense of foreboding settle in. The revelry felt hollow, the laughter tinged with an unshakeable tension.

"What was that about?" he asked Horace, who had fallen silent, staring into the distance.

"Nothing that concerns you, Thomas," Horace replied tersely.

"But it does concern me! You've been acting strange for weeks, and now she shows up out of nowhere? What is going on?"

Horace sighed, running a hand through his thinning hair. "Madam Hawthorne is not just anyone, Thomas. She is someone from my past—a past I wish to forget."

"But you can't ignore her. She knows something."

"Leave it be, lad. There are things best left undisturbed."

Thomas clenched his jaw, frustration boiling within him. "I can't just stand by while you're in danger. I have to find out what she wants."

"Danger?" Horace's gaze sharpened. "You think you can protect me? You're still an apprentice. You don't understand the world we live in."

"Then teach me! I can help you!" Thomas urged, but Horace shook his head.

"It's too late for that. Just focus on your work. The festival will end soon, and we can return to normalcy."

The words felt hollow, a facade Thomas couldn't accept. The festival may have been a celebration, but the true dangers lay hidden beneath the surface, ready to erupt like a clock winding down to its final tick.

As the last rays of sun disappeared behind the horizon, Thomas found himself standing at the edge of the village, gazing up at the clock tower that loomed over Eldridge. The clock, a towering symbol of time itself, seemed to mock him with its unyielding march forward.

Determined to protect his mentor, Thomas resolved to uncover the truth behind Horace's past and the enigma of Madam Hawthorne. He knew that the clock was ticking, and with each passing moment, the danger grew ever closer.

The next day, with the festival behind them, Thomas decided to take a trip to the local archives, hoping to find more information about Horace's past and his connection to Madam Hawthorne. The village records were stored in a dusty old building on the outskirts, where time seemed to stand still among the yellowed pages and fading photographs.

Inside, the musty smell of old books filled the air as he approached the librarian, an elderly woman with sharp eyes and a kind smile. "What can I do for you, young man?" she asked, peering over her spectacles.

"I'm looking for information on Horace Dobbins and anyone connected to him, particularly a Madam Hawthorne," he said, trying to keep his voice steady.

The librarian's expression shifted, a flicker of recognition crossing her face. "Ah, Horace... a talented clockmaker. But there's more to his story than just timepieces. What do you wish to know?"

"Anything about his past, particularly regarding his dealings with Madam Hawthorne. I feel there's a connection I need to understand."

The librarian hesitated, her gaze drifting towards a shelf filled with old newspapers. "Very well. But be warned, young man—some stories are better left untold."

Thomas nodded, determination flooding his veins. He followed her to the shelf, where she began to pull out yellowed newspapers, each one a window into a past he was only beginning to grasp.

Hours passed as they sifted through articles and clippings, uncovering snippets of a life once lived. There were mentions of Horace's early successes, his rise to prominence as a clockmaker, but also whispers of a scandal that involved him and a series of peculiar incidents tied to the village's history.

Then, amidst the pages, he stumbled upon a headline that sent a jolt of shock through him: "Mysterious Deaths Linked to Eldridge Clockmaker!"

His heart raced as he read the article, detailing a series of unexplained deaths that had befallen several villagers around the time Horace gained notoriety. The reports hinted at foul play, with accusations directed towards Horace, though no evidence was ever found.

"Is this true?" Thomas asked, his voice barely above a whisper. "Did people really die because of him?"

The librarian nodded solemnly. "It's a dark chapter in Eldridge's history. Many believed he was cursed, that his clocks were somehow connected to the tragedies. It tarnished his reputation, and people grew fearful of him."

"Madam Hawthorne," Thomas murmured, the pieces beginning to fall into place. "She must have played a role in this."

"Indeed," the librarian confirmed, pulling out another article. "She was known to have a close relationship with Horace back then. Some claimed they were involved in a romantic entanglement, while others whispered of a partnership in his craft."

"What happened to her?"

The librarian hesitated, her fingers tracing the edge of the article. "She vanished shortly after the scandal broke. Some say she left Eldridge, while others believe she met a more sinister fate. No one truly knows."

A shiver ran down Thomas's spine. The mystery of Madam Hawthorne deepened, intertwining with the very fabric of Eldridge itself.

With newfound determination, he thanked the librarian and left the archives, his mind racing with the implications of what he had discovered.

Returning to the workshop, Thomas found Horace deep in thought, surrounded by the familiar ticking of clocks. "Did you find what you were looking for?" Horace asked without looking up.

"More than I expected," Thomas replied, steeling himself for the confrontation. "I know about the deaths, and I know about Madam Hawthorne."

Horace's shoulders tensed, and he turned to face Thomas, his expression unreadable. "You shouldn't have delved into that. It's the past for a reason."

"It's not just your past, it's our future too! If she's back, there's a reason for it."

"Enough!" Horace snapped, his voice sharp. "You're playing with forces you don't understand. Leave it be, Thomas."

But Thomas refused to back down. "I can't. Not when there's so much at stake. We have to confront her before it's too late."

Horace's gaze softened, a flicker of regret crossing his features. "You're brave, lad. Braver than I was at your age. But some battles are not worth fighting. You could lose everything."

"What could I possibly lose?"

Horace hesitated, the weight of his past hanging heavy in the air. "You could lose yourself. I lost my way once, chasing shadows and phantoms. It nearly cost me everything."

Thomas took a step forward, the urgency of the moment propelling him. "Then let me help you. If she's a threat, we need to stop her together."

Horace's eyes darkened, the storm of emotions swirling within him. "Very well. But if we're to confront her, we must do it wisely. I will not have you thrown into danger."

That night, they devised a plan, discussing strategies and potential outcomes. Thomas felt a sense of purpose igniting within him, a burning desire to protect Horace and uncover the truth once and for all.

As the days passed, the tension between them lingered like an uninvited guest. They continued their work, but the specter of Madam Hawthorne loomed large.

One evening, as Thomas polished a beautiful mantle clock, he heard the unmistakable sound of the workshop door creaking open. He turned to see Madam Hawthorne standing in the threshold, her silhouette framed by the fading light.

"Good evening, gentlemen," she said, her voice smooth and seductive. "I see you're still hard at work. How charming."

"Madam Hawthorne," Horace greeted, his voice steady but strained. "What do you want?"

"Oh, just a friendly visit," she replied, gliding further into the workshop. "I've heard the festival was a success. I wanted to congratulate you on your fine work."

Thomas stood frozen, unsure of how to respond. The air was thick with tension, each second stretching into eternity.

"Your clocks have always held a certain allure, Horace," she continued, a glint in her eye. "But it seems some secrets still linger. I wonder what you've been hiding."

Horace stiffened, his demeanor shifting from defensive to wary. "I have nothing to hide from you, Madam."

"Oh, but I beg to differ." She stepped closer, her gaze piercing through the veneer of calm. "I know about the watch. I know about the past you've tried so hard to forget."

"Enough!" Horace's voice thunder
ed, filled with a mix of anger and fear. "You have no right to intrude on my life any longer."

Her smile faded, replaced by a cold glare. "Do you think you can escape it? The past has a way of catching up with us, Horace. And when it does, it brings the truth with it."

"What truth?" Thomas interjected, stepping forward. "What are you implying?"

Madam Hawthorne's eyes flicked to him, a hint of amusement dancing within. "Ah, the apprentice. So eager to play hero. You have no idea what you're stepping into."

"Then enlighten me," Thomas challenged. "If you know something about Horace's past, you owe it to him to tell the truth."

She regarded him for a moment, her expression shifting to one of contemplation. "Very well, if it's the truth you seek. But be warned—it may not be the truth you want to hear."

As the clock in the corner chimed the hour, the workshop fell into an eerie silence. Thomas held his breath, anticipation electrifying the air around them.

"Years ago, Horace and I were not just colleagues; we were partners in both craft and life," she began, her voice laced with nostalgia. "But with success came jealousy, and with jealousy came chaos."

"What chaos?" Thomas pressed, sensing the weight of unspoken secrets.

"The village was rife with suspicion. People whispered about my influence over Horace's work, suggesting that my presence brought misfortune. When the deaths occurred, they turned on us both."

Horace's jaw clenched, memories flooding back. "I lost everything," he muttered, pain evident in his voice. "The accusations destroyed my reputation."

"And you left, didn't you?" Madam Hawthorne continued, her gaze fixed on Horace. "You abandoned your craft, your passion, all because of fear."

"Fear of what?" Thomas interjected, frustration mounting. "What truly happened?"

Madam Hawthorne's eyes softened, a glimmer of sadness breaking through her steely demeanor. "There were rumors of dark forces at play—of a curse placed upon Horace and his clocks. I tried to protect him, but the damage was done."

"Curses don't exist," Horace snapped, anger boiling to the surface. "They were merely rumors fueled by ignorance."

"But what if they weren't?" Madam Hawthorne challenged, her voice low and dangerous. "What if there was truth in those whispers? What if the hands of time do indeed hold power?"

Thomas felt a chill run down his spine. The tension in the air thickened as they exchanged heated words, each one a revelation unraveling the layers of their shared history.

"I came back to warn you, Horace," Madam Hawthorne said, her tone shifting from accusatory to earnest. "The past is stirring, and it seeks to reclaim what it lost. We must confront it before it consumes us."

"How can we trust you?" Horace replied, skepticism lacing his voice. "You vanished without a trace, leaving me to bear the weight of your choices."

"I had my reasons," she shot back, frustration evident. "But I've returned to help you. We must face the truth together, or it will tear us apart."

Thomas stood at the crossroads of their confrontation, torn between the conflicting emotions swirling around him. "What do you suggest?"

"We must investigate the origins of the curse," Madam Hawthorne replied, determination settling in her features. "There are old records hidden away in the village archives—records that may hold the key to unraveling this mystery."

Horace opened his mouth to protest, but Thomas interjected. "If it's the only way to protect you, then we must do it. We can't allow the past to dictate our future."

With a reluctant nod, Horace acquiesced. "Very well. But I will not allow my life to be dictated by shadows and fears."

The three of them set out that evening, determined to uncover the truth lurking in the archives. As they entered the old building, the air felt heavy with anticipation, each creak of the floorboards echoing the weight of their collective past.

They spent hours combing through records and books, searching for any hint of the curse that had haunted Horace for so long. Each piece of paper they turned over revealed a web of secrets, intertwining the fates of the villagers with the clockmaker's legacy.

As they worked late into the night, Thomas felt the tension rise, each revelation pulling them closer to the edge of the unknown. Then, buried among the pages, he discovered an old journal, its leather cover cracked and worn.

"This might be it," he breathed, opening it carefully.

Inside were sketches of intricate clocks and notes detailing strange occurrences that had plagued the village. Thomas's heart raced as he read about a clockmaker who had come before Horace, a man rumored to have dabbled in dark arts, his clocks said to be cursed.

"They believed he forged a pact," Thomas murmured, glancing at Horace. "A pact with forces beyond comprehension."

Madam Hawthorne leaned closer, her expression shifting from curiosity to concern. "This is dangerous knowledge. We must tread carefully."

"But we can't back down now," Thomas replied, determination igniting within him. "If this curse is real, we need to know how to break it."

As they delved deeper into the journal, they discovered a passage that sent shivers down their spines:

"When the clock strikes thirteen, the past will awaken. Only through sacrifice can the truth be unveiled."

"What does it mean?" Horace whispered, his voice trembling with trepidation.

"It means we must face whatever darkness lies ahead," Madam Hawthorne replied, her expression resolute. "We must be willing to confront our fears and make sacrifices for the truth."

"But at what cost?" Thomas questioned, unease creeping in. "What if the truth leads to more pain?"

"Sometimes, the truth is the only path to healing," Madam Hawthorne asserted, her eyes fierce.

As the clock in the corner chimed midnight, a sense of dread settled over them. The hands of time were moving, and with each tick, they felt the weight of their choices bearing down upon them.

"We need to prepare for what's to come," Horace said, his voice steadying. "There's no turning back now."

With newfound resolve, they left the archives, ready to face whatever awaited them. As they stepped into the cool night air, the village lay shrouded in darkness, the weight of the past lingering like a shadow behind them.

Days turned into weeks as they raced against time, uncovering more secrets and gathering allies among the villagers. But with each revelation came more danger, whispers of the curse spreading like wildfire, igniting fear in the hearts of those who once revered Horace.

Then came the night of the festival, an event that was supposed to celebrate their triumph over adversity, but instead became a catalyst for chaos. As the villagers gathered in the square, the atmosphere shifted; tension crackled like electricity, and the air was thick with anticipation.

Thomas, Horace, and Madam Hawthorne stood at the forefront, determined to unveil the truth. With a microphone in hand, Thomas addressed the crowd, his voice steady but urgent. "Ladies and gentlemen, we stand before you not just as craftsmen and artisans but as guardians of truth."

He felt the weight of their gazes upon him, a mix of curiosity and skepticism. "We have uncovered a dark chapter in our village's history, one that connects us all. The clockmaker's legacy is intertwined with the fate of Eldridge, and we must confront it together."

Murmurs rippled through the crowd, the atmosphere shifting from celebration to uncertainty.

"The curse that has haunted us for generations can no longer remain a secret," Madam Hawthorne added, her voice rising above the din. "But it is only through understanding our past that we can hope to reclaim our future."

A wave of fear washed over the villagers, some backing away, while others drew closer, intrigued. Horace stepped forward, his presence commanding. "I have borne the burden of this curse for too long. It is time we face it together, for the sake of our village and our lives."

Just as the tension reached its peak, the clock tower struck thirteen, the chimes resonating through the square like an ominous warning. The ground trembled beneath their feet, and a chilling wind swept through, snuffing out lanterns and plunging the village into darkness.

Gasps filled the air as shadows flickered around them, a tangible manifestation of the past coming alive. The villagers scrambled, fear gripping their hearts as they searched for safety.

"Stay together!" Thomas shouted, his voice rising above the chaos. "We must confront whatever is happening!"

Suddenly, figures emerged from the shadows—lost souls from the past, their faces twisted with pain and longing. They drifted toward Horace, their eyes filled with anguish.

"Horace Dobbins," one of them spoke, a voice echoing through the night. "You cannot escape your fate. The time has come to pay the price."

"What do you want?" Horace's voice wavered, fear flooding his features.

"The pact must be fulfilled," the figure continued, reaching out towards him. "Only through sacrifice can the curse be broken."

"Sacrifice?" Thomas echoed, dread creeping in. "What kind of sacrifice?"

"Only one life can restore balance," the spirit replied, its eyes hollow and haunting. "Choose wisely, for time is unforgiving."

Madam Hawthorne stepped forward, her voice firm. "No! We will not stand idly by while you threaten him. We will find another way!"

But the spirits swirled around them, their whispers growing louder, drowning out reason. The

villagers watched in horror, torn between fear and desperation, as time itself twisted and turned before them.

As the clock continued to toll, Thomas felt a surge of anger and resolve. "I refuse to let this happen! We can break the curse without sacrificing anyone!"

"But how?" Horace asked, desperation lining his voice.

"Together!" Thomas shouted, rallying the villagers. "We must unite against the darkness. We can't allow fear to dictate our lives any longer!"

As the spirits closed in, the villagers joined hands, forming a barrier against the shadows. Their voices rose in unison, a powerful chant that resonated through the air, pushing back against the darkness.

With each repetition, the shadows shrank, and the spirits faltered, their anguished expressions transforming to confusion. Thomas felt a warmth envelop him as the energy surged, fueled by their collective hope.

The clock struck the final hour, the chimes echoing with newfound strength. The shadows dissipated, and the spirits began to fade, their voices turning to whispers of gratitude.

As the night wore on, the village began to breathe again, the weight of the curse lifting as light returned to Eldridge.

Horace looked at Thomas, awe evident in his gaze. "You did it, lad. You broke the curse."

But Thomas shook his head, humbled. "We did it together. This village is stronger than any curse."

Madam Hawthorne stepped forward, a hint of a smile gracing her lips. "You've shown true bravery, Thomas. You've faced the past and emerged victorious."

As dawn broke over Eldridge, the village awoke to a new reality, one free from the shackles of the past. The clock tower stood tall, a symbol of resilience and unity.

Together, they rebuilt, reclaiming their heritage and forging a future unbound by the shadows of yesterday. Horace returned to his craft, his passion reignited, while Thomas embraced his role as an apprentice, ready to shape the world around him.

And as the clocks continued to tick, the village thrived, a testament to the power of truth, unity, and the unwavering hands of time.

3. Uncovering the Motive

THE MOON HUNG LOW OVER the sleepy village of Haverhill, casting an ethereal glow on the cobblestone streets that wound their way through the heart of the town. The silence was almost oppressive, broken only by the soft rustle of leaves in the night breeze. Inside the dimly lit sitting room of Rosewood Manor, however, a tense conversation was unfolding, one that would unveil secrets long buried and motives that ran deeper than anyone could have anticipated.

Detective Eliza Hart sat in an armchair, her keen eyes studying the faces of those gathered around her. The flickering light of the fireplace illuminated the anxious expressions of the guests who had been summoned there after the shocking events of the previous evening. A death, they all knew, could unravel the very fabric of their lives, especially when that death was shrouded in mystery and suspicion.

Among them was Lady Margaret Pembroke, the matriarch of the manor and a woman whose sharp wit was matched only by her formidable presence. She looked more frail than usual, her hands trembling slightly as she clutched her teacup. Next to her sat her son, Jonathan, a brooding figure with dark hair that fell over his forehead, casting shadows over his eyes. His jaw clenched, betraying his inner turmoil. Across from them was Dr. Charles Aldridge, the town's physician, who had been the first to arrive at the scene of the crime. His brow was furrowed, and the lines on his face deepened with the weight of the tragedy.

"Thank you all for coming," Eliza began, her voice steady and commanding. "I know this is a difficult time for everyone, but it is imperative that we uncover the motive behind this heinous act. Someone here knows more than they are letting on."

The room fell silent, the air thick with unspoken words and hidden truths. Eliza leaned forward, her gaze shifting from one face to another. "Let us begin with the events leading up to last night. Dr. Aldridge, can you recount what you found when you arrived at the scene?"

Dr. Aldridge cleared his throat, his fingers nervously tapping against his knee. "I was called shortly after midnight. The manor was eerily quiet when I entered, but the sight of Mr. Pembroke... it was horrifying. He was slumped over in the study, a pool of blood pooling beneath him." He hesitated, swallowing hard before continuing. "It appeared he had been struck from behind with a heavy object. There was no sign of struggle."

Eliza noted the way Lady Pembroke's knuckles turned white as she gripped her teacup tighter. "And was there anything unusual in the room? Any signs of forced entry?"

"None that I could see," Dr. Aldridge replied, shaking his head. "The windows were locked, and the door was secured from the inside. It was as if the killer had been someone he knew."

A murmur of agreement rippled through the group. Eliza's gaze fell on Jonathan. "What about you, Jonathan? Where were you at the time of the incident?"

Jonathan's expression hardened, his jaw tightening. "I was in my room, asleep. I didn't hear anything until my mother came to wake me."

"Did you hear anything unusual before that? Any voices?" Eliza pressed.

He hesitated, then said, "No, nothing."

Lady Pembroke interjected, her voice trembling. "Jonathan was always a heavy sleeper. It's possible he didn't hear anything."

Eliza raised an eyebrow, sensing the tension. "And what of you, Lady Pembroke? You were quite close to your husband. Did he mention anything unusual before the incident?"

She took a shaky breath, the color draining from her face. "He had been anxious about something... but he wouldn't tell me what. He insisted that it was nothing to worry about, but I could see the strain in his eyes."

Eliza noted this with interest. A secret burden often held the heaviest motives. "Dr. Aldridge, did Mr. Pembroke have any enemies that you were aware of?"

The doctor frowned, deep in thought. "Mr. Pembroke was a businessman. He had his fair share of rivals, but none I would consider dangerous. He was well-respected in the community."

"But respected does not mean liked," Eliza pointed out. "Every person has their secrets, and sometimes it's the ones closest to us that harbor the darkest intentions."

"Are you implying that someone in this room could be the killer?" Jonathan snapped, his voice rising. "How dare you! We're all in mourning here!"

Eliza held up her hand to quell the rising tempers. "I am not accusing anyone, but we cannot rule out the possibility that the killer is among us. We must explore all avenues." She paused, allowing her words to sink in before continuing. "What about the clockwork collection in the study? The one Mr. Pembroke was so passionate about?"

Lady Pembroke's expression shifted, her eyes narrowing slightly. "He had a fascination with clocks, yes, but it was merely a hobby. I don't see how that could relate to his murder."

"Perhaps not in a direct sense, but hobbies can often lead to obsession. Was there anyone in particular he was working with on this collection?" Eliza probed.

Jonathan shifted uncomfortably in his seat. "He had spoken of collaborating with a local artisan, but I can't recall his name. He seemed more excited about the project than anything else."

"An artisan, you say?" Eliza's interest was piqued. "And what about the financial aspect? Was he investing a significant amount of money into this?"

"Perhaps," Jonathan said hesitantly. "But my father was always good with finances. He wouldn't jeopardize our family's wealth on a mere whim."

Eliza nodded, considering this new information. "Dr. Aldridge, did you notice anything unusual about Mr. Pembroke's finances during your last consultations?"

The doctor frowned again, his brow furrowing. "I'm afraid I wouldn't know much about that. I only treated him for minor ailments."

"Then we must look further," Eliza concluded. "I intend to speak with the townsfolk. If there are any whispers or rumors about Mr. Pembroke's dealings, they will come to light."

Lady Pembroke's voice trembled as she spoke. "Please, Detective, just find out who did this. I cannot bear the thought of more scandal in our family."

Eliza leaned back in her chair, her mind racing with possibilities. The clock was ticking, and every passing moment brought them closer to the truth — or deeper into a web of lies.

As the night wore on and the shadows lengthened, Eliza felt the weight of the mystery pressing upon her. Secrets were like gears in a clock: intricate, interlocking, and sometimes hidden from view. But she was determined to uncover the motive that lay beneath the surface, no matter where it led her.

The next morning, as the first rays of sunlight broke over the horizon, Eliza set out into the village, her resolve strengthening with each step. The streets were still damp with dew, and the faint scent of blooming flowers filled the air, masking the underlying tension that gripped Haverhill.

Her first stop was the local tavern, The Rusty Key, where the townsfolk often gathered to share gossip over mugs of ale. As she entered, the lively chatter subsided, and all eyes turned to her.

"Detective Hart!" a voice called out, belonging to Old Tom, the barkeeper. "What brings you here so early?"

"I'm looking for information regarding Mr. Pembroke and his recent death," Eliza replied, her tone firm. "I believe someone here may have heard something that could be of help."

The crowd murmured among themselves, and a few exchanged glances that spoke volumes. Eliza's instincts told her there was more to this than met the eye.

"Aye, Pembroke was a fine man," Old Tom began, leaning on the bar. "But he had his share of enemies. People don't like it when others get ahead."

"What kind of enemies?" Eliza pressed, sensing the flicker of intrigue.

"Folks in business, you know. He was always trying to expand his reach. Some didn't take kindly to his methods," he said, rubbing the stubble on his chin. "But it's all hush-hush, if you catch my drift."

"Who in particular?" Eliza's curiosity intensified.

Old Tom glanced around the room, lowering his voice as if sharing a secret. "There's a rumor about a man named Cedric Marsh. They say he had a falling out with Pembroke a while back over a land deal. Never trusted that man, I say."

Eliza made a mental note of the name. "And where might I find this Cedric Marsh?"

"He runs the mill on the outskirts of town. You can't miss it. Just follow the river until you reach the old stone bridge, and it'll be on your left," Old Tom instructed.

"Thank you, Tom," Eliza said, determination igniting within her. As she stepped outside, the morning sun warmed her face, and she felt invigorated by the new lead.

The walk to the mill was a pleasant one, with birds chirping cheerily in the trees and the gentle sound of water flowing nearby. But as Eliza approached the mill, she couldn't shake the sense of unease that settled in the pit of her stomach. The mill stood tall and imposing, its worn facade a testament to the years it had endured.

As she entered, the rhythmic sound of machinery filled the air, drowning out her footsteps. The scent of freshly ground grain hung heavily, mingling with the dust motes that danced in the sunlight.

Cedric Marsh was a burly man, with calloused hands and a weathered face that spoke of hard work. He looked up from his task, surprise flickering across his features as Eliza approached.

"Can I help you?" he asked, wiping his hands on his apron.

"I'm Detective Eliza Hart, and I'm investigating the murder of Mr. Pembroke," she said, her tone direct. "I understand you had some business dealings with him."

Cedric's expression darkened. "Aye, we had our differences. Pembroke was a hard man to negotiate with."

"What exactly happened?" Eliza inquired, her interest piqued.

"We were supposed to strike a deal over some land he wanted for his expansion, but he pulled out at the last minute, claiming it was too risky. I invested time and money into that deal, and it cost me dearly," Cedric replied, anger flashing in his eyes.

"Did you threaten him?" Eliza probed.

"Not directly. But I did make it clear I was unhappy with how things turned out. That doesn't mean I killed him!" Cedric exclaimed, his voice rising defensively.

Eliza studied him closely. "Where were you last night, Mr. Marsh?"

He hesitated, his gaze darting away. "I was here, working late. I have orders to fulfill."

Eliza sensed his unease. "Do you have anyone who can verify your whereabouts?"

"I... I don't," Cedric admitted, his voice dropping. "But you can't think I would resort to murder over a business deal!"

Eliza took a step closer, her instincts guiding her. "I'm not here to accuse anyone. I just want the truth."

He sighed heavily, rubbing his temples. "I may have been angry, but I didn't want him dead. I just wanted to teach him a lesson. Someone else might have taken it too far, though."

"Who do you mean?" Eliza pressed, sensing she was onto something.

"Rumors around town suggest Pembroke was involved in some unsavory dealings with unsavory folks. I wouldn't be surprised if he had more enemies than just me," Cedric muttered, his expression darkening.

"Do you have names?" Eliza inquired, her heart racing with the possibilities.

"Just whispers, really. There's talk of him dealing with some shady investors from out of town. I'd steer clear of that crowd if I were you," Cedric replied, his voice low.

"Thank you for your honesty, Mr. Marsh," Eliza said, making her way toward the door. "I'll look into it."

As she stepped outside, the sunlight felt warm against her skin. With each new revelation, the puzzle pieces began to fit together, but the picture was still far from clear. She had to dig deeper.

Her next stop was to speak with the local tavern owner, who often served as an informal hub of information. She needed to know if there was any truth to Cedric's claims about Pembroke's dealings.

Returning to The Rusty Key, Eliza found the tavern abuzz with patrons, their conversations a mixture of laughter and whispers. Approaching the bar, she caught the eye of Old Tom.

"Back again, Detective?" he grinned, wiping down the counter.

"I need to know more about Mr. Pembroke's dealings with the outsiders," Eliza said, her tone serious. "Cedric Marsh mentioned some shady investors."

Tom's demeanor shifted instantly, his face growing somber. "I didn't want to say too much before, but you might want to speak to Mrs. Margaret Finch. She's been going on about strange folk coming to town and talking to Pembroke."

"Where can I find her?" Eliza asked, her interest piqued.

"She lives in that little cottage by the river, just past the bridge. You can't miss it," Tom said, nodding toward the door.

Eliza thanked him and made her way through the village once again. As she walked, her thoughts raced. Who were these investors, and what were their intentions with Pembroke?

Margaret Finch's cottage was a quaint, ivy-covered home that seemed to blend seamlessly into the landscape. Eliza knocked on the door, and it creaked open to reveal a woman in her late sixties, her expression a mix of curiosity and concern.

"Detective Hart, isn't it?" Margaret greeted, her eyes twinkling with intelligence. "I've heard about the unfortunate event."

"I'm here to ask you about Mr. Pembroke and any dealings he might have had with outsiders," Eliza said, stepping inside.

Margaret led her to a cozy sitting room filled with the scent of blooming roses. "Pembroke had his fair share of visitors, that's for sure. I saw a couple of strangers hanging around the tavern a few weeks back, always asking about him."

"Did they say anything specific?" Eliza probed.

"They were looking for investments. I overheard them discussing some shady business deals. They seemed eager to make connections in Haverhill," Margaret replied, her voice low.

"Do you remember their names?" Eliza asked, her heart racing with excitement.

"I wish I could, dear. But I only caught a glimpse of them. They were handsome fellows, dressed sharply, but there was something unsettling about them," Margaret said, her brow furrowing. "You could feel it in your bones."

Eliza took mental notes, each piece adding to the growing tapestry of mystery surrounding Pembroke's death. "Thank you, Mrs. Finch. You've been very helpful."

As she stepped back outside, a chill crept into the air. The pieces were slowly coming together, but the motives remained tangled like the gears of a broken clock.

Eliza returned to Rosewood Manor, her mind spinning with the information she had gathered. She needed to regroup and analyze what she had learned.

Gathering her thoughts in the sitting room, she realized they needed to confront Jonathan and Lady Pembroke with what she had uncovered. The tension in the room was palpable as she prepared to lay out her findings.

"Lady Pembroke, Jonathan," Eliza began, drawing their attention. "There is much to discuss regarding your husband's death."

They exchanged anxious glances, and Eliza could feel their apprehension as she spoke. "It seems Mr. Pembroke was involved with some unsavory characters from out of town, people who were eager to invest in his businesses. There's a possibility that these individuals may have had a motive to harm him."

Lady Pembroke gasped, her hand flying to her mouth. "You mean he had enemies?"

"Possibly," Eliza replied, watching their reactions closely. "But we must not overlook the potential for motives from within this very household. Each of you has a vested interest in the family's legacy."

Jonathan's face turned ashen. "You think my mother could be involved? How dare you! She loved my father!"

"Love doesn't preclude motive, Jonathan," Eliza stated firmly. "The financial burden of the business, coupled with your father's secrecy, could have driven anyone to desperation."

Lady Pembroke's composure began to falter. "I would never! I loved him, despite his faults. He was a difficult man, but he was my husband."

Eliza took a step closer, her voice steady. "Tell me the truth, Lady Pembroke. What did your husband say about his dealings? Did he mention anyone in particular?"

"He was worried about the future," she admitted, her voice barely a whisper. "He mentioned feeling trapped. But I thought it was just his usual anxieties."

"Did he ever discuss the clockwork collection with anyone? Could it be tied to these outsiders?" Eliza pressed.

"I don't know!" Lady Pembroke's voice trembled. "He was so secretive about that collection. It was as if he was hiding something."

Jonathan clenched his fists, his frustration boiling over. "What are you implying? That my father was involved in something illegal?"

"We need to explore every possibility," Eliza insisted, feeling the urgency of the moment. "Every family has secrets, and it's time to bring them to light."

As the conversation deepened, Eliza felt a knot tighten in her stomach. The intricate gears of this case were starting to align, but the truth still eluded her. With each revelation, the stakes rose higher, and she could sense that the clock was ticking down to an inevitable confrontation.

Determined to get to the bottom of this mystery, Eliza planned her next steps. The shadows of suspicion were growing darker, but she was resolute in her mission to uncover the motive behind the clockwork murders. Every second counted as she plunged deeper into the tangled web of deceit, betrayal, and hidden truths that surrounded the Pembroke family.

As dusk fell over Haverhill once more, Eliza gathered her notes and prepared to confront the forces at play. The clock was still ticking, and with each passing moment, she felt the weight of the case pressing down on her shoulders. She was determined to unearth the truth, no matter the cost.

The heart of the village pulsed with secrets, and Eliza was prepared to unveil them all. In the world of clockwork mysteries, she was the detective who would stop at nothing to reveal the motives hidden beneath the surface, racing against time to ensure that justice would be served before the last grain of sand slipped through the hourglass.

4. A Web of Lies

THE AFTERNOON SUN CAST a warm glow over the small village of Eldridge, illuminating the narrow cobblestone streets and quaint thatched-roof cottages that lined them. The air was thick with the scent of blooming flowers, a deceptive aroma that masked the darker secrets hidden beneath the surface. In this seemingly idyllic setting, tension simmered just below the surface, as if the very stones of the village were privy to the unspoken truths that bound its inhabitants in a web of lies.

At the heart of Eldridge stood the imposing figure of Hargrove Manor, a stately Victorian house that had witnessed generations of triumph and tragedy. Its ivy-covered walls were home to the affluent Hargrove family, who had long enjoyed the privilege and prestige that came with their wealth. However, whispers of discontent echoed through the halls, and the air was thick with a sense of foreboding.

As the clock struck three, Lady Eleanor Hargrove, matriarch of the family, prepared for her weekly tea gathering. With a keen eye for detail, she meticulously arranged the delicate china and polished the silverware, but beneath her composed exterior lay a troubled mind. Eleanor had always prided herself on her ability to maintain control over her family's affairs, yet recent events had left her feeling vulnerable.

Her son, Charles, had returned from London with an air of mystery surrounding him. Once a promising young man, he had become a shadow of his former self, consumed by an obsession with his late father's business dealings. Eleanor had noticed the change in him—his eyes no longer sparkled with youthful enthusiasm but were instead clouded with suspicion and paranoia. Whispers of financial ruin and betrayal danced in the air, and Eleanor feared that the web of lies was tightening around them.

As the guests arrived—old friends and acquaintances—Eleanor greeted them with a practiced smile, but inside, her heart raced. Among them was Miss Agnes Thornton, a close family friend who had always been a source of support, yet Eleanor felt an inexplicable tension whenever they met. Agnes, with her keen intellect and probing questions, had a way of uncovering truths that many preferred to keep hidden.

"Eleanor, darling, how lovely to see you," Agnes said, her voice lilting with warmth as she entered the drawing room. "Your home always feels so welcoming."

"Thank you, Agnes. I do my best to keep the spirit of the house alive," Eleanor replied, gesturing toward the plush armchairs arranged around the fireplace. "Please, take a seat. I'll fetch the tea."

As Eleanor moved toward the kitchen, she couldn't shake the feeling that Agnes was observing her, dissecting her every move. The women had shared many secrets over the years, but now it felt as though a great chasm had opened between them, one that neither dared to cross.

The conversation flowed easily as the guests sipped their tea and nibbled on delicate pastries. Laughter echoed in the room, but Eleanor sensed an underlying tension in the air. It was as if everyone was aware of the elephant in the room—the mounting pressure surrounding Charles's business ventures and the ominous specter of financial ruin.

"Charles, my dear," Agnes interjected, turning her gaze toward him, "I've heard some rather unsettling rumors about your father's estate. Is there any truth to the whispers of mismanagement?"

Charles's demeanor shifted, a flicker of anger flashing across his face. "I assure you, Miss Thornton, my father's affairs are none of your concern."

"Ah, but aren't we all affected by the decisions made within these walls?" Agnes replied, her tone light but her eyes sharp. "We care for you, Charles. It's only natural that we inquire."

Eleanor's heart raced as she watched the exchange unfold. She could sense Charles's frustration boiling beneath the surface, and she feared that Agnes's probing had only deepened the rift between them. "Agnes, perhaps we should discuss lighter matters," she suggested, desperate to steer the conversation away from the contentious topic.

"Of course, Eleanor," Agnes conceded, though her gaze lingered on Charles, a knowing look in her eyes. "But the truth has a way of surfacing, doesn't it?"

As the gathering continued, Eleanor's mind raced with thoughts of the web of lies that had ensnared her family. Secrets whispered behind closed doors, hidden agendas, and unspoken truths threatened to unravel the carefully crafted facade of their lives. With every passing moment, she felt the walls closing in, and the weight of the truth bore down upon her like a heavy shroud.

As twilight descended upon Eldridge, the guests began to depart, leaving Eleanor alone with her thoughts. The flickering candlelight cast dancing shadows across the room, and she found herself lost in a spiral of uncertainty. She longed for clarity, but the more she searched for answers, the more elusive they became.

That evening, as she retired to her chamber, Eleanor found herself unable to sleep. The rhythmic ticking of the ornate clock on the mantle seemed to echo in her ears, a constant reminder of the time slipping away. She couldn't shake the feeling that something was amiss, that the truth lurked just beyond her grasp.

In the days that followed, Eleanor's unease grew. Charles's behavior became increasingly erratic, and his obsession with uncovering the truth behind his father's death consumed him. He spent hours poring over old ledgers and correspondence, determined to unearth secrets buried in the past. Eleanor watched helplessly as her son spiraled further into a world of paranoia and suspicion.

One afternoon, while rummaging through the attic for a forgotten family heirloom, Eleanor stumbled upon an old trunk. Its weathered exterior was covered in dust, and the lock had long since rusted shut. Driven by curiosity, she pried it open, revealing a collection of letters, photographs, and documents that told a different story—one that challenged everything she thought she knew.

As she sifted through the contents, a sense of dread settled in her stomach. The letters spoke of shady dealings, financial troubles, and a long-standing feud with a rival family. The truth began to weave itself into the tapestry of her life, each revelation tightening the threads of the web that ensnared them all.

Determined to confront her son, Eleanor sought him out in his study, where the dim light barely penetrated the gloom. "Charles," she called softly, but he remained absorbed in his work, oblivious to her presence.

"Charles!" she insisted, stepping closer. "We need to talk."

He finally looked up, his expression a mixture of exhaustion and frustration. "Not now, Mother. I'm on the verge of discovering something monumental."

"Monumental or not, we cannot continue like this. Your obsession is tearing us apart," Eleanor pleaded.

"Is it obsession if I'm simply trying to uncover the truth?" he retorted, his voice rising. "You don't understand the stakes involved. If I don't find out what really happened, our family name will be destroyed."

Eleanor took a deep breath, trying to remain calm. "I understand that, Charles, but at what cost? We're losing each other in this pursuit."

He fell silent, his eyes clouded with conflict. "I just need to piece together the last puzzle. Once I do, everything will make sense."

"What if the truth is more painful than the lies?" Eleanor countered, her heart aching for her son. "What if it's a truth that shatters our family?"

"Then we must face it together," he said, though doubt flickered in his eyes.

Days turned into weeks, and as the investigation deepened, the web of lies surrounding the Hargrove family tightened with every revelation. Eleanor watched helplessly as Charles delved deeper into the past, his health declining under the weight of his obsession. He spent sleepless nights poring over old documents, barely eating, consumed by his need for answers.

As Eleanor reflected on the unfolding events, she found herself drawn to Agnes once more. Despite the tension between them, she sensed that Agnes held a key to the truth. With a heavy heart, she invited her friend to visit, hoping to unearth the wisdom that had always guided their relationship.

"Agnes, thank you for coming," Eleanor said, pouring tea into delicate china cups. "I need your perspective on something troubling."

"Of course, my dear," Agnes replied, her demeanor warm yet cautious. "What weighs on your mind?"

Eleanor hesitated, her thoughts racing. "Charles is consumed by the past, and it's tearing him apart. I fear that the truth he seeks may be too dangerous for him to uncover."

Agnes studied her intently, her fingers delicately tracing the rim of her cup. "The past has a way of catching up with us, Eleanor. Sometimes, it's better to let certain secrets remain buried."

"But at what cost?" Eleanor pressed. "Our family's legacy is at stake."

"Perhaps it's not the legacy itself that matters, but the bonds we forge in the process," Agnes suggested, her voice softening. "We must remember that truth can be a double-edged sword."

As the conversation unfolded, Eleanor began to realize that Agnes had seen through the web of lies long before she had. There was a depth of understanding in her friend's eyes that spoke of shared struggles and sacrifices made in the name of love.

"I'm afraid, Agnes," Eleanor confessed, her voice trembling. "I'm afraid of losing my son to the darkness of the past."

Agnes reached across the table, her hand resting gently on Eleanor's. "You must remind him that family is worth fighting for, no matter the cost. The web may be tangled, but the threads of love can still bind us."

Inspired by Agnes's words, Eleanor resolved to confront Charles once more, to urge him to see beyond the lies and embrace the truth that lay

within their family. As the sun dipped below the horizon, casting a golden hue over Eldridge, she felt a flicker of hope ignite within her.

The following day, Eleanor found Charles in his study, surrounded by stacks of papers and photographs. "Charles," she began, her voice steady, "we need to talk. It's time to stop chasing shadows and focus on what truly matters."

He looked up, weary but attentive. "What do you mean?"

"I've discovered some things about your father's dealings—things that may change how you view this entire investigation," she explained, her heart pounding. "But first, we need to acknowledge the impact of our pursuit. We must prioritize family over legacy."

Charles's brow furrowed as he absorbed her words. "You've found something?"

"I have," Eleanor admitted, her voice filled with urgency. "But we must confront this together, without the shadows of doubt hanging over us."

In that moment, she could see the flicker of understanding in his eyes. Perhaps the truth they sought could still bind them, even amidst the web of lies that had ensnared their family.

Together, they began to unravel the tangled threads of their history, piecing together the truth that had long been obscured by deception. Each letter, each photograph, revealed a story that had been hidden for far too long. As they worked side by side, Eleanor felt a sense of unity blossoming between them, as if the weight of their shared burden was beginning to lift.

Weeks passed, and the once oppressive atmosphere of Hargrove Manor began to shift. Eleanor and Charles worked tirelessly to uncover the truth behind the family's past, illuminating the shadows that had lingered for so long. The web of lies began to unravel, revealing the intricate connections that bound them to their history.

But just as they felt the weight of their discovery begin to lift, a sudden tragedy struck. One evening, while Charles was out gathering more information, Eleanor received a chilling phone call. A neighbor had found Charles's car abandoned at the edge of town, the engine still warm, and a sense of dread washed over her.

Panic seized Eleanor as she rushed to the scene, her heart racing. The quiet streets of Eldridge suddenly felt menacing, and the shadows grew long as she approached the car. A crowd had gathered, and whispers filled the air—rumors of foul play, of a confrontation gone wrong.

"Lady Hargrove, is it true your son has gone missing?" one of the onlookers asked, her voice laced with concern.

"I... I don't know yet," Eleanor stammered, her mind racing. "He was just here, working on the investigation."

As the hours ticked by, dread settled like a heavy fog. Eleanor was tormented by questions—had Charles uncovered something dangerous? Had he fallen victim to the very lies he sought to expose?

When night fell, a frantic search ensued. Villagers banded together, scouring the surrounding woods and fields, calling out for Charles. Eleanor's heart ached with fear and uncertainty, and as the moon cast its silvery glow over Eldridge, she felt the weight of despair pressing down upon her.

Finally, as dawn broke, hope flickered when a figure emerged from the tree line. It was Charles, disheveled and weary but alive. Relief flooded Eleanor's heart as she rushed to embrace him.

"Where were you?" she cried, her voice trembling. "We were so worried!"

"I was following a lead, Mother," he explained, his voice hoarse. "I uncovered something significant, but it led me into a dangerous situation."

"What do you mean?" Eleanor urged, pulling back to look into his eyes. "What did you find?"

Charles hesitated, a shadow crossing his face. "The truth about our family's past is darker than I could have imagined. There are those who want to keep it buried, and they will stop at nothing to silence anyone who dares to speak out."

Eleanor's heart raced as he continued. "I found documents that implicate some of the most prominent families in Eldridge. There's a connection to my father's death—one that goes beyond mere business dealings. It involves betrayal and greed."

As Charles recounted the details, Eleanor felt the web of lies tightening once more. The very fabric of their family was at stake, and the truth they sought threatened to expose not only their past but the darkest secrets of the village itself.

"We can't let fear dictate our actions," she urged, her voice steady. "We must stand together, even if it means confronting those who would do us harm."

With renewed determination, they resolved to reveal the truth, no matter the cost. As they began to piece together their findings, the connections between the Hargrove family and the rival families in Eldridge became alarmingly clear. Each revelation painted a picture of greed and betrayal, and as they dug deeper, the web of lies began to unravel before their eyes.

The more they uncovered, the more dangerous their pursuit became. Shadows lurked around every corner, and threats came in whispers, yet they pressed on, fueled by a determination to reclaim their family's legacy.

One fateful evening, as they prepared to reveal their findings to a gathering of trusted allies, a sudden knock at the door shattered the calm. Eleanor's heart raced as she exchanged a worried glance with Charles. "Who could it be at this hour?"

As she opened the door, the figure that stood before her sent chills down her spine. It was Agnes, her expression grave. "Eleanor, you must listen to me. There are people who want to stop you—who will do anything to keep the truth hidden."

"Agnes, we're on the verge of exposing a scandal that runs deep," Eleanor replied, her voice trembling. "We can't turn back now."

"I understand that," Agnes said urgently. "But I fear for your safety. The web of lies is more intricate than you realize, and the danger is very real."

Eleanor felt a shiver run through her. The stakes had never been higher, and yet she could not back down. "We're prepared to face whatever comes our way, Agnes. We've come too far to turn back now."

As they gathered their allies, the atmosphere in the room crackled with tension. Eleanor could feel the weight of their collective determination, a palpable energy that seemed to echo through the walls of Hargrove Manor. They were united in their quest for the truth, and for the first time in weeks, hope began to blossom amidst the shadows.

In the following days, they organized a meeting with the key figures in Eldridge—those who held the power to help them expose the truth. With each passing moment, Eleanor felt a surge of adrenaline, fueled by the anticipation of what lay ahead.

As the day of the meeting arrived, Eleanor and Charles stood at the entrance of the grand hall, their hearts pounding in unison. The room was filled with faces both familiar and unfamiliar, a gathering of those who had the ability to shape the future of Eldridge.

"Thank you all for coming," Eleanor began, her voice steady despite the whirlwind of emotions swirling within her. "Today, we stand united in our pursuit of truth—a truth that has long been shrouded in lies and deception."

Charles stepped forward, holding up the documents they had painstakingly gathered. "We have uncovered evidence that connects the Hargrove family to the very heart of the corruption that plagues this village. This is not just our story; it is a story that belongs to all of you."

The room fell silent, anticipation hanging heavy in the air. As Charles began to present their findings, Eleanor felt the tension in the room shift. It was as if the walls themselves were listening, and the weight of history pressed down upon them.

But just as the presentation reached its climax, a sudden commotion erupted at the back of the hall. A group of men, faces grim and determined, burst into the room. Their presence loomed large, a stark reminder of the power dynamics at play.

"Enough of this nonsense!" one of the men shouted, his voice booming. "You're meddling in affairs that don't concern you."

Eleanor's heart sank as she recognized the leader of the rival family, a man known for his ruthlessness. "We have a right to expose the truth," she retorted, her voice steady despite the fear gripping her.

"You will regret this decision," he warned, a chilling smile playing on his lips. "You have no idea what forces you're dealing with."

In that moment, Eleanor understood the gravity of their situation. The web of lies was not just a construct of deceit; it was a living, breathing entity that sought to protect its own.

With their safety at stake, Eleanor and Charles made a hasty decision. "We must leave, now," Charles urged, urgency lacing his voice.

As they made their way through the chaos, Eleanor felt a mix of dread and determination. They had come too far to turn back, but the reality of their situation weighed heavily on her heart.

In the days that followed, they went into hiding, moving cautiously through the shadows of Eldridge. The walls of Hargrove Manor had once felt like a sanctuary, but now they felt like a prison. The truth they sought to uncover had transformed into a dangerous game, and each day felt like a ticking clock counting down to an unknown fate.

During this time, Eleanor and Charles communicated discreetly with their allies, sharing the evidence they had gathered while remaining vigilant against those who sought to silence them. The stakes were high, and the risk of exposure loomed large, but they were determined to fight back.

With each passing day, the web of lies continued to tighten around them, and the danger grew more palpable. They could feel the shadows closing in, but Eleanor refused to succumb to fear. She drew strength from the knowledge that their pursuit of truth was worth the risk.

Then, one fateful evening, as they sat in a dimly lit room, a knock at the door sent shivers down Eleanor's spine. "Charles, did you invite anyone?" she whispered, her heart racing.

He shook his head, his expression tense. "Stay quiet."

As they exchanged worried glances, the door creaked open, and a figure stepped inside. It was Agnes, her face pale and her eyes filled with urgency.

"You must leave, Eleanor," Agnes urged, her voice trembling. "They're coming for you."

Eleanor felt a surge of panic as she turned to Charles. "We can't run forever," she said, desperation in her voice. "We need to fight back."

"There's no time," Agnes insisted, her eyes darting toward the door. "You're in grave danger, and if you don't act now, it could be too late."

With a heavy heart, Eleanor made the decision to flee once more. They gathered their belongings and slipped into the night, guided by Agnes's instincts as they navigated the labyrinthine streets of Eldridge.

As dawn broke, they found refuge in a small cottage on the outskirts of the village, hidden away from prying eyes. It was there that they devised a plan to expose the truth once and for all, determined to shine a light on the dark corners of their history.

Days turned into weeks, and with Agnes's assistance, they began to assemble a coalition of allies—those who had also been touched by the web of lies. It became clear that they were not alone in their struggle, and together, they began to gather the evidence necessary to confront those who had sought to silence them.

As the day of reckoning approached, Eleanor felt a sense of purpose igniting within her. She was no longer merely a mother fighting for her son; she was a woman determined to reclaim her family's legacy and expose the darkness that threatened to engulf them.

On the day of the planned confrontation, the tension in the air was palpable. They had gathered at a discreet location, surrounded by trusted allies who were equally invested in the pursuit of truth. Eleanor stood before them, her heart racing as she addressed the group.

"We've come together today not just as individuals but as a united force against the lies that have haunted our families for far too long," she declared, her voice steady and resolute. "Together, we will reveal the truth and ensure that the shadows that have plagued Eldridge are banished for good."

With each passing moment, Eleanor felt the weight of her family's history lifting. They had transformed the web of lies into a tapestry of resilience and hope. As they prepared to face their adversaries, she knew that no matter the outcome, they had already won by choosing to stand together.

As the sun dipped below the horizon, casting a warm glow over the gathering, Eleanor felt a sense of peace wash over her. They were ready to confront the darkness, armed with the truth and the strength of their unity.

In that moment, she realized that the web of lies that had ensnared them was not just a burden; it had forged connections that would endure long after the truth had been unveiled. The bonds of family, friendship, and loyalty would triumph over the shadows, and together, they would emerge stronger.

As the clock chimed, marking the beginning of a new chapter in their lives, Eleanor felt a flicker of hope ignite within her. The web of lies would no longer define them; they would reclaim their story, one truth at a time.

5. The Final Clue

THE AIR WAS THICK WITH tension as Detective Hart stood in the dimly lit study of the late Mr. Abernathy, the renowned clockmaker. The polished wooden surfaces gleamed faintly in the golden light of the flickering lamps, casting long shadows that danced upon the walls adorned with intricate timepieces of every conceivable design. Yet, amidst the elegance of the room, a sense of foreboding hung heavy in the atmosphere.

Only days ago, Abernathy had been found lifeless at his workbench, surrounded by the very creations that had defined his life. The investigation into his untimely demise had revealed a web of secrets, betrayal, and suspicion, each thread more sinister than the last. And now, as Hart meticulously examined the cluttered desk strewn with gears, cogs, and half-finished clocks, he felt the pressure of time closing in around him. He was determined to solve this case before another life was extinguished.

A gentle tap at the door pulled him from his reverie. The door creaked open to reveal Clara, Abernathy's once devoted apprentice, now burdened with the weight of grief and fear. Her usually bright eyes were clouded, and her hands trembled slightly as she stepped into the room.

"Detective Hart," she said, her voice barely above a whisper. "I believe I have something that might help you."

Hart raised an eyebrow, intrigued. Clara had been an invaluable source of information since the investigation began, her loyalty to Abernathy unwavering even in the face of tragedy. She approached the desk, a small leather-bound notebook clutched tightly in her hands.

"This was his," she continued, placing it gently on the surface. "I found it hidden behind one of the clocks. I wasn't sure if I should show it to you, but—"

"May I?" Hart interjected, reaching for the notebook.

Clara nodded, her apprehension palpable. As he flipped through the pages, Hart was met with Abernathy's neat, precise handwriting. Sketches of clock designs filled the pages alongside annotations that spoke of various inventions and theories, but one entry caught his attention immediately.

"Clara, look at this," he said, pointing to a detailed sketch of a clock with an unusual mechanism. The clock featured an intricate arrangement of gears that appeared to be linked to a series of numbers—an encoded message, perhaps.

She leaned in closer, her brow furrowing. "I've never seen anything like that. Do you think it's connected to... what happened?"

"I suspect it is. Abernathy was known for his eccentric designs, but this... this seems deliberate. It's as if he were trying to communicate something important," Hart replied, his mind racing.

Clara's gaze shifted from the sketch to Hart, fear etched across her features. "Do you think he knew he was in danger?"

Hart closed the notebook, a sense of unease settling over him. "It's possible. He might have been trying to protect himself or even warn someone. We need to understand this mechanism fully. If Abernathy left us a clue, it could lead us to the truth."

"Where do we start?" Clara asked, her determination igniting.

"The gears," he said, a plan forming in his mind. "If we can decipher the arrangement he sketched, we may find out what he was trying to convey. I'll need your expertise. Can you help me?"

Clara nodded, a spark of hope igniting in her eyes. "I'll do everything I can."

Together, they set to work, poring over Abernathy's notes, discussing every possible interpretation of the mechanisms. The hours slipped by unnoticed as they pieced together the cryptic puzzle, their collaboration a dance of intellect and intuition. The ticking of the clocks around them formed a rhythmic backdrop, a constant reminder of the urgency of their task.

As the night deepened, they finally reached a breakthrough. Hart, leaning back in his chair, stared at the design laid out before him. "If we interpret the gears in this manner, it could represent a series of coordinates."

Clara's eyes widened. "Coordinates? You mean... locations?"

"Yes," he replied, excitement building. "Abernathy might have encoded where something important is hidden. It could be the key to unraveling the motive behind his murder."

"But what could he have hidden? And why?" Clara pondered aloud, her brow furrowed in concentration.

Hart glanced at the sketch again, his mind racing. "It could relate to the missing blueprints for his latest invention—a revolutionary clock that could change everything. If someone wanted to steal his designs, they might have been willing to kill to keep him quiet."

Clara's expression hardened. "You think he was killed for his work?"

"I believe it's a strong possibility," Hart replied, his voice steady. "But we must act quickly. If this is indeed a clue, others may be looking for it as well."

They quickly gathered their things and set off towards Abernathy's workshop, located a short distance away. The moon hung high in the sky, casting an ethereal glow over the quiet streets. As they approached the workshop, Hart's instincts kicked into high gear. The air felt charged, as if the night itself were alive with secrets.

Inside the workshop, the familiar smell of oil and wood greeted them. The clocks ticked in unison, an eerie chorus that underscored the gravity of their mission. Hart led Clara to the back of the room, where Abernathy had kept his most prized creations. Among the dusty shelves and half-finished projects, there lay a locked cabinet, its wooden surface ornate yet worn.

"This cabinet..." Hart murmured, examining the lock. "If Abernathy concealed something important, it could be inside here."

Clara stepped forward, a look of determination on her face. "I can try to pick the lock. Abernathy taught me a thing or two about mechanisms."

Hart nodded, stepping aside as Clara knelt before the cabinet. With deft fingers, she worked the lock, her concentration palpable. As the final click echoed in the stillness, she looked up at Hart, her eyes sparkling with triumph.

"It's open!" she exclaimed, pushing the door ajar.

Inside, they found an array of clocks, each more exquisite than the last. But nestled at the back was a small box, intricately carved and adorned with symbols that matched those in Abernathy's sketches.

"Here it is," Hart breathed, pulling the box from its resting place. He opened it slowly, revealing a set of delicate blueprints, meticulously rolled and protected from the elements.

Clara gasped. "These must be the blueprints he was working on! This is incredible!"

"Yes, but we need to be cautious. If someone was willing to kill for these, they'll stop at nothing to get them back," Hart cautioned, carefully examining the documents.

The blueprints detailed a remarkable clock that integrated technology with art, a piece that could revolutionize the industry. Yet, it was clear that this design also held secrets—mechanisms that hinted at a purpose beyond mere timekeeping.

"Look here," Clara pointed to an inscription at the bottom of one of the sheets. "It says, 'To those who seek to control time, know that it cannot be tamed.'"

Hart's brow furrowed. "A warning or a challenge? This may have been what Abernathy intended to convey. He knew the potential of his work and the danger that accompanied it."

Before they could discuss further, a noise echoed from the front of the workshop—a soft shuffle, then the unmistakable sound of footsteps. Hart's heart raced as he motioned for Clara to be silent.

They crept towards the door, peering through the crack. A figure loomed in the shadows, their face obscured by a hat pulled low. Hart instinctively reached for his pocket, feeling the comforting weight of his revolver.

"Stay close," he whispered to Clara, his pulse quickening. "We may have company."

As the figure stepped into the light, Hart's breath caught in his throat. It was Victor, Abernathy's estranged brother—a man whose motives had been under scrutiny since the beginning of the investigation.

"Victor!" Hart called out, stepping into the open. "What are you doing here?"

Victor froze, his expression a mix of surprise and defiance. "I came to see what you've found, Hart. I won't let you take everything from me."

Clara moved beside Hart, her eyes narrowed. "You were always lurking in the shadows, weren't you, Victor? Did you think you could just steal Abernathy's work and get away with it?"

"I have a right to my brother's legacy!" he shouted, his voice trembling with emotion. "He never appreciated my genius. He always looked down on me, and now you want to take what's left?"

Hart took a step closer, his tone firm. "You think murder is the answer? Your brother was trying to protect his work, and you killed him!"

"I didn't kill him!" Victor retorted, his voice rising in desperation. "But I needed those blueprints! You don't understand what it means to be overlooked, to be forgotten!"

"You're wrong," Hart replied, his gaze unwavering. "Abernathy was a brilliant man, but his work wasn't meant to be twisted for personal gain. It was meant to inspire, to bring beauty into the world."

Victor's shoulders slumped, the fight seemingly leaving him. "And what of my beauty? What of my ideas? I was always in his shadow."

"Then step out of it," Clara interjected, her voice steady. "You have a choice. You can either continue this path of destruction or honor your brother's memory by creating something new."

For a moment, silence hung in the air, tension palpable.

Victor's expression shifted, confusion and anger warring within him. Then, in a swift motion, he lunged towards the blueprints, desperation fueling his actions.

Hart reacted instinctively, grabbing Victor's arm to stop him. "Don't make this worse! You have no idea what you're risking."

But Victor's eyes were wild, his desperation morphing into rage. "You think you can just take everything from me? I will not let that happen!"

With a sudden movement, he broke free from Hart's grip, sending them both crashing to the floor. Clara gasped, scrambling to grab hold of the blueprints that threatened to slip from their grasp.

In the chaos, Hart felt a surge of determination. "We can't let him take them!" he shouted, fighting against Victor's grip.

"I'll make you pay for this!" Victor snarled, his anger boiling over.

But just as Victor reached for the box again, a loud crash reverberated through the workshop, the sound of wood splintering echoed as one of the clocks fell from the shelf, shattering against the ground. The distraction was enough to shift the balance, and Hart managed to pin Victor to the ground, the blueprints safely in Clara's possession.

"Enough!" Hart shouted, his voice fierce. "You don't have to do this!"

Victor's eyes blazed with fury as he struggled against Hart's hold. "You think you can take everything from me? You think you're the hero in this story?"

"Right now, you're the villain," Hart replied firmly, feeling the weight of the moment pressing down on them. "But you can change that."

Clara knelt beside them, her voice steady. "You don't have to follow this path. You can still make something of yourself, Victor. Abernathy wouldn't want this for you."

The fire in Victor's eyes flickered, uncertainty creeping in as he met their gazes. Slowly, his struggles began to weaken. "I just wanted to be recognized... to be seen."

"You can be," Hart replied, releasing his grip slightly. "But not like this. Not through violence. Honor your brother by creating, not destroying."

Victor's breath came in ragged gasps, the fight fading from his body as he finally seemed to understand the gravity of his actions. "What have I done?" he murmured, the weight of his choices crashing down upon him.

In that moment, Clara reached out a hand to him, her expression filled with compassion. "It's not too late. You can still honor his legacy. Let us help you."

With a defeated sigh, Victor lowered his head, the rage that had consumed him dissipating into resignation. "I don't know what to do now."

"Start by telling us the truth," Hart said, rising to his feet and helping Victor up. "Why did you really come here tonight?"

Victor's gaze fell to the floor, shame washing over him. "I wanted the blueprints. I thought if I could just have them, I could prove myself. I thought it would give me the recognition I craved. But I didn't kill him... I swear."

Hart studied him closely, searching for any sign of deception. "Then who did? You know something, don't you?"

"I heard him arguing with someone... someone he mentioned only in whispers. A man named Mortimer. I don't know who he is, but Abernathy was terrified of him," Victor confessed, his voice trembling.

"Mortimer?" Clara repeated, exchanging a glance with Hart. "Why was Abernathy afraid?"

Victor took a shaky breath, steeling himself. "He was working on something groundbreaking, something that could change the industry forever. But Mortimer... he was a ruthless businessman. He wanted control over Abernathy's designs."

Hart nodded, piecing the information together. "So, Abernathy feared for his life. He didn't trust Mortimer and hid the blueprints to protect his work."

Victor glanced up, a flicker of realization dawning. "That's why he was working on that strange clock... it was a safety mechanism, a way to protect himself from Mortimer's greed."

"Then we need to find Mortimer," Hart said, his voice resolute. "If he was involved in Abernathy's death, we must bring him to justice."

With newfound determination, Clara turned to Victor. "We can help you, but you must be honest with us from now on. This isn't just about you anymore."

Victor nodded, the weight of responsibility settling upon him. "I'll do whatever it takes to make this right."

As they stepped out of the workshop into the crisp night air, Hart felt a renewed sense of purpose. The final clue had led them to an unexpected ally, and together, they would seek justice for Abernathy and uncover the truth behind the clockwork murders. The gears of fate were turning, and time was on their side.

With urgency fueling their actions, they set off into the night, determined to confront Mortimer and uncover the secrets that had cost Abernathy his life. The final clue was just the beginning, and Hart knew that every tick of the clock brought them closer to the heart of the mystery.

6. Betrayed by Time

THE SUN DIPPED LOW in the sky, casting elongated shadows across the cobbled streets of the quaint little town of Elderwood. With each passing moment, the golden hue of dusk turned to a murky grey, and a chill crept in, as if the very air carried whispers of secrets long buried. The townsfolk, having grown accustomed to the peaceful rhythm of their lives, paid little mind to the unsettling shift in atmosphere that enveloped them.

At the heart of Elderwood stood the old clock tower, its hands frozen at six o'clock—an eternal reminder of the fateful night when tragedy struck. It was a time that had marked the end of one life and the beginning of an enigma that would haunt the town for years to come. Many claimed the clock tower was cursed, its silence echoing the unheeded warnings of those who had tried to unearth the truth.

Detective Amelia Hart, known for her tenacity and sharp intuition, had recently returned to her hometown after years of service in London. The allure of Elderwood, with its picturesque landscapes and close-knit community, had beckoned her back, but beneath the surface lay a darkness that was all too familiar. The town had a way of holding onto its secrets, and Amelia was determined to uncover the mysteries entwined with her childhood.

As she strolled through the town square, the echoes of laughter from children playing nearby mingled with the distant chime of the remaining working clocks. Elderwood was alive, yet the clock tower loomed ominously, a monument to lost time and forgotten stories. Amelia felt an inexplicable pull towards it, as if it were a compass guiding her to a truth that had long evaded her grasp.

The memory of her childhood friend, Eleanor, flashed in her mind. Eleanor had been vibrant, full of life, with dreams that reached as high as the tower itself. But that night—the night of the accident—had shattered everything. Amelia could still hear the panicked voices, the sirens, the frantic whispers of adults trying to shield their children from the harsh reality that sometimes, tragedy strikes without warning.

She approached the clock tower, her heart racing as she took in the crumbling façade. Vines snaked their way up the stone walls, reclaiming what had once been a symbol of progress and hope. As she reached the entrance, she was greeted by a chilling silence, the kind that wraps around you like a heavy fog. The door creaked open under her touch, revealing a narrow staircase spiraling upwards into darkness.

With each step, the memories flooded back. She remembered how she and Eleanor would climb to the top of the tower, their laughter mingling with the sound of ticking clocks. Those carefree days felt like a lifetime ago. Now, the tower stood as a monument to the betrayal of time itself.

Amelia reached the top, her breath hitching as she stepped into the lantern room. The view was breathtaking—Elderwood sprawled below, cloaked in twilight, with the distant hills silhouetted against the fading light. But her gaze was drawn to the large clock face, its hands eerily still. She reached out to touch the cold glass, and a shiver coursed through her.

Just then, a sound caught her attention—a faint rustling behind her. Whipping around, she found herself face-to-face with an unexpected visitor. It was Charles, Eleanor's brother, his face pale and drawn, as if the weight of the past had taken a toll on him.

"Amelia," he said, his voice barely above a whisper. "I didn't think you'd come back here."

"Neither did I," she replied, studying his expression. "But I had to know... what really happened that night."

Charles looked away, his gaze fixed on the clock. "You think it's time that betrayed us? Or was it something more?"

The question hung in the air, heavy with unspoken truths. Amelia stepped closer, wanting to break through the wall of grief that surrounded him. "Eleanor deserved justice, Charles. We all did. We can't let the past consume us."

"Justice?" he scoffed, a bitter edge to his tone. "What good is justice when time has already made its choice?"

Amelia's heart sank at his words. It was true that time had a cruel way of erasing memories, twisting them into something unrecognizable. But she refused to accept that they were powerless. They had a chance to reclaim their narrative, to rewrite the ending that had been forced upon them.

Suddenly, a glimmer of movement caught Amelia's eye—a small, silver key nestled among the dust and debris of the lantern room. She bent down to retrieve it, her fingers brushing against its cool surface. "What do you think this unlocks?" she mused aloud.

Charles's brow furrowed as he took a step closer. "It looks like the key to the old workshop... the one that belonged to the clockmaker. But it's been abandoned for years."

"Perhaps it's worth a visit," Amelia suggested, a surge of determination igniting within her. "If there are any answers to be found, it will be there."

Reluctantly, Charles nodded, and together they descended the staircase, the weight of their shared history pressing heavily upon them. The air felt electric with possibility, a shared sense of purpose binding them together once more.

As they stepped outside, the world had transformed. Night had fallen, draping Elderwood in a shroud of stars. The moon illuminated their path as they made their way to the clockmaker's workshop, located on the outskirts of town. With every step, Amelia felt the pulse of the town beneath her feet—the stories of its people, their heartaches, and the lingering scent of betrayal.

When they arrived at the workshop, its door stood ajar, as if inviting them inside. The building was cloaked in shadows, the once-vibrant paint now peeling and faded. Inside, the scent of wood shavings and oil lingered in the air, remnants of a time when the clockmaker's hands had deftly crafted mechanisms that told stories through their intricate designs.

Amelia felt drawn to the workbench, cluttered with tools and half-finished clocks. She brushed her fingers over the dusty surfaces, her mind racing with questions. "Do you remember how Eleanor loved to watch him work?" she asked Charles, hoping to evoke a glimmer of the joy that had once filled their lives.

"Yes," he replied, his voice thick with nostalgia. "She used to say the clocks had their own personalities, that they could tell you when to be happy and when to be sad."

"Perhaps they also hold the key to the truth," Amelia said, her resolve strengthening.

They searched through the workshop, unearthed secrets lying in wait. Behind a stack of old blueprints, Amelia discovered a journal, its pages yellowed with age. She opened it, her heart racing as she began to read. The entries detailed the clockmaker's life, his passion for his craft, and hints of a darker undertone—a struggle with his own creations, and an obsession with time that had consumed him.

"Look at this," she called to Charles, pointing to an entry that caught her eye. "He mentions a prototype—a clock unlike any other. It was designed to manipulate time, to rewind it, even."

Charles leaned over her shoulder, his brow furrowed. "But that sounds impossible. Time can't be reversed."

"Can it?" Amelia challenged, her curiosity piqued. "What if the clockmaker's designs weren't just figments of his imagination? What if he found a way to make it real? What if he was trying to right a wrong?"

The thought sent a shiver down her spine. The idea of tampering with time was both exhilarating and terrifying. "We need to find this prototype," she declared, her mind racing with possibilities. "It could hold the answers to what happened that night."

Together, they scoured the workshop for clues, but the night grew late, and exhaustion began to creep in. As they were about to give up, Charles stumbled upon a hidden compartment beneath the floorboards. He pried it open, revealing a small, ornate clock, intricately designed with strange symbols.

"This must be it," he breathed, lifting it from its resting place.

Amelia's heart raced as she took in the clock's beauty. "What do you think it does?"

"Only one way to find out," he replied, his voice steady despite the uncertainty that hung in the air.

As he set the clock on the workbench, its hands began to move, ticking slowly at first before gaining momentum. A soft hum filled the room, and Amelia felt a strange pull, as if the clock was awakening something deep within her.

Suddenly, the room around them shimmered, the shadows deepening as the air thickened. Amelia's pulse quickened, and she grabbed Charles's arm, uncertainty flooding her mind.

"Is it supposed to do this?" she asked, her voice barely above a whisper.

"I don't know," he admitted, eyes wide as they watched the clock.

Then, as if by some unseen force, the world around them shifted. The walls of the workshop faded, replaced by the bright lights of the town square, bustling with life. Amelia gasped as she realized they were standing in the very same square, only it was filled with townspeople, laughter ringing in the air.

"It's... it's like we've gone back in time," Charles stammered, his eyes wide with disbelief.

"Look!" Amelia exclaimed, pointing to a group of familiar faces gathered nearby. There, among the crowd, stood Eleanor—alive and vibrant, just as she had been before the tragedy.

Tears pricked at Amelia's eyes as she watched her friend, the sight filling her with a bittersweet longing. "We have to go to her," she urged, but Charles grabbed her arm, a look of caution in his eyes.

"Wait! We don't know what this means. If we intervene, what could happen?"

The clock continued to tick, its hands moving faster, and Amelia felt the urgency of the moment. "But if we don't try, we'll never have the chance to understand what happened. We can't let time betray us again!"

With a shared look of determination, they stepped into the crowd, weaving their way toward Eleanor. Each heartbeat echoed with a mix of hope and dread.

"Eleanor!" Amelia called out, her voice cutting through the noise. The girl turned, her face lighting up with recognition as she rushed forward.

"Amelia! Charles! How are you—?"

But before Eleanor could finish her sentence, a shadow fell over them. The laughter faded, replaced by an oppressive silence. The air grew heavy, charged with the weight of the moment.

"Stay away from her!" a voice boomed from behind. Amelia turned to see a figure approaching, cloaked in darkness, a menacing presence that sent chills down her spine.

"Who are you?" she demanded, stepping protectively in front of Eleanor.

"I am time itself," the figure replied, their voice echoing through the square. "You tread on dangerous ground. The past is not yours to alter."

Amelia's heart raced as the figure advanced, the clock's ticking growing louder in her ears. "But we have to understand! We need to know what happened that night!"

"Some truths are better left buried," the figure warned. "You cannot rewrite history without consequences."

As the figure reached out, a flash of light enveloped them, and Amelia felt herself being pulled away, the clock's hands moving faster than ever.

In an instant, the square vanished, replaced by the dim light of the workshop. They stumbled back, disoriented and breathless. The clock lay silent, its magic dissipated.

"What just happened?" Charles gasped, looking around as if expecting the town square to reappear.

"I think we touched something we shouldn't have," Amelia said, her heart heavy with the weight of their encounter.

"We can't give up," he insisted, determination hardening in his gaze. "We need to figure out what we learned. There must be a way to find the truth without changing the past."

Amelia nodded, steeling herself for the challenge ahead. "Let's look for more clues in the journal. We need to understand the clockmaker's work and what he was trying to achieve."

As they returned to the journal, Amelia's fingers trembled with anticipation. She turned the pages carefully, searching for any mention of the prototype and its possible effects. Hours slipped away, but as the night deepened, their resolve only grew stronger.

They discovered blueprints outlining the clockmaker's theories and experiments, revealing a mind obsessed with controlling time. "He believed that if one could understand the mechanics of time, one could manipulate it," Amelia read aloud. "But it's unclear whether he succeeded or failed."

"Perhaps it's a warning," Charles suggested. "What if he discovered something that led to Eleanor's accident? Something he was trying to fix?"

"Then we need to find the truth," Amelia replied, her heart racing. "The truth about the clockmaker and what really happened that night."

The days turned into weeks as they plunged deeper into the clockmaker's world. They interviewed townsfolk, piecing together fragments of memory like a jigsaw puzzle. Some spoke of Eleanor's dreams, while others whispered of the clockmaker's descent into madness.

As they gathered information, the picture became clearer. The night of the accident had not been a mere mishap; it was the culmination of a series of events that had spiraled out of control. The clockmaker's obsession had created a rift in time, and Eleanor had become an unwitting victim.

One evening, as they combed through the final entries in the journal, a sense of urgency washed over Amelia. "We're running out of time, Charles," she said, her voice laced with desperation. "We need to confront the past before it consumes us."

Charles nodded, his expression solemn. "But how do we do that? We can't simply travel back and change what happened. We need to find a way to expose the truth without rewriting history."

Amelia's mind raced as she considered their options. "What if we set a trap? If we can recreate the conditions of that night, we might be able to draw out the truth without altering anything."

"Do you think it will work?" Charles asked, skepticism creeping into his tone.

"It's worth a try," Amelia replied, determination flaring in her chest. "We can't let the town continue to be haunted by this. Eleanor deserves justice, and so do we."

Together, they prepared for the night of reckoning. They meticulously crafted a plan, gathering materials and recreating the circumstances leading up to the fateful moment. The clockmaker's workshop would serve as their stage, and with each passing hour, their anticipation mounted.

When the night arrived, they stood in the dim light of the workshop, the clock ticking steadily as they waited. Shadows danced on the walls, and a sense of foreboding enveloped them.

"Are you ready?" Charles asked, his voice low.

Amelia took a deep breath, her heart pounding in her chest. "Ready as I'll ever be."

As the clock struck midnight, the air thickened, and the world around them shimmered once more. The workshop faded, and they found themselves back in the town square, the cacophony of laughter ringing in their ears.

But this time, they were prepared. They moved through the crowd with purpose, searching for the clockmaker, for the answers they desperately needed. The tension in the air was palpable, and Amelia felt the weight of time pressing down on her.

Then, out of the corner of her eye, she spotted him—the clockmaker, standing near the fountain, his expression distant and haunted. "There!" she exclaimed, pulling Charles along as they made their way through the throngs of people.

"Excuse me!" Amelia called out, pushing her way to the front. "We need to speak with you!"

The clockmaker turned, surprise flickering in his eyes as he took in their determined expressions. "What is it you want?"

"You need to tell us the truth about Eleanor," Amelia pressed, her voice steady despite the gravity of the moment. "What happened that night?"

His face fell, and for a moment, it seemed as if he might flee. But then he straightened, and the weight of remorse settled upon him. "I did not mean for any of this to happen," he said, his voice thick with sorrow. "I was blinded by my obsession with time, and it cost me everything."

"What do you mean?" Charles demanded, urgency lacing his words. "Tell us!"

"The prototype," the clockmaker whispered, his eyes filled with regret. "It was never meant to hurt anyone. I thought I could control it, that I could make time bend to my will. But I was wrong. I lost Eleanor that night because I could not see the dangers of my own creation."

Amelia's heart raced as she listened, a mixture of anger and compassion swirling within her. "And what happened? How did she die?"

"I was working on the prototype, trying to unlock its potential when the accident occurred," he confessed, tears brimming in his eyes. "I didn't see her. I thought she was safe, but... time betrayed me, just as it has betrayed you."

His words cut through her, and Amelia felt a rush of emotion. "You must make it right," she urged. "We can't let this go on any longer. The town deserves to know the truth!"

The clockmaker nodded, determination igniting within him. "I will tell them. I will make amends for the past."

As the clock struck again, the crowd began to dissolve, the world around them shifting once more. This time, they felt the pull of time receding, and Amelia grasped Charles's hand, fear and hope intertwining.

With a deep breath, the clockmaker stepped forward, ready to confront his demons and reveal the truth.

Amelia and Charles watched as he began to speak, the weight of his confession lifting from his shoulders. The past was unraveling, the threads of time slowly coming undone, and in that moment, they felt a glimmer of hope.

Perhaps they could rewrite their story, not by altering the past but by embracing the truth. Time would continue to march forward, but they would no longer be betrayed by its passage. The echoes of their history would resonate through the town of Elderwood, forever intertwined with the memories of those who had come before.

As the clocktower chimed, the hands began to move once more, and the future unfolded before them—a promise of new beginnings, forged from the ashes of their shared past.

Together, they stood at the precipice of time, ready to embrace whatever lay ahead, united by the bonds of friendship, love, and the unyielding power of truth.

Chapter 10: Time Runs Out

1. The Murderer Revealed

As the clock struck twelve, a heavy silence enveloped the room. The guests at the opulent manor, gathered for the grand reveal of the evening's mystery, held their breath. Detective Eleanor Hart stood at the centre of the drawing room, her gaze sweeping across the anxious faces before her. The flickering candlelight cast long shadows, creating an atmosphere thick with tension.

"Thank you all for your patience," Eleanor began, her voice steady but laced with urgency. "Tonight, we have not merely gathered for an evening of entertainment; we are here to uncover the truth behind the tragic events that have unfolded in our midst."

Whispers broke out among the guests. Fear and anticipation gripped them. Everyone knew that at least two lives had been lost in the past week, and now, they felt the weight of suspicion pressing heavily upon their shoulders.

Eleanor took a step forward, her sharp mind racing as she recalled each detail she had gathered. "This was not simply a matter of fate or misfortune. We are facing a calculated murderer, one who has planned each step with meticulous care. The first victim, Gregory Thornton, was discovered in his study, an antique clock lying shattered beside him, its hands frozen at precisely ten o'clock. The second, Lady Margaret, met a similarly tragic fate, found in the garden at the stroke of midnight, the very time the clock struck when Gregory was killed."

Gasps echoed through the room as Eleanor continued. "This was no coincidence. Each murder had a purpose, and the clock itself is a key witness, one that tells a story not just of time but of betrayal, revenge, and a long-buried secret."

"But how could you possibly know all this?" interrupted Mrs. Beatrice Fairweather, a stout woman with a penchant for dramatics. Her eyes darted nervously as she clutched her pearls. "We all know that the clock can be unreliable. It's a mere mechanism!"

Eleanor shot her a piercing glance. "Ah, Mrs. Fairweather, you've unwittingly pointed out the very crux of the matter. The clock is a metaphor, a symbol of the hidden machinations at play here. It is not just the time that it shows; it signifies moments of our lives, memories tied to each tick. Every person in this room has their own history, their own connection to the events we are unraveling."

As she spoke, Eleanor felt the tension in the air rise. She took a deep breath, steeling herself for what was to come. "Now, let us delve deeper into our little mystery. Each of you has your own reasons for being here, for knowing Gregory and Lady Margaret. And, as we dissect these motives, we will find the murderer among us."

Eleanor raised her hand, gesturing toward a large board behind her, cluttered with photographs, snippets of conversations, and timelines that she had painstakingly arranged. "Let us start with Gregory Thornton. A man of ambition, wealth, and significant influence, he was adored by some and reviled by others. The question we must ask is: who would have benefited from his death?"

"His business rival, perhaps?" offered Mr. Edmund Blake, a tall man with an air of sophistication, adjusting his spectacles. "Gregory had many dealings that could have been seen as hostile."

"Indeed," Eleanor acknowledged, her gaze fixed on him. "Mr. Blake, you are correct in your assumption. But Gregory was also known for his charity work, helping the underprivileged in our community. A life so filled with contradictions cannot simply end without reason."

She turned to Lady Margaret's portrait, the lady of the manor, whose smile seemed to mock them all in her everlasting beauty. "Now, Lady Margaret—what do we know of her? She was adored by all who met her, but behind that charm lay secrets of her own. A complicated past that may have entwined with Gregory's fate."

The room shifted uncomfortably, a collective realization dawning among the guests. Lady Margaret had not only been a friend but had also shared a dark history with many present.

Eleanor continued, her voice unwavering, "What if I told you that Lady Margaret was in possession of a secret that could have destroyed Gregory's reputation? A secret tied to her past, involving a young man, Charles, who disappeared mysteriously years ago. Would that not provide sufficient motive for murder?"

Gasps of shock echoed through the room. Faces blanched, and it was as if a veil had been lifted, revealing hidden truths lurking beneath the surface.

"I dare say that each of you holds a piece of the puzzle," Eleanor continued, her keen eyes locking onto each guest in turn. "Let us begin our examination, starting with the most likely suspect—Mr. Blake. You were seen leaving the study moments before Gregory's death."

"I was merely going for a walk," Mr. Blake replied hastily, though his voice quivered slightly.

"A walk?" Eleanor pressed, not letting him off the hook. "A convenient alibi, but let's not forget the antique clock in the study. It was found in pieces, and I have reason to believe you were the last person to see it intact."

Mr. Blake's face turned crimson, and he stammered, "I... I merely admired it. It was a valuable piece, and I—"

Eleanor cut him off. "Admired it, you say? Or did you tamper with it, knowing it would serve as an ideal diversion when you decided to confront Gregory?"

A tense silence fell upon the room as the guests exchanged glances, weighing the implications of Eleanor's words.

"It's easy to point fingers," chimed in Mrs. Fairweather, her voice a mix of fear and defiance. "What about you, Eleanor? You have been investigating this case with a fervor that seems... personal."

Eleanor's gaze sharpened. "I assure you, Mrs. Fairweather, my motives are purely professional. But you have also danced around your connection to the victims. What is your relationship with Gregory and Lady Margaret? It is not lost on me that you were one of the last to speak to both of them."

Mrs. Fairweather's eyes widened. "I only wished to offer my condolences! I had nothing to gain from their deaths!"

"Or perhaps everything to lose?" Eleanor suggested, sensing the shift in the atmosphere. "Your past dealings with them may have placed you in a precarious position. The desperation to maintain your social standing could have driven you to unspeakable acts."

As the accusations flew back and forth, Eleanor turned her attention to the quietest member of the group—Lady Eleanor Harrington, who had been watching with wide eyes, her fingers clasped tightly in her lap.

"Lady Harrington," Eleanor began gently, "You have remained eerily silent throughout this discussion. I would like to hear your perspective on these events."

Lady Harrington looked startled, her voice barely above a whisper. "I—I have nothing to say. I barely knew either of them."

"But you did know them," Eleanor pressed, feeling the tension in the air. "You were in attendance at their last gathering. You must have seen something, heard something that could point us in the right direction."

A tremor coursed through Lady Harrington's body, and for a moment, Eleanor thought she might faint. But then, as if gathering her courage, she spoke. "I did hear a heated argument between Gregory and Lady Margaret. It was about... Charles."

Eleanor's heart raced. "Charles? The man who disappeared?"

"Yes," Lady Harrington confirmed, her voice gaining strength. "I overheard them arguing about the past. It was clear that Gregory held something over Lady Margaret's head."

"And that something could very well be the motive behind the murders," Eleanor concluded, a sense of triumph coursing through her. "But I fear there is more to this story than meets the eye."

As the night wore on, Eleanor pieced together fragments of information from each guest, uncovering their hidden motives and their shared histories with the victims. Yet, despite all the revelations, one thing became painfully clear: the murderer was still among them, lurking in the shadows, waiting for the opportune moment to strike again.

Finally, after what felt like hours of questioning, Eleanor gathered everyone into the drawing room once more. The atmosphere was tense, the air thick with anticipation.

"Tonight, we stand on the precipice of unveiling the truth," she declared, her voice commanding attention. "I have heard your stories, gathered your secrets, and now I am ready to reveal the murderer among us. The clock has struck midnight, and it is time for the truth to emerge."

A shiver ran through the crowd as they braced themselves for the truth. Eleanor took a deep breath, prepared to expose the lies that had twisted their lives together and shattered the peace of their community.

"Before I unveil the identity of the murderer, let us consider the clues we have gathered," she continued, pacing the room. "We have a clock, a shattered clock, representing both the fragility of time and the fragility of human life. Each tick reminds us of the seconds lost, moments that can never be reclaimed."

She paused, locking eyes with each guest. "The broken clock signifies the moment of Gregory's death, but it also symbolizes the emotional clocks of each individual here. We have all endured moments of betrayal, moments of passion and regret. It is these very moments that bring us closer to the truth."

"But why did you suspect Mr. Blake initially?" someone interjected, their voice quivering.

Eleanor turned her gaze towards Mr. Blake. "His connection to Gregory was undeniable, as was his opportunity. But as I delved deeper into the

motives of each individual, it became apparent that the clues led me elsewhere."

The guests exchanged nervous glances, their breaths hitching in anticipation.

"Mrs. Fairweather, you claimed to have been a mere acquaintance of both victims. But it is no secret that you once harboured feelings for Gregory. Your jealousy, perhaps, was a motive for murder?"

Mrs. Fairweather gasped, but before she could respond, Eleanor pressed on. "And Lady Harrington, you have your own ties to this tragedy. Your secrets were tied to the very fabric of the past. Your silence has only fueled the fire of suspicion."

Lady Harrington's hands trembled, but she held her ground, meeting Eleanor's gaze with defiance. "I won't be your scapegoat, Detective!"

Eleanor raised an eyebrow, intrigued by the rising tension. "Scapegoat? No, my dear Lady Harrington, I seek to uncover the truth. But the truth is complex, tangled in the lies we tell ourselves."

It was then that the truth struck Eleanor like a bolt of lightning. She had spent so much time looking at the larger picture that she had overlooked the most significant detail—the clock itself, which had been a constant presence throughout the investigation.

"The answer lies within the very mechanisms of time," she declared, her voice unwavering. "The murderer is someone who has lived in the shadows, someone who has been manipulating the gears of this situation for their own benefit."

The guests looked bewildered, but Eleanor pressed on, determined to bring the truth to light. "The killer is none other than Mr. Edmund Blake."

Gasps of shock erupted from the crowd, but Eleanor continued, unfazed. "You have been playing a game all along, haven't you? A game of deception. You knew about the clock and its significance. You knew that breaking it would cause chaos, diverting suspicion away from you. You believed you could remain in the shadows, hidden from view."

Mr. Blake's face darkened as he took a step back, the walls closing in around him. "This is absurd! I would never—"

"But you did," Eleanor interrupted, her voice firm. "You were present at both murder scenes, and you had everything to gain from Gregory's downfall. His death cleared the path for your business, didn't it? And Lady Margaret's death? It served to further bury the truth, to eliminate anyone who might uncover the dark history that bound you all together."

As the reality of Eleanor's words sank in, a tension crackled in the air. Mr. Blake's façade crumbled, revealing the desperation lurking beneath.

"You don't understand!" he shouted, his voice breaking. "I had no choice! Gregory was going to ruin everything I had built! And Lady Margaret... she knew too much!"

Eleanor watched him, a mix of sympathy and resolve filling her heart. "You chose a path of destruction rather than facing the consequences of your actions. And now, you must pay for your crimes."

At that moment, the weight of the truth pressed down on everyone in the room. The clock's hands continued to tick, marking the passage of time—a relentless reminder of the choices they had made and the lives that had been lost.

As the guests stood frozen in shock, the reality of what had transpired sank in. The murder had been a web of deceit, each thread intricately woven together by desperation, jealousy, and greed.

Eleanor turned to the remaining guests, her voice softening. "Tonight, we have uncovered the truth, but the path to healing will be long. Each of you must reckon with the choices you have made and the darkness that has touched your lives."

The clock chimed once more, its echo resonating through the hall. With that sound, the tension slowly began to dissipate, replaced by a somber understanding of the fragility of life and the consequences of their actions.

In the end, the clockwork had revealed not only the murderer but also the intertwined fates of all present. Each guest, haunted by their pasts, was now left to ponder the future—a future marked by the shadows of their decisions, but also by the glimmer of hope for redemption.

2. The Last Move

THE CLOCK STRUCK TEN as Detective Arthur Hart settled into his favorite armchair, the worn leather creaking beneath him like an old friend. The flickering glow of the fire cast dancing shadows across the room, but his mind was far from the comfort of the hearth. Instead, it was consumed by the events of the past few weeks, each moment a piece in a puzzle that had yet to reveal its complete picture.

The recent murders had left the small town of Ashwick in a state of paralyzing fear. The first victim, Benjamin Hargrove, a local watchmaker known for his eccentricities, was found lifeless in his workshop, his body slumped against the very clock he had dedicated his life to perfecting. It was a gruesome sight, one that haunted Hart's dreams. The second murder, that of Lady Evangeline Sinclair, a prominent socialite, was equally disturbing, occurring mere days after Hargrove's demise. Both murders were linked by a single thread—an intricate clockwork mechanism found at each crime scene.

As the investigation deepened, so did the shadows that surrounded the case. Hart had spent countless hours poring over the evidence, examining each detail with meticulous care. The townspeople whispered about a curse that had befallen Ashwick, but Hart was not one to succumb to superstition. He believed in facts, in the tangible. Yet, as he traced the timeline of the murders, he couldn't shake the feeling that there was something deeper at play, something that intertwined the lives of the victims and the community in a sinister dance.

With a sigh, he pushed himself up from the chair and reached for the stack of papers cluttering his desk. Among them lay the latest letter he had received—an anonymous tip that hinted at a connection between the victims and a hidden past. The handwriting was neat and precise, a stark contrast to the chaos that had enveloped Ashwick.

"Meet me at midnight in the old clock tower," it read. "All will be revealed."

It was a dangerous proposition, one that could lead him to the truth or put him in the crosshairs of a killer. But Hart knew he had little choice; the weight of the case pressed heavily on his shoulders. With determination, he slipped the letter into his pocket, donned his coat, and set out into the night.

The streets of Ashwick were eerily quiet, the kind of stillness that set his instincts on edge. Shadows loomed like specters in the dim light of the gas lamps, and a chill ran down his spine as he approached the clock tower. It stood tall against the night sky, its silhouette both imposing and familiar. Hart had spent countless hours there in his youth, fascinated by the intricate workings of the clocks, the very same that now seemed to mock him.

As he ascended the creaking staircase, each step echoing in the silence, he couldn't help but reflect on how time had transformed. Once a source of wonder, it now felt like a relentless adversary, ticking down the moments until the next tragedy would strike. At the top, he paused, catching his breath, and took a moment to survey the room. Dust motes floated in the air, illuminated by the moonlight streaming through the cracked windows.

"Detective Hart," a voice broke the silence, smooth and measured, reverberating off the stone walls. He turned sharply to see a figure emerging from the shadows, cloaked in a dark trench coat, the brim of a hat obscuring their features.

"Who are you?" Hart demanded, his hand instinctively reaching for the revolver holstered at his side.

The figure chuckled, a sound both disarming and menacing. "You can call me Elysia. I have information that may interest you."

"Information? Or another riddle?" Hart shot back, his patience wearing thin. He had grown weary of cryptic messages and half-truths.

"Both, I suppose," she replied, stepping into the light. Her face was pale, with striking green eyes that glimmered with an intensity that sent a shiver through him. "But you'll want to hear what I have to say, Detective. The clock is ticking."

Elysia moved closer, her voice lowering to a conspiratorial whisper. "There's a connection between Hargrove and Lady Sinclair that no one else has discovered. They were part of something much larger, something that has been hidden for decades."

"What are you talking about?" Hart's brow furrowed as he tried to piece together her words. "What larger thing?"

"An old society," she continued, glancing around as if the walls themselves had ears. "They called themselves the Clockmakers, a group dedicated to the preservation of time and its secrets. Hargrove was one of them, and Lady Sinclair—she was set to expose the truth."

"Expose what truth?" Hart pressed, the pieces of the puzzle beginning to shift.

"The truth about a missing invention," Elysia said, her voice steady but urgent. "An intricate clockwork device designed to manipulate time itself. Hargrove believed it had been lost, but he found clues leading him to its location. Lady Sinclair was close to unveiling everything when she was killed."

Hart felt a rush of adrenaline. "Where is this device now?"

"I can't tell you that just yet," Elysia replied, her eyes darting to the door. "They're watching. We need to be careful. If you want the answers, you'll have to trust me."

"Trust is a luxury I can't afford right now," Hart said, his mind racing. "You could be the killer for all I know."

"Then let's not waste time," she insisted. "We need to act fast before it's too late. Meet me at the old mill tomorrow night. I'll show you what you need to see."

Before he could respond, she turned and disappeared down the stairs, leaving Hart alone in the shadowy tower. His heart raced, but he knew he couldn't let this opportunity slip through his fingers. He had to follow her lead.

The following day passed in a blur. Hart spent the hours scrutinizing the evidence he had gathered, piecing together the fragments of a story that was becoming increasingly complex. The clockwork murders were no longer just about the victims; they were a thread connecting past and present, a web spun from secrets that had festered in the darkness for far too long.

As dusk fell, Hart made his way to the old mill. It had long since ceased to operate, a relic of a bygone era, but it had become a gathering place for those seeking refuge from the prying eyes of the town. The air was thick with anticipation as he approached, the sound of water rushing in the nearby stream providing a haunting backdrop.

Elysia was already there, her silhouette outlined against the setting sun. She turned to him as he approached, a serious expression on her face.

"Did anyone follow you?" she asked, her voice tense.

"I don't think so," Hart replied, glancing around the empty space. "What did you want to show me?"

Elysia nodded and beckoned him to follow her inside the mill. The interior was dimly lit, dust motes swirling in the beams of fading light. In the corner, hidden beneath a tattered tarp, was a large wooden crate. Elysia lifted the tarp, revealing a series of intricate clock components, gears, and springs, all meticulously arranged.

"This is it," she said, her voice barely above a whisper. "The remnants of the invention. Hargrove was close to completing it, but someone wanted to stop him."

Hart studied the pieces, feeling a sense of urgency wash over him. "But how do we find the rest? What about the bodies?"

"The clockwork device is the key," Elysia explained. "Hargrove believed it could alter time, allowing him to prevent the deaths he foresaw. But someone didn't want that secret to get out."

"Who?" Hart pressed, frustration bubbling beneath the surface. "Who would go to such lengths?"

Elysia hesitated, her eyes narrowing as if she were trying to read his thoughts. "There's a figure lurking in the shadows—a puppet master pulling the strings. I've only heard whispers, but they say he's part of the old society, perhaps even its leader."

"And you think this person is responsible for the murders?" Hart asked, his mind racing.

"I do," she confirmed. "But we need to be cautious. They're powerful, and they won't hesitate to eliminate anyone who threatens their plans."

As they discussed their next steps, a loud crash interrupted their conversation. Hart's instincts kicked in, and he instinctively reached for his revolver. "Stay behind me," he ordered, scanning the darkness beyond the crate.

Suddenly, the door to the mill burst open, and figures clad in dark clothing flooded in. They moved with purpose, and before Hart could react, he was surrounded.

"Detective Hart," one of them sneered, his voice laced with contempt. "We've been waiting for you."

Hart felt a surge of adrenaline as he assessed the situation. There were too many of them, and they were closing in fast. He raised his weapon, but they were already upon him, and in an instant, the world around him descended into chaos.

A scuffle ensued, and Hart fought with every ounce of strength he possessed. But as the figures wrestled him to the ground, he caught a glimpse of Elysia, her expression one of horror and helplessness. In that moment, everything seemed to blur, the shadows of the past merging with the urgency of the present.

And then, just as suddenly as it had begun, it was over. Hart lay on the floor, gasping for breath, the intruders gone, leaving behind only the echo of their footsteps and a lingering sense of dread.

• • • •

"ARE YOU OKAY?" ELYSIA rushed to his side, her eyes wide with concern.

"I'm fine," he managed to say, pushing himself up. "But we need to get out of here. They'll be back."

As they stumbled outside, Hart knew they had only scratched the surface of the truth. The clockwork murders were a ruse, a distraction from something far more sinister. They had to uncover the full extent of the conspiracy, and quickly.

The next few days were a whirlwind of investigation, danger, and deception. Hart and Elysia delved deeper into the shadows, uncovering fragments of a story that spanned generations. They learned of betrayals that ran deep within the community, of alliances forged in secrecy, and of a clockwork device that could alter the very fabric of time.

With each revelation, the stakes grew higher. The puppet master remained elusive, but Hart was determined to uncover the truth. He had become a pawn in a game far greater than he had anticipated, and he was prepared to make his final move.

Their investigation led them to a hidden chamber beneath the clock tower, a place where the old society had once gathered to discuss their most guarded secrets. It was there that they uncovered the final piece of the puzzle—the blueprint for the clockwork device, its intricate design promising unimaginable power.

"This is it," Elysia said, her voice trembling with excitement. "With this, we can expose everything."

But just as they began to formulate a plan, a figure emerged from the shadows, the same one Hart had glimpsed in the mill—the puppet master himself. He wore a mask, his identity concealed, but there was no mistaking the malice in his eyes.

"You've come quite far, Detective," he said, his voice smooth yet chilling. "But this is where your journey ends."

Hart's heart raced as he prepared for a confrontation, knowing that this was the moment he had been waiting for. The last move in a game that had threatened to consume him.

"You're behind the murders," Hart accused, refusing to back down. "You wanted to silence Hargrove and Lady Sinclair because they were close to revealing your secrets."

The puppet master chuckled, a sound devoid of warmth. "Secrets? My dear detective, it's not the secrets that matter. It's the power that comes with controlling time itself. Hargrove was a fool, and Lady Sinclair was merely a means to an end."

As he spoke, Hart's mind raced, searching for an opening, a way to turn the tide in this high-stakes game. "You think you can control time? You're playing with forces you don't understand."

"Oh, but I do," the puppet master replied, stepping closer, his presence both menacing and magnetic. "And now, you'll pay the price for your meddling."

In a flash, the confrontation erupted into chaos, a dance of shadows and light. Hart and Elysia fought with everything they had, their determination fueled by the truth they sought to uncover. But the puppet master was cunning, his movements precise as he evaded their attacks.

Just as it seemed they might be overwhelmed, Hart caught sight of the blueprint lying on the ground, the intricate design glowing in the dim light. In that moment, he understood—it was not just a blueprint; it was a weapon, a key to the very heart of the clockwork device.

With renewed resolve, he lunged for it, seizing the chance to turn the tide. "This ends now!" he shouted, holding the blueprint aloft. "You can't control time, but we can expose the truth!"

The puppet master faltered, a flicker of uncertainty crossing his face. "You think you can stop me?"

In that instant, Hart felt the weight of the past and the promise of the future collide within him. "You've underestimated the power of truth, and the lengths to which I'll go to protect it."

With a swift motion, he unveiled the blueprint, the designs catching the light in a way that illuminated the dark chamber. The puppet master recoiled, realizing too late the significance of what he had lost.

In the ensuing chaos, the confrontation reached a fever pitch. Elysia and Hart fought as one, their movements synchronized in a desperate attempt to reclaim the power that had been taken from them. And as they closed in on the puppet master, the weight of time hung heavy in the air, a reminder of the stakes they faced.

In the final moments of the struggle, Hart could see the realization dawning in the puppet master's eyes. "You may win this time, Detective," he spat, his voice laced with venom. "But time has a way of catching up with us all."

With that, the puppet master made his escape, slipping into the shadows like a wraith, leaving behind only the echoes of his threats and the remnants of a shattered conspiracy.

Hart and Elysia stood together in the aftermath, breathless and battered but triumphant. They had uncovered the truth, exposed the lies that had plagued Ashwick, and taken the first steps toward healing the wounds that had festered for too long.

As they emerged from the clock tower into the dawn light, Hart felt a sense of renewed purpose wash over him. The clock had struck its final hour for the puppet master, and though the scars of the past remained, he knew they had the power to shape a brighter future.

In the days that followed, the truth began to unravel, the pieces falling into place as the town of Ashwick came to terms with the dark legacy it had harbored. Hargrove's inventions were celebrated, Lady Sinclair's memory honored, and the clockwork device, once a source of fear, transformed into a symbol of resilience.

Detective Hart had faced the darkness and emerged stronger for it. Time had indeed passed, but with each tick of the clock, he was reminded of the importance of truth, justice, and the power of choice.

As he returned to his armchair, the warmth of the fire surrounding him, he knew that this was not the end. The clockwork murders had revealed the intricacies of human nature—the capacity for both good and evil—and he was prepared to continue his pursuit of justice, one case at a time.

The clock continued to tick, but for Hart, it had become a reminder not of fear, but of the possibilities that lay ahead. The last move had been played, but the game was far from over.

3. A Desperate Chase

THE NIGHT WAS CLOAKED in an eerie stillness as Detective Harold Finch sprinted through the narrow alleys of Fairview, his heart pounding with a mix of determination and dread. The streetlamps cast long shadows, their flickering lights barely illuminating the cobblestone path ahead. Time was of the essence; he could not allow the elusive murderer to slip through his fingers again.

Earlier that evening, Finch had received a cryptic note, its edges frayed, and the ink smudged, warning him of the imminent danger. "At midnight, the clock will strike, and the hunter will become the hunted," it read. His instincts told him the message was more than a mere threat—it was a taunt. Someone was playing a game, and he was their unwitting pawn.

As he rounded a corner, he caught a glimpse of a figure darting into the shadows, their silhouette barely discernible in the dim light. Without hesitation, Finch pursued. The figure moved with remarkable speed, ducking under awnings and weaving through the throng of late-night pedestrians, their frantic pace suggesting desperation.

"Stop!" Finch shouted, but his voice was swallowed by the night.

The figure glanced back, their features obscured by a wide-brimmed hat. Finch could feel the adrenaline surging through his veins, propelling him forward. He tightened his grip on the flashlight, the beam cutting through the darkness, illuminating the path just ahead. Each step echoed like a drumbeat, marking the rhythm of a chase that felt both exhilarating and perilous.

They dashed past the old clock tower, its hands frozen at ten minutes past eleven, a silent witness to the unfolding drama. Finch had always found the clock tower oddly foreboding, a relic of the past that seemed to mock the passage of time. Now, it stood as a reminder of the urgency of his mission. He could not afford to let the figure escape; the clock was ticking, and with it, the chance to uncover the truth.

The chase led him to the outskirts of the town, where the streets became less familiar, overgrown hedges spilling onto the pavement. The figure slowed, and Finch saw an opportunity to close the distance. They veered into a darkened alleyway, an unlit passage that promised concealment and escape.

Finch followed, the adrenaline dulling the fear that crept into the edges of his mind. As he entered the alley, the air felt thick with tension. It was a dead end, a narrow space flanked by high walls that seemed to close in on him.

"Why are you running?" he called out, trying to break through the silence that surrounded them. "I just want to talk!"

The figure hesitated, and for a fleeting moment, Finch thought he might finally catch a glimpse of their face. But the moment passed, and they turned to scale the wall, agile and desperate. Finch's heart sank as he watched them ascend, every instinct screaming that this was a crucial moment. He reached for his radio, his fingers trembling slightly.

"Control, this is Detective Finch. I'm in pursuit of a suspect heading towards the old mill. I need backup—now!"

There was a brief crackle before the voice on the other end responded. "Understood, Finch. Units are on their way."

He could hear the thud of footsteps approaching, and for a moment, hope flickered within him. But it was soon eclipsed by the realization that he needed to act quickly. The figure was halfway up the wall, and time was not on his side.

With a burst of energy, he lunged forward, gripping the figure's ankle just as they reached the top. They cried out, startled, and in that instant, Finch managed to pull them down. They tumbled to the ground, landing in a heap of limbs and fabric.

"Get off me!" the figure spat, struggling against him.

In the darkness, Finch could finally see their face, illuminated by the pale glow of the moon. It was a woman, her eyes wide with panic and defiance. He recognized her immediately; she was a prominent local artist, known for her enigmatic paintings that often depicted shadows and light intertwined.

"Clara!" he exclaimed, momentarily taken aback. "What are you doing here?"

"Let me go!" she shouted, writhing in his grasp. "You don't understand!"

"Understand what?" Finch pressed, his voice urgent. "You're in danger. You need to come with me."

"I can't! You don't know what's at stake!" she retorted, her breath coming in quick gasps.

Just then, a sudden noise erupted from the entrance of the alley, shattering their tense exchange. The sound of footsteps echoed ominously, and Finch felt a chill run down his spine.

"They're coming," Clara whispered, her fear palpable.

Before he could respond, he heard the unmistakable sound of sirens approaching. The cacophony of light and sound filled the air, sending a jolt of adrenaline through his veins.

"Over there!" Finch shouted, pointing towards a nearby door that led into the mill. "We need to hide!"

Clara hesitated for just a moment before nodding, and together they sprinted toward the entrance. The door creaked as they pushed it open, and they slipped inside just as the first police cars screeched to a halt outside.

Inside the mill, the air was heavy with the scent of damp wood and rust. Finch scanned the room, his instincts telling him to find a place to conceal themselves. The shadows seemed to dance around them, flickering in the faint light that filtered through the dusty windows.

"Why were you running?" Finch demanded, his voice low as they crouched behind a stack of crates.

"I didn't kill him!" Clara insisted, her voice trembling. "I swear, I was framed!"

"Who? Framed for what?" he pressed, desperate for clarity amid the chaos.

"The artist—Evelyn Moore. She was found dead, and I was the last person to see her! I came to confront her about the stolen painting, but when I arrived, she was already...gone," she explained, her voice quivering with emotion.

Finch's mind raced as he pieced together the puzzle. Evelyn had been a controversial figure in the art world, and her death had sent shockwaves through Fairview. "And you thought you'd find the real killer?"

"I thought I could confront whoever was responsible! But someone saw me leaving, and now they're trying to pin it all on me!"

As she spoke, the sound of voices drifted from outside. Police officers were interviewing witnesses, searching for clues, their shouts piercing through the stillness.

"We need to get out of here," Finch whispered urgently, glancing toward the door. "If they find us, we'll both be in trouble."

"Where do we go?" Clara asked, her eyes wide with fear.

"Follow me," he said, leading her deeper into the mill, past machinery that loomed like ancient giants, their metallic surfaces covered in dust. The atmosphere was thick with tension, each sound amplified in the silence.

They moved cautiously, keeping close to the walls, their footsteps muffled by the layers of grime that had accumulated over time. Finch's mind raced with questions, but he knew that first, they had to escape the immediate danger.

Suddenly, a loud crash reverberated through the building, causing them both to freeze. Finch's heart raced as he instinctively reached for his radio.

"Control, this is Finch. I need backup—urgently!"

He could hear the chaos outside, the shouts growing louder. It was clear that someone was closing in, and the walls of the mill suddenly felt constricting.

"We have to hide!" Clara hissed, her eyes darting around the room.

Finch spotted a narrow staircase leading to the upper levels, partially hidden behind a stack of crates. "This way!" he urged, and they darted toward it, climbing quickly, their breaths ragged.

As they reached the top, Finch pulled Clara into a small room filled with forgotten relics and dust-covered furniture. The atmosphere was thick with the smell of mildew, but it offered them a temporary refuge.

"We can wait here until it calms down," he said, pressing a finger to his lips to signal silence.

Clara nodded, her eyes wide with apprehension. They could hear footsteps and muffled voices from below, the tension palpable in the air.

"What if they find us?" she whispered, her voice barely above a breath.

"Then we'll have to think fast," Finch replied, scanning the room for anything they could use as an escape route or a weapon.

They settled into silence, the only sound the distant commotion outside. Finch's mind raced with possibilities. He had never expected to find himself in such a precarious situation, but the weight of Clara's predicament pressed on him heavily.

"Tell me everything you know about Evelyn," he urged, breaking the silence as the sound of footsteps grew fainter.

Clara took a deep breath, the tension in her shoulders easing slightly. "Evelyn was a genius, but she had enemies. She was working on a new collection that could have changed the art world, but people were jealous. She was trying to reclaim a stolen piece, and I know it meant a lot to her," Clara explained, her voice steadier now.

"What was the painting?" Finch asked, intrigued.

"The Clockwork Heart," she said, her expression turning serious. "It was a masterpiece, and everyone wanted it. I thought if I could just confront her, maybe we could work together. I didn't expect to find her dead."

· · · ·

FINCH PROCESSED HER words, the pieces of the puzzle starting to align. "And you believe the killer is still out there?"

"Yes," Clara replied firmly. "I know it. Someone is trying to silence anyone who gets too close to the truth."

Just then, a loud thud echoed from below, followed by the unmistakable sound of a door slamming shut. Clara's eyes widened, and Finch felt a surge of urgency.

"We need to move now," he said, taking her hand.

They crept back to the staircase, their hearts racing as they descended quietly. Finch peered out cautiously, listening for any signs of danger. The commotion had subsided somewhat, but he knew they couldn't linger.

"Let's get to the back entrance," he whispered, leading the way.

As they made their way through the darkened hallways, Finch's mind raced with plans. They needed to find evidence that would exonerate Clara and expose the true murderer.

The back entrance loomed ahead, a flickering light shining through the cracks in the door. Finch pushed it open slowly, and they stepped outside, the cool night air washing over them.

"Where to now?" Clara asked, her voice filled with uncertainty.

Finch glanced around, spotting a narrow path that led toward the woods. "We need to get somewhere safe. I have a contact who can help us."

They dashed toward the woods, the shadows enveloping them as they moved deeper into the trees. The sounds of the town faded, replaced by the rustling of leaves and the distant calls of night creatures.

As they reached a clearing, Finch halted, turning to face Clara. "Listen, I need you to trust me. We're going to find the real killer, but we have to stay one step ahead."

"I do trust you," she said, her expression softening. "But I'm scared."

"I know," Finch replied, offering a reassuring smile. "But we'll get through this. Together."

With newfound determination, they continued their journey through the darkened woods, the moonlight guiding their path. The night was far from over, but Finch felt a renewed sense of purpose.

They would uncover the truth, and in doing so, perhaps find redemption in the shadows of the past.

4. The Clock Strikes Twelve

THE CLOCK STRUCK TWELVE, its chimes resonating through the grand hall of Ashbury Manor, a stately edifice nestled amid the rolling hills of the English countryside. The sound reverberated in the air, mingling with the murmurs of the gathered guests, each lost in their own thoughts and intrigues. The evening had promised to be a celebration of sorts—a gala in honor of Lady Arabella Fairchild, the manor's owner, and the esteemed philanthropist known for her exquisite taste and lavish soirées. Yet, as the clock's final chime faded, a palpable tension hung in the atmosphere, as if the very walls themselves were holding their breath.

Lady Arabella, adorned in an opulent gown of emerald satin that accentuated her graceful figure, stood at the center of the room, a radiant smile on her face. Her dark hair, elegantly arranged and sparkling with jeweled pins, framed her delicate features. But beneath her polished exterior lay an undercurrent of anxiety, perceptible only to those who had known her long enough to recognize the subtle shifts in her demeanor.

Among the guests were the elite of society—prominent figures from politics, business, and the arts, each with their own agendas and secrets. Sir Reginald Hargrove, a shrewd businessman with a reputation for ruthlessness, engaged in quiet conversation with his wife, Lady Hargrove, a woman of quiet strength and unwavering loyalty. Across the room, Professor Harold Thorne, a well-respected historian, animatedly discussed ancient civilizations with the strikingly beautiful Miss Lydia Bennett, who was often the center of attention wherever she went.

As the guests mingled, a sudden chill crept through the hall, unnoticed by most but acutely felt by Lady Arabella. The evening had begun in good spirits, but with each passing hour, the atmosphere thickened with an unspoken tension, as if the very fabric of the night was woven with threads of foreboding.

Just as the clock struck its final note, a commotion erupted at the grand entrance. The heavy oak doors swung open with a creak, revealing a figure shrouded in shadows. Gasps echoed through the room as the intruder stepped into the light—a tall man, his features obscured by a wide-brimmed hat and a long trench coat that swept the floor. Silence enveloped the hall, the once lively conversations dying away as all eyes turned toward the stranger.

"Good evening, ladies and gentlemen," he announced, his voice smooth yet commanding, slicing through the tension like a knife. "I trust I am not too late for the festivities?"

Lady Arabella's smile faltered momentarily, but she quickly regained her composure. "Not at all, sir. I do believe we were just about to begin the evening's toast. May I ask your name?"

"Of course," he replied, removing his hat to reveal tousled dark hair and a face that bore an enigmatic expression. "I am Inspector Lionel Graves, and I must apologize for my unconventional entrance. I have urgent matters to discuss."

Whispers erupted among the guests, each one wondering what could possibly warrant the presence of a detective at such a gathering. Lady Arabella's eyes narrowed slightly, her heart racing as she instinctively sensed the gravity of the situation. "Inspector Graves, may I ask what brings you here tonight?"

"It is a matter of utmost importance, my lady," he said, his tone lowering to a conspiratorial whisper. "I regret to inform you that there has been a murder in the vicinity. And I have reason to believe that one of your guests may be involved."

The room erupted into chaos as the guests reacted with shock and disbelief. Gasps and cries of horror filled the air, and a palpable fear began to ripple through the crowd. Lady Arabella raised her hand to quiet them, her voice steady despite the storm brewing within her.

"Please, everyone! Let us not jump to conclusions. Inspector Graves, do you have any further details about this unfortunate event?"

The inspector cleared his throat, his gaze sweeping across the anxious faces of the guests. "A local farmer was found dead on his property not far from here. The circumstances surrounding his death are suspicious, and I must question each of you to determine if any of you were near the scene."

As he spoke, Lady Arabella's mind raced. The clock had struck twelve, marking not just the hour but the onset of a night fraught with uncertainty. She had invited these individuals into her home, each one seemingly more charming than the last, but now she could not shake the feeling that beneath their polished exteriors lay hidden truths waiting to be unearthed.

With a resolute nod, she addressed the crowd once more. "I understand this is alarming news, but I implore you to remain calm. Inspector Graves will conduct his inquiries here, within the confines of Ashbury Manor, where we can ensure everyone's safety. Until the matter is resolved, I ask that no one leaves the premises."

The guests exchanged uneasy glances, uncertainty etched on their faces. The inspector's presence loomed like a dark cloud, shrouding the evening in an unsettling gloom. Lady Arabella gestured for the inspector to take a seat at the grand dining table, where they would commence the questioning.

"Now, Inspector, I believe it is best we start with the facts," she said, her voice steady despite the turmoil within. "Who was the victim, and what do we know about him?"

"The victim was Samuel Treadwell," Inspector Graves replied, his tone grave. "A local farmer known for his reclusive nature. His body was discovered in the barn, and preliminary examinations suggest foul play."

Murmurs rippled through the guests once more. The name struck a chord, and Lady Arabella felt a shiver run down her spine. She had seen Samuel Treadwell's figure pass through her estate from time to time, a solitary man going about his business. But what had he done to provoke such violence?

"Was he known to any of us?" Lady Arabella inquired, her gaze sweeping the room. "Surely someone here must have encountered him."

Professor Thorne cleared his throat. "I believe I may have spoken to him on a few occasions while researching local history. He was an odd fellow, always reluctant to share much about himself."

"Odd, indeed," murmured Miss Lydia, her brow furrowed. "I heard he kept to himself and was rarely seen outside his property. There were whispers in the village about strange happenings around his farm."

As the conversation continued, Inspector Graves took careful notes, his eyes flicking between the guests as if attempting to gauge their reactions. Lady Arabella felt a tightening in her chest, her instincts warning her that something was amiss.

The inspector paused, his gaze piercing. "I must remind you that while I gather information, your cooperation is paramount. I will be asking each of you questions regarding your whereabouts prior to the discovery of the body."

With that, the evening took on an air of interrogation. One by one, the guests were ushered into another room, each one emerging with an air of anxiety hanging over them. Lady Arabella watched, her heart heavy with dread, as her friends and acquaintances revealed fragments of their lives, each testimony weaving a more intricate web of secrets.

As the clock continued its steady ticking, the realization dawned on Lady Arabella: there was a murderer among them. The very walls of Ashbury Manor seemed to harbor the weight of untold stories, and as she glanced at the inspector, she knew that unraveling the truth would not only expose the culprit but could also shatter the facade of their lives forever.

Hours passed, and the interrogation wore on. Inspector Graves remained composed, though Lady Arabella could see the strain etched across his features as he diligently pieced together the fragments of the case. Each guest presented a different narrative, some shaken by fear, others steadfast in their alibis.

Finally, it was her turn. As she stepped into the dimly lit study, the inspector regarded her with keen eyes. "Lady Arabella, thank you for your patience. I understand this evening has been trying for you."

"Indeed, Inspector," she replied, a tremor of unease in her voice. "But I assure you, I am innocent of any wrongdoing. My only concern is for the victim and ensuring justice is served."

"Of course," he said, his tone professional yet softening. "I have no reason to suspect you. However, I must ask—what were you doing prior to the discovery of Mr. Treadwell's body?"

"I was preparing for the evening's festivities, overseeing the arrangements for the gala," she explained, her brow furrowed. "I had no contact with Mr. Treadwell that evening, but I did see him a few days prior when he passed by the estate."

"Did he seem agitated? Anything out of the ordinary?" the inspector pressed, his pen poised above the notepad.

"Not particularly," she replied, recalling the brief encounter. "He was his usual self, though there was a flicker of concern in his eyes as he glanced at the estate. I assumed it was merely his nature to be wary of others."

"Interesting." The inspector noted her response, his expression thoughtful. "I would like to ask about your relationships with the other guests. Did you notice any tensions or disputes among them?"

Lady Arabella hesitated, her mind racing through the evening's interactions. "There were moments of unease, yes. Sir Reginald and Professor Thorne appeared to have a disagreement earlier in the evening regarding a business matter. And Miss Lydia seemed particularly interested in engaging with anyone who would listen."

"Noted," he replied, jotting down her observations. "I appreciate your candor, Lady Arabella. Please know that I will leave no stone unturned in this investigation."

As she exited the study, a wave of dread washed over her. She had expected a lively evening of celebration, yet here they were, ensnared in a web of suspicion and fear. The clock continued its relentless ticking, each passing second a reminder that the night was far from over.

Back in the grand hall, the guests awaited their turn, the air thick with apprehension. Lady Arabella felt their eyes upon her, each one a mix of curiosity and concern. It was then that she realized the evening would not conclude until the truth was laid bare.

As the clock inched toward one o'clock, Inspector Graves called for everyone's attention. "Ladies and gentlemen, I appreciate your cooperation thus far. The situation is delicate, and I must ask for your continued patience."

Gasps of disbelief rippled through the crowd, and Lady Arabella sensed the rising tide of fear. "Inspector, surely there must be a way to ensure everyone's safety," she interjected, her voice unwavering despite the chaos surrounding them. "We cannot allow panic to take hold."

"You are correct, Lady Arabella," he replied, his eyes scanning the room. "However, I cannot overlook the possibility that the murderer remains among us. I would like to propose a temporary measure—until the investigation is resolved, I suggest we confine ourselves to the manor."

A murmur of agreement rippled through the guests, but Lady Arabella could sense the underlying tension. The once-celebratory atmosphere had morphed into a chamber of distrust, where every glance could be construed as a challenge, every whisper as a potential threat.

The inspector continued, "I will be conducting a final round of questions, but I also implore you to share any information you may have about Mr. Treadwell. Even the smallest detail could prove vital."

As the night wore on, the questioning resumed, and Lady Arabella found herself pacing the hall, unable to shake the feeling of impending doom. The clock loomed overhead, its relentless ticking mirroring the rising urgency within her.

She paused by a large window overlooking the grounds, the moonlight spilling across the manicured lawns, casting eerie shadows that danced along the walls. It was a stark contrast to the chaos within, and for a moment, she longed for the simplicity of life before the night had turned dark.

Suddenly, a thought struck her. Samuel Treadwell had been an enigma—a man with secrets buried beneath layers of silence. If she could uncover something, anything, about his past, perhaps it would illuminate the darkness surrounding his death.

Determined, she returned to the gathering, her mind racing with possibilities. She sought out Professor Thorne, who was deep in conversation with Lady Hargrove. "Professor, might you have any further insight into Samuel Treadwell's life?" she asked, urgency lacing her tone.

The professor regarded her with surprise. "Why, Lady Arabella, I may have some information that could prove useful. I once encountered Treadwell at a local history society meeting. He spoke of his family lineage, mentioning a long-lost heirloom that had been passed down for generations—a timepiece of great significance."

"A timepiece?" Lady Arabella echoed, her curiosity piqued. "Could this heirloom be connected to the circumstances of his death?"

"Perhaps," he mused, stroking his chin thoughtfully. "He mentioned it was tied to a family feud—a story of betrayal and regret. I never probed deeper, but the tension surrounding the subject was palpable."

Lady Arabella's heart raced. The clock had struck twelve, ushering in a night of revelations, and now it seemed that time itself held the key to unlocking the mystery of Samuel Treadwell's death. "If you would, Professor, please share any additional information you may have regarding this heirloom. I suspect it may be the missing piece we need to solve this tragic puzzle."

As the night wore on, the tension within Ashbury Manor escalated. The guests exchanged wary glances, and the shadows grew longer, hinting at the secrets lurking just beneath the surface. The clock continued to tick away the minutes, marking time as it slipped further into uncertainty.

The inspector, having concluded his inquiries, gathered the guests once more. "I appreciate your patience as we delve deeper into the investigation. The presence of a murderer among us weighs heavily on my conscience, but I assure you, we will uncover the truth."

As the words hung in the air, a sudden crash echoed from the kitchen, shattering the fragile calm. The guests gasped, eyes wide with fear. Lady Arabella's heart raced as she exchanged a quick glance with Inspector Graves.

"Stay here!" he commanded, his voice firm. "I will investigate."

With that, he strode toward the kitchen, leaving the guests in a state of hushed panic. The clock's ticking grew louder, a reminder that time was of the essence. Lady Arabella clenched her fists, her resolve strengthening.

She could not remain idle while chaos reigned. Summoning her courage, she followed the inspector into the kitchen, where the scene unfolded like a nightmare.

The cook, Mrs. Fletcher, stood over a broken platter, her face pale with shock. "I— I dropped it," she stammered, eyes darting around the room. "I didn't mean to cause a commotion!"

Inspector Graves's sharp gaze took in the chaos, and he approached Mrs. Fletcher. "Did you see anyone suspicious in the hallway before this incident?"

"N-no, Inspector. I was simply preparing refreshments when I heard the noise from the hall," she replied, her voice trembling. "I didn't mean to startle anyone."

Lady Arabella stepped forward, sensing an opportunity. "Mrs. Fletcher, were you aware of Mr. Treadwell's murder?"

The cook's eyes widened, her hands shaking as she clutched the counter. "I heard whispers, yes, but I never met the man. He kept to himself, always a shadow in the background."

"Then tell me," Lady Arabella pressed, "have you noticed anything unusual around the manor? Any visitors or strange occurrences?"

Mrs. Fletcher hesitated, her brow furrowed in thought. "Well, there was a man who came by a few days ago. He was asking about the grounds, something about old ruins near the estate."

"Did you get a name?" Inspector Graves interjected, his tone urgent.

"Not his name, no," she admitted, "but he seemed very interested in the history of the manor. He left a business card, I think—something about antiques."

As she rummaged through a drawer, Lady Arabella's heart raced. Could this man be connected to Samuel Treadwell's death? Time was slipping through their fingers, and with every passing second, the weight of the night's mysteries pressed heavier upon her.

"Here it is!" Mrs. Fletcher exclaimed, producing a worn card. "Mr. Roderick Blake—antique dealer."

Inspector Graves accepted the card, his expression serious. "Thank you, Mrs. Fletcher. This could be significant. We need to find Mr. Blake and ascertain what he knows."

With the urgency of the moment propelling them, Lady Arabella and Inspector Graves exited the kitchen, rejoining the other guests in the grand hall. The clock struck one, each chime reverberating with a sense of impending doom.

"Ladies and gentlemen," Inspector Graves called, his voice firm and unwavering. "We have a potential lead in this investigation. A man named Roderick Blake may hold vital information regarding the events surrounding Mr. Treadwell's death. Until we locate him, I ask for your cooperation and vigilance."

As the inspector's words settled over the gathering, Lady Arabella could sense the shifting dynamics among the guests. Eyes darted around the room, suspicion weaving through their ranks as they considered the implications of Blake's involvement.

With a collective sense of determination, they set about searching the manor for any clues that might lead them to Roderick Blake. Lady Arabella felt a surge of adrenaline coursing through her veins, each heartbeat urging her to uncover the truth.

The minutes turned into an hour as they scoured the estate, retracing their steps and probing for any sign of the elusive dealer. Lady Arabella's thoughts raced as she pondered the potential connections between Samuel Treadwell, Roderick Blake, and the sinister events of the night.

Just as the clock ticked toward two o'clock, a commotion erupted near the library. Lady Arabella rushed to the scene, her heart pounding. The inspector stood at the doorway, his expression a mix of shock and anger.

"What is it?" she asked, breathless.

"Roderick Blake has been here," the inspector replied, pointing toward a discarded coat draped over a nearby chair. "And it seems he left in a hurry."

"Why would he abandon his coat?" Lady Arabella wondered aloud, her mind racing with possibilities.

"Perhaps he sensed we were onto him," Inspector Graves replied, his eyes narrowing. "Or perhaps he knows more than he's letting on."

As the clock chimed once more, marking the passage of time, Lady Arabella felt the weight of the night settle heavily upon her shoulders. They were running out of time to solve the mystery, and the stakes had never been higher.

With renewed resolve, she turned to the guests. "We must find Roderick Blake. If he holds the key to uncovering the truth, we cannot let him slip away."

The group set off once more, determined to uncover the secrets hidden within the shadows of Ashbury Manor. As the clock continued its steady ticking, the night unfolded with a sense of urgency, each moment leading them closer to the truth—and deeper into the heart of darkness.

Time had become their adversary, and the clock was ticking down to a final revelation. The mystery of Samuel Treadwell's murder was not just a matter of time; it was a battle against the

very fabric of deception that had woven itself through their lives.

The night pressed on, and with it came the realization that the clock had struck twelve, heralding the arrival of an evening fraught with danger, betrayal, and the promise of revelation. The players had assembled, and the stage was set for the truth to be unveiled, whether they were ready or not.

5. The Countdown

THE NIGHT WAS THICK with anticipation, each second echoing like the tick of a clock in a hushed room. Detective Albert Hart stood at the center of the dimly lit drawing room of Foxglove Manor, his gaze sweeping over the anxious faces of the guests gathered around him. The room, adorned with ornate furnishings and gilded frames, seemed to hold its breath. The air was thick with tension, an unspoken dread hanging like a dark cloud above their heads.

Just hours ago, the invitation to this exclusive gathering had seemed harmless, a chance to revel in the company of the elite. However, that feeling had swiftly dissipated when the first scream pierced the night, shattering the illusion of safety that the manor had long been known for. The scream had come from the library, where they had found Lord Ambrose Mortimer sprawled across the floor, his lifeless body surrounded by the very clocks that had fascinated him for decades.

"Six o'clock," Albert murmured, glancing at the ornate grandfather clock that dominated the room, its pendulum swinging steadily. "That was the time of death."

The guests exchanged uneasy glances, their earlier merriment extinguished like a candle snuffed by an unkind wind. Each person present had a reason to fear, as the invitation had hinted at a dark secret lurking within the walls of Foxglove Manor. But it was the timing of Lord Mortimer's death that set the tone for the evening. The clock struck six, and with it, the countdown had begun.

"Now, everyone," Albert began, his voice steady, though inside he felt the adrenaline coursing through his veins. "We must remain calm. This is not the first time a murder has taken place at a gathering such as this. We can unravel this mystery, but I need your cooperation."

Lady Penelope, the widow of the deceased, clutched a silk handkerchief, her face pale. "Who would do such a thing?" she whispered, her voice trembling. "And why? Ambrose had no enemies, at least none that we knew of."

"Ah, but therein lies the crux of the matter," Albert replied, his keen eyes narrowing. "Even the most beloved figures often harbor secrets. Lord Mortimer was known for his vast collection of rare clocks, but what you may not know is that he was also a man deeply involved in the local financial affairs. It is possible that someone saw an opportunity to rid themselves of him."

The room was silent, save for the rhythmic ticking of the clocks. Albert could see the gears turning in their minds as they contemplated the implications. He gestured toward the library door. "We should return to the scene of the crime. Perhaps we can find something that will shed light on the motive and the murderer."

As they entered the library, the flickering candlelight cast long shadows on the walls, creating an atmosphere both foreboding and intimate. The room was lined with shelves filled with books, their spines dusty from years of neglect. Yet, it was the collection of clocks that captured Albert's attention. Each timepiece was unique, with ornate carvings and delicate movements, but all were eerily still now, their hands frozen in time.

Albert knelt beside Lord Mortimer's body, examining the lifeless form for clues. "He had a watch," he noted, reaching for the pocket of the deceased's waistcoat. "Perhaps it will tell us something."

As he retrieved the watch, he noticed it was set to six o'clock, matching the grandfather clock in the hall. "Curious," he murmured. "It seems our dear lord had an obsession with punctuality."

Lady Penelope stepped closer, her eyes wide with fear. "You think this was premeditated? That someone wanted him dead?"

Albert nodded slowly, the pieces beginning to form a picture in his mind. "It is highly likely. But the question remains—who among us would be so ruthless?"

Just then, the manor's door creaked open, and a figure stepped inside. It was Inspector Graves, a seasoned officer known for his brusque demeanor and sharp intellect. "I received word of the murder, Detective Hart. I trust you have everything under control?"

"Everything is under control," Albert replied, his voice steady, though he felt the pressure mounting. "But time is of the essence. We must uncover the truth before the clock strikes again."

Graves surveyed the room, his eyes narrowing as he focused on the guests. "It seems you have quite a gathering, Hart. Care to enlighten me on the situation?"

Albert took a deep breath. "Lord Mortimer was found dead here, surrounded by his clocks. Each guest received an invitation hinting at a hidden agenda, and now we must unravel this web before more lives are lost."

Graves nodded, his expression serious. "Let us not waste time, then. We'll need to interview each guest. Secrets have a way of revealing themselves when pressed."

As the two men moved to gather the guests, Albert could feel the urgency in the air. The countdown had begun, and they were racing against time to solve a murder that threatened to shatter the lives of everyone present.

The guests were assembled in the drawing room once more, their faces a mix of fear and curiosity. Albert took a moment to observe them, noting the tension in their postures and the way they avoided each other's gazes. It was clear that the atmosphere had shifted, and with it, the facade of camaraderie had crumbled.

"Ladies and gentlemen," Albert began, his voice firm yet calm, "we are gathered here not just to mourn Lord Mortimer but to seek justice for his untimely death. I will need your full cooperation as we proceed. I trust that you will answer my questions honestly, for the truth has a way of coming to light, even in the darkest of hours."

He began with Lady Penelope, who was still visibly shaken. "Lady Penelope, I must ask you—what were your last interactions with Lord Mortimer before his death?"

She hesitated, her gaze flickering toward the clock. "We had a disagreement about finances, I must confess. He was deeply involved in some investments that I believed were ill-advised. I wanted him to reconsider, but he was resolute. It was only a discussion, though—nothing more."

Albert noted her words carefully, sensing an underlying tension. "And what of the rest of you? Were there any signs of animosity among the guests?"

One of the guests, a business partner of Lord Mortimer, spoke up. "There was a heated discussion earlier this evening regarding the manor's financial affairs. Ambrose was adamant about a new investment, and I feared he might be making a grave mistake. But I would never wish him harm."

Albert's attention shifted to another guest, Miss Clara, a young woman who had been a childhood friend of Lord Mortimer. "Miss Clara, how did you find out about Lord Mortimer's death?"

"I was in the garden, picking flowers when I heard the scream," she replied, her voice trembling. "I rushed inside but was too late to help him."

Albert could see the genuine distress in her eyes, but he also sensed something more—a deep-seated fear that she was struggling to articulate. "Did you see anyone suspicious near the library?"

"No, I did not," she replied, shaking her head vigorously. "But I did overhear Lady Penelope discussing her concerns with Lord Mortimer."

The room fell silent, all eyes turning to Lady Penelope, who now looked more agitated. "I spoke to him out of concern, not malice!"

"Yet concern can often cloud judgment," Albert said, his tone even. "And what of you, Mr. Leighton?" he asked, turning to the business partner. "You had a vested interest in Lord Mortimer's decisions, did you not?"

"Yes," he admitted, his voice tight. "But my interest was purely financial. I had no reason to harm him. The investments were a matter of personal gain, but I would have never considered murder."

"Interesting," Albert said, his mind racing as he pieced together their alibis and motivations. Each guest had a motive; each one could have acted out of desperation or fear of loss. "As time is of the essence, we must consider every angle. I will need to see Lord

Mortimer's office. Perhaps there are documents or correspondence that can shed light on this matter."

Albert led the way to Lord Mortimer's office, the air growing heavier with each passing minute. As they entered, he noted the meticulous organization of the room—books lined the shelves, and papers were neatly stacked. Yet, it was the desk that caught his attention. A silver clock sat atop it, its hands frozen at six o'clock, matching the others.

"Remarkable," he said, running his fingers over the clock's surface. "The very moment he died."

As he rifled through the papers, he came across a letter, its contents alarming. It was a threat—an ultimatum from an unknown sender. "This changes everything," he said, showing it to Graves. "Someone wanted Lord Mortimer to comply with their demands. But what were those demands? And why did he ignore them?"

Graves frowned. "We need to get this to the constable. Perhaps they can trace the handwriting or the source of the letter."

Just then, a commotion erupted outside, drawing their attention. Albert rushed to the window, peering out to see a figure darting away from the manor, a cloak billowing in the wind. "Quick! After them!" he shouted, adrenaline surging as he dashed toward the door.

The two men raced outside, determination driving them forward. The night was alive with the sound of footsteps pounding against the cobblestones, the distant chime of the clock marking the passage of time. They could see the figure weaving through the trees, disappearing into the shadows of the garden.

"Stop!" Albert called, but the figure only quickened their pace. With every heartbeat, Albert felt the weight of the investigation pressing down on him. He knew that if they didn't catch this person, the truth would remain elusive, hidden behind layers of deceit.

As they rounded the corner, Albert stumbled upon a small clearing, illuminated by the moonlight. The figure had disappeared, leaving only a faint rustling in the bushes. He paused, listening intently, his instincts telling him they were not alone.

"Albert!" Graves whispered urgently, his voice low. "We need to regroup. This may be a trap."

Just as he said it, a shadow loomed behind them. Albert turned, instinctively reaching for his pocket, but before he could react, a hand clamped down on his shoulder.

"Detective Hart," a voice hissed, low and menacing. "You're meddling in matters far beyond your understanding."

Albert recognized the figure as one of the guests from earlier, a man who had been quiet throughout the evening. "What do you want?" Albert demanded, trying to mask his surprise.

The man's eyes glinted in the moonlight, filled with a mixture of fear and anger. "You're too late. You cannot change what has already been set in motion."

"Then perhaps you can tell me what it is you're hiding," Albert pressed, refusing to back down.

But before the man could respond, the night erupted into chaos. A shot rang out, echoing through the trees, and Albert instinctively pushed Graves to the ground, narrowly avoiding the bullet.

"Run!" Albert shouted, adrenaline coursing through him as they dashed toward the safety of the manor. The countdown had taken a deadly turn, and they were no longer simply racing against time—they were in a fight for their lives.

As they reached the door, Albert's mind raced with questions. Who had fired the shot? And what deeper secrets lay hidden within the walls of Foxglove Manor?

Inside, the atmosphere was charged with panic. Guests were huddled together, whispers of fear spreading like wildfire. "What happened?" Lady Penelope cried, her voice trembling.

"A gunshot," Albert replied, his expression grave. "We have to secure the premises. Someone is trying to kill us, and I fear it is only the beginning."

The urgency in his voice propelled them into action. Albert began to assign tasks, instructing Graves to check the windows and ensure they were secure while he interviewed the remaining guests. They had no time to lose, for the countdown was ticking away.

As he moved through the room, he could see the fear etched on their faces. "Listen closely, everyone," he said, projecting authority. "We are in danger. It is imperative that you do not leave this room until we ascertain who among you is capable of murder."

One guest, a nervous young man, stepped forward. "But Detective, we can't stay here! What if the murderer is among us?"

"Precisely," Albert replied, his gaze piercing. "That is exactly why we must remain vigilant. The moment you leave this room is the moment you put your lives in jeopardy."

Lady Penelope clasped her hands together, her voice quivering. "What do we do?"

"First, I need each of you to recount your whereabouts during the gunshot," Albert instructed, his tone firm. "Then we will compare alibis and see if anyone's story doesn't add up."

As they began to share their accounts, Albert listened intently, noting the inconsistencies that began to emerge. The room was heavy with tension, and each second felt like an eternity as they fought against the encroaching darkness.

Suddenly, the clock chimed once more, the sound echoing ominously through the room. Six times it rang, each toll a reminder of the life that had been extinguished and the danger that still lurked within.

"Time is running out," Albert said, his voice steady despite the chaos around him. "We must find the truth before more lives are lost."

He turned to the guests, his heart pounding. "Now, let's find out who among you is the true enemy. The countdown has begun, and we cannot afford to fail."

As the investigation unfolded, Albert felt the weight of the world pressing down on him. Every tick of the clock resonated in his mind, a constant reminder that the clock was ticking, and time was not on their side.

Through the chaos, one thing became clear: within Foxglove Manor, secrets lay thick as fog, and only by unraveling the threads of deceit could they hope to escape the shadow of death that loomed over them.

The countdown had started, and with it came the realization that not everyone would survive to see the dawn.

6. An Unforgiven Crime

IN THE QUIET VILLAGE of Aldersfield, nestled between rolling hills and dense woodlands, an air of tranquility prevailed. It was the sort of place where every face was familiar, and the sound of laughter echoed through the cobbled streets. Yet, beneath this idyllic surface lay an unsettling tension, like the coiling of a spring just before it snaps. This tension was most palpable in the large, ivy-clad manor that loomed at the edge of the village—Hawthorne House.

The manor, with its intricate woodwork and grandiose windows, had been the pride of Aldersfield for generations. However, it had become a mausoleum of memories since the tragic events that unfolded a year prior. The untimely death of its owner, Mr. Edward Hawthorne, had left the village reeling. The circumstances surrounding his demise were as murky as the waters of the nearby lake, and whispers of foul play lingered in the air.

It was a misty autumn morning when Inspector Harold Finch arrived in Aldersfield, his presence felt like a harbinger of change. A man of average height with a keen intellect and an unyielding sense of justice, Finch had garnered respect throughout his years on the force. He had been summoned by an anonymous letter hinting at a revival of the case—a crime that had long been buried under layers of grief and silence.

The villagers were initially hesitant to speak with Finch. They had long since learned to keep their secrets hidden, preferring to protect their own rather than confront the ghosts of the past. Nevertheless, Finch's persistence was unwavering. He began his inquiries at the local inn, The Silver Stag, where the townsfolk gathered for gossip as much as for drink.

"Mr. Hawthorne was a good man, if a bit reclusive," said Margaret, the innkeeper, her hands wringing a cloth as she cleaned a glass. "He kept to himself after his wife passed away. You'd hardly see him in town, and then—" She paused, glancing around the room as if the walls had ears. "Then came that dreadful night."

Finch leaned in, encouraging her to continue. "What happened that night?"

"He was found dead in his study, you know. They said it was a heart attack, but..." Her voice trailed off, and her eyes flicked toward the door as if fearing someone might overhear.

"But what?" Finch pressed gently.

Margaret sighed, her demeanor shifting. "There were rumors. Some folks believed he was murdered. They said there was a struggle—things were knocked over in that room. But no one wanted to believe it."

"Did anyone see anything unusual?" Finch asked, sensing a thread he could unravel.

"Only the gardener, old Tom. He swore he heard shouting from the house, but who listens to a gardener?" Margaret rolled her eyes. "Still, he vanished after the funeral. Poor fellow probably couldn't bear the memories."

As Finch continued his inquiries, he became increasingly aware of the web of fear and denial that enveloped the villagers. It was as if they had collectively agreed to forget the tragedy that had befallen them. But Finch was not so easily deterred. He knew that the truth lay buried beneath their reluctance to confront it.

After a long day of questioning, Finch made his way to Hawthorne House. The imposing structure stood dark against the twilight sky, its windows like vacant eyes watching him approach. He had obtained permission from the estate's current owner, a distant cousin of Mr. Hawthorne, to investigate the house. Finch felt a thrill of anticipation mixed with trepidation; he was stepping into the very heart of the mystery.

The air inside the manor was thick with dust and the scent of old wood. Finch moved cautiously through the dimly lit halls, his footsteps muffled by the faded carpet beneath him. As he entered the study, a chill ran down his spine. The room was just as it had been the night of the incident—bookshelves lined with leather-bound volumes, a mahogany desk strewn with papers, and a shattered vase lying in the corner.

It was then that Finch noticed something unusual. A small, ornate clock on the desk had stopped. He picked it up, examining the intricate engravings that adorned its surface. The hands were frozen at ten minutes past eleven, the exact time of Mr. Hawthorne's death according to the coroner's report. A cold realization washed over him: the clock was more than a mere timepiece; it was a silent witness to the events that had transpired.

Finch set the clock back down, his mind racing with possibilities. He scanned the room for any other clues that might reveal what had happened that fateful night. As he turned to leave, something caught his eye—a scrap of paper half-hidden under the desk. He crouched to retrieve it, and his heart quickened as he read the hastily scrawled note.

"Meet me at the clock tower. Midnight. You know the truth."

The note was unsigned, but its implications were clear. Someone had intended to confront Mr. Hawthorne that night, someone who believed they held the key to the mystery. Finch knew he had to find out who had written it.

The following day, he revisited The Silver Stag, hoping that with the added urgency of the note, someone might finally speak up. He approached old Tom, the gardener, who had returned to the village under a pseudonym. Finch found him hunched over a pint, lost in thought.

"Tom," Finch said, sliding into the seat across from him. "I'd like to talk to you about Mr. Hawthorne."

The gardener looked up, his eyes widening in recognition. "I've told you everything I know," he muttered, a tremor in his voice.

"No, I don't think you have," Finch replied, leaning forward. "I found a note. It mentions a meeting at the clock tower. You were there that night, weren't you?"

Tom's expression shifted from surprise to fear. "I didn't mean to. I was just trying to protect him."

"Protect him from what?" Finch pressed, his curiosity piqued.

"There were people after him," Tom whispered, glancing around as if he feared they might be listening. "He got mixed up in something dangerous. I was told to keep an eye on him, but I never thought it would come to this."

"Dangerous how?" Finch demanded.

"Money," Tom said, his voice barely above a whisper. "He was involved in something illegal. There were threats made—people didn't want him to speak. I was supposed to warn him, but I didn't get there in time."

Finch felt a surge of urgency. "Did you see anyone that night? Did you hear anything?"

"I heard shouting," Tom admitted, his face pale. "But I didn't see who it was. I was too far away. I thought maybe it was just an argument, but I knew it wasn't right. When I arrived, it was too late."

Finch's mind raced with possibilities. He knew he needed to find out who had threatened Mr. Hawthorne. As he left the inn, he felt a sense of purpose solidifying within him. The truth was beginning to unfurl, and with it came the chilling realization that the villagers weren't just protecting their own—they were hiding from a danger that lingered just beneath the surface.

As the sun dipped below the horizon, Finch made his way to the clock tower, the very place mentioned in the note. The structure loomed over the village like a sentinel, its bells silent for years. He had a feeling that this was where the threads of the past would lead him.

As he climbed the creaking stairs, each step echoed in the empty space, heightening the tension in the air. The view from the top was breathtaking, offering a panorama of the village and the surrounding woods. But Finch's attention was drawn to the clock itself. It was still and silent, its hands frozen as if trapped in time.

Suddenly, he heard a noise behind him, and he turned to see a figure emerging from the shadows. "You shouldn't have come here," the voice warned, low and menacing.

"I need answers," Finch said, standing his ground. "Who are you?"

The figure stepped into the light, revealing a woman with sharp features and a determined gaze. "I'm the last person you want to be questioning."

"Then you must know something about Mr. Hawthorne," Finch countered.

"I know a lot more than you think," she replied, crossing her arms defiantly. "But it's not for you to uncover."

"Why not? Is it because you're involved?" Finch probed, sensing that he had struck a nerve.

"Edward was my brother," she said, her voice trembling with emotion. "And I won't let you tarnish his memory with your accusations."

"Your brother was mixed up in something dangerous," Finch stated. "And I believe someone wanted him dead."

"You don't know anything!" she shouted, her composure slipping. "Edward was a good man. He made mistakes, yes, but he didn't deserve this."

"Then help me find out what happened," Finch urged. "We need to find the truth."

The woman hesitated, her resolve faltering as she looked into Finch's earnest eyes. "You don't understand. If you dig too deep, you'll unearth more than just a crime. You'll uncover secrets that will destroy this village."

Finch felt a sense of foreboding wash over him. "Sometimes the truth is more important than the comfort of lies."

With that, the woman turned and fled down the stairs, leaving Finch standing alone in the tower. He realized that time was running out, and if he was to uncover the truth about Edward Hawthorne's death, he would need to act quickly.

Returning to
the village, he pieced together the information he had gathered so far. He decided to confront Margaret, the innkeeper, again. There was something about her demeanor that suggested she knew more than she let on.

When he arrived at The Silver Stag, the atmosphere was thick with tension. The usual chatter was muted, and the villagers exchanged wary glances as Finch entered. He made his way to the bar where Margaret was wiping down the counter.

"Margaret, I need to ask you some questions about Edward," he began.

Her expression hardened. "I've told you everything I know, Inspector."

"No, you haven't. You're hiding something. I can feel it," Finch pressed.

Margaret glanced around the room before leaning closer. "Fine. But you didn't hear this from me. There was talk of a deal gone wrong. Edward was supposed to be meeting someone that night—a man named Walter Stokes."

"Who is Walter Stokes?" Finch asked, intrigued.

"He's not someone you want to cross. He's involved in some shady business—money laundering, extortion, you name it. Edward got caught in his web, and I fear it didn't end well for him," she confessed.

"Where can I find him?" Finch demanded, urgency clawing at him.

"Last I heard, he was staying at the old inn on the outskirts of town. But be careful; he's dangerous," she warned.

With a newfound determination, Finch set out toward the old inn, his heart pounding in anticipation of what he might find. The journey felt like an eternity as he navigated the winding roads that led away from the village. The sun was setting, casting an eerie glow over the landscape, and shadows danced around him as if whispering secrets long forgotten.

Upon reaching the inn, Finch was met with an unsettling silence. The building appeared neglected, its windows dark and foreboding. He knocked on the door, and after a moment, it creaked open to reveal a disheveled man with unkempt hair and a wary gaze.

"What do you want?" the man asked, eyeing Finch suspiciously.

"I'm looking for Walter Stokes," Finch replied, stepping inside.

The man hesitated, glancing around as if he feared being overheard. "He's not here."

"Where is he?" Finch pressed, refusing to back down.

"He left town," the man mumbled. "And I suggest you do the same before you get yourself into trouble."

Finch's instincts told him the man was lying. "I know about Edward Hawthorne and the deal that went wrong. If you know anything, now is the time to speak up."

The man shifted nervously, his eyes darting to the door. "I don't want any part of this," he said, his voice trembling.

Finch took a step closer. "Then you'll have to live with the knowledge that an innocent man was murdered. Are you really willing to let that happen?"

Finally, the man relented. "Alright, alright. Walter was here the night Edward died. They argued about money. I heard shouting. Then... then I heard a crash."

"A crash?" Finch echoed, urgency bubbling within him.

"Yeah. It sounded like something breaking. But then it went quiet. I didn't want to get involved, so I left," the man admitted, his voice barely a whisper.

Finch's heart raced. "Did you see Walter leave?"

"Not really. I was too scared," he stammered. "But he's dangerous, Inspector. If you're looking for him, you need to be careful."

Finch nodded, his mind racing. The pieces were falling into place, but he still needed more evidence to confront Stokes. He thanked the man and left the inn, his resolve stronger than ever.

As he returned to the village, he pondered his next move. He knew he had to find Stokes before he vanished completely. With each passing moment, he felt the weight of time pressing upon him. The truth was within reach, but it eluded him like sand slipping through his fingers.

The following day, Finch arranged a meeting with the local constable, hoping to gather additional resources for the search. He met Constable Richards at the village hall, where the atmosphere was thick with anxiety.

"Inspector, you're not going to believe this," Richards said, his brow furrowed with concern. "There's been another incident."

"What do you mean?" Finch asked, dread creeping into his voice.

"Walter Stokes was found dead in his hotel room," Richards revealed, his tone grave. "The manager discovered him this morning. It looks like foul play."

Finch felt a chill run down his spine. "We need to investigate immediately. Stokes may have known more than he let on about Edward's death."

As they arrived at the inn, a crowd had gathered outside, drawn by the commotion. Finch pushed his way through the throng, his heart racing. He entered the room to find Stokes lying motionless on the bed, a look of terror frozen on his face.

"Looks like he didn't go quietly," Richards remarked, surveying the scene.

Finch examined the room, searching for any clues that might reveal what had happened. A half-empty bottle of whiskey lay on the table, and the curtains were drawn tightly, shrouding the room in darkness. The air felt heavy with foreboding.

"Do you see that?" Finch pointed to a scrap of paper lying on the floor near the bed.

Richards picked it up, and Finch could see a hastily written message. "I know what you did," it read. "You'll pay for your betrayal."

"This could mean something," Finch mused, his mind racing. "It suggests that Stokes was involved in something far more sinister than we realized."

"Who would want him dead?" Richards wondered aloud.

"I suspect it has to do with Edward's death," Finch replied, piecing the puzzle together. "If Stokes was threatening someone, perhaps they silenced him to prevent the truth from coming out."

"Do you think it could be connected to the villagers?" Richards asked, uncertainty creeping into his voice.

"It's a possibility," Finch admitted. "We need to gather more information, but time is running out."

As they left the inn, Finch's instincts kicked into high gear. He felt the eyes of the villagers upon him, watching and waiting for him to uncover their secrets. The tension in the air was palpable, and he knew he had to confront the very heart of the matter.

Returning to Hawthorne House, he combed through the evidence he had collected, searching for any leads that could provide clarity. His gaze fell upon the broken clock, its hands forever frozen in time. It was a symbol of the tragedy that had unfolded and the unanswered questions that lingered.

That evening, Finch called for a meeting at the village hall, determined to confront the villagers about the events that had transpired. The hall was filled with anxious faces, their expressions a mix of fear and curiosity.

"Ladies and gentlemen," Finch began, his voice steady and commanding. "I have gathered you here to address the events surrounding Edward Hawthorne's death. We cannot continue to live in the shadows of secrets and lies."

Murmurs rippled through the crowd, and Finch pressed on. "I believe that someone here knows the truth, and it's time to bring it to light. If we do not confront our fears, they will consume us."

Margaret stepped forward, her expression defiant. "You don't understand, Inspector. We've lived in this village for generations. We protect our own, no matter the cost."

"Even at the cost of justice?" Finch countered, his eyes locking onto hers. "Edward was a good man who did not deserve this fate. If you care about this village, you will help me uncover the truth."

A heavy silence fell over the hall as the villagers exchanged glances. It was then that Tom, the gardener, stood up, his voice shaky but determined. "I'll speak. I saw things that night. I was afraid, but I cannot let this continue."

Finch felt a surge of hope. "What did you see, Tom?"

"I saw a shadowy figure leave the house just after the shouting stopped," Tom admitted, his voice gaining strength. "I couldn't recognize them, but they had a distinctive coat—a dark, long one."

"Did you see their face?" Finch asked, leaning in.

"No, but I know it was someone who didn't belong in the house. I wish I had done something sooner," Tom replied, his voice heavy with regret.

"Did you recognize the coat?" Finch pressed, urgency flooding his words.

Tom hesitated. "I think it belonged to someone in the village, but I can't be sure."

Finch's mind raced as he contemplated the implications of Tom's revelation. If they could identify the coat, it could lead them directly to the killer. "We need to gather the villagers and see if anyone recognizes it."

As the meeting concluded, Finch felt a renewed sense of determination. The truth was finally within reach, but the shadows of the past loomed larger than ever.

The following day, Finch and Richards organized a gathering to display the coat, urging the villagers to come forward with any information. The atmosphere was tense, filled with anticipation as they unveiled the dark coat.

"Does anyone recognize this?" Finch asked, scanning the crowd.

A collective silence fell over the room until an elderly woman stepped forward, her voice trembling. "That coat belongs to Arthur."

"Arthur? Who is he?" Finch inquired.

"He's a recluse who lives on the outskirts of town. He keeps to himself, but he has a reputation," she explained.

"Where can I find him?" Finch asked, sensing that they were closing in on the truth.

"He usually spends his time at the old mill," she replied. "But be careful. He can be... volatile."

With newfound urgency, Finch and Richards set off toward the mill, their hearts racing with anticipation. As they approached the crumbling structure, the weight of the investigation pressed upon them. They found Arthur hunched over a table, sketching something in the dim light.

"Arthur!" Finch called, stepping into the room. "We need to talk."

The man looked up, startled. "What do you want?" he snapped, his eyes narrowing.

"We're investigating Edward Hawthorne's death," Finch replied, keeping his tone steady. "We found a coat that belongs to you."

Arthur's face paled, and he rose to his feet. "I don't know what you're talking about."

"Don't lie to me," Finch pressed, his voice firm. "We have witnesses who saw you near the manor that night."

"I was nowhere near there!" Arthur shouted, panic creeping into his voice.

"Then explain the coat," Finch demanded.

"I—I left it behind," Arthur stammered. "But I wasn't involved. I had nothing to do with it!"

Finch stepped closer, narrowing his gaze. "Tell me what you know, and this will end better for you."

Arthur's defenses crumbled, and he slumped back into his chair. "Fine. I had an argument with Edward a few days before he died. He owed me money, and I needed it back. But I didn't kill him! I swear!"

"Then who did?" Finch pressed, sensing that he was finally getting closer to the truth.

"I don't know! I heard him arguing with someone that night, but I didn't see their face," Arthur admitted, desperation etched on his features. "I just wanted my money."

Frustrated, Finch stepped back, knowing that time was slipping away. The pieces of the puzzle were still scattered, and he needed to find a way to connect them.

As he left the mill, a thought struck him. The note he had found at Hawthorne House. If Stokes had known about the money, he could have been the one threatening Edward. If he had confronted him about the debt, it could have led to a confrontation.

Returning to the village, Finch decided to review Stokes' affairs. He spoke to the manager of the inn where Stokes had been staying, hoping to gather more information.

"Stokes was a ruthless man," the manager said, his voice low. "He was always involved in something shady. I remember seeing him arguing with someone in the tavern just before he died."

"Who was he arguing with?" Finch asked, his pulse quickening.

"I couldn't see their face," the manager replied. "But they were both agitated. I thought it was just a typical bar fight, but now..."

Finch's mind raced. "Now it feels more significant, doesn't it?"

"Indeed," the manager said, his brow furrowed in concern. "You should speak with the villagers who were there that night. They might have seen something."

Finch nodded, determination swelling within him. He had to find those villagers and unravel the connections between Edward, Stokes, and the shadowy figure who had left the house that night.

Days passed, and as Finch continued to gather evidence, he began to see the connections between the villagers' lives and the events surrounding Edward's death. He spent countless hours piecing together testimonies, each one revealing a deeper layer of deception.

Finally, he gathered the villagers once more at the village hall, ready to confront them with what he had learned. "I have gathered enough evidence to believe that Edward was not just an innocent victim," Finch began, his voice echoing through the hall. "He was involved in a web of deceit that ultimately led to his demise."

Gasps filled the room, and Margaret stepped forward. "You don't understand! He was just trying to make a living!"

"By involving himself with dangerous people?" Finch pressed. "Someone wanted him dead, and I believe you all know who that someone is."

The villagers shifted uneasily, their expressions a mix of guilt and fear.

"Tom, you mentioned hearing shouting," Finch continued. "Who was arguing with Edward?"

Tom hesitated but finally spoke up. "It was Arthur. They were arguing about money."

"Arthur?" Finch echoed, turning his gaze toward the recluse. "What do you know about the money?"

Arthur's face paled. "I was angry! I needed that money, and I didn't care how I got it!"

"Did you kill him?" Finch demanded.

"No! I swear! I didn't know he was dead until later!" Arthur shouted, desperation in his eyes.

"Then who did?" Finch pressed. "The truth is out there, and I will find it!"

Suddenly, a voice rang out from the back of the hall. "It wasn't him!"

All eyes turned to see the woman from the clock tower step forward, her expression fierce. "I was there that night. I saw everything."

Gasps erupted in the room as the villagers exchanged shocked glances.

"I watched from the shadows as Stokes confronted Edward," she continued. "They argued about the money, and then Stokes—he was furious! I couldn't believe what I was witnessing."

"Why didn't you come forward sooner?" Finch asked, urgency in his tone.

"I was scared," she admitted, her voice trembling. "I didn't want to put myself in danger. But I can't let Edward's memory be tarnished any longer."

"Then tell us what happened," Finch urged.

"They were arguing when Stokes pushed Edward. He fell, and then—" She hesitated, pain etched on her features. "Then I saw Stokes take out a knife. It was an accident, I swear!"

Finch felt a rush of adrenaline. "We need to find Stokes and confront him about this."

The villagers erupted into chaos, their fear spilling over into panic. "He's dangerous! He'll kill us all!" they cried.

Finch steadied himself, raising his hands to quiet the crowd. "I need you to trust me. If we come together, we can stop this once and for all."

As the villagers calmed down, Finch organized a search party to find Stokes. The fear that had gripped Aldersfield for far too long would finally come to an end. Together, they set out into the night, determination fueling their steps.

The search led them to the old clock tower, a place where shadows danced in the moonlight. As they approached, Finch's heart raced. It was there that the truth would be revealed once and for all.

"Stokes!" Finch called, his voice echoing in the stillness. "We know what you did! You can't run from the truth!"

The wind howled through the tower, and they heard a faint sound—a figure darting through the shadows. Finch and the villagers pursued, their footsteps pounding against the ground.

"Stop!" Finch shouted, his voice resonating with authority. "We just want to talk!"

But the figure was fast, darting into the woods surrounding the tower. Finch felt a surge of urgency as they continued the chase, the darkness enveloping them.

Finally, they cornered Stokes at the edge of a clearing, panting and wild-eyed. "You won't take me back!" he shouted, his voice filled with desperation.

"We just want the truth," Finch replied, his tone steady. "You can't keep running forever."

"I didn't mean for it to happen!" Stokes cried, fear etching his features. "It was an accident! I just wanted my money back!"

"You killed Edward!" Finch pressed, his heart pounding. "You can't hide from that."

Suddenly, Stokes lunged, and the villagers gasped as he brandished a knife. But Finch was ready. He had anticipated this moment, and he lunged forward, wrestling the knife from Stokes' grasp.

"You're finished!" Finch shouted, pinning Stokes to the ground. "The truth will come out!"

As Stokes was restrained, Finch felt a sense of closure wash over him. The shadows of Aldersfield were beginning to lift, and justice was finally within reach.

As the dawn broke over the village, Finch gathered the villagers once more. "Edward Hawthorne was a victim of circumstances, but his death will not go unpunished. We have the truth, and it will set this village free."

The villagers erupted into cheers, their fears dissipating with the light of the new day.

In that moment, Finch knew that he had not only solved a crime but also restored a sense of hope to Aldersfield. The shadows that had lingered would finally be banished, and the village could begin to heal.

As the villagers celebrated, Finch stood quietly, reflecting on the journey that had brought them to this moment. The clock that had once stood as a testament to tragedy now symbolized a new beginning. The echoes of the past would forever remain, but they would no longer hold power over the present.

And so, as the sun rose over Aldersfield, Finch felt a sense of fulfillment wash over him. He had uncovered the truth, and in doing so, had brought light back to a village shrouded in darkness. The clockwork of their lives would continue, ticking forward, guided by the lessons learned from the past.

Chapter 11: The Clockwork Legacy

1. Aftermath and Reflections

The early morning sun cast a muted light over the small village of Eldershire, its rays struggling to penetrate the thick fog that clung to the ground like a shroud. As the townsfolk went about their routines, the weight of recent events hung heavily in the air, a palpable tension that could not be dismissed.

Detective Inspector Charles Hart stood at the edge of the village square, his hands tucked into the pockets of his overcoat, deep in thought. It had been a fortnight since the last of the Clockwork Murders had been solved, yet the echoes of that turbulent time reverberated through the cobbled streets. The town had experienced a reckoning, the revelation of dark secrets and hidden lives weaving a tapestry of intrigue that was both disturbing and fascinating.

He recalled the frantic search for the murderer, each clue meticulously pieced together like the delicate gears of a finely crafted clock. The thrill of the chase, the puzzle that needed to be solved—these were familiar sensations for Hart. Yet now, with the case closed, he felt an unsettling emptiness within him. Justice had been served, but at what cost?

The first victim, Gregory Fenton, had been a prominent figure in the village—an eccentric clockmaker whose creations were coveted by collectors far and wide. His untimely death had set off a chain reaction, revealing a world of envy and deceit lurking beneath the surface of Eldershire's quaint exterior. As Hart walked the familiar path to the local café, he pondered the lives that had been irrevocably altered.

In the wake of Fenton's death, many had come forth with their grievances, shedding light on a man who was as enigmatic as he was talented. The villagers had whispered of his cruelty, the way he had treated his apprentices with disdain. Yet there were those who had loved him fiercely, their loyalty unwavering even in the face of his faults. It was this dichotomy that fascinated Hart—the complexity of human nature and the blurred lines of morality.

As he settled into a corner table at Mrs. Flanagan's café, the aroma of freshly brewed coffee mingled with the scent of baked goods. The warmth enveloped him, providing a temporary solace from the chilling memories that haunted him. He glanced out the window, observing the townsfolk going about their business, their expressions ranging from somber to indifferent. Had they already forgotten, he wondered? Or had they merely chosen to bury the past beneath a veneer of normalcy?

Mrs. Flanagan bustled over, her apron dusted with flour, a bright smile contrasting sharply with the melancholy atmosphere. "Good morning, Inspector! What can I get you today?"

"Just a coffee, thank you," Hart replied, forcing a smile. He admired her resilience, the way she seemed to embody the spirit of the village. But even she, with her warm demeanor, couldn't dispel the shadows that lingered.

As he sipped his coffee, his mind wandered back to the final confrontation with the murderer, the revelation that had rocked the very foundations of Eldershire. In a chilling twist, the killer had turned out to be someone Hart had least expected—one of Fenton's most trusted apprentices, a young man named Thomas. Driven by jealousy and a desperate need for recognition, Thomas had orchestrated a series of gruesome murders, each more calculated than the last.

Hart had been astonished by the sheer audacity of it all. Thomas had been a bright and promising talent, a young man with dreams of surpassing his mentor. But in his quest for greatness, he had succumbed to darkness, allowing envy to cloud his judgment. It was a tragic end to what could have been a remarkable career.

The case had garnered attention beyond Eldershire, drawing the interest of journalists eager to sensationalize the story. Headlines had screamed of the "Clockwork Murders," capturing the imagination of the public. But for Hart, it was not a tale of thrills and chills; it was a somber reflection on ambition, the lengths to which one would go to achieve success, and the devastating consequences of betrayal.

Just then, the café door swung open, and a gust of cold air swept through the room. Hart turned to see Evelyn, the widow of Gregory Fenton, stepping inside. Her eyes, once bright with life, now seemed dulled by grief. She had been a constant presence throughout the investigation, a woman caught in the crossfire of love and betrayal.

"Inspector," she said, her voice barely above a whisper. She approached his table, her hands trembling slightly. "May I join you?"

"Of course, Mrs. Fenton," Hart replied, gesturing to the empty chair across from him. He noted the way her fingers brushed against the edge of the table, seeking comfort in the familiar gesture.

"I heard the news about Thomas," she began, her gaze fixed on a point beyond the window. "It's hard to believe that someone so young could be capable of such horror."

Hart nodded, his heart heavy. "Envy can drive a person to unthinkable lengths. It's a tragic truth."

Evelyn's eyes glistened with unshed tears. "Gregory was flawed, as we all are. But he never deserved to die like that. I keep wondering if there was something I could have done to prevent this."

"Sometimes, there are no signs, no warnings. People wear masks, and it's only when the facade crumbles that we see the truth," Hart replied gently.

"Do you think he ever truly cared for me?" she asked, her voice quivering. "Or was I just another part of his collection?"

The question hung in the air, heavy and loaded. Hart understood her pain; he had seen it mirrored in the eyes of others affected by the murders. It was a question without an easy answer, a reflection of the complexities of love and ambition.

"Love can be as intricate as a clock," Hart mused, "filled with moving parts that can either work in harmony or collide tragically. It's often difficult to discern the difference."

Evelyn sighed, the weight of her grief evident in her posture. "I wanted to believe in him, in us. But now... now it feels like everything was built on a lie."

Hart reached across the table, placing a comforting hand on hers. "You must remember that his actions do not define you. You are more than the shadows cast by his choices."

For a moment, they sat in silence, each lost in their thoughts, the world outside continuing to move with an unsettling indifference. Hart's mind wandered to the future of Eldershire. The village would heal, as it always did, but the scars of the Clockwork Murders would remain, a testament to the fragility of trust and the darkness that could lurk within even the brightest of souls.

As they spoke, the café filled with the sounds of laughter and chatter, the mundane rhythm of life continuing unabated. Hart observed the villagers, their lives intertwined, each one carrying their own burdens and secrets. He recognized that while the murders had been a catalyst for change, the underlying issues that had plagued the village remained unresolved.

"What will happen now?" Evelyn asked, breaking the silence. "Will the village ever truly recover?"

"Recovery takes time, but I believe the people of Eldershire are resilient," Hart replied. "They will find a way to move forward, though it may not be easy."

"I hope so," she whispered, her gaze drifting out the window again, her mind seemingly a million miles away. "I hope they find peace."

As the days turned into weeks, Hart found himself drawn deeper into the tapestry of Eldershire. He walked the streets, engaging in conversations with locals, piecing together their stories, their hopes, and their fears. It became clear that the murders had exposed not just the darkness within individuals, but the fractures within the community itself.

Gossip swirled like the autumn leaves, whispers of past grievances and resentments surfacing in the wake of the tragedy. Neighbors who once greeted each other with warm smiles now cast sidelong glances, suspicion mingling with fear. The unity that had defined Eldershire for generations was slowly unraveling, replaced by an undercurrent of distrust.

Yet amid the disarray, Hart noticed flickers of hope. Some villagers, determined to restore their community, began organizing meetings to discuss ways to foster understanding and healing. It was heartening to see, a reminder that even in the darkest of times, there were those willing to strive for a brighter future.

One crisp afternoon, as the sun dipped low in the sky, Hart attended one such meeting at the village hall. The atmosphere was charged, a mixture of apprehension and anticipation. He took a seat at the back, observing the assembled townsfolk—faces lined with worry, eyes brimming with uncertainty.

The mayor, a stout man with thinning hair and a voice that carried authority, addressed the crowd. "We are gathered here today to discuss how we can rebuild our community after the tragedies we've faced. We must not let fear dictate our lives."

Hart listened intently as voices rose and fell, opinions clashing like the gears of a clock in disarray. Some advocated for tighter security measures, while others emphasized the need for understanding and compassion. The debate raged on, a reflection of the complexities they all faced.

Eventually, Evelyn stood up, her presence commanding attention. "I know many of you have suffered losses, but we must remember that we are stronger together. We can't allow fear to divide us any further. We owe it to ourselves and to those we lost to create a community that supports one another."

Her words resonated through the hall, a call to action that echoed in the hearts of those present. As discussions continued, Hart felt a renewed sense of purpose. Perhaps, amidst the pain, there was a path forward, one that could lead to healing.

In the weeks that followed, Hart remained an integral

part of these community gatherings. His insights, shaped by his experiences during the investigation, proved invaluable as the villagers navigated their way through the aftermath of the Clockwork Murders. Together, they began to address the rifts that had formed, forging connections that transcended their past grievances.

Time marched on, and slowly but surely, Eldershire began to heal. The fog that had blanketed the village lifted, revealing the beauty that lay beneath. Children's laughter returned to the streets, and the café once again buzzed with chatter and warmth.

Yet for Hart, the shadows of the past lingered. The memories of the case, the lives shattered, weighed on his conscience. He knew that even as the village emerged from its mourning, he could never forget the lessons learned in those dark days.

One evening, as he strolled through the now-bustling market square, he spotted Evelyn at a stall, selecting fresh produce. He approached, a smile spreading across his face. "You seem to be enjoying the market."

She looked up, her eyes lighting with warmth. "It's nice to see life returning to Eldershire. I've even started baking again."

"Your cakes were the talk of the village," he remarked, recalling the delightful pastries she used to make.

"Perhaps I'll host a gathering soon," she said, her voice carrying a hint of excitement. "A chance for everyone to come together, to celebrate life."

Hart felt a swell of hope. "That sounds like a wonderful idea. It's time for the village to remember the good things."

As they chatted, Hart sensed a change within Evelyn—a newfound resilience. The tragedy had forged her into someone who could embrace life, despite the scars left behind. He admired her spirit, a reflection of the village itself.

Days turned into weeks, and soon, Evelyn's gathering came to fruition. The village hall was adorned with colorful bunting, and the aroma of baked goods wafted through the air, enticing townsfolk to come together. Laughter echoed as families mingled, the joy infectious.

Hart observed the interactions around him, feeling a sense of satisfaction. The Clockwork Murders had left indelible marks on the village, but here, amidst the laughter and shared stories, he witnessed the resilience of the human spirit. In embracing their past, the people of Eldershire were forging a brighter future.

As the evening wore on, Hart found himself lost in conversation with the villagers, their stories weaving a rich tapestry of life in Eldershire. He realized that amidst the shadows, there existed a profound beauty—a community that, while flawed, was willing to confront its demons and emerge stronger.

As the sun set, casting a golden glow over the gathering, Hart felt a sense of closure wash over him. The memories of the

Clockwork Murders would always remain, but he had learned to embrace the lessons they imparted. Life was a fragile thing, a clock with delicate gears that could so easily be disrupted.

With a renewed sense of purpose, Hart knew he would continue to protect the village he had come to love. He would stand by its residents, helping them navigate the complexities of their lives. In the face of darkness, there would always be light, and together, they would forge a future that honored the past while embracing the possibilities ahead.

And so, as the laughter and warmth enveloped him, Detective Inspector Charles Hart understood that healing was a journey—a winding path shaped by love, loss, and the unbreakable bonds forged in the face of adversity. In Eldershire, the clock continued to tick, each moment a testament to the resilience of the human spirit, a reminder that time, though relentless, could also be a source of hope.

2. An Unsolved Mystery

THE SUN WAS DIPPING below the horizon, casting a golden hue over the quaint village of Windermere, where time seemed to have stood still. Nestled among rolling hills and shimmering lakes, the village was a picture of serenity, yet a pall of unease hung in the air. It had been two weeks since the mysterious death of Reginald Crowley, the local clockmaker, and whispers of intrigue filled the cobbled streets.

Reginald was a man of peculiar habits, with an obsession for precision that bordered on the obsessive. His workshop, filled with the rhythmic ticking of clocks, had been a hub of creativity and craftsmanship. But when he was found lifeless among the gears and springs of his creations, it sent shockwaves through the community. No signs of struggle, no obvious cause of death—just an enigmatic stillness that left everyone perplexed.

The villagers gathered at the local pub, The Timekeeper's Rest, to discuss the strange events surrounding Reginald's death. A group of them huddled around a table, voices low, faces drawn with concern.

"Do you think he was murdered?" whispered Mrs. Hargreaves, her hands trembling around her mug of ale.

"Not a chance," scoffed Mr. Thompson, a burly man with a bushy beard. "He probably just had a heart attack. That man worked himself to the bone, tinkering with those infernal clocks."

"But there were those strange sounds coming from his workshop the night he died," interjected young Thomas, the baker's apprentice. "I heard it myself. It was like something ticking down... counting down."

The pub fell silent, the weight of Thomas's words sinking in. Reginald had been known to keep to himself, his only companions the timepieces he crafted. But in the days leading up to his death, there had been rumors—hushed conversations in the shadows of the marketplace, furtive glances exchanged among the townsfolk. It was as if Reginald had stumbled upon a secret, one that someone wanted to keep buried.

As night fell, the chilling autumn air crept into the pub, wrapping around the villagers like a shroud. An old man, known to everyone as Mr. Green, raised his glass, his voice quavering but resolute. "We must not let this go unsolved. Reginald deserves justice, and we owe it to him to find out the truth."

The air crackled with a mix of fear and determination. And with that, a new resolve settled over the group. They would not let the mystery of Reginald Crowley's death fade into obscurity.

Meanwhile, across the village, in a cozy cottage adorned with creeping ivy, sat Eliza Bennett, a local schoolteacher with a penchant for puzzles. She had watched the events unfold from the sidelines, her curiosity piqued by the unsettling nature of

Reginald's death. As she sat in her armchair, a novel resting in her lap, she couldn't shake the feeling that something was amiss.

Eliza had known Reginald for years. She had often visited his workshop to marvel at his intricate creations, each telling its own story through the delicate dance of its hands. But now, as she recalled their conversations, a chilling thought crept into her mind: had Reginald been trying to convey something before his untimely demise?

The next morning, driven by an insatiable desire for answers, Eliza set out for Reginald's workshop. The place was shrouded in an eerie silence, the door slightly ajar as if inviting her in. She stepped inside, her heart pounding in her chest. Dust motes danced in the rays of sunlight filtering through the grimy windows, illuminating the chaos of gears and tools scattered across the workbench.

As she examined the room, she noticed a clock on the wall, its pendulum swinging rhythmically. It was unlike any she had seen before, ornate and elaborate, with engravings that seemed to tell a story of their own. She approached it, her fingers brushing against the cool metal, and suddenly felt an inexplicable chill.

Then she saw it—a small drawer at the base of the clock, slightly ajar. With a sense of trepidation, she pulled it open, revealing a collection of sketches and notes. They were hastily drawn diagrams of various clocks, accompanied by scribbled calculations that made her heart race. But what caught her attention was a single sheet, the words "THE COUNTDOWN" scrawled across the top in Reginald's distinctive handwriting.

Eliza's mind raced as she pieced together the fragments of information. The countdown—was it a reference to a specific time? Or something more sinister? She quickly pocketed the sketches, knowing they could hold the key to understanding Reginald's final days.

Over the next few days, Eliza delved into her investigation, reaching out to the villagers for more information about Reginald's recent behavior. She learned of strange visitors to his workshop, shadowy figures who appeared at odd hours, their intentions cloaked in secrecy.

One evening, as she returned home, she noticed a figure lurking in the shadows near the village square. It was a man she recognized—David Pritchard, a reclusive historian who had recently moved to Windermere. Rumor had it that he had been researching the town's history, but Eliza couldn't shake the feeling that he was hiding something.

"Good evening, Miss Bennett," he greeted her, his voice smooth but lacking warmth.

"Good evening, Mr. Pritchard," she replied, studying him closely. "I couldn't help but notice your frequent visits to Reginald's workshop."

He stiffened, his eyes darting away for a moment before settling back on her. "Reginald was an interesting man. I was merely curious about his work."

"Curious, or perhaps something more?" Eliza pressed, her instincts telling her he knew more than he let on.

He chuckled softly, a hint of sarcasm in his tone. "In a small village like this, curiosity can lead to... unfortunate consequences."

His words hung heavy in the air, and Eliza felt a shiver run down her spine. She could sense the tension simmering beneath the surface, the secrets that lay buried among the village's quaint charm.

As days turned into weeks, the investigation began to unravel more threads than Eliza had anticipated. She discovered a connection between Reginald's death and a series of thefts targeting antique clocks in nearby towns. Each theft had been accompanied by a mysterious message, cryptic and unsettling—like a countdown to something far more nefarious.

One evening, driven by a relentless pursuit of the truth, Eliza summoned the courage to confront David Pritchard once more. She found him at The Timekeeper's Rest, nursing a drink in the corner. As she approached, she noticed the tension in his demeanor, as if he was preparing for a confrontation.

"Mr. Pritchard," she began, her voice steady. "I need you to tell me what you know about Reginald Crowley."

He glanced up, irritation flickering across his face. "Why are you so intent on digging up the past? Reginald was a clockmaker, nothing more."

"Nothing more?" Eliza challenged, her resolve unwavering. "He was a man who died under suspicious circumstances, and I intend to find out why."

His eyes narrowed, and for a moment, she thought he might break. But then, he leaned back in his chair, a sly smile creeping across his lips. "Some mysteries are best left unsolved, Miss Bennett. Perhaps you should let sleeping clocks lie."

His words were a taunt, a challenge that ignited her determination. Eliza could feel the walls closing in around her, the threads of mystery tightening their grip. But she was resolute; she would not be intimidated.

In the days that followed, Eliza continued her investigation, driven by the urgency of uncovering the truth. She gathered the villagers once more at The Timekeeper's Rest, determined to share her findings and rally them to join her cause.

As the villagers assembled, she stood before them, her heart racing with anticipation. "Reginald's death is not merely a tragedy; it is a mystery that demands our attention. I believe there are connections to the recent thefts of antique clocks, and I urge you all to share any information you might have."

Whispers rippled through the crowd, and Eliza could see the flicker of hope in their eyes. Together, they began to piece together the puzzle, sharing stories of strange sightings and unexplainable events surrounding Reginald's last days.

It became clear that Reginald had stumbled upon something significant—something that had put him in danger. The notion that he had been targeted for his knowledge and skills fueled their resolve to seek justice on his behalf.

But as they delved deeper into the enigma, Eliza couldn't shake the feeling that the answers lay just beyond her reach. Each revelation led to more questions, and the sense of impending danger grew stronger.

One fateful night, Eliza found herself back at Reginald's workshop, determined to uncover the final piece of the puzzle. Armed with her notes and sketches, she searched for clues that might illuminate the mystery surrounding his death.

As she rummaged through the disarray of tools and clock parts, her heart raced with the anticipation of discovery. And then, amidst the chaos, she stumbled upon a hidden compartment at the back of the workshop.

With trembling hands, she pried it open, revealing a collection of antique clock faces—each marked with a different date and time. It was as if Reginald had been meticulously documenting something, and she felt a sense of urgency wash over her.

Suddenly, the door cre
aked open behind her, and she spun around, heart pounding. There stood David Pritchard, his expression dark and foreboding. "I warned you, Miss Bennett. You should have left this alone."

"Why are you so intent on stopping me?" she demanded, her voice steady despite the fear coursing through her veins.

"Because some secrets are meant to stay buried," he replied, his tone chilling. "And Reginald's fate is a warning to those who dig too deep."

With that, he lunged toward her, but Eliza was quick. She grabbed a clock from the workbench and hurled it at him, the glass shattering as it connected. The chaos of the moment gave her the opening she needed. She dashed past him, heart racing as she fled the workshop into the dark night.

As she sprinted through the streets of Windermere, she could hear David's footsteps behind her, closing in. Panic surged within her, but she pressed on, determined to reach the safety of the village square.

With each pounding step, Eliza's mind raced, piecing together the fragments of the mystery that had haunted her. Reginald had unearthed something—something dangerous that someone was willing to kill for.

Finally, she burst into the square, gasping for breath as she glanced back. David was nowhere in sight, but she knew he wouldn't stop. She had to gather the villagers, to warn them of the impending danger.

In the heart of the square, she raised her voice, calling for the others to gather. "Reginald uncovered something important—something that has put us all at risk. We must band together to protect ourselves and find the truth!"

The villagers emerged from their homes, confusion etched on their faces, but the urgency in Eliza's voice ignited a fire within them. They formed a circle around her, their solidarity a shield against the encroaching darkness.

As the night wore on, they strategized, pooling their resources and knowledge to confront the mysteries that lay ahead. Eliza felt a sense of determination swell within her—a belief that together, they could unravel the secrets that had plagued Windermere.

Days turned into nights as the investigation intensified. Eliza, fueled by the support of the villagers, began to make connections that had eluded her previously. They scoured the town for information, tracing the origins of the antique clocks and the figures who had been seen visiting Reginald.

Through their efforts, they uncovered a clandestine network of clockmakers who had been operating in the shadows, stealing valuable designs and sabotaging their competitors. Reginald had unknowingly become a target—a threat to their operations.

As the pieces of the puzzle began to fall into place, Eliza realized that they needed to confront David Pritchard directly. He was the key to understanding the full extent of the conspiracy and the reason behind Reginald's death.

One evening, armed with the knowledge they had gathered, Eliza and a small group of villagers set out to confront David at his cottage. The air was thick with tension as they approached, the shadows of the trees looming overhead like silent sentinels.

Eliza knocked on the door, her heart racing. After a moment, it swung open, revealing David's cold, calculating gaze. "What do you want?" he demanded, his tone dripping with disdain.

"We know about the network," Eliza stated firmly, refusing to be intimidated. "Reginald was murdered because he posed a threat to your operation. We want answers."

His expression shifted, a flicker of surprise flashing across his face before it hardened. "You have no idea what you're meddling in, Miss Bennett. This is bigger than you can imagine."

"Then tell me," she pressed, her resolve unwavering. "We're not backing down until we know the truth."

With a resigned sigh, David stepped aside, allowing them into the dimly lit cottage. The air was thick with the scent of dust and secrets, and as they entered, Eliza's eyes were drawn to the clock on the wall, its pendulum swinging methodically.

"We're not just clockmakers; we're guardians of time," David said, his voice low. "What we create can shape history, and

Reginald's innovations threatened to expose us. He knew too much."

The gravity of his words weighed heavily on Eliza as she processed the implications. "So you killed him to protect your interests?"

"He was a fool," David spat, his anger bubbling to the surface. "And now you'll share his fate if you don't leave this alone."

But Eliza stood firm, her determination unwavering. "I won't be intimidated. We deserve justice for Reginald."

Before David could respond, the sound of approaching footsteps echoed outside. The villagers had come, emboldened by their shared purpose. They had banded together, ready to confront the darkness that threatened their community.

With a renewed sense of strength, Eliza turned to David, determination etched on her face. "It's over. You can't silence us any longer."

In that moment, she knew the truth was within reach. With the support of her friends and neighbors, they would unearth the secrets that lay hidden beneath the facade of their village—a truth that would finally bring justice to Reginald Crowley and expose the darkness lurking in Windermere.

As they stood together, united in their quest for answers, Eliza felt a surge of hope. The countdown was drawing to a close, and together, they would unravel the mystery that had haunted their village for far too long.

3. The Clockmaker's Gift

IN THE QUAINT VILLAGE of Eldridge, where the cobblestone streets twisted like the winding gears of a clock, there stood an unassuming shop nestled between a bakery and a bookshop. The faint scent of aged wood and oil hung in the air, mingling with the sweet aroma of pastries from next door. This was the workshop of

Horace Eldridge, the village clockmaker, a man whose talent was only rivaled by his secrecy.

Horace was a tall figure with a gentle demeanor, his spectacles perched precariously on the bridge of his nose. His hands, though calloused and stained with oil, moved with the delicacy of a surgeon as he tended to his intricate creations. Clocks of every size and design adorned the walls of his shop — from grandiose grandfather clocks that reached the ceiling to delicate pocket watches that glimmered under the soft glow of gaslight. Each tick resonated through the space, creating a symphony of time that echoed the passage of moments in the lives of the villagers.

Yet, beneath the harmonious façade of the ticking clocks, a peculiar stillness lingered, a sense of something lurking just out of sight. The townsfolk revered Horace not only for his craftsmanship but also for the air of mystery that surrounded him. Whispers circulated about the enigmatic clockmaker's past, suggesting he had once dabbled in secrets far darker than mere timekeeping.

One fateful autumn afternoon, a stranger arrived in Eldridge, cloaked in shadow and intrigue. He was a tall man with a sharp jawline and piercing eyes that seemed to analyze everything around him. The villagers watched with a mix of curiosity and apprehension as he entered Horace's shop, the bells above the door tinkling softly to announce his arrival.

"Good day," the stranger greeted, his voice low and smooth. "I've heard much about your talents, Mr. Eldridge."

Horace looked up from the intricate gears he was assembling, a flicker of unease crossing his features. "And who might you be, sir?"

"A collector," the stranger replied, stepping closer. "I've traveled far and wide in search of the rarest timepieces, and it is said that your craftsmanship is unparalleled."

With a hesitant nod, Horace gestured for the man to follow him to the back of the shop, where his most prized possessions lay hidden behind glass cases. The stranger's gaze swept across the clocks, eyes glinting with desire as he took in the meticulous details and ornate designs.

"Impressive," the man mused, reaching out to touch a finely engraved pocket watch. "But I'm not merely interested in clocks, Mr. Eldridge. I seek something... extraordinary."

Horace's brow furrowed, unease creeping in. "I'm afraid I don't have anything of that sort."

"Ah, but I believe you do." The stranger leaned closer, his voice a conspiratorial whisper. "The legends surrounding your family's legacy speak of a clock unlike any other, one said to possess extraordinary powers. A clock that can alter the very fabric of time."

The air grew thick with tension, and for a moment, Horace's heart raced. The stories his grandfather had told him as a child flooded back — tales of a clock hidden away, imbued with a magic that could bend reality. But they were just stories, he reasoned. Myths that should remain buried in the past.

"I know nothing of such things," Horace replied, his voice steady. "The clocks I create are merely mechanical. There is no magic here."

The stranger straightened, a glint of annoyance flashing in his eyes. "You would do well to remember, Mr. Eldridge, that legends often hold a grain of truth. And those who possess the gift of time are rarely ordinary clockmakers."

As he spoke, the door of the shop creaked open, and a young woman entered, her auburn hair cascading over her shoulders. Clara Hawthorne was a familiar face in Eldridge, known for her vibrant spirit and inquisitive nature. She had often visited Horace's shop, captivated by the intricacies of his creations.

"Horace, have you seen—" she began, but her words caught in her throat as she noticed the stranger. "Oh, I'm sorry, I didn't mean to interrupt."

The stranger regarded her with an unsettling smile. "Not at all, my dear. I was just admiring the craftsmanship of this fine clockmaker."

Clara's eyes darted between the two men, sensing the tension in the air. "Is everything all right?"

"Quite so," Horace assured her, forcing a smile. "Just a discussion about clocks."

The stranger inclined his head. "Indeed. But I must take my leave for now, Mr. Eldridge. I trust our paths will cross again."

As he exited the shop, the bells tinkled softly once more, leaving behind an unsettling silence. Clara turned to Horace, concern etched on her face. "Who was that man? He seemed... strange."

"A collector," Horace replied, his mind still lingering on the man's unsettling words. "But I suspect there is more to him than meets the eye."

Days passed, and the stranger's visit weighed heavily on Horace's mind. He resumed his work, focusing on the intricate gears and mechanisms that brought life to his clocks. Yet, he couldn't shake the feeling that he was being watched, as if unseen eyes were scrutinizing his every move.

Then, one evening, as dusk settled over the village, a loud knock echoed through the shop. Horace hesitated before opening the door to find Clara standing there, breathless and wide-eyed.

"Horace, you need to come quickly!" she exclaimed, glancing around nervously. "It's about the stranger."

"What do you mean?" he asked, his heart racing.

"I overheard some villagers talking. They saw him near the old mill, and they think he's been digging around there." Clara's voice trembled with urgency. "They believe he's searching for something."

Horace's stomach tightened at the mention of the mill. It was a relic of the past, long abandoned and shrouded in legend. "What could he possibly want there?"

"I don't know, but we have to find out," Clara urged. "We can't let him uncover whatever he's looking for."

With a shared determination, the two set out toward the mill, their footsteps echoing in the cool evening air. As they approached, the dilapidated structure loomed ahead, its windows dark and foreboding.

"Stay close," Horace whispered, his heart pounding. "If that man is indeed searching for something, we need to be cautious."

As they entered the mill, the musty scent of decay enveloped them. Shadows danced across the walls, and the creaking floorboards sent chills down their spines. They crept deeper inside, following the faint sound of rustling and scraping.

Suddenly, they stumbled upon a dimly lit room at the back of the mill. The stranger stood there, his back turned, illuminated by the flickering light of a lantern. In front of him lay a large wooden chest, its surface intricately carved with swirling patterns.

"What are you doing?" Horace demanded, stepping forward.

The stranger turned slowly, a sly smile creeping onto his lips. "Ah, Mr. Eldridge. I see you've decided to join me."

Clara gasped, her eyes widening as she caught sight of the chest. "What is that?"

"Something that holds great significance," he replied, his gaze glinting with a mix of pride and obsession. "The clock that can change time, as your grandfather spoke of."

Horace's heart sank. "You're mad! That's just a story. There's no such clock."

"Is there?" The stranger leaned closer to the chest, his fingers hovering over the latch. "Perhaps the legends were right all along. Perhaps your family's legacy is far more valuable than you realize."

With a swift motion, he threw open the chest, revealing a collection of dusty gears, broken clock faces, and an ornate timepiece that shimmered with an otherworldly glow.

Horace recoiled in shock. "No! You can't—"

But before he could finish, the stranger seized the clock and held it aloft, its hands spinning wildly as if caught in a vortex. The room trembled with energy, and a sudden rush of wind blew through the mill, extinguishing the lantern's flame.

Clara clutched Horace's arm, her heart racing. "What's happening?"

"I don't know!" Horace shouted, panic rising in his chest. "We have to get out of here!"

The stranger's laughter echoed in the darkness as the clock's hands began to slow, ticking ominously. "You cannot escape the power of time, Horace Eldridge! It belongs to me now!"

In a desperate bid for freedom, Horace and Clara turned to flee. They raced through the winding corridors of the mill, the walls seeming to close in around them. The sound of the clock's ticking grew louder, drowning out their footsteps.

Just as they reached the exit, a blinding light enveloped them, and the world around them shifted and blurred. Time itself felt as if it were unraveling, threads of reality twisting together and apart.

Then, with a final jolt, they stumbled into the cool night air, gasping for breath. The mill stood behind them, unchanged, as if the chaotic encounter had never happened.

"What just happened?" Clara panted, glancing back at the mill.

"I think... I think we escaped whatever that was," Horace replied, his voice shaky. "But the clock... it's not just a clock. It holds power."

They stood there, trying to grasp the gravity of what had just occurred. A chilling realization settled over Horace. The clockmaker's gift was not merely craftsmanship; it was a burden, a legacy that had entwined his family for generations.

As they made their way back to the village, Horace's mind raced with questions. Who was the stranger? What did he truly seek? And more importantly, what would happen if the power of the clock fell into the wrong hands?

Days turned into weeks, and the encounter at the mill haunted Horace's thoughts. Clara often visited, bringing fresh pastries from the bakery and sharing tales of the village, but the weight of the clock loomed heavily in his mind.

"I can't shake this feeling," he confessed one evening, as they sat together in his workshop. "That man was searching for something, and I fear he won't stop until he finds it."

Clara looked at him, her expression serious. "We can't let him. If the legends are true, we must protect that clock."

With newfound determination, Horace delved into his family's history, scouring old journals and documents that had long been neglected. He uncovered tales of a hidden clock, crafted by his great-grandfather, said to have the ability to manipulate time itself. But with each revelation came a chilling warning: the clock's power could corrupt the heart of even the most virtuous.

One fateful evening, as the sun dipped below the horizon, casting long shadows across the workshop, a loud knock echoed through the door. Horace's heart raced as he exchanged a wary glance with Clara.

"Who could it be?" he asked, moving cautiously toward the door.

As he opened it, he was met with the imposing figure of the stranger, now accompanied by two menacing-looking individuals. The stranger's smile had vanished, replaced by an expression of cold determination.

"I warned you, Mr. Eldridge," he said, his voice low and threatening. "You should have left well enough alone."

"Stay back!" Horace shouted, stepping protectively in front of Clara.

"Do not be foolish. I am here for what rightfully belongs to me." The stranger's eyes glinted with greed. "The clock is my birthright."

In that moment, Horace realized that the true threat lay not only in the clock's power but in the lengths to which the stranger would go to possess it. This was no ordinary collector; he was a man consumed by obsession, driven by a desire that transcended mere timekeeping.

"Leave us!" Clara interjected, her voice steady despite the fear coursing through her veins. "You have no right to demand anything from us."

The stranger's gaze flickered toward her, and for a brief moment, uncertainty passed over his features. "You do not understand the stakes, my dear. This is not just about a clock; it is about the very essence of time."

Horace's heart raced as he felt the weight of Clara's hand gripping his arm. They stood united against the impending threat, but he knew that words alone would not deter the stranger's hunger for power.

With a sudden surge of courage, Horace took a step forward. "You can't control time. It's a force beyond any man's grasp. We will never give it to you."

The stranger's expression darkened, and he motioned to his companions. "Then we will take it by force."

In an instant, chaos erupted. Horace and Clara sprang into action, darting around the shop as the stranger's men advanced. Clocks shattered as they crashed into furniture, the air filled with the sound of splintering wood and the frantic ticking of time slipping away.

Horace spotted the ornate clock resting on the workbench, its hands frozen at midnight. With adrenaline pumping through his veins, he dashed toward it, determination fueling his every step.

"Clara, cover me!" he shouted, grabbing the clock as the world around him spun with chaos.

Just as he grasped it, the stranger lunged, his hand outstretched, but Clara intercepted him, a fire ignited in her eyes. "You won't get it! Not while I'm here!"

With a powerful shove, she pushed the stranger back, giving Horace the precious seconds he needed. He turned the clock over, desperately seeking the mechanism that would allow him to unlock its true potential.

As the struggle intensified, the shop became a battleground, the sound of chaos melding with the relentless ticking of the clocks. Time itself seemed to warp around them, and Horace could feel the weight of the clock in his hands.

"Horace, hurry!" Clara's voice rang out, filled with urgency.

With a final twist of the clock's key, the gears whirred to life, and a bright light erupted from within. The air crackled with energy as the room transformed around them. Time rippled, and the very fabric of reality seemed to bend.

"Stop!" the stranger bellowed, but his voice was drowned out by the surge of power emanating from the clock.

In that moment, Horace realized the true gift of the clock: not merely the ability to manipulate time, but the power to reveal the truth. The struggles, the fears, and the darkness that lingered in the hearts of men were laid bare.

The light enveloped them, and for a brief instant, they stood in a realm where time held no sway. Memories, regrets, and aspirations cascaded around them like a symphony of moments frozen in time.

But then, as quickly as it began, the light receded, and they found themselves back in the shop, the clock's hands now moving steadily forward. The stranger and his companions lay sprawled on the floor, disoriented but unharmed.

Horace turned to Clara, his heart pounding. "We did it. We stopped him."

She nodded, relief flooding her features. "But at what cost?"

As the dust settled, Horace realized that the clock was no longer just a relic of the past; it had become a symbol of their triumph over darkness. They had protected their legacy, but the burden of that legacy remained.

Together, they stood in the dim light of the shop, surrounded by the ticking clocks that whispered of time's unyielding march. The clockmaker's gift had revealed itself, not as a tool of power but as a reminder of the choices that shape their lives.

Days turned into months, and life in Eldridge slowly returned to normal. The stranger was never seen again, but his presence lingered like a shadow over the village. Horace continued to craft his clocks, pouring his heart into each creation, knowing that time was a delicate balance between hope and despair.

Clara remained by his side, her spirit unyielding. Together, they faced the future, united by their shared experience and the knowledge that the clockmaker's gift was not merely a legacy but a bond that would endure through the ages.

And so, in the heart of Eldridge, the clockmaker's workshop continued to tick, a sanctuary where time flowed freely, and the echoes of their adventure would forever be etched in the annals of history.

As the seasons changed and the years passed, Horace and Clara became the guardians of the clockmaker's legacy, weaving stories of love, loss, and the intricate dance of time. The clocks they crafted became not just instruments of measurement, but vessels of memory, each telling a story that transcended the boundaries of time itself.

In a world where moments are fleeting, the clockmaker's gift endured, a testament to the resilience of the human spirit and the enduring power of time.

4. A New Beginning

IN THE DIM LIGHT OF the early morning, as the sun peeked timidly over the horizon, the small town of Everwood stirred to life. Nestled amidst lush green hills and the whispering pines, Everwood was a place where time seemed to stand still. It was the kind of town where everyone knew each other's names and secrets were kept as closely as one might guard a family heirloom. However, the stillness of the town belied the tension brewing just beneath the surface.

Detective Eliza Hart stood at her window, her gaze sweeping over the cobblestone streets. The familiar sights were beginning to feel foreign to her. After months away, working cases in bustling cities, the quaintness of Everwood now felt like a ghostly echo of her former self. She had returned not just to the town of her childhood but to the weight of unresolved questions and unhealed wounds.

As she turned away from the window, the sound of the clock ticking reminded her that time, relentless as it was, continued to move forward. It had been a year since the events that had turned her world upside down, a year since she had lost her mentor, Chief Inspector Harold Finch, under circumstances shrouded in mystery and tragedy. The memory of that fateful night haunted her like a specter. It was time to confront the past, and with it, the specter of her own fears.

The morning sun brightened the office of the Everwood Police Department, illuminating the old wooden desks and worn-out chairs that had witnessed countless stories of heartache and triumph. As Eliza settled at her desk, she could hear the familiar bustle of her colleagues. Constable Matthews was arguing with the new recruit over the best way to brew coffee, while Sergeant Roberts was engrossed in a newspaper, shaking his head at the latest scandal. It was comforting, yet strange; the normalcy of it felt like a cruel reminder of the turmoil that had engulfed her life.

The sound of footsteps interrupted her thoughts, and she looked up to see Inspector Martin Walsh entering the office. Tall and broad-shouldered, Walsh carried an air of authority that had always put Eliza at ease. His eyes, however, bore a hint of concern as he approached her desk.

"Welcome back, Eliza," he said, a warm smile breaking through his stern facade. "I trust your time away was restorative?"

"Restorative?" she echoed with a slight laugh, shaking her head. "I don't think that's the word I would use."

Walsh leaned against the edge of her desk, crossing his arms. "I can only imagine. There are still whispers around town about what happened with Finch. People are curious. They're looking to you for answers."

Eliza sighed, the weight of his words settling heavily in the air. "I'm not sure I have any answers, Martin. Not yet."

"We need to move forward," he said, his voice firm yet gentle. "And there's a case that could use your keen instincts."

At that moment, a young officer burst into the room, breathless and wide-eyed. "Inspector Walsh, we've got a situation at the old clock tower. It's bad."

Eliza felt a cold chill run down her spine. The clock tower, a relic from Everwood's past, had long been a source of local legends and ghost stories. Its mechanisms were said to be cursed, its chimes foretelling doom. "What's happened?" she asked, her heart racing.

"Body found at the base of the tower. It looks like foul play," the officer stammered.

Eliza exchanged a glance with Walsh. This was the beginning—an unexpected turn that would inevitably plunge her deeper into the mysteries of Everwood. "Let's go," she said, her mind already racing with possibilities.

The drive to the clock tower was tense, the air thick with unspoken words. Eliza gazed out the window, watching the scenery rush by. The quaint houses, with their flower-laden gardens, seemed oblivious to the darkness creeping into their midst. What had once been a peaceful town was now the backdrop for a sinister drama, and Eliza was determined to unravel the threads before it was too late.

As they arrived at the tower, the scene was already swarming with officers and curious onlookers. The old structure loomed above them, its weathered stone bearing the weight of countless seasons. Eliza felt a shiver as she stepped out of the car. The familiar sight of the clock tower now felt ominous, its hands frozen at the hour of tragedy.

The body lay sprawled at the foot of the tower, lifeless and stark against the cobblestones. It was a young man, his features pale and serene, as if he were merely sleeping. But the twisted angle of his neck told a different story. Eliza knelt beside him, her heart pounding in her chest.

"Who is he?" she asked, her voice steady despite the turmoil within.

"His name is Simon Granger," a voice behind her responded. It was Officer Carter, a bright young recruit with a penchant for detail. "He was a local clockmaker, known for his intricate designs. We believe he was last seen at a gathering at the town hall last night."

Eliza frowned, piecing together the fragments of information. "Did anyone see him leave?"

"Not that we know of," Carter replied. "But we're interviewing witnesses. There was quite a crowd."

Walsh approached, studying the scene with his keen eyes. "This wasn't an accident. Someone wanted him dead. The question is, why?"

Eliza felt the weight of the world pressing down on her shoulders. The clock tower had become a backdrop for another tragedy, and the intricate machinery of time and fate was set into motion once more. "We need to look into his life, his connections. If this was a murder, there will be a motive hidden somewhere."

As the officers began to cordon off the area, Eliza and Walsh exchanged glances. They had both known that her return to Everwood would not be without its challenges, but they had not anticipated this. The sense of urgency stirred something deep within Eliza—a spark of determination ignited by the tragedy before her.

With a deep breath, she turned to Walsh. "Let's gather what we can. I want to speak to the last people who saw him. Maybe we'll find out more about what he was involved in."

They worked tirelessly through the day, interviewing townsfolk and piecing together Simon's last known whereabouts. Eliza learned that he had recently completed a project for a private collector, a restoration of a rare clock rumored to hold more than just the time. Whispers of hidden mechanisms and secrets began to surface, each thread pointing towards something deeper and more dangerous than she had anticipated.

As the sun began to set, casting long shadows across the cobblestones, Eliza and Walsh found themselves in the quiet of the local library, sifting through records and old newspapers. The musty scent of aged paper filled the air, a comforting reminder of the stories waiting to be uncovered.

"Look at this," Walsh said, his finger tracing a passage in an old article. "It mentions a feud between Simon and another clockmaker, Jasper Hargrove. Apparently, Hargrove accused him of stealing designs."

"Jealousy can lead to dark places," Eliza murmured, her mind racing. "If Hargrove was involved, we need to find him."

The library clock chimed, its deep resonant sound echoing through the stillness, a reminder of the time that was slipping away. They had to act quickly before the threads of this mystery unraveled further. Eliza felt an urgency within her, a calling that pushed her forward.

The following morning, armed with their newfound information, Eliza and Walsh sought out Jasper Hargrove. His workshop was nestled at the edge of town, cluttered with unfinished clocks and discarded gears, a testament to the man's obsession. The air inside was thick with the scent of oil and wood shavings, and the ticking of countless clocks filled the space with an eerie rhythm.

As they approached, Eliza noticed Hargrove's demeanor shift. He was a wiry man with sharp features, his brow furrowed as he peered up from his workbench. "What do you want?" he snapped, defensiveness etched across his face.

"We're here to ask you about Simon Granger," Eliza said, maintaining her composure. "He's dead. We believe you might have had a reason to be angry with him."

Hargrove's expression twisted into a mixture of anger and sorrow. "Simon was a thief! He stole my designs and claimed them as his own. But I didn't kill him!"

"Where were you the night he died?" Walsh pressed, his tone firm.

"I was at the tavern, drinking with friends!" Hargrove exclaimed, his voice rising. "Ask anyone!"

Eliza exchanged a glance with Walsh, weighing their options. "You may not have killed him, but you might know something about his last project. The restoration of a rare clock?"

At the mention of the clock, Hargrove's eyes flickered with something akin to fear. "That clock... it's cursed. Whoever possesses it will meet a grim fate. I warned Simon to leave it be."

The revelation sent a chill down Eliza's spine. Cursed clocks? It sounded like the stuff of legends, but she knew there was often truth hidden in tales. "Where can we find this clock?" she demanded.

"Simon's client," Hargrove replied reluctantly. "A collector named Lord Edward Blackwood. But be careful—he's a man with many secrets of his own."

The name resonated in Eliza's mind as they left Hargrove's workshop, her determination solidifying. The pieces of the puzzle were slowly coming together, yet the shadows of danger loomed larger with each revelation. The clockwork of fate was ticking, and she needed to act before it struck midnight once more.

Their next destination was Blackwood Manor, an imposing structure that loomed over the hills like a guardian of the town's secrets. The estate was known for its grandeur but also its isolation, a reflection of Lord Blackwood's reclusive nature. As they approached the entrance, Eliza felt a sense of foreboding settle in the pit of her stomach.

"Stay sharp," Walsh whispered as they walked up the winding path. "We don't know what we're walking into."

With a firm knock, they were greeted by a butler with a stoic expression. "Lord Blackwood is expecting you," he said, leading them through opulent halls adorned with portraits of ancestors whose gazes seemed to follow them. The air was thick with the scent of polished wood and antiquity.

When they entered the drawing room, Lord Blackwood stood by the fireplace, a tall man with salt-and-pepper hair and a commanding presence. His eyes were sharp, assessing them with an intensity that made Eliza's skin prickle.

"Detective Hart, Inspector Walsh. To what do I owe the pleasure?" he inquired, his voice smooth yet laced with an underlying tension.

"We're investigating the death of Simon Granger," Eliza replied, keeping her tone steady. "He was working on a restoration for you. We need to know more about the clock."

Blackwood's demeanor shifted, and for a moment, Eliza caught a glimpse of something—fear, perhaps? "Ah, Simon. A talented craftsman, indeed. But the clock... it has brought nothing but misfortune."

"What do you mean?" Walsh pressed, leaning closer.

"The clock holds secrets—secrets I'd rather not unveil. Simon became obsessed with it, and I feared it would lead to his demise," Blackwood admitted, his voice dropping to a whisper.

"Where is it now?" Eliza asked, her heart racing.

"In the cellar. But I caution you, be wary. It is said to be cursed. Many have come to harm because of it," he warned, his gaze piercing through her.

Ignoring his warning, Eliza nodded toward Walsh, and they exchanged determined glances. The clock was a key piece in this unfolding mystery, and they needed to see it for themselves.

As they descended into the dimly lit cellar, the atmosphere grew heavier. Shadows danced along the walls, flickering with the light of their lanterns. And then they saw it—the clock. It stood tall and majestic, its intricate gears exposed, as if waiting for someone to set it in motion.

Eliza approached it cautiously, her breath hitching in her throat. There was something mesmerizing about its design, yet it felt foreboding. "What's the story behind it?" she murmured, glancing back at Walsh.

Blackwood's voice echoed behind them, filled with apprehension. "It was built by an ancient craftsman, known for infusing his work with a sort of magic. The clock counts down not just the hours, but also the days of those who possess it."

Eliza's heart raced as she examined the clock. "What do you mean?" she pressed.

"It is said that it predicts the end of its owner's life," Blackwood replied, his tone grave. "When the hands align at midnight, doom follows."

The implications sent a shiver down Eliza's spine. This clock was not just an object; it was a harbinger of death. "Did Simon believe this?"

"Absolutely," Blackwood replied. "He became increasingly obsessed. He wanted to discover its secrets, and I fear that obsession cost him his life."

As they stood there, the weight of the clock's presence grew heavier. It was a sinister reminder of the fragility of life and the inexorable march of time. Eliza's thoughts swirled as she considered the threads of fate intertwining around them.

"Do you still possess the clock?" Walsh asked, breaking the heavy silence.

"No," Blackwood replied, his voice strained. "After Simon's death, I had it removed. I couldn't bear to keep it any longer."

"Where did it go?" Eliza asked, her voice steady.

"To a storage facility. I intended to sell it, but I feared the repercussions," he said, his expression darkening.

Eliza's mind raced with possibilities. The clock's story was far from over. If it had passed through the hands of multiple owners, perhaps they would lead her to the truth. "We need to find that storage facility," she said, determination hardening her resolve.

As they left Blackwood Manor, Eliza felt the weight of the clock's legacy pressing on her shoulders. The past was a tangled web, and she was determined to unravel it. With Walsh by her side, they set off to uncover the next piece of the puzzle.

The search for the storage facility led them to the outskirts of town, where a large warehouse loomed amidst the rusting machinery of abandoned factories. The air was thick with anticipation as they approached the entrance, and Eliza felt the hairs on the back of her neck stand on end.

"Ready?" Walsh asked, his voice low.

"Let's go," Eliza replied, steeling herself.

Inside, the musty smell of forgotten items hung heavily in the air. Boxes piled high were covered in dust, each one a repository of untold stories. As they searched through the maze of clutter, Eliza's heart raced with the thrill of discovery.

"Over here!" Walsh called, and Eliza hurried to his side.

There it was—the clock, wrapped in layers of protective cloth, standing sentinel amidst the forgotten relics. It looked almost majestic in its isolation, as if it had been waiting for someone to acknowledge its existence once more.

Carefully, they unwrapped it, revealing the intricate craftsmanship and the eerie beauty of its design. Eliza felt a chill as she traced her fingers over the gears, her thoughts racing. The clock was a testament to time itself—beautiful, terrifying, and ultimately inescapable.

"What do you think?" Walsh asked, his voice barely above a whisper.

"I think we're about to learn a lot more than we bargained for," Eliza replied, a sense of foreboding creeping in. "We need to know who else has come into contact with it."

As they carefully examined the clock, Eliza noticed something odd—a small inscription hidden beneath the base. It was a name: "Evelyn Hawthorne."

The name struck a chord, sending ripples of recognition through her mind. Evelyn Hawthorne was a renowned historian, a woman with an insatiable curiosity about the town's past. Eliza had heard whispers of her over the years—a reclusive figure who had spent her life uncovering the secrets of Everwood.

"Do you think she could help us?" Walsh asked, watching her intently.

"Possibly," Eliza replied, already contemplating the possibilities. "But we need to find her first. She might have insights about the clock that we're missing."

With renewed determination, they set out to locate Evelyn. The search took them to the outskirts of town, where the Hawthorne estate stood isolated, surrounded by wild overgrowth and forgotten gardens. The mansion was an imposing structure, its grandeur faded but still striking.

As they approached, Eliza felt a mix of anticipation and trepidation. The door creaked open, revealing a dimly lit interior filled with the scent of aged paper and dust. It was as if time had stood still within these walls.

"Evelyn?" Eliza called softly, stepping inside. "Are you here?"

From the shadows, a figure emerged—Evelyn Hawthorne. Her silver hair framed her face like a halo, and her eyes sparkled with an intelligence that seemed to pierce through the layers of time. "Who seeks me?" she inquired, her voice melodic yet commanding.

"Detective Eliza Hart and Inspector Walsh," Eliza introduced herself. "We're investigating the death of Simon Granger, and we believe you might know something about a clock he was restoring."

Evelyn's expression shifted, and a flicker of recognition crossed her face. "Ah, the clock. It has a troubled history, one that intertwines with the very fabric of this town."

Eliza felt a shiver of anticipation. "Can you tell us more?"

"Of course," Evelyn replied, motioning for them to follow her into a study filled with books and artifacts. "But be warned: some truths are best left buried."

As they settled in, Evelyn began to weave a tale of intrigue and mystery, recounting the origins of the clock and the people who had possessed it. The clock was said to have been crafted by a master clockmaker whose family had been cursed for generations. Each owner met an untimely end, their lives marked by tragedy and despair.

"Simon was drawn to the clock, believing he could break the curse," Evelyn said, her voice steady. "He was not the first to attempt this."

Eliza listened intently, her heart racing. "Did anyone else try to uncover its secrets?"

"Yes, many have," Evelyn replied, her gaze distant. "But the clock demands a toll. It cannot be understood without sacrifice."

"Sacrifice?" Walsh echoed, leaning forward. "What do you mean?"

"Those who seek its power often pay a heavy price," she warned. "Simon may have learned too late that some mysteries are better left unsolved."

The weight of her words hung heavy in the air, a reminder of the darkness lurking just beneath the surface of Everwood. Eliza felt the pieces of the puzzle falling into place, yet there were still questions left unanswered. What had Simon uncovered? And who else was entangled in this web of fate?

"Do you have any idea where the clock came from before it reached Simon?" Eliza asked, determined to follow every lead.

Evelyn's brow furrowed as she searched her memory. "It passed through many hands, but the last known owner was a man named Alistair Hargrove—Jasper Hargrove's father. He was said to have been obsessed with its powers."

Eliza felt a spark of recognition. "So, the obsession runs in the family?"

"Indeed," Evelyn replied. "And it is rumored that Alistair's death was the culmination of his pursuits. He believed he could control the clock's power, but it consumed him instead."

The implications of Evelyn's words reverberated within Eliza's mind. The clock was not just an object; it was a testament to the human desire for control and the consequences of seeking the unattainable.

As they continued to talk, Eliza realized that Evelyn was a repository of knowledge—a living library of Everwood's past. Yet, amidst the tales of tragedy, there was also hope. Perhaps together, they could uncover the truth and break the cycle of despair that surrounded the clock.

Days turned into weeks as Eliza, Walsh, and Evelyn delved deeper into the mystery. They interviewed townsfolk, unearthed long-forgotten records, and pieced together the connections that linked Simon to the clock and its previous owners. With each revelation, they uncovered the dark legacy of the clock, a history marked by obsession, greed, and untimely deaths.

The clock's curse was not merely a myth; it was a warning—a reminder of the consequences of tampering with the unknown. But as they uncovered the truth, Eliza felt a glimmer of hope. Perhaps it was not too late to change the course of fate.

One stormy evening, as rain lashed against the windows, Eliza gathered her thoughts in her small office. The shadows danced around her, echoing the turmoil within. She could feel the weight of the clock's legacy pressing down on her, but she refused to let it consume her.

The door creaked open, and Walsh stepped inside, shaking off the rain. "We've found something," he said, a sense of urgency in his voice.

Eliza's heart quickened. "What is it?"

"We traced the clock's history to a hidden chamber in the old clock tower," he revealed. "There are records of its construction, and it may hold the key to breaking the curse."

Eliza felt a surge of determination. "Then we need to go there. It's time to confront the past."

Together, they made their way to the clock tower, the storm raging around them. As they ascended the creaking staircase, the air thickened with anticipation. The chamber was dark, illuminated only by the flickering light of their lanterns.

"Look over here," Walsh called, shining his light on a hidden compartment within the wall. It was filled with dust-covered scrolls and artifacts, remnants of a time long past.

As they carefully examined the contents, Eliza's heart raced. The scrolls detailed the clock's construction, along with incantations and rituals that had been performed to harness its power. It was a treasure trove of knowledge, but also a warning of the dangers that lay ahead.

"What do we do with this?" Walsh asked, glancing at her with uncertainty.

"We use it to understand the curse," Eliza replied, her voice steady. "If we can break it, we can free the clock from its dark legacy."

As they delved into the texts, the storm raged outside, a reminder of the turmoil within Everwood. But with each revelation, Eliza felt a sense of clarity emerging from the chaos. They were on the brink of discovering the truth, and she was determined to see it through.

Days turned into weeks as they pieced together the rituals, uncovering the key to breaking the curse that had haunted the clock for generations. They worked tirelessly, fueled by a sense of urgency and purpose. And with every step, Eliza felt the burden of the past lifting, replaced by hope.

Finally, the day arrived when they would attempt the ritual to break the clock's curse. The air was charged with anticipation as they gathered in the old clock tower, the very heart of the mystery that had gripped Everwood.

"Are you ready?" Walsh asked, his voice steady but laced with tension.

Eliza nodded, determination shining in her eyes. "We must do this together. It's our only chance."

As they began the ritual, the clock chimed, its sound resonating through the chamber like a heartbeat. The air crackled with energy, and Eliza felt the weight of the clock's legacy pressing down on her. This was their moment—the moment to confront the darkness that had plagued them for so long.

With each incantation, they called upon the forces of time and fate, seeking to break the chains that bound the clock to its tragic history. The room was filled with an otherworldly light, and Eliza felt a sense of liberation washing over her.

And then, with one final chime, the clock's hands began to move, the gears shifting in a symphony of sound. Time, once stagnant, began to flow again, breaking the cycle of despair that had gripped Everwood.

As the light enveloped them, Eliza felt a surge of warmth—a promise of new beginnings. The clock, once a harbinger of death, had transformed into a symbol of hope and renewal.

When the light faded, they stood in the chamber, breathless and awed. The clock, now ticking steadily, had shed its dark legacy, its curse lifted.

"We did it," Walsh whispered, disbelief mingling with relief.

Eliza nodded, her heart swelling with a sense of accomplishment. They had unraveled the mystery, confronting the shadows of the past and emerging victorious. But more than that, they had reclaimed their town, transforming it from a place of fear into one of hope.

As they stepped outside, the storm had passed, and the sky was painted in hues of gold and pink. The townsfolk, once shrouded in whispers and secrets, were now free to embrace the light of a new beginning. Everwood would no longer be defined by its past; it would rise anew, a testament to resilience and the strength of the human spirit.

And as Eliza stood on the threshold of a new chapter in her life, she knew that the journey was far from over. The clock's hands were still ticking, each second a reminder of the beauty of life and the power of redemption. She was ready to embrace whatever came next, knowing that every ending was simply a new beginning waiting to unfold.

5. The Town's Dark Secret

THE TOWN OF ELDRIDGE had always been a quiet place, nestled between rolling hills and dense forests, with its cobblestone streets winding like a river through the heart of the community. It was a picturesque setting, seemingly untouched by the frenetic pace of the outside world. Children played in the meadows, neighbors exchanged pleasantries, and the scent of fresh bread wafted from the local bakery. Yet, beneath this serene facade lay a murky undercurrent, a dark secret that clung to the town like a thick fog.

It was a chill autumn morning when Detective Lydia Harrington arrived in Eldridge, drawn not by the promise of its idyllic scenery but by a letter delivered to her office the previous week. The letter was brief, cryptic, and unsettling, written in a spidery hand: "There are truths buried in Eldridge that should never see the light of day. Find the clockmaker; he knows." Lydia's instincts told her that this was not merely a case of small-town gossip. It was a call to uncover the hidden layers of a town that had, for too long, shrouded itself in silence.

As she stepped out of her car, the crisp air bit at her cheeks. The locals eyed her with a mix of curiosity and suspicion, as if they could sense that her arrival heralded an unwelcome intrusion into their comfortable lives. Lydia took a moment to adjust her coat, its weight a reminder of the responsibility she bore. She was not here for tea and small talk; she was here to unravel a mystery, and she had no intention of leaving until she had uncovered the truth.

Her first stop was the Eldridge Historical Society, a quaint building that had seen better days. Inside, the dusty shelves were lined with leather-bound tomes chronicling the town's history. The curator, Mrs. Agnes Beasley, was a woman of indeterminate age, with a keen eye that seemed to miss nothing. Lydia introduced herself, and Mrs. Beasley's expression shifted from guarded to intrigued.

"What brings you to our little corner of the world, Detective?" she asked, her tone friendly yet cautious.

"I received a letter regarding the clockmaker," Lydia replied, watching for any flicker of recognition in the older woman's eyes.

Mrs. Beasley's brow furrowed. "Ah, old Mr. Winslow. He's been retired for years, but his workshop is still on the edge of town. The man was a genius, you know. Created the most remarkable clocks."

"Do you know where I can find him?" Lydia pressed.

"He keeps to himself," Mrs. Beasley warned, her voice lowering conspiratorially. "But if you're determined, take the road past the old church. His shop is at the end of the lane."

As Lydia thanked Mrs. Beasley and stepped back into the sunlight, she couldn't shake the feeling that the curator knew more than she let on. The townspeople had a way of guarding their secrets, and it was clear that Mr. Winslow's clockmaking skills weren't the only remarkable thing about him.

Following Mrs. Beasley's directions, Lydia drove past the quaint church with its weathered steeple, the path becoming narrower and more overgrown as she approached the workshop. The trees loomed overhead, their branches reaching out like skeletal fingers, casting shadows across the road. When she finally arrived, she found herself staring at a dilapidated building, the windows clouded with dust and the door hanging slightly ajar.

Pushing the door open, Lydia was greeted by a cacophony of ticking and whirring sounds. The interior was cluttered with clocks of all shapes and sizes, their rhythmic ticking blending into an odd symphony. At the back of the room, an elderly man with a shock of white hair was hunched over a workbench, focused intently on a delicate mechanism.

"Mr. Winslow?" she called, stepping further into the workshop.

The man looked up, squinting as if trying to place her. "Who are you, and what do you want?"

"I'm Detective Lydia Harrington. I'm investigating a matter that pertains to your work," she explained, watching his reaction closely.

His expression hardened. "I have no interest in your investigations, Detective. This is my sanctuary."

"I received a letter suggesting you know something important about Eldridge's past," Lydia pressed, unwilling to back down.

For a moment, Winslow hesitated, the gears in his mind visibly turning. Finally, he sighed and gestured for her to sit. "Very well, but my time is limited. What do you wish to know?"

Lydia took a seat, feeling the weight of the moment. "What happened in Eldridge? What secrets are buried here?"

Winslow leaned back in his chair, his gaze drifting to the clock on the wall, its hands frozen at 3:15. "This town has always been a place of shadows. There are things people prefer to forget. Years ago, a series of tragedies struck, and the clockmaker became the scapegoat. I lost my business, my reputation, and the community I loved."

"What kind of tragedies?" Lydia asked, intrigued.

"A child went missing, and soon after, another tragedy followed. The townsfolk were desperate for someone to blame, and I happened to be the last one seen with the child." Winslow's voice was laced with bitterness. "They said I had lured her away with promises of wondrous clocks."

Lydia felt a shiver run down her spine. "Did you have anything to do with it?"

"Of course not! I was only trying to help. But once the rumors began, it was impossible to convince anyone otherwise. The town turned its back on me, and I retreated here, away from their judgment."

Lydia noted the pain in his eyes, a flicker of truth in his words. "And the child? Did anyone ever find her?"

Winslow shook his head slowly. "No. The case went cold, and life resumed as if nothing had happened. But those of us who remained knew that something darker lurked beneath the surface."

Determined to dig deeper, Lydia inquired about the letter that had led her to him. "Who wrote to me about you?"

A shadow crossed Winslow's face. "It could have been anyone. The fear and guilt of that time linger like a specter. Perhaps someone wants the truth to come out after all these years."

Before Lydia could press further, there was a sudden commotion outside the workshop. The door swung open violently, and a young woman burst in, her face pale and eyes wide with fear. "Mr. Winslow! You must come quickly!"

"What is it, Clara?" Winslow asked, his voice steady despite the chaos.

"It's— it's happening again!" she stammered, her breath hitching in her throat.

Lydia exchanged glances with Winslow, sensing an urgent need to uncover more. "What do you mean?" she asked, moving closer to the young woman.

"There's been another disappearance," Clara gasped, gripping the edge of the workbench as if it were the only thing anchoring her to reality. "A child has gone missing from the village. Just like before!"

The implications of her words hung heavy in the air. Lydia felt a sense of urgency wash over her. She had arrived in Eldridge to uncover its past, but now it seemed that the town's dark secrets were clawing their way back to the surface.

Without hesitation, Lydia turned to Winslow. "We need to go. You might know something that could help find this child."

As they raced out of the workshop, Clara leading the way, Lydia couldn't shake the feeling that the clock was ticking, both for the missing child and for the town itself. The echoes of the past were threatening to repeat themselves, and this time, she was determined to uncover the truth before it was too late.

The village square was alive with frantic energy as townsfolk gathered in hushed clusters, their faces etched with worry. Lydia's heart raced as she scanned the crowd, looking for any sign of the missing child. Clara led them to a group of mothers, their eyes glistening with unshed tears. The air was thick with fear and uncertainty.

"Did anyone see what happened?" Lydia asked, stepping into the circle of anxious faces.

One of the mothers, a woman named Margaret, stepped forward. "I saw her playing near the old clock tower. She just... vanished." Her voice trembled as she spoke, and her hands shook visibly.

"Did you see anyone else nearby?" Lydia pressed.

Margaret shook her head, her eyes filling with tears. "No, just the usual kids. I thought she was safe."

Lydia felt a knot tighten in her stomach. The old clock tower loomed in the distance, its shadow stretching ominously across the square. It was a relic of a different time, much like the town itself, and it was clear that its presence was deeply intertwined with the unfolding tragedy.

"We should search the clock tower," Lydia suggested, determination sharpening her resolve. "It's possible the child went there."

Clara nodded, her expression grim. "I'll gather some volunteers to help."

As Clara rushed off, Lydia turned to Winslow. "What do you know about the clock tower? Is there a way to access it?"

"It's been locked for years," he replied, the weariness in his voice palpable. "After the tragedies, the townsfolk deemed it cursed. But I have the key. I can help you."

The two of them made their way toward the tower, the ground crunching beneath their feet as they walked. As they approached, the imposing structure loomed overhead, its ancient stones weathered and cracked. Lydia felt a chill run down her spine, as if the very air surrounding the tower was saturated with secrets.

With a shaky hand, Winslow

produced an old, tarnished key from his pocket. He inserted it into the lock, the sound of metal grinding against metal echoing ominously in the silence. With a heavy push, the door creaked open, revealing a dark interior filled with dust and cobwebs.

"Stay close," Lydia instructed, her instincts kicking in as they entered. The dim light filtered through the grime-covered windows, casting eerie shadows that danced along the walls.

Inside, the clock tower was a labyrinth of gears and mechanisms, remnants of a bygone era. Lydia couldn't help but feel a sense of history weighing down on her, as if the walls themselves held the memories of the past. But she had no time for reverie; there was a child's life at stake.

They climbed the narrow staircase, each step echoing like a heartbeat in the oppressive silence. Lydia felt a growing sense of urgency, knowing that every second counted. As they reached the top, the chamber opened up to reveal the massive clock face, its hands frozen in time.

"Where could she be?" Lydia muttered, scanning the room for any signs of the missing child.

Winslow moved to the window, peering out at the village below. "If she came here, she may have climbed up to the ledge," he said, his voice filled with dread.

Without hesitation, Lydia stepped toward the window, her heart racing as she leaned out to look down. Below, the square was bustling with townsfolk, their worried faces turned upward. But no child was in sight. The fear of what might have happened clawed at her insides.

Just then, a faint sound caught her attention—a soft giggle, almost childlike, drifting through the stillness. It was coming from behind a stack of old crates at the far end of the room. Lydia's heart surged with hope as she gestured for Winslow to follow her.

They moved cautiously, the sound growing clearer as they approached. Behind the crates, nestled among the dust and shadows, was a small girl, her hair disheveled but her expression innocent.

"Why are you hiding?" Lydia asked, her voice gentle yet firm.

The girl looked up, her wide eyes brimming with curiosity. "I was playing a game," she replied innocently. "But then I got scared."

Relief flooded through Lydia as she knelt beside the girl. "It's alright now. We need to get you back to your mother."

As the girl reached for her, Lydia felt Winslow's hand on her shoulder, urging her to look closer. She turned her head just in time to see something glinting beneath the crates. With a frown, she crouched down to inspect it, her heart pounding.

What she found sent a chill racing through her veins—a small locket, half-buried in the dust. It was unmistakably the same locket worn by the child who had disappeared all those years ago.

"What is this?" Lydia asked, her voice barely above a whisper.

Winslow's expression darkened as he examined the locket. "It belonged to the first victim. It should not be here."

The implications were staggering. The missing child had somehow stumbled upon a connection to the very tragedy that had haunted Eldridge for years. And the clock that once marked time had now become a conduit for the town's hidden horrors.

Lydia quickly gathered the girl in her arms, relief and urgency mingling as they descended the tower. The townsfolk had gathered below, their faces etched with concern. Clara rushed forward, her eyes wide as she caught sight of the girl.

"She's safe!" Lydia called out, holding the child close.

Cheers erupted from the crowd, but the weight of the locket hung heavy in Lydia's mind. As they made their way back to the square, she realized that the dark secrets of Eldridge were far from buried. They were alive, pulsing beneath the surface, waiting for someone to unearth them.

With the girl safely returned to her mother, Lydia turned her attention back to Winslow. "We need to figure out how this locket ended up here. It can't be a coincidence."

Winslow nodded, a haunted look in his eyes. "The past has a way of creeping back, doesn't it?"

As night fell over Eldridge, Lydia knew that the clock was ticking once again. The dark secret of the town had been momentarily silenced, but it was clear that the echoes of the past were far from finished. The mystery surrounding the clockmaker and the tragedies of Eldridge needed to be unraveled before it was too late.

Determined to uncover the truth, Lydia gathered her notes and set out to interview the townsfolk once more. She had no intention of letting the darkness consume Eldridge any longer. The clock was ticking, and she would not rest until she had pulled every thread of this tapestry of secrets.

As she made her way through the winding streets, she couldn't shake the feeling that she was being watched. The townsfolk exchanged glances, their eyes revealing a mixture of fear and something else—something deeper that lurked beneath the surface.

Arriving at the local tavern, Lydia took a seat at a corner table, scanning the room filled with patrons who murmured quietly among themselves. The tavern was known as a gathering place for the locals, and she hoped to glean more information about the clockmaker and the child's disappearance.

"Detective Harrington," a voice called out, breaking her train of thought. It was Clara, her expression a mix of determination and concern. "Can I sit?"

"Of course," Lydia replied, motioning for her to join.

"I heard about what happened at the clock tower. Thank goodness the girl is safe," Clara said, her voice trembling slightly. "But what about the locket?"

"I need to know what you can tell me about the past," Lydia urged, leaning forward. "Anything that could lead to the truth."

Clara took a deep breath, glancing around the room as if checking for eavesdroppers. "There's something I've always heard—something the elders used to whisper about the clockmaker. They say he made more than just clocks. Some believed he dabbled in darker things, even claiming he could stop time."

Lydia raised an eyebrow, intrigued. "Stop time?"

"It sounds absurd, I know," Clara continued, her eyes wide with fear. "But there are legends of him crafting timepieces that could trap moments, holding onto them forever. When the first child disappeared, it was said he was experimenting with one of those pieces."

The atmosphere in the tavern felt charged, as if the walls themselves were listening. "Have you ever seen one of those clocks?" Lydia asked, her curiosity piqued.

"No," Clara admitted, her voice barely above a whisper. "But I know a few people in town who still have their family heirlooms from him. Perhaps you could speak with them?"

"Absolutely," Lydia replied, her mind racing with possibilities. "The more I learn about Winslow, the more I feel like the answers are hidden in plain sight."

Clara smiled faintly, her enthusiasm returning. "I'll gather some names for you. If anyone knows about those clocks, it will be them."

As Clara left to gather information, Lydia couldn't help but wonder if the clockmaker's legacy was more sinister than she had initially believed. The clock was ticking, and with every passing moment, the weight of the town's dark secrets pressed heavily on her shoulders.

With the tavern quieting down for the night, Lydia decided to take a stroll through the town square, hoping to clear her mind. The moon hung low, casting silvery beams on the cobblestones, illuminating the paths where children had once played. But now, shadows danced in the corners, and she could almost hear the whispers of those long gone.

As she wandered past the old clock tower, she caught sight of a figure lingering in the darkness. It was a young man, his face obscured by the shadows. Lydia's instincts kicked in, and she approached cautiously.

"Can I help you?" she asked, her voice steady.

The figure turned, revealing a nervous smile. "I'm sorry to disturb you. I saw you at the tavern earlier. I'm Aaron, a friend of Clara's."

Lydia studied him carefully. "What brings you out here at this hour, Aaron?"

"I've heard things, you see. About the clockmaker and the tragedies. I thought you might be interested," he said, shifting nervously.

"Go on," Lydia encouraged, intrigued by his sudden willingness to share.

"There's a rumor that the clockmaker's last creation, the one before he vanished, was hidden away in the tower. They say it has the power to reveal the truth—if you can find it," Aaron whispered, glancing around as if someone might overhear.

Lydia felt a rush of excitement. "If that's true, we need to find it. But why do you care?"

"My sister was one of the first victims," he said, his voice cracking. "I want to know what happened to her, to finally uncover the truth that's haunted this town for so long."

The darkness of his words hung heavy in the air, but Lydia could sense a glimmer of hope amid the sorrow. "We'll find the truth together, Aaron. I promise you that."

As they made their way back to the clock tower, Lydia felt the weight of history pressing down on her. The town's dark secret was about to be unveiled, and she wouldn't stop until the last tick of the clock revealed its hidden truths. Together, they would confront the shadows and bring light to the mysteries that had long been buried.

The door creaked open once again, revealing the tower's interior, and Lydia led the way, her determination unwavering. The clock's frozen hands loomed above, and the air crackled with anticipation.

"What do we look for?" Aaron asked, his eyes wide with hope and fear.

"Anything that seems out of place," Lydia replied. "The clockmaker was a master craftsman. He would have hidden his final creation carefully."

They began to search the room, moving among the dust-laden gears and forgotten memories. Lydia's heart raced with every moment, knowing that they were on the brink of uncovering something monumental.

Suddenly, Aaron's voice broke through her thoughts. "Lydia! Over here!"

She rushed to his side, where he knelt beside a trapdoor partially concealed by a pile of old papers. "Do you think it leads somewhere?" he asked, a glimmer of excitement in his eyes.

"Only one way to find out," she replied, her heart pounding in anticipation. Together, they pried the door open, revealing a dark staircase that spiraled downward into the unknown.

Taking a deep breath, Lydia led the way into the abyss, each step echoing like a heartbeat. The air grew cooler as they descended, the darkness enveloping them like a shroud.

At the bottom, they found themselves in a dimly lit chamber filled with old machinery, but it was the sight of a peculiar clock at the far end that captured their attention. It was unlike anything Lydia had ever seen—intricate gears whirred and ticked, and the clock face shimmered with an otherworldly light.

"This must be it," Lydia whispered, her heart racing.

As they approached the clock, Aaron reached out, entranced by its beauty. "What does it do?" he wondered aloud.

"Only one way to find out," Lydia said again, her curiosity piqued. Together, they examined the clock, searching for a way to unlock its secrets.

As they explored, Lydia noticed a small inscription engraved along the side. "It says, 'Time reveals all truths,'" she read aloud, her voice barely above a whisper.

"Then we must set it in motion," Aaron suggested, glancing around for any means to do so.

Lydia nodded, her heart racing. "Let's see if we can wind it up." They carefully manipulated the gears, and as the clock began to tick, a low humming filled the room.

Suddenly, the clock face began to glow brighter, illuminating the chamber in an ethereal light. The gears turned with increasing speed, and a vision began to materialize before them—a swirling image of Eldridge as it once was, with scenes of laughter and joy interspersed with moments of sorrow.

Lydia watched in awe as the memories of the town unfolded, each tick of the clock revealing glimpses of the past. But as the images continued to swirl, she felt a shift in the air, a darkness creeping in as the scenes shifted to the tragedies that had plagued Eldridge.

"No," Lydia gasped, realizing what was happening. "This is the truth—the dark secret of the town."

As the clock continued to tick, they saw the faces of those who had been lost, including the first child who had vanished. The echoes of laughter turned into cries for help, and Lydia's heart ached for the families left behind.

"This is why it was hidden," Aaron whispered, tears streaming down his face. "They wanted to forget."

But as the clock struck a final chime, the vision faded, leaving them in silence once more. The weight of the truth hung heavy in the air, and Lydia felt a sense of purpose rekindle within her.

"We have to share this," she said firmly, her eyes meeting Aaron's. "The town needs to know. We can't let fear silence the truth any longer."

Together, they climbed back up the staircase, the memory of what they had seen etched in their minds. As they emerged into the cool night air, Lydia knew that the path ahead would not be easy, but the clock had started ticking anew.

With every step they took toward the village square, the weight of the town's dark secrets pressed down on them. Lydia was resolute; the truth would not be buried any longer. Eldridge had to confront its past if it ever hoped to move forward.

As they reached the square, the townsfolk were still gathered, anxiously awaiting news. Clara spotted them first and rushed forward, her expression a mixture of concern and hope.

"Did you find anything?" she asked, her eyes wide.

"We need everyone to gather around," Lydia announced, her voice steady. "There's something important we must share."

The crowd fell silent, eyes focused on her. Lydia felt the gravity of the moment as she looked around, realizing how intertwined their lives had become.

"Years ago, a tragedy struck Eldridge. Children went missing, and lives were forever altered," she began, her voice unwavering. "But we've uncovered the truth—the dark secret that has haunted this town for far too long."

Gasps echoed through the crowd, and Lydia pressed on, recounting what she and Aaron had witnessed in the clock tower, the visions of the past and the importance of confronting their history. The townsfolk listened intently, their expressions a mix of disbelief and dawning comprehension.

"It's time to stop living in the shadows," Lydia urged. "The clockmaker may have made mistakes, but his final creation has shown us the truth. We must face our past if we ever want to heal."

As she spoke, Lydia noticed the faces in the crowd shift, fear giving way to determination. The whispers of the townsfolk grew louder, conversations igniting as they processed the revelations.

"Do you really believe we can change things?" Clara asked, stepping forward with uncertainty.

"We have to believe it," Lydia replied earnestly. "We owe it to those we lost. We owe it to ourselves."

As the night wore on, the townspeople began to share their own stories, memories long buried surfacing in the light of Lydia's revelations. The atmosphere shifted from one of despair to a collective resolve, each voice adding to the tapestry of truth that had long been frayed.

Lydia stood back, watching as the community began to come together, united in their quest for healing. And in that moment, she felt a sense of hope blossoming within her, a belief that even the darkest secrets could be unraveled, one tick of the clock at a time.

As dawn broke over Eldridge, the sun's rays illuminated the town in a warm glow, a stark contrast to the shadows that had once loomed over it. Lydia knew that the work was far from finished, but the clock was ticking in a new direction, and for the first time in years, the town was ready to embrace the light.

In the days that followed, the community worked tirelessly to honor the memories of those lost, transforming the dark legacy of Eldridge into a story of resilience and hope. The clock tower, once a symbol of despair, became a gathering place for remembrance and healing.

And as Lydia prepared to leave Eldridge, she felt a bittersweet sense of closure. The past had been laid to rest, but its echoes would always resonate. The clock had begun to tick anew, marking not only the passage of time but the journey toward redemption.

With one last glance at the town that had captured her heart, Lydia knew she would carry its story with her, a reminder that even in the darkest of places, the truth would always find a way to shine through.

6. Time Heals All Wounds

THE WIND HOWLED THROUGH the narrow streets of Thistlewood, a quaint village tucked away in the English countryside. It was the kind of place where time seemed to stand still, where the cobbled lanes twisted around ancient buildings, and secrets lay buried beneath layers of ivy and moss. But within the cozy homes and warm hearths, whispers of unrest echoed louder than the wind outside.

At the heart of the village stood a grand old clock tower, its face cracked but still resolute, its hands eternally turning in a slow dance with time. The clock had witnessed countless events — joyous celebrations, tragic losses, and everything in between. Today, however, its ticking seemed particularly ominous.

Detective Eliza Hawthorne had returned to Thistlewood after a decade spent in the bustling streets of London. The city had swallowed her whole, its chaos drowning out the whispers of her childhood. Yet, the village called her back, an unshakeable pull that she could no longer ignore. Eliza had come to find solace, to heal from her own wounds, but she soon discovered that the past is never truly buried.

As she stepped into the familiar yet foreign landscape of her youth, memories flooded her mind. The laughter of children playing in the meadows, the scent of freshly baked bread wafting through the air, and the warmth of her grandmother's embrace enveloped her like a comforting blanket. But among these sweet recollections lay shadows of sorrow — the tragic death of her younger brother, William.

It had been a rainy afternoon, the kind where the clouds hung low and the ground was slick with mud. Eliza remembered the frantic search for him, the panic that gripped her heart as she ran through the woods behind their home. Hours turned into an eternity before they found him, lifeless beneath the old oak tree, a victim of a terrible accident. The village mourned, but for Eliza, the wound never truly healed. It had festered, becoming a part of her, haunting her every step.

Now, as she walked the winding paths, she felt the weight of those memories pressing down on her. They had called her back not just to reminisce but to confront the ghosts of her past. But she hadn't expected the village to have its own set of secrets, dark and twisted, waiting to unravel.

News of a series of mysterious deaths had gripped Thistlewood in a vice of fear. First, it was the baker, Mr. Jennings, found dead in his shop, surrounded by the sweet scent of pastries and the chilling echoes of his last breath. Then came the schoolteacher, Miss Callahan, whose body was discovered in the village square, her expression frozen in a mixture of surprise and terror. The clock tower had struck midnight on both occasions, and as the villagers gathered to mourn, an unsettling realization began to creep in — time itself seemed to be the harbinger of death.

As Eliza delved deeper into the town's happenings, she encountered old friends and enemies alike. The village was a tapestry of intertwined lives, each thread holding a story, a secret, or a hidden grudge. There was Thomas, her childhood friend, now the local constable, who wore his authority like a heavy cloak, burdened by the expectations of his role. And then there was Mrs. Hargrove, the enigmatic widow with a penchant for gossip and a sharp eye for the unspoken.

"Ah, Eliza! Back from the big city, are we?" Mrs. Hargrove had exclaimed, her voice laced with curiosity and a hint of malice. "You've come just in time to witness our little troubles. Thistlewood is not what it used to be, I assure you."

Eliza met her gaze, steady and unwavering. "What do you mean, Mrs. Hargrove? It seems quite picturesque to me."

"Picturesque? Perhaps. But beneath that charm lies a darkness. We've had two deaths in quick succession, and the villagers are growing restless. They whisper of a curse, a reckoning, if you will. I do hope you're not here to unearth old memories," she replied, her eyes sparkling with mischief.

Eliza frowned, the familiar ache of her brother's memory tightening around her heart. "I'm here to help, not to cause trouble. Do you know anything about the deaths?"

"Rumors abound, dear. Some say it's the work of the old clock tower — that it's cursed. Others think it's the work of someone among us, hiding in plain sight. You know how it goes in small villages; everyone has a theory." Mrs. Hargrove leaned closer, lowering her voice. "But I fear that if we don't uncover the truth soon, more lives will be lost."

The days turned into a blur of investigation as Eliza and Thomas worked together to piece together the threads of the mystery. The villagers were reluctant to share their fears, their stories laced with superstition and suspicion. Each interview revealed more layers of distrust, and Eliza found herself caught in the web of their lives.

"Do you believe in curses, Eliza?" Thomas asked one evening as they sat in the village pub, the flickering candlelight casting dancing shadows on the walls.

"Not really. I believe in human nature — our capacity for good and evil. It's much more complex than a simple curse," she replied, her eyes searching his. "But I do think the clock tower holds significance. It's been here longer than any of us and has witnessed more than we can imagine."

As they gathered clues, a pattern emerged. Each victim had a connection to the clock tower, and with every tick of its hands, Eliza felt a pull toward the truth hidden within its walls. Yet, the closer she got, the more perilous her journey became. The villagers' fear morphed into hostility, and suspicion ran rampant. Eliza found herself facing threats disguised as friendly warnings.

"Leave it be, Eliza. Some things are better left buried," warned an old woman with eyes that seemed to hold centuries of wisdom and sorrow.

But Eliza was undeterred. With each day, the tension escalated. The clock's hands continued their relentless march forward, ticking away the seconds, minutes, and hours until the next death. It felt as though the village was held in a cruel grip of time, each moment dragging heavy with foreboding.

Then came the night that changed everything.

A thunderstorm raged over Thistlewood, lightning illuminating the sky in jagged bursts. Eliza stood at the window of her childhood home, the rain lashing against the glass like the furious whispers of the villagers. As she watched the storm, a flicker of movement caught her eye — a shadow darting beneath the clock tower.

With a sense of urgency, she grabbed her coat and rushed out into the tempest. The wind howled, nearly knocking her off her feet, but determination drove her forward. As she approached the tower, the air crackled with electricity, and the ground beneath her felt alive.

Inside, the clock's mechanism ticked loudly, a heartbeat echoing in the silence. She stepped closer, the shadows stretching ominously around her. And then she heard it — a muffled cry from the dark recesses of the tower. Eliza's heart raced as she followed the sound, her instincts guiding her.

In a small alcove, she found a hidden compartment, the door slightly ajar. Her breath caught in her throat as she pushed it open, revealing a scene that would forever haunt her. There, sprawled on the floor, was the lifeless body of Mrs. Hargrove, her face frozen in terror, surrounded by shattered clock parts.

Eliza's scream was swallowed by the storm outside as she stumbled back, the weight of the revelation crashing down on her. The village's darkness had claimed another victim, and the clock's relentless ticking was a grim reminder that time would not stop for grief.

With Mrs. Hargrove's death, the pieces of the puzzle began to align in Eliza's mind. The clock tower, the deaths, the whispers of a curse — it was all connected in a way she had yet to fully understand. But now, with the stakes higher than ever, Eliza knew she had to uncover the truth before more lives were lost.

Returning to the village, Eliza felt the tension in the air shift. The storm had passed, but the atmosphere was charged with something far more dangerous — fear. The villagers had gathered in the square, their faces pale and drawn, eyes darting suspiciously among one another.

Eliza stepped forward, her voice steady and clear. "We need to talk about the deaths and what they mean for all of us. This isn't a curse; it's a crime, and it's time we faced the truth together."

Murmurs of dissent rose among the crowd, but Thomas stood by her side, his presence lending her strength. "We're not here to point fingers but to protect one another. We need to uncover the truth, not just for ourselves but for those we've lost."

The villagers shifted uneasily, but Eliza pressed on. "Mrs. Hargrove was right. We're all interconnected in this web of life and death. We can't allow fear to dictate our actions. We must band together and find out who is responsible for these murders before it's too late."

In that moment, the clock tower chimed, echoing through the square like a tolling bell. Eliza could see the flicker of understanding dawning on some of the faces before her. They were weary of living in fear, weary of losing those they loved.

As they began to share their stories, the atmosphere shifted. The villagers opened up about their connections to the victims, their fears, and their suspicions. Together, they formed a web of truth, unraveling the lies that had fester
ed for too long.

Through their shared experiences, Eliza pieced together a timeline of events leading to the deaths. Each victim had held a secret, a connection to the clock tower, and each secret had been buried beneath layers of time, waiting for the right moment to surface.

Eliza stood at the center of it all, the weight of her brother's memory guiding her. She understood now that healing would come not just from uncovering the truth but from acknowledging the pain they had all suffered. The wounds of the past had festered long enough, and it was time to stitch them closed.

As the villagers shared their stories, the clock tower stood sentinel, a reminder of time's relentless march. With every tick, they inched closer to the truth, and as the final pieces fell into place, Eliza felt a sense of clarity wash over her. The murderer was among them, hiding in plain sight, manipulating the clock's hands to serve their own twisted desires.

When the last piece of evidence fell into place, the truth hit Eliza like a bolt of lightning. She called a meeting in the village square, gathering everyone together under the watchful eye of the clock tower. With trembling hands, she laid out the facts, exposing the web of deceit that had ensnared them all.

As she spoke, the villagers shifted uncomfortably, glancing at one another with dawning realization. The murderer was not just a stranger lurking in the shadows but someone they all knew, someone who had played their part in the tragedy that had unfolded.

With the evidence laid bare, Eliza turned to face the crowd. "The clock has ticked down to this moment, and it's time we take action. We must confront the one who has caused us so much pain and suffering."

At that moment, as if summoned by fate, the clock struck once more, its deep chime resonating through the air. And from the crowd, a figure stepped forward, the weight of guilt heavy upon their shoulders.

It was Thomas.

"I did it," he confessed, his voice trembling. "I thought I was protecting you all. I thought if I could control time, I could keep the village safe from its own secrets. But I was wrong. I've only brought more pain."

The air hung thick with shock, the realization rippling through the crowd. Eliza's heart sank as she processed the betrayal of her childhood friend. But as she looked into his eyes, she saw not just guilt but a deep sorrow, a wound that ran as deep as her own.

"Time may heal all wounds, but it cannot erase the truth," Eliza said, her voice steady. "We all carry the burden of our pasts, but it's how we face them that defines us."

In that moment, as the clock tower chimed one final time, the villagers began to understand the true meaning of healing. It was not about forgetting or running away; it was about facing the darkness together, about embracing their shared pain and transforming it into strength.

With Thomas's confession, the village began to mend. The clock tower, once a symbol of fear, now stood as a testament to resilience. Time would continue to pass, but the villagers would face the future united, ready to heal their wounds together.

As Eliza stood beneath the clock tower, she felt the weight of her brother's memory lift. The echoes of the past would always remain, but she had learned to carry them with grace. Time may have left its scars, but it had also woven a new tapestry of hope.

In the days that followed, Thistlewood transformed. The villagers gathered to remember their lost loved ones, to celebrate life in all its complexity. The clock continued to tick, a reminder of the moments they had shared and the ones yet to come.

Eliza knew that time would always hold its mysteries, but she had found solace in the connections they had forged. The village would heal, not just from the wounds of the past but from the strength they had discovered within themselves.

As she looked up at the clock tower, she realized that while time may heal all wounds, it also teaches us to cherish every moment, to embrace the love and loss that shape our lives. And in that understanding, she found her peace.

The shadows of the past may linger, but in the light of hope, they could never fully take hold. Eliza had come home not just to uncover the truth but to remind the village that healing is a journey best traveled together.

And so, as the clock chimed, marking the passing of another day, Eliza knew that Thistlewood would forever be a place of resilience, a sanctuary for those who dared to confront their truths and embrace the healing power of time.

Milton Keynes UK
Ingram Content Group UK Ltd.
UKHW030746221024
449869UK00001B/40